Critical Acclaim for the Sudden Quiet Trilogy

"Veith has written a dark and poignant dystopian thriller."
  -Publishers Weekly

"We the Anishinaabe Nation, believe in channeling knowledge from the stars. Veith's trilogy will send shivers of truth down your spine."
  -Courtney Miller, medicine person, activist, and dancer.

"Veith is one hell of a fine writer. I flew through the first dozen pages and lost myself in the following four hundred."
  -Tom Powers, *Michigan in Books*

"Veith's trilogy is haunting, deep, and raw, yet the Native American, mystical and nature elements soothed me throughout my reading. Wow. I don't often read this genre, but I look forward to finishing the trilogy."
  -Debra Payne, author of *The Burden of Sparrows*

"Veith effortlessly places the reader in familiar landscapes which have been dramatically eroded beyond recognition."
  -BookLife Review

"This trilogy mesmerizes with its Tolkien references, Anishinaabe culture, local lore and historic maps. The books are spellbinding!"
  -Jennifer Harsha Carroll, artist and editor

"I commend anyone intrepid enough to imagine an American future in these dark and uncertain times. The Sudden Quiet trilogy is a deeply felt visit to that strange time-to-come. It made me want to try living there for a spell."
  -James Kunstler, author of the *World Made by Hand*

Dark Straits

SUDDEN QUIET: BOOK II

Dark Straits

Joshua Veith

Readers are encouraged to go to www.MissionPointPress.com to contact the author or to find information on how to buy this book in bulk at a discounted rate.

Published by Mission Point Press
2554 Chandler Rd.
Traverse City, MI 49696
(231) 421-9513
www.MissionPointPress.com

ISBN: 978-1-965278-21-5
Library of Congress Control Number: 2024921549
Printed in the United States of America

Cover Design credit to Janella Williams, photograph by Shawn Malone

As an author and educator I strive to be an Indigenous ally. At the end of this book I acknowledge the many mentors that have guided me on my path. Any fault in portraying Native language or customs is mine alone and in no way reflects my excellent teachers.

This book is dedicated to authors everywhere, especially the unknown, the unpublished—lonely alchemists transmuting the dross of existence into literary gold. Write on!

'To such dark straits, alas! now brought
are ye I love, for whom I fought.
Nor further with you can I go—'

—J.R.R. Tolkien, "The Lay of Leithian," 1925

CAST of CHARACTERS:

Beaver Islanders

Samantha

Miinan

Mukwa

Tom Doyle

The Naturals

Dr. Chow

Brian

Nighthawk

Old Law

125th Griffins

Rangers

Howlers

Panzer Pharm

Bob Campbell

Chosen

Red Liz

XCons

Aghori

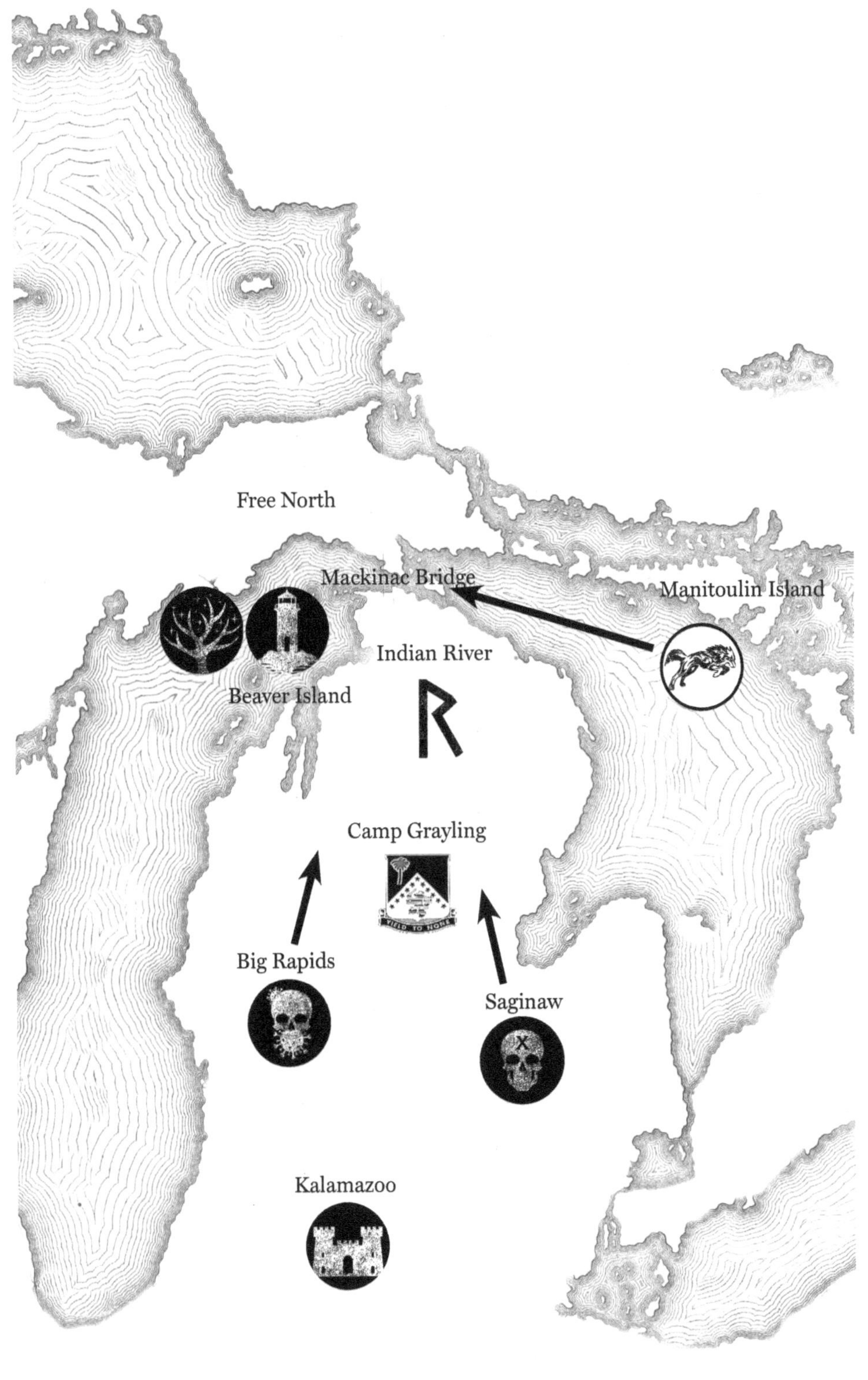

Free North
Mackinac Bridge
Manitoulin Island
Indian River
Beaver Island
Camp Grayling
YIELD TO NONE
Big Rapids
Saginaw
Kalamazoo

Map created by Ed Wojan and Jeff Cashman of Beaver Island

Welcome to Beaver Island

THE LONG JUNE DAY, dusking at last, had been a weary one, and the two doctors were tired. They'd been screening passengers and livestock since the ferry docked at dawn. The big boat was almost empty; every test result had been negative.

Virus-free, the newcomers—self-named Naturals—were re-settled in the state forest by the island's friendlier families. But there were grumblers too, guts squeezed by fear. Incredulous, they shook their heads at this welcome, disbelieving the two doctors and their diagnostic tools.

"Elena, Diana, you're the last ones to be screened. Are you both ready?" Doc Newsome, Beaver Island's resident physician, had been introduced to the athletic women, both Sentinels—a militant faction of Naturals. Elena, fair and blonde, and Diana, dark and tall, both nodded their consent. All day the two women had supervised: reassuring, facilitating the offload, answering questions. Doc Newsome and his two island nurses—masked, gloved, and garbed in PPE—entered names and data in the ledger.

Dr. Chow—a fellow Natural, a mainlander—swabbed the muscled women, sampling blood from each. Upon docking, Chow was the first one tested. Virus-free, Doc Newsome welcomed Chow's assistance in screening the rest. Chow, gloved and gowned, carefully handed the vials to Newsome's nurse, Sean. Their serum was tested by two different kits: the first for antigens, indicating virus; the second for antibodies, evidencing exposure. These point-of-care tests weren't perfect, but short-comings were balanced by the uniformity of results.

Newsome dictated the final entry to Registered Nurse Mathew, hand-scribing the log. Laptops and HIPPA protocols, dead for two years, were relics from before. "Patient Elena, number 203, viral-antigen test, negative. Antibody test, positive. Patient Elena is not a carrier of virus and has antibodies against it. She is cleared to exit quarantine."

As Mathew finished and closed the journal, he looked up at Elena, hand-in-hand with Diana, her partner and ELF comrade. "Welcome, both of you, to Beaver Island."

The two athletes crossed the gangway, stepping from the ferry to the unknown shore. Screenings over, nurses and doctors packed up; they'd meet the next morning to plan for the future. Dr. Chow waved farewell from the ferry as Doc Newsome and his nurses stepped ashore, removed their personal protection, and were carted off by a farmer and his horse-powered wagon.

In the nautical twilight, a low planet smoldered, reflecting red light. The June moon, a day past full, would rise soon. Daniel Chow stood alone at the rail, filling his lungs with cool night air. There was much to process. Unlike the rest of the Naturals, he'd spend his night on board.

Elena and Diana were ashore; the resettlement was in their competent hands. Seeking solace, Chow tried popping his anxiety-bubbles as they formed: the uniformity of test results, Doc Newsome's competency, the kits they'd used, various equipment Chow longed for, and all his professional worries.

He tried filling his mind with emerging stars, with wave-lap and wind. But the doctor kept remembering Keith Two-Crow, their savior, gunshot, blasted from the ferry's bow this morning. Chow flinched from the fresh trauma-scar, adding it to his list. He bore plenty—everyone did. Naturals might be shielded from infection, but no antibodies immunized heartache—the face of his wife, his two sons from before.

Tomorrow's conference with Newsome and the islanders would be intense. He'd need hard evidence, and lots of it. Dr. Chow, duly diligent, had been collecting data since collapse, compiling a year and a half worth of hand-scribbled notes. Now where had Pastor George stowed Chow's saddlebag of journals? Had the Lutheran minister—another Natural—mentioned a storage locker?

Chow guessed this "green-shielded" business would be first on Newsome's list, as it should be; nothing was more important. In his time with Naturals on the mainland, Chow's science was often stymied. He hoped Newsome's clinic had equipment that could help—maybe a generator? Without electricity, everything was harder.

Chow turned his back on the town of St. James and its placid harbor, focusing instead on searching the ferry for those records. The tanker-truck they'd stolen from Charlevoix still squatted on deck, freighted with unspoiled fuel. The gang they'd stolen from—Chosen, super-spreaders of contagion—had armed the ferry with machine guns looted from National Guard armories. Approaching Beaver Island, the refugees—called elves by some—dismounted the guns, replacing them with white banners instead. Keith Two-Crow, unfurling one in a sign of peace, was murdered by a Beaver Island boat captain, firing out of fear.

Dr. Chow unpocketed his penlight, entered the ferry, and began combing compartments, looking for his misplaced ledgers.

Cowboy Discovered

THE FERRY'S ENGINES HAD SLOWED, then stopped. In the sudden quiet, had Bob heard singing? Then a rifle shot, followed by a splash? The hymn resumed as the big engines were put in gear. They'd bumped against something solid—a dock, a pier? Finally, the throaty engines were choked, this time for good. For the rest of the day, he heard commotion on deck and the braying of livestock.

The man, Bob Campbell, called "Cowboy" since collapse, was biding time in the brig. Confined in a ferry cabin, he'd been in and out of consciousness. Bob was starving, gasping with thirst. His hands were flex-cuffed to a stanchion behind his back. Too tight, the plastic chafed him, almost to the bone.

How many days had it been? Cowboy figured five? Maybe a week? For the first few, he was checked on daily by one of Liz's gang. They'd provided a dog bowl of water, and got their kicks from kicking him. He hadn't tasted food since his man Mikey betrayed him. Bob's last visitor had been one of Liz's lieutenants. Cowboy knew her from downstate, from the chaos of early collapse. The woman's name was Lacy and she had a thing with Red Liz, her boss. Lizzy was famous for her appetites. Cowboy should know, he'd been on her menu—bad boy du jour.

Lacy, like Cowboy, like Liz, had been "chosen" by the Stinger variant for survival. Like most Chosen, immunity powered her piracy. Lacy, days earlier, had stepped in from the passageway and flicked on a light, dogging the hatch behind her. She'd pit-ied him with a long look. "Not gonna lie, Cowboy, you've seen better days."

No shit. Cowboy kept quiet.

He squinted in the glare. Lacy blurred above him. Bruised, his body tensed, but she wasn't in a kicking mood. The tattooed Chosen wore a biker jacket and was sheathed in a miniskirt. "Liz doesn't know what to do with you. Up to me you'd be dead already."

She could do it too; this bad Barbie was a bitch.

"What happened to you, man? You used to be something, a real inspiration." Lacy removed the jacket—*Born to Kill*—from her bullet-toned body, both arms stylishly tattooed. Eyeballing her inky erotica, Cowboy's monkey-brain went ballistic. His captor cozied closer. "Let me make things easier for you, Bob. Loosen those cuffs, get you some food, how does that sound?"

Cowboy didn't move. Lacy's scent was straight sex; his libido lurched. She'd use this against him in a second, her easiest trick.

The Viral sighed, stretching her limbs. "It's not a trap, Cowboy. I want information. Like, what's the deal with these Naturals? The ones kicking your ass? On the radio, you called them 'elves.' Your man Mikey thinks they're immune, that the virus can't touch 'em. What do you think?"

Cowboy made an effort to dull his senses. Many Chosen were hyper-sexual, and Lacy's pull was powerful. Her interrogation continued. "A fuckin' game changer if they're immune. Downstate, Sharkey, the Big Boss, would be interested, don't you think? Panzer might promote the person that brought this intel. Would you like a piece of that promotion, Bob?"

He stared at the deck, willing her to walk away. Instead, she sauntered closer. Well-versed in manipulation, Lacy scissored over him, each well-razored leg a guillotine. Bob couldn't help it, he peeked. *God damn it!* She wore nothing under her skirt.

Lacy was the cat and Bob, her prey. She twitched a feline grin, purring, "Perhaps it's another kind of piece you're interested in?"

She eased herself down, miniskirt sliding higher. Face to face, socially undistanced, she grinded against him, giving his ear a catlike nip. The pleasure receptors in Bob's brain exploded. He was in real danger, and his body could care less. Desperate, he chafed his cuffs together, hard. For a few seconds, pain was prioritized in his sex-addled cortex. He leaned away, rejecting Lacy's proffered trade-goods. The woman felt him turn off and was not amused. With startling quickness she gripped his filthy hair, slamming his skull hard against the bulkhead.

Concussed, Cowboy blinked stars. Then Lacy drove her knee into his plexus. He spasmed, gasping for life. The Chosen succubus straightened, admiring her handiwork. "That's all the time I've got today. Boss Liz has a plan to mop up these Nats, maybe tonight. She'll tidy the mess you've left us. Honestly though," the Viral shook her head, "they don't even use guns. How'd you let a band of primitives do you like that, Bob?"

Cowboy couldn't breathe, couldn't speak. He fucking hated that trick.

"Maybe I'll bring back a she-elf to keep you company, since you're buddies and all." She nudged his dog bowl with her boot. "I was supposed to water you, wasn't I? Knew I forgot something." She hitched up her skirt and squatted. Bob looked away as her gush filled his bowl. He whiffed its acrid brine as she stood, grabbed her jacket, and left, shutting the hatch behind her.

That had been a couple days ago, maybe more? Eventually, coerced by thirst, he tried a sip of her cooled piss. It hadn't gone well. Then the ferry had been moved—by Liz? Hours later, there'd been that singing, then the gunshot, the splash.

Mind muddled by solitary confinement, body parched and hollowed out by hunger, Bob thought he heard footsteps outside his compartment. Someone approached. Lacy again? Or another fucking Chosen? He should be terrified, but thirst overruled him. His hatch creaked open. A penlight pinned his shackled self. Diagnostic, a medical voice addressed him: "Now, what do we have here?"

Old Law

DATE TIME GROUP: 070930RJUN21

LOCATION: Northwest Lower Michigan

The single Humvee rolled to a stop. Smoking wreckage blocked M-31, the coastal road between Petoskey and Charlevoix. Sunrise lit the pennant of the 125th Infantry Regiment, a yellow griffin and its motto, "Yield to None." This unit of Michigan's National Guard traced the history to the Civil War. If the griffin was surprised to find itself fighting in another one, it gave no sign.

The doors of the armored vehicle opened. Several figures emerged wearing M50 gas masks and level-4 MOPP gear. They carried M4 assault rifles in the low-ready position, covering each other as they waded through vehicular carnage. US Army Captain Frank Young, a fire chief in the civilian world—the world that had ended—projected orders through his mask: "Keep your gear on, men. Corpses could be contagious. Sergeant, let's get a kill-count and figure out what happened here last night. Meet back here in twenty."

Captain Young climbed the embankment and gazed upon Lake Michigan, deep and impossibly blue. Out of sight and upwind, he pulled off his mask, gulping unfiltered air. No matter how many times he witnessed it, he couldn't abide the char of human flesh. After a career fighting fires, plus two combat tours in Afghanistan, Frank knew he should be over it. Well, he wasn't.

For a minute, he breathed freely. Gulls and terns cartwheeled over the combers. Then Young masked up, called to duty again.

Safely sealed inside the Humvee, the three men decontaminated, removing masks, mopping sweat from their faces. "Sergeant Booker?"

Anthony Booker, from Detroit, was a reservist in the Guard. Brokenhearted like most, he was a widower and grieving father. Sergeant Booker reported, "No shell casings, Captain, or evidence of a firefight. I'd say the damage was done by M18s, claymores, a whole daisy string chained together. A big ol' tree is blocking the road; looks like a planned ambush, though who up here would whack Chosen is beyond me."

Captain Young nodded; whoever planted the mines knew their business. With rocky embankments on both sides, the lethality in the blast radius appeared a hundred percent.

"Specialist Cruz, you get a body count?"

Alfonso Cruz, from Saginaw, was a combat medic. Pre-collapse, he'd deployed with Captain Young and his buddy Booker to Kunduz. Together, they'd seen some shit. The specialist gave his assessment, saying, "We got ten vehicles, sir, all shredded. Looks like four or five occupants in each. Let's call it plus forty KIA."

"Any chance one of our perps got cooked?" Captain Young took a flyer from the stack and studied it.

"Well Captain, here's the interesting part." Cruz pointed at a woman's mugshot. "Says here that our Liz drives a red F-250. Sir, you wanna guess what vehicle was leading this here column?"

"No shit? What about a body, Specialist? We got a positive ID on Liz McGee?"

"Not that lucky, sir. Her truck's the only empty one."

Young smoothed his non-regulation mustache. Resisting the

urge to gripe, he issued orders to his men. Thirty minutes later, they departed the scene.

A woman, badly wounded, skulked in tree shadow. With blood-shot eyes she watched the Humvee depart, bumping south towards Charlevoix, its yellow griffin pissing in the wind. She crawled to the nearest utility pole; half her body had been seared. Her scalp was bald on one side. Where her left breast had been, a wound oozed, half-cauterized. With her good arm she filched the flyer tacked up by the soldier.

Wanted by order of the US Army:

Member of the Chosen 'Red' Liz McGee

Member of the Chosen 'Cowboy' Bob Campbell

Descriptions, aliases, crimes (alleged) and photos below

Order to be enforced by all units identifying as Old Law

Signed, LTC J.R. Dennis

Battalion Commander 125th Infantry Regiment, 37th IBCT

The creature wheezed as it deciphered the descriptions and pho-tos. Laughing, then coughing, it let the flyer fall. Lizard-like, it scuttled over the embankment to lap warm water from a puddle by the shore, wincing as sunlight aggravated its many wounds. When sated, Red Liz scurried back to shade.

PART 1:
Old Friends and New Arrivals

Canoes in a Fog, Lake Superior by Frances Anne Hopkins

Weaving with Wood

A TEENAGE GIRL SAT BESIDE A MAPLE TREE, both listening to water-song. The Jordan was one of two rivers on Beaver Island. Its Indigenous name, ethnically-cleansed, was forgotten by all except the river itself, who tried whispering it to Miin—Peace maybe? Sanctuary?

The Naturals, after three months on the island, had both. Prosperous in their refuge, they'd left the depeopled mainland and its Viral gangs behind them. For a season now, they'd found respite in the island's interior, sheltered by the strong arms of two rivers. Miin was expecting visitors, but in a gridless world, time's hourglass was less granular. The message from Samantha—Miin's foster-gran and Anishinaabe elder—had stated, "Expect visitors in the morning." Samantha's apprentice had been sitting since daybreak.

The September day was golden; the sun's arc had shallowed. Equinox approached, green leaves feasting on photons while they could. Already whole branches had flamed out, blazing with orange and red. As chloroplast factories met their quota—stored sucrose—they were shuttered till spring.

Back in June, some 200 Naturals had disembarked from the stolen ferry. Miin, a Native, an islander, had been aboard. She'd been sent by Samantha, along with two companions, to scout the mainland. Their leader was Keith Two-Crow, an old-timer, a Vietnam veteran with a mountain-man beard. Keith, parting the blockade, had been murdered in June. Shot by a boat captain, his body splashed into the harbor. The third scout, Mukwa—her foster brother, a bear of a man—dove from the ferry to retrieve the blasted corpse. St. James Bay had purpled, Keith's red blood diluted by Michigan's infinite blue.

Island council, despite angry voices, granted land to the asylum seekers inside the state forest. This gift—of life, really—was appreciated by the transplanted Naturals. Miin, ever a go-between, had been tasked by Samantha, island's eldest, to greet yet another delegation. Miinan, Anishinaabemowin for blueberry, would again lead a tour of the ELF encampment. The barefoot diplomat had done this before.

Miin's maple was aflutter with anticipation, its fibrous roots sipping from the river. So far, the narrow bridge remained empty. Island automobiles had been idled by collapse. Fuel was rationed for the fleet and for the health clinic's generators. Island council—grudgingly—allowed Naturals and their flocks to homestead in the interior, hoping their green thumbs and animal husbandry could provide calories, reducing the cull of the coming winter.

The teenager wove sticks while she waited. Sweet-blooded, her maple companion was curious. Miin arranged her creations for inspection—a basket, a hat, a ship. The branches dipped down, millions of stomata opening and closing, sniffing her signature, the flavor of her pheromones. Sightless, the barky old one brailled the girl's character with twiggy fingers. Miin had introduced herself and the sentient tree reciprocated, emitting complex chemicals expressing its life story and mood for the day. These salutations were slow; Miin translated what she could. Like any traveler ignorant of dialect, effort matters, and any attempt is appreciated.

When Miin spied approaching visitors and bowed out, the tree bowed too, saving the girl's signature, posting Miin's scent profile on the island's wood-wide-web. The forest remembered past tree-talkers and stored such data, not in clouds, but in roots and the symbiotic fungi between them. Such talkers were once common, but a century had passed since a new name was added. This block-chain of mycorrhiza was accessed by the dendritic denizens of the island. The names of past tree-talkers were recalled, and Miin's, which she'd shared, was added to the loamy ledger: Miinan, Blueberry, Miin.

The old tree sighed as the young two-legs greeted the new arrivals—others of her kind. The maple adjusted its leafy panels; photon-focused, it resumed its shift, sweetening sunlight into sugar.

The Delegation

REUNITING ON THE JORDAN RIVER BRIDGE, Samantha and Miin, foster and fosterling, hugged each other hard. The slanting light of September illuminated the former roommates. Since Miin returned from the mainland, they'd seen each other seldom, both too busy helping others acclimate to the new status quo. Born in another age, the white-haired elder studied her protégé at arm's length. "You've got that treeish look again, Miinan. I can see the green-light in your eyes."

"Just chatting with the locals, nothing wrong with being neighborly."

Samantha grinned. "Speaking of neighbors, of course you remember our visitors?"

Miin welcomed the four islanders that followed. "Mr. Greene, good to see you again. Your farm shares a border with this forest. We're lucky to have you and your family so close. Thank you for coming, not just today, but all your prior visits too."

Shawn Greene had been an ally to Samantha, convincing islanders it was in their interest to offer sanctuary to Naturals. The capable man nodded and said, "Always good to see you, Miin. I've mentioned this before, but my wife and I were terrified when Samantha told us you were scouting the main. I'm glad you're back on Beaver where you belong."

Miin nodded, turning to the next visitor. "Doc Newsome, I believe this is your first visit? I'm sure you'll find our camp healthy and sanitary. By the way, thank you for screening the ferry and declaring us virus-free. That morning back in June seems like forever ago."

The tall man smiled agreeably. He had been the island's resident physician for decades, delivering its babies, certifying the deceased. Collapse had canceled his retirement.

Miin moved on. "Deputy Williams, good to see you too, though I don't think you'll be needing your sidearm."

Travis Williams, island-born, flinched a bit. "I know it, Miin. Just part of my uniform, OK?"

Miin looked critical. The sheriff's deputy continued, "Let me say how sorry I am about Keith's death. Did you know he was a veteran? Vietnam. Decorated too. I admired him, and so did many on the island."

"Thank you," Miin answered carefully. "But why did you free the man that shot him? Shouldn't there be a trial?"

The gathering grew awkward as the deputy got defensive. "Bill Ferny was released on his own recognizance. He can be called back at any time. Meanwhile, his behavior, especially towards these Naturals, will be closely monitored."

Miin held eye contact with the island's only lawman.

"Miin, Keith's shooting was complicated. We have no judge. I did the best I could. Many called it self-defense. If I could redo that morning, believe me, I would."

Miin did believe him. She respected Williams and the badge on his uniform. He'd gone out of his way to supply her adopted Uncle Keith with sheriff department surplus. Two-Crow, forever *Semper Fi*, used the weaponry to ambush Chosen, allowing ELF refugees to escape.

Blueberry smirked at his sidearm. The combat training of Naturals, especially the Sentinel squads, made his precious pistol seem like a toy. The Sentinels, led by Elena and her partner Diana, eschewed modern weaponry. Their proficiency with bow, spear, and blade had bested heavily armed Chosen on multiple occasions.

Miin knew this training continued; replacements were recruited to replace those killed or missing. June had been a bloody month for the Sentinels. Squirrel, Diving-Duck, Matador, Tigre, Bull, Thorn, his squad—all were lost. There'd been no shortage of volunteers. Beaver Island's safety was only temporary. Naturals, especially ELF extremists, anticipated fighting ahead. Most were prepared to do their part. When XCons and hell hounds attacked their encampment near Petoskey's Bear River, unarmed Naturals had been slaughtered as well. Their school teacher, old Ms. McIntyre, principled till the end, died shielding her students from X-branded mass shooters.

Miin looked, but her fellow scout Mukwa wasn't there. Miin and Mukwa—unrelated by blood, both fostered by Samantha—had much in common despite a decade's difference in age. They came from broken families, raised by Sam and the island's remnant Ojibwe. The siblings loved Keith Two-Crow. The old man's death created a vacuum, a void in the canopy; a mighty tree had been felled. Miin filled this hole—and her heart—with community, with teaching, with new growth. She tended green-talents, pushing them like tendrils, looking for light in darkness, seeking solace in the midst of mass death.

Her foster brother? Not so much. The big man was a mess. Scouting the mainland, Mukwa had fallen hard for Nighthawk, a Sentinel archer, a real hothead, a militant. Miin knew the awkward couple shared a tent—and not much else—near the edge of the state forest. Samantha intuited her thoughts. The Anishinaabe elder gave her fosterling a look. They would discuss Muck's malaise later.

Miin turned her attention toward welcoming the last delegate on the bridge, though it pained her. "Captain Doyle, I'm surprised to see you here."

Delegate Doyle

"BE LYING IF I DIDN'T SAY THE SAME," Doyle grumbled. "Like the deputy said, if I could do it over, I would."

The commercial fisherman didn't offer his hand—Doyle doubted she'd take it. Miin didn't seem so young anymore. Seen some shit, no doubt, scouting the main. Had a way of boring right through you with those brown-green eyes. What had crone Sammy called it? Her "treeish" look? Like having a blinking contest with a damn oak.

Doyle, a gill-netter, had mending to do, so he did. "I'm here to apologize, Miin. To you and your brother Muck—I mean Mukwa—as well. If Dr. Chow is around, I'd say the same to him."

She gaped; they all did. Doyle held course. "I let you kids down, broke a promise. Keith's dead because of me. Not an easy truth to live with. I'm sorry."

In all his decades on the water, greenhorn to captain, Doyle could count his apologies on one calloused hand. What happened next surprised him even more. Miin moved in close. Seizing his rough hands with her tender ones, she tugged him down and kissed a scruffy cheek. Doyle backed water in alarm. *What the fucking hell?*

"I, for one, forgive you, Captain." Red-faced, Doyle stumbled in retreat before finding his sea legs again. Miin pressed on, "The aid you gave us, the evacuation you promised, put you in an impossible position with other captains and your duties to the island. I recognize that. I'm sure Keith did too. It's time to move on."

His cheek felt cool where she'd smooched it, like ferns in the shade. Doyle scented green leaves and sap. He resisted the urge to touch his face—had his whiskers grown mossy? Dignity kept his hands stowed at his side. Her acceptance was shocking—more than he deserved. *And what the hell would Annie think?*

His giggling wife would never let this go. Doyle looked at Greene, at Newsome, at Williams. The islander men had the decency to look away. *Kissed on the cheek by an Indian girl! Blushing like a damn schoolboy!* He cleared his throat, steadied rudder, and resumed course. "How 'bout we get down to business? See what you Nats been up to these past months?"

The delegates followed Miin and Samantha across the bridge. Doyle checked the river for the fall run of salmon—too early. He crossed over with the rest, noticing a sign woven from sticks and vines. A stylized tree had been formed, and the words, "Welcome to ELF Country!"

Though a first for Doyle, there'd been plenty of visitors. Miin nodded at the sign: "Back on the mainland, I wondered the same. Apparently, the ELF were eco-activists from the last century. Earth Liberation Front they called themselves. Mother Nature's insurgents, wrecking logging equipment, setting lab mice free, torching bulldozers, that sort of thing. Some Naturals took a shine and I guess it stuck. Elves is a nickname some use, though most outsiders, of course, roll their eyes."

Rolling his own, the deputy interrupted, "I trust their terrorist days are behind them? Not much here for them to sabotage."

Miin grinned. "The island is safe, if that's what you're asking. Most Naturals are against technology. A religious thing—or maybe spiritual? Others could explain it better. Covee and its variant are Earth's way of de-modernizing the world. They believe their connection with nature has shielded them. Relying on technology might remove this shielding. With some exceptions, it's why they won't use modern weapons or vehicles. They wouldn't even allow Keith's CB radio in their camp."

Shawn Greene nodded, Deputy Williams looked doubtful, Doc Newsome stayed neutral. Doyle didn't know what the hell to think. The whole thing seemed kooky. Ojibwe mumbo jumbo. But he'd said a mouthful already.

The tour continued; it was a lot to take in. Miin introduced the delegates to at least a dozen Naturals. Doyle noted multiple ethnicities, and a whole mix of ages, from babies in slings to old folks stacking wood. Most had earthy names that sounded hippie, but they were serious people—athletic and grim, like they could handle themselves in a fight.

Some of the harder ones—Miin's "Sentinels"—looked like they'd seen killing, maybe done some themselves. It reminded Doyle of the first summer of collapse, when his Beaver boats enforced the blockade. Back then, it was kill or be killed; fleeing disease in anything that could float, desperate mainlanders were rammed by the fleet. He remembered shots fired, boat decks set aflame. The price had been high, but contagion—thank Christ—was kept from their shore. Grid down, and out of medicine, they had their share of deaths, but none had been stung or died from disease.

Doyle had a head for numbers. Two hundred refugees disembarked back in June. Pre-collapse, there'd been 300 islanders living year-round on Beaver. Thirty islanders died that first winter, culled by a lack of calories, of insulin, of heat.

Samantha had advocated for resettlement, insisting that hosting Naturals would boost their own chances. Her mentee Miin, as tour guide, emphasized the winter preparations. Many Naturals lived in walled tents with woodstoves, or constructed wigwams of bent wood with sturdy roofs. Some families burrowed into sandy hillsides, timbering their inner rooms and framing doorways. Squinting up at the canopy, Mariner Doyle saw tree platforms and hammocks swaying uncomfortably high in the pinetop rigging.

No adults sat idle, and even their kids were industrious, making games of gathering acorns, splitting kindling, and the like.

Most impressive to Doyle was their livestock. Islanders had been mostly meatless for a year and a half. The herds of pigs and sheep made him drool. Pens had been constructed and the Natural in charge, a Lutheran pastor named George, explained that more animals were at pasture, shepherded by the camp's teenagers, an arrangement that suited everyone. "These kids don't know how good they have it," George sighed. "Given the choice between a meadow and middle school, I'd have picked meadow every time."

The pastor, in muddy boots, urged the delegates to bring Father Peter next time, the popular—and profane—priest of Holy Cross Church. George had heard the rumors: Father Peter rarely wore his collar, would rather be hunting, gambling, and swearing with parishioners than cloistered in his church.

Deputy Williams, acting DNR as well as sheriff, interviewed ELF fishermen mending nets and smoking filets. He had the same stern talk with folks skinning squirrels and scraping hides outside their tents. Doyle approved of the lawman's tone. With licenses and bag limits long gone, Williams emphasized conservation. Way ahead of the lawman, Naturals nodded. Sustainability was their thing.

Continuing the tour, Miin introduced the delegates to farmer Rodriguez and farmer White, the same-sex couple in charge of crops. ELF garden plots looked tidy; the soils weren't great, but decent fields had been found, and cultivation commenced. Doyle admitted these tree-huggers had green thumbs, with a work ethic to match. They'd been irrigating the interior, diverting streams, constructing channels. The coming harvest appeared to be a good one. Though, like every fisherman Doyle knew, the farmers were superstitious of success, loath to discuss bushels and crop yields.

Doyle saw his fellow delegates were impressed. So far, every question had been answered. Greene was in his element, crawling into root cellars to inspect non-electric preservation. Doc

Newsome approved the camp's latrines and drinking water situation. No weaponry or Sentinel types had been seen since their arrival, but the sheriff's deputy kept an eye peeled for potential violence. Nothing they'd seen pointed to trouble. The Naturals were preparing for winter; there'd been no drunkenness, no sloth. If any of the refugees blamed Ferny for Keith's killing, they didn't show it. If Samantha's intent had been to put the delegates at ease, Doyle confessed the old bird had succeeded.

"Just one more question before we go." Doyle, back on the bridge, squinted at Miin, at Samantha, at tall Diana who joined them. "If our island is threatened again, will your people fight? Will you help defend this place if we have to?"

Jordan—the river border of ELF Country—burbled towards the big lake, singing of wetlands, peace, and millennia of finned migration. The delegates, prepped for departure, waited impatiently for an answer. Miin and Samantha looked to Diana. The Sentinel, even weaponless, had a predatory vibe. The militant locked bright eyes on doubtful Doyle. "We will fight," Diana said, then paused, overhearing the river's refrain, "though let's pray—to Gaia, to God—that we don't have to."

With that, the delegation thanked their hosts and crossed over, exiting the sylvan sanctuary. The men walked towards Greene's farmstead and the horse and wagon that would carry them north to St. James and the harbor.

Miin called out to Shawn Greene, "If your kids have finished chores, send them over!"

"Will do, thank you Miin, *miigwech*! Sarah and I might come too."

Samantha, Miin, and Diana farewelled the delegates with raised hands. Doyle shook his head at the three women, at the woven sign behind them. "Earth Liberation Front," he muttered, "hippies, Indians, and freaks." Still, he grudged, they seemed capable enough. Rather fight with 'em than against. Plus, they'd brought him the damn ferry and a tanker of diesel to keep his boats fueled up, and some generators too.

Judas Doyle, still haunted by the canceled evacuation, had one more apology to make. He'd looked, but Chow hadn't been in camp. Nats said the doctor had been spending time in Newsome's clinic testing theories. Doyle would stop in on his way back to Annie, eat crow one more time, and put these damn apologies astern. He'd visit the lighthouse too, go over the logs, make sure his watchers stayed sharp at their stations. No telling what loomed over the horizon. The next incoming vessel might be a plague ship; instead of truce flags and flocks it could be pirates, pox, and pillage. Orneriness returning, his familiar ballast, Doyle stumped off the bridge and out of ELF Country.

Mukwa's ELF Problem

A BEAR TATTOO—he'd sketched it himself—clawed his neck and a broken heart bruised his sleeve. Mukwa grew his hair long, longing for Keith, his murdered mentor. He heard about Miin's delegates only after they'd departed ELF Country. Probably for the best, he had history with three of the four. Years ago, Deputy Williams handcuffed him a couple times, overnighting the bulky boy in the island's tiny jail. Mukwa wasn't proud of his angsty self, the Muck-punk he'd been before fleeing off-island.

Doc Newsome, another delegate, had dosed him once for chlamydia; Mukwa was fine skipping that reunion too. He had nothing against Shawn Greene, but Tom Doyle had been a delegate as well. Captain Coward, back in June, had promised evacuation. Remembering the man's betrayal still raised his hackles. Keith Two-Crow had been killed by Ferny, one of Doyle's captains. Again, it was best that Mukwa missed their visit, but his own day hadn't been any better.

Nighthawk was in one of her moods. The woman was pissed all the time. She hated it here—hated the island, her insular role. Most of all, Hawk hated him. Her eye-rolling, her cringing at his touch, hurt worse than a whole quiver of arrows.

Muck had spent his day arguing, soothing, chasing, and pleading. Actually, most of his days were like this. A few hours of couples combat exhausted him more than their entire exodus from the mainland. Yes, they'd been sleep-deprived, traumatized, and hounded by Cons, but at least they'd had love. Hawk showed affection then; they'd had each other's backs. Fighting with each other, instead of against, they'd been unstoppable—scything through Charlevoix's Chosen while Diana hijacked their precious ferry. He knew he shouldn't live in the past, but he kept playing their highlight reel—Hawk and Mukwa's greatest hits.

Mukwa missed the delegation, and Sam and Miin too, because earlier in the day Hawk had ascended a white pine, perching there ever since. She'd taken flight at breakfast after he suggested some alone time together, offering—again—a guided tour of his island. She hadn't reacted, staring ahead with dead eyes. When he asked if she was going to finish her eggs, she'd tossed her plate and bolted from the table.

Muck, bits of egg on his face, hulked against the trunk and looked up but couldn't see her. He'd treed her like a lovesick pup. The Sentinel archer could really climb. He sat doggedly, waiting on his master. A kind word from above would set his tail to wagging; he'd bark and do backflips for the merest smile. But those days were gone, probably for good. Mukwa's heart was heavy, bile gnawing his gut. Would they weather this storm? He hoped so. Even the strongest northers gusted themselves out, subsiding after a three-day blow.

Mukwa scented Hawk's friend before he saw her; olfaction was a green-skill he'd been honing. The approaching woman, gnat-sized and gymnastic, was a Sentinel and squad-mate, war-named Sparrow. The ELF warrior stopped when she saw him, shaking her braided head in disgust. "You can't keep chasing her, Mukwa. It's not healthy for you guys. Honestly, it's kind of pathetic."

He gazed at the ground between his knees. "Think I don't know that? Think I'm proud? Shit, Sparrow, help me out. What the hell should I do?"

She offered a strong arm to the big bruin, and gruntingly hauled him to his feet. "I don't know, but it's not this. Let's walk."

Mukwa resisted, looking up at the crown.

"Dude, she's not there. She jumped a few trees, came down and found me. Told me you were stalking her again."

A growl gripped his throat. *Stalking?* Damn. She wasn't wrong though. Sparrow flitted south along a path. He followed her away from camp and deeper into the state forest. The little woman flew through the understory, Mukwa huffing to keep her in view. Pines gave way to maples, then beech trees, their smooth skins girthy with age. She led him to a clearing, sat herself on a sandy bluff, and invited him to do the same. Island-raised, he'd never been here before; Mukwa had spent his cub years closer to town.

Sparrow's perch was a good one. The both gazed south, September's sun slanting upon the landscape. Below them was an inland lake, then a buffer of woods, then the bare, duney shoulders of Lake Michigan. The big lake dazzled, a diaspora of diamonds. A sandy breeze scooped up their signatures, pushing them towards the interior. Sparrow closed her eyes, self-soothing. Mukwa tried focusing on the moment and unfortunately succeeded—all he felt was pain.

He just couldn't shake Nighthawk from his head, his heart. He'd trade every tree and dune for one genuine smile, one embrace, one hint she still had feelings for him.

Sparrow glanced at Mukwa, sighed and said, "Look man, I've known her since collapse. We qualified as Sentinels together, and we've been squad-mates for over a year. This whole depressed Romeo thing will only push her away. You need to knock it off."

"Think I don't know that? If I could, I would, believe me."

"Mukwa, you need to understand it's not about you. Hawk's not the only one having trouble adjusting. Most Sentinels I know, especially those that fought, are having a tough time, way tougher than other Naturals. Now why do you think that is?"

Sparrow wanted an answer; maybe the gymnast was suffering herself. Mukwa thought it through before replying, "Probably feels weird being guests? You guys are used to being in charge, self-sufficient. Then all of a sudden you're begging for somewhere to stay."

Sparrow brightened. "Keep going Oso, there's hope for you yet."

They shared a sad smile hearing Mukwa's nickname again. Two Sentinels, Matador and Tigre, were killed by XCons in the night attack that exiled the elves from ELF Country. Ever winking, the two brothers had delighted their squad, cracking crude jokes about Mukwa's bear nature.

The big man kept thinking out loud. "Maybe she's grieving too? Lots of Sentinels were killed or went missing, and Nighthawk knew them way better than me."

Sparrow nodded approval. "For sure that's part of it. Hardest for me aren't the deaths we witnessed, like Squirrel and Diving-Duck; it's the others, the missing. Like Bull. Like Thorn and his squad. Drives me crazy thinking we stranded them in hostile country. What if they're prisoners? Enslaved? Experimented on? Makes it hard to enjoy all this peace. Just remember, Oso, it's not all about you."

Mukwa got it, he really did.

"And something else," Sparrow opened up, "don't go repeating it, certainly not to her, but Hawk's turned extreme about the virus and what our mission should be. She's vulnerable, radicalized. Mukwa, I worry."

He pulled his eyes from the horizon. "What are you talking about?"

Sparrow waited. Mukwa's Sentinel-status wasn't clear. He'd come to the Front as an outsider, a scout from Beaver Island. Yes, he'd proven himself in combat, but in this lull, his limbo status returned. She decided on full disclosure. "You know the ELF name? Its origin story? Eco-terrorists from the '90s?"

Sentinel philosophy hadn't really been his strength, but Mukwa nodded—yes, he was generally aware.

"You've heard our shaman, Brian, preaching about Lovelock, Gaia, and Tolkien's talking trees? Naturals believe we're shielded by our nature-bond, our rejection of technology."

Mukwa started to glaze over; this felt like school. When was lunch? Muck, ever the class clown, waited for the bell.

Sparrow slowed her speech. "There's a faction, a splinter group, that has issues with our role here. Are we betraying Gaia and Her virus by helping these locals? Are we interfering? Endangering our own green-shielding through association? Shouldn't Gaia decide who lives and who dies?"

Sparrow left it at that, letting Mukwa take it in. Muck, too often mocked, had little love for his fellow islanders—most of them, anyway. But this was too much theory. He knew Nighthawk would be interested though. Her mental skills, like all her powers, were next-level. Elves never talked about their past lives, but he knew she'd been well-educated, some kind of crusader for conservation?

"If you're worried, Sparrow, then what should we do? Hawk and I share a tent. One of these nights she might not show."

"I don't know, Mukwa, I really don't. I wish Matador were here. Dude really had a way of soothing her down, giving her purpose. He had that effect on all of us."

Oso hung a heavy limb on her shoulder. "I miss him. Tigre too. I miss them both."

The sun brushed the scene with golden strokes. Every leaf was a solar panel, storing charge, green energy for the future. Lake Michigan remained empty, above and below. No boat wakes marred the blue. No contrails crisscrossed the sky. Killed by contagion, most combustion engines had coughed their last. Trucks, Cessnas, and chainsaws had died, gasping for gas.

The diminutive elf mock-elbowed Muck and the scenic spell was broken. Together they got to their feet. "You wanted advice, right?" she asked.

He wouldn't like it, but nodded anyway.

"Give her some space, man. Find somewhere else to sleep. Do your own thing for a while. Hang with Miin, or go visit your people."

Athletic, the little Sentinel spun and sprinted away. He let Sparrow go; she was faster by far. He had a lot to process and steeled himself not to return, not to see Nighthawk. Mukwa felt relieved. He needed to buck up, leave Hawk the hell alone. But what to do next? Again, he felt a loss-pang for Keith. Not that Two-Crow had been friendly, but there'd been respect, and at the end, a leathery kind of love. He had nightmares of Keith's killing, diving for his body, the blood in the bay. Or worse, cradling his corpse, but then both eyes would pop open, Keith locking arms around Mukwa till water filled both their lungs.

Shit. Ol' Muck was a mess; he had healing to do. His foster-gran Samantha was a healer. The Natural, Grace, had strong medicine too. Miin, his foster-sis, knew both women well.

When in doubt, return to your roots. Anything was better than tossing in his tent, obsessing over if she'd show or what her mood would be like. He was done with all that—he fucking hoped so, anyway.

Mukwa pulled out his pocket notepad and thumped to the ground. From his vantage on the bluff, he sketched the big lake—still empty—then turned his gaze inland. A low spot in the landscape, a kettle lake, glowed more emerald than the rest: Cranberry Bog. Samantha's shack was near that hollow, a place of power. Crow, Bear, and Blueberry, the three scouts, had been bonded there. Samantha, silver-haired, had shown them a vision of their quest, mirrored in spring water. If green-shields had indeed been given, the bog had bestowed them.

As good a destination as any.

He put away his pad, his pencil. The mocked man stood tall, sniffing for scent. Mukwa, a skin-changer, dropped on all fours, scooting through the brush. Low to the ground, he shuffled towards the interior.

Bogged Down

MUKWA KNEW FROM PAST EXPERIENCE that surrender was the key to finding Sam's sanctuary. The harder he tried, the more gran's shack receded, the more scratched and bug-bitten he became. He didn't need Sparrow's head-shrinking to see the same lesson applied to him and Nighthawk. Hawk was a wild thing; the sharp-eyed Sentinel would never fly towards his whistle. Even if she did, if she landed right on Muck's fist, Hawk would lose half of who she was. High fliers abhorred a cage. Hooded and jessed was not how he wanted her. Mukwa paused, bleeding openly, as once again the path petered out, ending in a barricade of brambles.

This was not the way. But, fuck, what was? *Nishiime*, little sister, Miin—what would she do? Thinking her name, summoning her soily signature, was like a cool breeze on hot skin. Mukwa's anxieties were wicked away, banished by the healing shadow Blueberry cast in this place.

"Miinan—*Sunlight on Berries*." Mukwa spoke slowly, namedropping his sis, a sylvan VIP. All the lifeforms were listening, nodding along, root, leaf, and twig. Approval wafted from the foliage, coded in complex chemicals. The bramble-bouncers relented, arterial footpaths unclogged, as Cranberry Bog—emerald heart of the island—rolled out its green carpet. Mukwa stooped low, hunched his shoulders, and with a humble gait took the path that was proffered.

His procession was noted by Samantha's familiars: owl, fox, and feline. Mukwa nodded to each sentry he passed. The forest opened up. There was Sam's garden, there her warped shack. The grove of maples gossiped about him behind leafy limbs; Muck knew they were talking trash, throwing shade. He knew they were right.

"Look what the cat dragged in." Samantha stroked the tabby that had reported him.

"*Aanii, nookomis*." Mukwa wasn't Native, but foster-gran didn't care. It wasn't skin or hair or blood quantum that mattered, but strength of spirit, and Samantha's foster—good ol' Muck—was a bear.

Sam cleared her throat as Mukwa slaked his thirst at the rain barrel. Mukwa doused himself with the dipper. "Granny, I don't want to hear it. Sparrow gave me an earful already, so save your advice."

Samantha grinned, pretending to scratch her cheek; the only finger she used was her middle one. Mukwa laughed from his belly, couldn't help it. Sammy was good medicine. The wise one zipped her lips, nodded at the woodpile and the maul, then turned her back on the bear and got busy in her garden. Mukwa rolled his muscled shoulders, hefted the hickory handle, and got to work. An hour later he wiped away sweat, admiring the face-cord he'd constructed.

The grove collected sunlight; that's what it did. Casting spells of green magic, the woody alchemists transmuted water, air, and earth. Photons, flung from the sun, became BTUs—batteries of fire for the long dark ahead. Mukwa's woodpile was a calendar of summer days, and Sam's woodstove a time machine. Fueled by chunks of maple, January became July.

Westering, the sun slipped below the treeline as Mukwa guzzled again from Sam's barrel.

"Best dip yourself in, too." His foster-gran wrinkled her nose for effect, nodding towards the bog path. Mukwa sniffed his pits and took the hint. He propped his splitter against the pile and flexed his stiff paws. He could feel blisters beneath the pale skin. Too long since he'd hefted a handle. At his peak, training with Matador's squad—spear, staff, and bow—he'd been a lean, mean, blade-wielding machine. In his three months back on-island, he'd let himself go slack. No wonder his Hawk had flown. Couldn't blame her, not one bit. Muck clawed off his soaked shirt, heading towards the cold spring to cleanse himself, inside and out.

Returning to the sugarbush refreshed, he greeted the place properly: *"Iskigamizigan."* Mukwa's calm was restored, his balance renewed. A fall breeze stirred the yellowing maples; gossip over, acceptance granted, they nodded to Mukwa in return. Samantha had made ready, nothing fancy or elaborate. A seashell, a braid of sweetgrass, and an eagle feather to speed the spirits. Mukwa entered the shack and breathed from his belly, floating to a chair. No words were spoken.

When the time was right Samantha nudged the sketchpad towards her artist. She filled a small jar with fruity wine. Keats' nightingale—perching on her bookshelf—came to mind, *beaded bubbles winking at the brim.* Her hulking foster took a sip. The smudge curled through the cabin. Samantha exited, no longer needed.

That I might drink, and leave the world unseen,

And with thee fade away into the forest dim.

Mukwa, left alone in the shack, was free to find himself. He opened to a blank page and began to make his own acquaintance. No noosed necks or Viral hounds this time. No nudes of Nighthawk either. Instead, he drew the slowly warping shack, green allies, and the medicine woman—his gran—dancing through her duties.

Traumas tamed, at least for now, Mukwa closed up his pad and stepped outside, shutting the shack door behind him. Samantha, barefoot, stood by the birdbath, gazing at its silvery surface. Reflecting on the past, she addressed him by saying, "Did you know that young Keith stacked wood, just like you did, when he returned from Vietnam?"

No, Mukwa hadn't heard this. Bereft, he kept quiet, barely breathing, hoping for more.

"Yes, Keith was drafted, became a Marine, served in helicopters. Like you, Mukwa, he did things, saw things, that no person should. Weighed down by sin, Keith fell, became trapped, stuck on the ground. Two-Crow lost his wings.

"I was auntie to him, *ozigosan*. We were both Nish, original people, but out of place on this too-Irish island. Our dark skins were drowning in a rising tide of white. When Keith was drafted it broke my heart. His too, though the lanky kid wouldn't say it. He wouldn't run either, though I urged him to. We had kin in Canada, but he never crossed that line. When Two-Crow returned from Asia he was broken. Said he felt corrupted, no longer deserving of island peace and its pleasures."

The afternoon light began to fade, as did Mukwa's pulse rate, his anxieties. He took it all in and bundled it away, strong medicine for future hurts. Samantha was satisfied: "Well, school will be out soon. Should we go find Miss Teacher?"

Mukwa looked up, spell broken. He offered his arm, but when Sam went to take it, he slung ol' granny—carefully!—over a broad shoulder. She giggled like a girl, light as a silver feather, tickling and beseeching till mighty Muck set her down. Arm in arm, an ancient beauty and a bruised beast, they left the bog smiling, heading for West Side Road, hoping to hitch a ride to Miin's mobile classroom of the day.

Tree Academy: Green Training

"FIND YOUR INNER TREE. Listen with your heart and feet."

It was September, and school was in session on Beaver Island. The district was ELF Country, Fox Lake the day's classroom. Students gathered around Big Birch, root-connected to hundreds. Years ago, hearing rumors of old trees, the Eastern Native Tree Society sent an emissary to the island—measuring, naming, stirring things up. According to ENTS the Big Birch, *Betula papyrifera*, had nurtured this grove for three centuries—4,000 full moons silvering its glade.

Highly qualified, Ms. Miin lectured the class, then bid her pupils to remove their footwear. Soon, a dozen pairs littered the leaves: worn out gym shoes from islander kids, Shawn and Amanda Greene's muddy boots, Miin's moccasins. Grace and Brian, as guest teachers, were barefoot already. Trained in best practices, Miin modeled respiration, filling her lungs—bronchial trees—with the outbreath of plants: green oxygen. She burrowed her feet in loam, stretching leafless limbs to the sky.

"The soil of your body will guide you. Your kinship with these rooted relatives is not as distant as you think."

Her pupils followed her lead. The gathering morphed treeish—fingers to twigs, torsos to trunks. Miin, as central sapling, was soon surrounded by a copse of aspiring sun-seekers.

"Feel the photons on your face, sift the scent of each drifting molecule. Seek the tree that is seeking you. You'll know when you find each other."

Using Sentinel hand-talk, Miin signed the group to scatter. A soft light slanted through the canopy; the sylvan banners of the school fluttered gold and green.

"Approach your tree, ask for consent. You'll know what is right. Your tree will tell you."

Miin, Grace, and Brian tiptoed amongst the novices, matchmaking humans with their cambium companions, though who was choosing whom was a question worth asking. When the pairings were complete and each primate stood beside its carboniferous cousin, Brian took up the lesson. The red-bearded man—wearing tie-dye and beaded dreads—helped the humans make their next connection.

"Be with the tree in a way that works for your body and the tree's body."

Brian demonstrated a respectful approach, a wordless introduction, how to ask permission and how to receive it.

"The first touch can be powerful," he continued, "so don't rush it. Be fully present in that moment when skin touches skin and your atoms intermingle."

Again, Miin, Grace, and Brian flowed from tree to tree, assisting with each bonding.

Brian went on, "You can lay in the roots, stand forehead to trunk, or swing yourself up into their branches."

Here he boosted an island boy who'd been beckoned by a white pine.

"Four million years ago we lived in trees; the memory—ours and theirs—remains green, as if it were yesterday."

When the initiates had completed introductions and further instruction was unnecessary, Grace—as safety officer—began patrolling the grounds. Miin and Brian shared the rooty lap of an old sugar maple, content with silence and pleased with their pupils.

A raptor glided above the treetops, curious about the scene below. It sent down a cry, querying this two-legged intrusion. Miin shouldered Brian and grinned. Aloft already, he smiled, eyes closed as his consciousness flew. If an islander had glanced, they'd have thought the man was napping. Miin was glad he was up there, eyes in the sky, another level of school security. She wished her friend happy flying.

As lead teacher, Miinan wanted feedback on the day's lesson. Her senses reported things were going well. The students were quiet; they didn't fidget and were focused on the learning task. The true test, though, was the trees. She inhaled their leafy exhalations, bartering carbon for oxygen, the ancient exchange. As her two eyes closed, a third blinked open—the stoma in her mind. Dormant brain-regions ignited. Barriers built of habit dissolved, brick by brick.

Distinctions between *self* and *outside-of-self* became blurry.

With dreamlike fluidity Miin was welcomed by the green world around her. Reluctantly, she maintained focus, resisting the urge to tunnel with worms, mingle with mycelia, or sip sugar through straws of xylem and phloem. Chlorophyll's electrons were vibrating by the billions. Miin frolicked through the photo-factories, then returned to earth to check on her charges.

The white pine—*biisaandago-zhingwaak* to the island's Indigenous—had much to say about he half-dozing in its burly arms. Michael Martin had made a good impression. The boy's scent-profile was already in the system—young Martin was known as a nimble climber. The rooted residents near his farm had posted to the group chat already, garnering a million green likes.

Meanwhile, Josie, eldest daughter of the Greenes, like Miin, had an affinity for *wiigwaasag*. There was a playfulness to birch trees that was hard to ignore. Teenage Josie maintained her bond through motion. Her slender form, sylph-like, danced— oh so proper—with Big Birch, the grandfather of the grove. Onlookers waved their branches in approbation, a thousand leaves rustling their applause.

Miin, still seated, continued her rounds; tree to tree, the teacher touched base. Brian twitched beside her, adjusting his flight-feathers to updrafts of air. All appeared well, above and below. The peaceful afternoon pointed towards what was possible in Gaia's green new deal.

A hooded intruder perched high above the scene. Cloaked by her camouflage, the dark elf had evaded school security. The shooter observed the day's lesson, drawing her own conclusions about the new world and Gaia's vision for it. This watcher, sensing the approach of visitors—an elderly woman and a too-familiar oaf—departed the scene, leaping branch to branch, a chameleon in the canopy.

The trees, organically omniscient, rooted for neither side, detrimentally neutral—as always—in human affairs.

Kilty's Hill

TWO VISITORS APPROACHED THE NEW SCHOOL, a silver-haired elder and a muscled bear. Smiling, the pair waited while Miin dismissed her pupils, one student gifting an apple—a McIntosh—to their all-time favorite teacher.

Samantha, eldest of the island's Anishinaabeg, spoke first. "Excellent lesson, Miinan. Your ancestors would be proud, *miigwech chi-miigwech!*"

Mukwa grinned too. "I'm no fan of school, but sis, that's the kind of class I might actually like." He opened his arms. Blueberry lost herself in foster brother's embrace.

"Don't kid yourself," she said, emerging with a smile. "Your green abilities are more active. Sitting under a tree would feel like detention soon enough."

Mukwa laughed, his second of the day; damn it felt good. He nodded towards her co-teacher. "What's up with Brian?" The rumpled shaman sat propped against the tree. "Head in the clouds again?"

Mukwa extended his arms, spreading his own wings. The trio—a blended family—laughed; the bruin felt more weight fall from his shoulders.

"Little sis, if you're not busy, Sam thought we might visit Keith's grave. Haven't been up there since the funeral, might do me some good."

Miin squeezed his rough paw. Foster brother looked a bit

less haunted; he'd been haggard since their exodus in June. Of course, she was in.

Three figures slowly climbed Kilty's Hill at twilight. The moon phase was waxing crescent, little warmth in its smile. Campfires winked from the settlement of Naturals below.

Sleepy squirrels watched the supplicants genuflect in their grove. Three deer—an old mama, a spike, and a doe—scent-checked the visitors before resuming their acorn repast. The three signatures were known, and none posed a threat.

The warm day eased into dusk, eager stars shining as the hemisphere darkened. Daylight's long summer reign was dimming. Atop the hill, a sapling had been planted over freshly turned earth. Keith's other grave marker was his .22 rifle, standing upright, rusted from three months in the rain. The trio sat themselves down and bowed heads, joining hands in a circle of power. Unseen, a squirrel family eavesdropped from above. Words were spoken, and a pipe was passed. Fragrant smoke soon tickled the leaves. More words were said, then a starry silence resumed.

The eldest, white-haired, lifted her lids and greeted the watchers. A squirrel kit chittered back before being hushed by its parents. Beneath their tree, the big man kept his eyes on the ground. A heaviness was in him, a weight that the whole grove could feel—thunder before a storm. The youngest was a girl, and her sadness burned bright. She gathered sticks as she sat, deftly weaving a nest.

The scolded squirrel was shocked, and looked to its parents. What was happening? The big oak they lived in bent down its branches. As above, so below—the oak's twiggy fingers repeated the girl's pattern. Now the whole canopy was chittering, even the heavy man looked up, baring a grin.

Vega, the first star, peeped brightly through the leaves, followed by a second, then a third; Altair and Deneb swanned through the sky.

A bell began to clang, and all ears bent towards its clamor. The three humans stood and quickly descended. Nearby, an osprey stirred himself to flight; a few powerful wingbeats, and the sandy island fell behind. A few more, and the flier spied the source of alarm.

A trio of oversized canoes approached Beaver Island from the darkening east. Paddles flashed in synchrony. Singing was heard from many strong voices.

Clang! Clang! Clang! the warning bell insisted.

Stroke! Stroke! Stroke! the newcomers replied.

Gaia's Guardians

SENTINEL NIGHTHAWK, furious, flew away from Miin's school as Sam and Mukwa approached. The ELF daughter—dark hearted—was unwilling to alter her neural pathways, her habitual thinking. And why should she? To be polite? To join with these islanders in unholy union? Spying on Miin's school only sharpened Hawk's suspicions.

Nighthawk followed the savor of roasting meat to a wooded hollow, the trysting place of her sisters-in-arms. She owl-called from shadow. The two fire-tenders unhooded themselves and signaled her to approach. Gray-clad, like herself, the Sentinel women hadn't eaten all day and were about to take their meal. The archer joined their fairy circle, removing her hood. Elena lifted rabbit-skewers from greasy flames. Diana pinched salt and the women sat silent as each composed their thoughts.

Eventually, Elena said grace: "We are thankful to these creatures. May they fuel our bodies as they were fueled by the forest. May they give us the strength we need to fight for Gaia and the wisdom to know Her mind."

Portions were divided; the campfire lit their faces as they broke their fast together. Soon, the tiny bones had been stripped and hands and faces scrubbed clean. The women sat cross-legged and stoked the flames. A crescent moon glinted sharply as dusk descended, earlier each passing day.

"Miin was at it again today. Training a batch of islanders by Big Birch."

Elena and Diana absorbed this news as Nighthawk continued, "She's a good teacher, and her talent is strong. It won't be long before those kids are shielded. One girl was dancing like a dryad already."

Diana sighed, the trained mariner sensing dangerous shoals ahead. Sentinel Nighthawk, an extremist, searched the flames, scrying further. "And it won't stop there. Once the kids are trained up, their parents will be next. Soon the whole damn island will be immune."

A sappy branch popped in a detonation of sparks. Elena sided with her partner Diana, saying, "It breaks my heart that this is bad. Are we really rooting for the virus?"

Nighthawk hissed, "We've been over this a million times. It's not that I want these folks to die; they took us in, didn't they? But we shouldn't be interfering. Gaia shielded us for a reason. She may have a reason for not shielding others. Her pandemic needs to play out without us butting in. That's all we're saying, right?"

"Yes, that's what we're saying." Elena sounded sad. "But it's hard when names and faces are attached. We've all killed Chosen, haven't we? Killed Cons too. Isn't that interfering?"

"Protecting Naturals is different!" Nighthawk countered. "Gaia selected us, after all. But going out of our way to immunize others, that's too far. It's playing God. That's what got humans in trouble in the first place."

Diana nodded as the first star—Vega—crowned herself queen. "The only thing that justifies our pain, the loss of loved ones, the collapse of everything, is having faith that there's a *reason* behind it. Whether there's such a thing as 'Gaia's will' or not, *She* is something I need to believe in."

"How can you doubt Her?" Hawk's anger kindled. "Gaia is everywhere! Her will is obvious! She's scrubbing the human filth from this planet before She suffocates. Some of us, She wants to survive. Others, like those Chosen bastards, She's using to spread Her virus. The vast majority of humans, including these islanders, She's scheduled for extinction. There's no holy mystery here. She's desperate, fighting for Her life. The last thing we should do is get in Her way."

Elena and Diana—knee touching knee—tended their silence, tended their campfire. Another star blossomed, then another—silver blooms in a garden of black sky. A barred owl proclaimed an evening hunt. Its primal voice gave the lie to Hawk's earlier signaling.

"Gaia's not the only one that's desperate." Elena spoke as calmly as she could, stirring embers with a stick. Nighthawk glared daggers across a gulf of flames.

"We're all struggling to adjust here," Elena continued, trying for therapy. "Our Sentinel skills aren't needed. The violence we've committed haunts us. Relationships aren't easy, and we're all—"

"What's going on between me and Mukwa has *nothing* to do with this!"

Elena raised a pale palm. "This isn't just about you two. I'm only saying that back on the mainland, our purpose was clear—"

"My purpose is *still* clear! I'm not the one attacked by doubts. I'm not letting some man get between me and *my* mission!"

The older women averted their eyes as Hawk vented further: "I'm not letting any men get in my way! Gaia has a chance here, maybe Her last, to restore balance. Male and female should be equal, damn it! You two know that more than most. A world cocky with testosterone is doomed to fucking fail!

"Just look at this island and their sausage fest 'council.' Fucking Doyle, that traitor! Or Doc Newsome and his 'exams.' That celibate priest, we know his type! Little Deputy Williams, compensating with that pistol of his!

"Shit, look at our own leadership. Chow's scheming almost got us slaughtered back in June. You two saved our asses! What thanks did *you* get? None! I'm telling you, Gaia needs us. The *world* needs us. The men need us too, though they'll never admit it."

Nighthawk's nosedive leveled off, her anger absorbed by leaf and needle until quiet resumed. The Sentinels let their fire fade. The thin moon descended, its silver blade pricking the heart of ELF Country. Night sounds resurfaced: crickets, leafy susurration, and water-song from a seeping spring.

Then, something else, from across a vast distance. A vibration of air, felt more than heard, a reverberation of sound. Their senses deciphered it—the faraway clang of a church bell.

The women sprang to their feet in alarm, sharp ears honing on the source. A different bell—lower-toned—took up the tolling. A coyote howled, then another, and another, as the pack coordinated its feral response.

Elena kicked out the fire. Diana hefted their gear—bows, packs, and quivers. When the horn of the Naturals began to blow, Gaia's daughters were already sprinting. Their shadowy forms flew north along the path as the doleful sound called the forest to arms.

Dr. Chow's Secret

BOB "COWBOY" CAMPBELL HAD BEEN a construction contractor in the before. He'd built a hundred homes, force-feeding McMansions to the already bloated burbs. Bob had married his high school sweetheart. Happy ever after, he and Ashley raised a daughter, their definition of delight. Pre-collapse, Bob saved enough to surprise his angel with college tuition. He'd kept it secret, saving the big reveal for Angela's sweet sixteen.

Both partners were happy in marriage, and kept things spicy. Bob loved country music, especially the old stuff, which he strummed on guitar. Despite some close calls, he'd stayed faithful, his wife too, till the variant—a real homewrecker—intervened.

His wife died in the passenger seat of Bob's truck, her lungs flooding with mucus. Ashley Campbell drowned in a cytokine storm. The ER staff, panic-sweating in flimsy PPE, stacked her sheeted corpse on the sidewalk. Toe-tagged, she played footsie with the fallen. Frozen by rigor mortis, they rested in peace.

When Bob the builder returned, wifeless, to his cookie-cutter home, his little girl had cut her own cords in the hot tub. Her "Dear Dad" note broke what was left of Bob Campbell. The persona that emerged was "Cowboy," red-eyed and wrathful, especially once he'd been "chosen."

Two years distant from this trauma, marooned on Beaver Island, Cowboy found himself confined, no longer in the brig, but in an isolated cabin with a view. His discoverer had freed him from the ferry, only to lock his ass in a cottage. Frying pan to the fire, supposedly for Bob's own good.

Cowboy's captor, during daily rounds, coerced Bob with calories into recording his before-times in a journal the medical man provided. The cabin's windows had been locked and barred by its previous owner. Bob bided his time gazing north at the dunescape and the big lake beyond. Each time his jailer departed, the heavy door was padlocked behind him. Cowboy half-heartedly tried all the exits, but escape was impossible, even if he wanted to. Beaver Island's resident patient was surprisingly content; Bob guessed he was being drugged.

His visitor eventually offered a name, "I'm Dr. Chow, but call me Professor," he'd suggested during his second visit to Bob's compartment in the ferry. "Many people do. And you are?"

For some reason—perhaps his days in solitary, or the man's medical demeanor—Cowboy told the truth. "Campbell, Bob Campbell. Now, *Professor*, please get me the *fuck* out of here."

They were both fit-looking men, dark hair salted with gray; Campbell and his clinician looked much alike. The professor explained how he'd found Bob by accident while looking for medical journals misplaced during a chaotic evacuation. After discovering the ferry compartment, the professor had taken a vial of Bob's blood, bandaged his abrasions, left food and water, and replaced his reeking shit-bucket. "I'll visit again soon," he'd promised.

The next day he returned, cut Bob's cuffs, and explained that for Campbell's safety he'd be quarantined in a remote cabin. This would be their secret; the professor was taking an awful risk. He'd given his patient an appraising look and said, "Mr. Campbell, you should know that you are on an uninfected island with paranoid people who would kill you for who you are, if they weren't killed by your virus first. Do you understand?"

Campbell, red-eyed, returned his look, the professor's frankness inspiring the same. "I'm an asshole Chosen with a deadly virus and the blood of innocents on my hands."

The medical man nodded, penciling his pad. "Interesting."

Campbell had been confined in the cabin since June. His chafed wrists had scabbed and he felt damn near healthy. The clinician had given Campbell a chart—pushups, sit-ups, jumping jacks, even jerking off. Bob, duly-diligent, performed each set, wiping his hands before initialing.

The season tiptoed towards October. A breeze, cooled by the big lake, frosted the tips of the leaves. The sun slanted further south each day, gilding dune grass as it sank. Bob's body had a nice floaty feel as he limbered up. His libido ebbed low, a relief. Bob appreciated the lack of horniness—his usual baseline of behavior. How nice to be free from his dick-tator, to declare independence from King Peter. He was recovering in a rustic spa. The chemicals that no doubt laced his food provided a calm, sparkly buzz: THC? CBD? Opiates?

Cowboy, early on, had asked the mystery man why.

The professor gave his patient a clinical look. "Mr. Campbell, I'm interested to learn if your viral load can be reduced, perhaps even eliminated. I apologize that you didn't volunteer, but given the precarious nature of your presence here, I hope you agree our experiment is for the common good?"

Cowboy had nodded, almost grinned. Virus-free? Was that even possible? Well, they were going to find out. Fine by him. After all, he hadn't aspired to be a murderous, lecherous D-bag. Plus, being stoned near a beach, with all his needs provided for, was hard to argue with. Better than arrowed by elves on the mainland, or lynched by these islanders as a super-spreader. No contest really. Why not make the most of it?

So Campbell complied. He journaled, he exercised, he ate his meals, and slept soundly for the first time since his wife and daughter died. Facing north, pleasantly high, he watched the dune shadows lengthen.

Daniel Chow—M.D. from U of M—carried food, a guitar, and poetry he'd checked out from the island's little library. The doctor watched his back as he took the path towards Sucker Point and his patient in the dunes. After discovering Campbell cuffed in the ferry, Chow had spent a sleepless night, then searched all morning till he found the perfect clinic for his infected client— an out of the way cabin with grates on the windows and a poorly hidden key for the door's big padlock.

Three months later, Chow's conscience was clouded; the risks were mind-numbingly high. The balance between scientific discovery and islander safety teetered on a scalpel's edge. The ethical strain—"first, do no harm"—was taking its toll. Chow was plagued by scenes of catastrophe: Campbell discovered—or escaped—his virus too. Then a rash of symptoms, lethal proteins ballooned by the breeze, mass die-offs, accusatory fingers, witch hunts, the slaughter of innocents, the piled dead.

Nearing the cabin—unfollowed, as far as he could tell—Chow weighed the gains: his patient's viral load was decreasing, this was indisputable. Campbell's baseline samples had been high, his system saturated with viral RNA. Chow ran each subsequent test twice, and the weekly results—decreasing load levels—appeared accurate.

Access to the Roche machine, neglected and dusty in the island's clinic, had been tricky, till Chow realized Doc Newsome wasn't technically inclined. The diagnostic tool wasn't even his. It had been installed ten years ago by med students from the university. Someone had been interested in disease variance over time, comparing islander immunity with populations on the mainland. Data gathered, dissertation written, they'd departed the island, leaving the Roche behind, another relic of before.

Chow had easy access to the machine and its software. His cover story to Newsome and the two nurses: he was monitoring the island for infection. The limiting factor was diesel for the generator. The tanker the ferry brought across made electrification of the clinic and its diagnostic machine less of an issue. Chow congratulated himself on his prescience back in Charlevoix—bringing the fuel truck on board had been his idea, quid pro quo, a petro-treat to sweeten the deal.

The setting sun, blood red, dripped upon the western horizon. Gulls and terns sifted the surf, collecting calories before last call. The isolated cabin appeared in its sheltered dune-fold. It had a woodstove for winter, but chimney smoke—scent and sight—would eventually give them both away. For a cover story, should Chow publicly shift his quarters from ferry to cabin? But then he'd have visitors, plus rooming with Campbell, rapist and murderer, wasn't a great idea, no matter the data.

Reading the man's journal had been as interesting as the lab results. Campbell had a good hand for sketching: nooses, street lights, and cages were common. Some of Chow's theories about super-spreaders had been upended. There was scant evidence his patient had a pre-pandemic predilection for violence—sexual or otherwise.

Rather, Campbell's entries indicated relative normalcy. So what explained his immunity and subsequent sociopathy? Chow knew that solving this epidemiological riddle might prove decisive, not just for Campbell, Naturals, and islanders, but for the entire *Homo* genus.

The doctor trudged through sand towards the cabin, its only occupant waving from the window. Campbell grinned and gave a thumbs up at the guitar case Chow was hauling. The M.D. fought his fraternal feelings, remembering that here, in this idyllic spot, a serial killer had been caged—a walking, talking weapon of mass destruction, rife with protein strands that, if loosed, would bring death to the 300 islanders Chow had promised—*Primum non nocere*—to protect.

Chow inserted the key and opened the padlock, hoping not to be murdered. Though only half-ELF in his beliefs, the healer's sharp ears had often overheard the Sentinel supplication. "Gaia guide me," Chow whispered, entering the knotty pine sanatorium.

Campbell received the guitar gratefully, popped the latches and began tuning by ear. "Welcome back, Professor," he said through a smile.

From St. James harbor, a sudden alarm began to clang. Coyotes joined in, call and response—from Indian Point on Beaver, to Garden Island across the strait—a feral chorus of calamity.

A Game of Cribbage

TWO FIGURES BATTLED OVER A TABLETOP, squinting in the early dusk. A young crescent fell through the branches of their backyard tree. A tire swing, never used, briefly bullseyed the moon. The cricket choir grew softer as their finale approached, the season's first frost.

The situation was serious; Doyle's brow furrowed in concentration. Annie, serene, sipped strawberry wine, the Mason jar hiding her smile. The next crib was hers. With any luck, she'd peg out and have her man skunked. Captain Doyle hated losing, no matter the contest. He had a reputation to protect as the island's highliner. When it came to hauls of whitefish, year after year, his boat, *Bloody Mary*, always topped the catch list.

For Annie, her win held extra savor. They'd bet big on the game: the stakes tonight were sexual. Her friend Samantha suggested it to spice up their sheets. Annie tried not to be hurt that Tom was trying so hard. She sipped at Sam's homebrew; flush with hearts, she allowed herself to feel frisky.

Their next hand was cut short by clanging from Whiskey Point's big bell. The quiet evening reverberated with alarm. Doyle dropped his cards—another 19 hand—and shot a look at his wife. Her grin vanishing, Annie nodded permission instead. "To be continued!" she threatened. "Farewell, Tom Doyle."

He scraped her cheek with a sandpaper kiss. "Adieu, Annie lass. Stand by the radio. I'll call when I know more." Tom stumped on sea legs to the garage, grabbed his go-bag, and disappeared, whistling as he walked—*For we've received orders, to sail back to Boston.*

Annie sighed, more disappointed than worried. With her captain it was always something.

Doyle quickly reached the docks. Boat crews were gathering, stowing weapons and gear as main engines roared to life. A greasy smell hovered over the harbor; the fug of diesel was Tom's strawberry wine. The captain jumped aboard *Mary* and ducked into his wheelhouse. Powering up the marine radio, he listened to the report from the tower: "Pan-Pan, Pan-Pan, Pan-Pan. This is Whiskey Light. Multiple craft spotted, bearing zero-four-five from the tower, moving slowly. They look like large canoes. Over."

Doyle keyed his mic. "*Bloody Mary* to tower. Roger, multiple craft, north north-east of the island. What direction are they headed? Over."

Static, then the watcher's voice answered, "Tower to *Mary*, hard to tell in twilight. They disappeared towards Garden Island. Over."

Doyle thought for a second as O'Donnell thumped aboard. Tom pointed his deckhand to the engine hatch, miming, *check the oil*. Doyle then keyed the mic again, saying, "*Mary* to Indian Point, Bauman you there? Can you see anything? Over."

Static before the reply came through: "Indian Point to *Mary*, negative, my scan shows nothing."

Doyle cursed. The deck plates vibrated as O'Donnell tickled *Mary's* engine to life. The captain eyed his gauges—oil pressure, RPMs, engine temp—as he formulated a defense plan. Just one fucking Viral, that's all it would take, and every islander he knew would be dead in a week. Another person thumped aboard. Gauges steady, he threw a backward glance towards his fishdeck. What in the hell?

O'Donnell was blocking a newcomer. That red-bearded hippy—*a damn Nat!*—tried pushing past him. O'Donnell gut-slugged the intruder with a cinderblock fist. The mainlander crumpled, gasping, "They—are—NOT—a—threat!"

The freak wheezed for breath.

"Bullshit!" roared Doyle. He vice-gripped one soft arm, O'Donnell the other. Together they heaved the longhair ashore.

"Throw lines, let's go!" Doyle straddled his wheelhouse as O'Donnell cast them loose. *Bloody Mary* bucked as Doyle geared her transmission. One-handed, he steered around the breakwater, squeezing the mic with the other. "Tower, keep your eyes open! Bauman, you too. I want reports on every stick of driftwood that fuckin' floats our way!"

He released the PTT, barking at O'Donnell, "Get yer rifle ready and get on the bow! Shoot anything that even looks like a swimmer!"

His man moved to comply. Doyle keyed again: "I want five boats with me, running dark! We'll fan out. Form a perimeter between Beaver and Garden. Hannigan, Keller, McCann, Ferny, and Miller, have your shooters ready and report. Everyone else, fuckin' standby!"

Doyle slammed the handheld into its cradle, mind revving—*current, visibility, fuel consumption, hours till daylight, threat-vectors....*

His radio crackled as captains called in. Looking astern, he could see their bow-waves glinting in starlight. Thank Christ it was calm. Thank Christ it was clear.

A casualty of his calculations, he'd forgotten poor Annie. Tom swore, as always, to make it up to her. Then the radio beeped with an incoming call.

"Tower to *Mary*, you hearing this Tom? Better take a listen!"

Doyle couldn't hear shit. He idled down, then cut the engine. He stepped on deck and stood in the sudden quiet. O'Donnell was on the bowsprit, silhouetted with his rifle. They'd left the harbor and were drifting darkly between the two islands. Nautical twilight had deepened. Their little boat floated beneath a galactic bowl, milky with stars. The alarm bell ceased its clangor, shouted down by a hundred throaty howls.

What the FUCK is that? Wolves? Coyotes?

Doyle's sun-splotched skin prickled at the eerie sound. Sure as shit, island-to-island, Garden-to-Beaver, those calls were communicating.

O'Donnell gravely shook his head. "Nothin' good 'bout that sound, Cap'n," the dour deckhand spat. "Nothin' good at all."

Voyageurs

THE COMMON LOON, *GAVIA IMMER*, sent a sight-picture to its uncommon symbiont—*the crescent moon, three islands of interest, the largest one inhabited by humans.*

The recipient, a boy, stood in the bow of the lead canoe. He translated, hand-signing the shift in course to steersmen, who adjusted their paddles. His mother sat beside him, a copper bowl of lake water on her lap; she stared intently at its surface. The men and women behind her, red-capped, propelled their craft with powerful strokes. Three oversize canoes, each with a crew of ten, plowed straight wakes across placid Lake Michigan.

Raising Hog Island off their starboard bow, the mother consulted her bowl. After a moment she shook her head, and they paddled on. In the twilight, Beaver Island loomed next, its tower spiking the purple sky. The seer lifted her head and spoke to her son's back, saying, "There's a watcher in that tower. If we can see them, they can see us."

Loon-focused, he replied, "That's kind of the whole point, isn't it, Mom?"

The woman didn't answer. Cradling the bowl, she consulted her cartography, mapping the way of the heart. She saw possibility here, an openness to alliance. In her eyes, the sky glowed green above the big island, an aura of ionic power. Tiny vibrations disturbed the surface of her bowl. A few seconds later, the sine waves resolved—distant bells were tolling alarm.

"Stop the boats!"

The boy stood in the gloaming, palms-down, signaling the others. As one, all paddles ceased, then backed water. Indeed, as they'd hoped, Beaver Island was inhabited. First contact had been made. The paddlers, tasked with a mission, became diplomats again. The steersman in the lead canoe, a large Métis man with powerful arms, addressed mother and son: "*Mon Dieu*, tell me we're not headed that way? I'm in no mood to get shot in the dark."

The boy shook his head, invisible to all but his mother. The woman answered, "There's a third island, Baptiste. Between the two we can see. They call it Garden Island. That's our destination tonight."

Baptiste, wearing a woolen cap, gave the order; his three canoes angled through the straits. Full dark had descended, the splinter moon pricking the western horizon.

His mother spoke. "Son, where is your loon? What does he see?"

The boy probed ahead with feathered feelers. "The loon is gone. There's a raptor about, osprey I think. Unusual after dark, might be something behind it?"

The medicine woman nodded. A sheen emanated from the pot, limning her face with reflected light. The loon-boy said, "We can beach on Garden for the night, but we'll have visitors by morning." As he spoke, his mother constructed a spirit-map of their environs.

Below them: finned fish, somnolent in the deep.

Above: astral birds, mythic migrators of the Milky Way.

The third island: a garden of graves, their neglected denizens long gone to seed.

Cartography complete, she placed the newest piece into her regional puzzle. The voyageurs beached their canoes, Kevlar keels scraping sand. The resident coyotes of Garden Island synced their voices in a chorus of welcome. Across a mile of open water, the bell on Beaver ceased clanging, its pure note overpowered by the atonal howling of *Canis latrans*.

The Arrest of Red Liz

THIRTY MILES SOUTHEAST, on the mainland, cramped in the cab of her stolen semi, Liz McGee watched Lake Michigan quench the fire of another fucking day. September's sun had waned in power, but still irritated her burns. The red-eyed lizard cringed from its light. When dusk descended at last, she opened the door and slithered painfully from the rig.

Three months prior, overconfident and overstimulated, she led her Chosen into a damn ambush. Pinned between embankments, road-blocked by a fallen tree, well-planted mines had blown her column to hell. The next day, a Humvee of Old Law cucks investigated, tacking up wanted posters on power poles. When the Guardsmen rolled away, Liz picked through the wreckage, gagging from gut-stench, checking bodies and scavenging what she could. Hard to tell, but someone might have survived? She hadn't found Cowboy's fucking fix-it man. But Mikey the mechanic—a known snitch—wouldn't make it far. Even if he did, he sure as shit wouldn't bring her any help.

A real pro had mined that road. Illogically, Liz blamed Cowboy. After her coup, her power grab, she had her ex locked inside the ferry, but still, she wouldn't put it past him. Had Bob somehow gotten his revenge? She'd betrayed him, after all. Following her orders, Bob's own man Mikey had tased his ass good. Red Liz wheezed as she crawled closer to the water's edge. Had Cowboy Bob pulled a Houdini? Well, Liz could guaran-fucking-TEE she'd have the final say.

Concussed and badly wounded, for weeks now this little park had been her home. Fisherman's Island had been printed in white letters on MDOT's shit-brown sign. Just south of Charlevoix, the pull-off offered shade, concealment, and an infinity of fresh water. Post-ambush, bare-assed and barely alive, she had limped back to Charlevoix. Arriving at her old HQ, Liz found out her ferry—with Bob locked inside?—had been stolen and the M-31 drawbridge lowered. But who did it? Her Chosen garrison was gone. Cowboy again? Doubtful, but she pinned it on Bob anyway—one more reason to hate her ex's guts. Planning his pain kept her going. Of course the ferry was gone, her fuel tanker too—clever bastard.

Wounds weeping and suffering from shock, she filched keys to a Chosen big rig and low-geared the semi south to her park. She tunneled it under some trees, out of sight. For three months now its squalid cab was her home-sweet-home. Luckily, the semi-trailer carried food and supplies, part of a Kalamazoo convoy sent by Sharkey, the Big Man, her boss.

The day breeze dropped with the sun, the lake's wrinkled face unfurrowed. Before leaving cover, Liz scanned her surroundings. No telling who, or what, might be out and about. She didn't know shit about local resistance. Cowboy had been mocked for saying "elves" on the radio. There could be AWOL Chosen around. Or XCons. Or local Hidden, unexposed to the variant, probably armed and paranoid as hell.

Recon complete, she slinked to the beach, stripping off clothes and pus-stained bandages. Liz worked the slide of her pistol, chambering a round, and placed her sidearm on the pile. In the twilight, she crawled to the water-mirror to inspect her nakedness. It wasn't pretty. Half-bald, a reptile reflected from the surface. Her singed hair hadn't grown back. Her perfectly matched tits, weapons-of-male-destruction, were disabled. Her left breast had been sheared by sharp metal, but its gooey scab was healing. Her right side was intact, but withered from trauma. Her flesh, seasoned by sweat, had been seared; her once-milky skin was clotted with scars. But she wasn't dead, not yet. Liz grinned and the lizard grinned back, flicking a tongue. *Go fuck yourself* ordered Lizzy's only fan.

Don't mind if I do.

Her body still had its urges. Liz paddled in the shallows, then plunged herself deeper. Cold on the outside, but oh so warm within. How was she even alive? How was she healing so quickly? And how the fuck could this still feel so good? The lizard tingled, inside and out. Caressed by a coast, she climaxed, ripples of pleasure emanating from her source. Waves subsiding, she barked out a laugh. Red Liz, once desired by all, now reduced to fucking a lake. Oh well, a girl's gotta make do.

Three sets of night vision ogled the green-tinted creature as it frolicked. If the Army captain and his two enlisted felt any stirrings, they kept it to themselves. The MOPP gear they wore against infection dampened their urges anyway. Specialist Cruz knelt near the semi-truck, Captain Young and Sergeant Booker observing the beach from cover. They carried M4s and flex-cuffs and were positioned for arrest.

Captain Young had sand-tabled the interdiction, stressing the contagious nature of their quarry, the importance of not breaking the seals on their chem-suits. They'd observed their target for two days. So far, so good.

When Liz emerged, naked and dripping, green-skinned through their goggles, Young's team executed their mission. While Cruz covered their six, Booker and the captain, using darkness, moved quickly to confiscate her weapon. Booker tossed the pistol in the lake and stepped clear with his carbine. The confused woman crouched, night-blind but alert. Captain Young slung his rifle and unholstered a Taser. Distanced from her droplets, he pronged the woman's torso, giving Red Liz the ride of her life.

Vibrated by volts, her half-scabbed face was a rictus of rage. *Fucking Cowboy!*

Liz McGee, wanted for a long list of atrocities, fell onto the fossilized coral of coastal Michigan. The virulent woman, a new kind of creature, lay cradled by Devonian stones, remnants of Pangea 300 million years before.

A Bigger Picture

DATE TIME GROUP: 192330RSEP21

LOCATION: Northwest Lower Michigan

The soldiers waited for their target to stop twitching. They maintained situational awareness, alert for emerging threats; they'd been surprised before. Their captain spoke first. Muffled by his mask, Young rasped through his respirator, "See those tattoos, Sergeant? Looks like a positive ID."

"Yes sir, pretty pervy stuff. I'd say that's our girl."

The wanted poster detailed the explicit ink that Liz wore.

"Sir, look at her wounds. She's a mess. How'd she survive those claymores? Trauma should have killed her months ago."

Frank Young, socially distanced, examined her figure through multiple lenses. "Strange times, Mr. Booker. Her viral load must be high, kept her going somehow. Fetch Cruz, and have him bring his med kit; we've got work to do."

"Yes sir. Just don't get too close. Can't trust volts on a Chosen."

Booker jogged heavily off the beach, his MOPP gear flopping in the dusk.

Captain Young, claustrophobic in his clammy suit, ordered his breathing to slow. He pulled his eyes from the naked woman and looked up for an astral bearing. Through his NVGs, the Big Dipper was a blur in a minty green sky. The Milky Way appeared melted, a starry smear.

When his men returned, they followed protocol for restraining a Viral. Their Tango's wrists and legs were cuffed tight, Cruz—combat medic and civilian EMT—bandaged her wounds, dressing her in clean scrubs, while Booker fetched their Humvee from the access road.

"Captain, her semi-trailer's pretty roomy. Maybe we confine her inside?"

Cruz and Young had backed away from the POW, awaiting Booker's return.

"Good idea, Specialist. Can't have her exhaling all over the Humvee."

"Gonna call someone? Or do we bring her in ourselves?"

"Guessing the CO will send for her, since this McGee was high on Colonel's list. We're not set up for Viral transport anyway. I'm hoping she'll give us something actionable, at least enough intel to make our next move."

The lizard began to stir, Petoskey stones clacking beneath the cuffed creature. They heard, then saw, their own vehicle approaching.

"Strap her to the litter. Mr. Cruz, let's get her into that trailer."

"You got it, Captain."

Thirty minutes and a sat-phone call later, Captain Young had his orders. Their colonel was sending a sealed ambulance and a gun-truck escort. The CO wanted McGee for murder, and for her close ties—allegedly sexual?—to Chosen leadership. Highest priority: the two-vehicle convoy would arrive before dawn, bringing fuel to top off Young's Humvee, keeping his team on station. Colonel Dennis urged anti-virus protocols, then wished them good hunting before signing off.

Tasking two vehicles, and a drum of diesel, was a big expenditure for their depleted force. Not much remained of Grayling's Guard unit. When the variant morphed and gained function, soldiers nationwide deserted en masse, prioritizing families.

"Old Law" consisted of the ragtag remnants of police, fire, and assorted first responders. Susceptible to Covee's STING response and short on everything including PPE, the white hats had been winnowed down.

Captain Young replaced the handheld in the charger, its brand name—Palantir—faded from use. The variant was winning everywhere. What remained of Old Law weakened, while Spreaders gained turf and resources by the day. At the HQ in Grayling, an operations map of Michigan—pinned and flagged—charted the expansion of Chosen, XCons, and other factions. Michigan's Guard couldn't halt their spread. Far-flung, its recon elements could do little more than gather intelligence and pinch an occasional perp. Without antivirals or effective vaccines, the war for Michigan would be lost without a real battle.

Camp Grayling maintained a US map as well. Patchy satellite comms and an occasional LRRP kept its lines blurry. Nationally, the situation was much the same. Six months prior, POTUS had been killed, allegedly by a female assassin. In the pogrom that ensued, the People's House had been pockmarked, its galleries becoming gallows. The VP, a weak fish, was sworn in. Then D.C. imploded. Fascist-trending units had gone haywire. The Keepers took new oaths as Proud Boys burned Pride flags. Up and down the DOD chain, Red attacked Blue. The fratricidal fire had been far from friendly.

Each region became isolate, with unique names for its Spreaders. Pockets of unexposed were shrinking. No one was making a stand anywhere. Old Law optimists, and Young was one, still held out hope for Navy ships at sea, or maybe staff in underground labs. But these hope-bubbles were easy to pop. The nation and its states had fractured; local units were on their own.

Globally, no help was coming. Nordic NATO had been nuked by the Rus. China's PRC had lost all its people. The only thing uniting the nations was collapse. Globally, the grid was gone. Planet Earth had lost its sparkle. Deaf and dumb, it rolled through the void, illuminated only by funeral fires.

Young detoured away from depression, steering his thoughts to the task at hand. Cruz and Booker secured their detainee in the trailer. Red Liz, lantern-lit by LEDs, lay strapped to her litter with a saline drip. The Viral glared at the captain as he pulled himself—awkward in PPE—into her container. His two men waited nervously just outside.

"Watch yourself, sir. Can't afford to lose you. She ain't worth it."

Young, muffled by his mask, recited the rights of a suspect from a laminated card, a mix of Miranda and UCMJ's article 31: "You have the right to remain silent. Anything you say can be used against you. You have the right to a fair trial. You have the right to an advisor. You have the right to know what you're accused of. Ms. McGee, do you understand these rights?"

The lizard spat venom in response, spewing virions at the hazmatted captain. Young heard Cruz and Booker cursing outside. Droplets of death splattered across his facemask. Heart hammering, Young stepped back from her litter. "Red Liz, you're accused of multiple counts of homicide, sexual assault, and human trafficking. Do you have anything to say for yourself at this time?"

A laugh wheezed from the broken squeeze-box as she beckoned him closer. Young put his palms up in refusal. She creaked out two syllables: "Cow-boy."

Young shook his helmet, hard of hearing. "Say again?"

Liz lifted her chin towards an unseen island, snarling, "COW-BOY!"

Strange Waters

DATE TIME GROUP: 210330RSEP21

LOCATION: Lake Michigan

A commandeered boat with an unnautical crew zig-zagged beneath the stars. Sergeant Booker, way over his head, manned the helm. A landlubber, he struggled to keep the compass needle pointed—NNW—towards Bob Campbell's last known location: Beaver Island. Only occasionally did the Detroit native succeed.

The three soldiers, ground-pounders all, had fussed unsuccessfully with the boat's electronics: no radio, no radar, no GPS, no sonar. But at least the gauges worked, the propeller turned, and their combat boots, so far, were dry. For their current mission—apprehending Campbell on Beaver—that was enough.

Yesterday, they'd handed off their hissing captive, trading fiery Liz for Army fuel. After she snitched on Campbell, they tried a dozen boats in Charlevoix's harbor, none of which had a crankable engine. Finally, at the Coast Guard station, they'd flattened a security fence with their Humvee, and the 45' Response Boat-Medium, secure in its berth, had answered their prayers. Scavengers had of course stripped her of finery, then pumped her fuel tanks dry; the boat had been battered, but for the most part seemed sound, and (hopefully) seaworthy. They struggled to fold down the mast to fit her under the lowered bridge, but after that, their transit had been smooth.

Their commanding officer, headquartered at Camp Grayling, had sent a two-vehicle convoy to take their captive into custody. Captain Frank Young, wearing hazmat, had interrogated Red Liz while waiting.

The woman, professionally bandaged by the EMT Cruz, was strapped to her litter. The lizard, laid low, gnashed its teeth. The only actionable intelligence Young received was that Bob "Cowboy" Campbell, a POI high on their perp list, had apparently been taken—accidentally?—to Beaver Island, some thirty miles offshore of Charlevoix.

Once Liz was safely transferred, Young's men had hitched the promised fuel-trailer to their Humvee. Following safety protocols, they'd decontaminated their musty MOPP gear and discussed next steps. Red Liz was hardly a credible source, but her hatred for Campbell was convincing and her snitching seemed sincere. The guardsmen agreed that Beaver Island was next. Captain Young argued that even if she was lying, the isolated island was worth investigating anyway.

Besides fuel, rations, and ammo, the relief convoy had shared the latest SITREP for northern Michigan. Recon elements reported massed movement of Chosen and XCon vehicles. It looked like a big push was planned, and all signs pointed north.

The convoy sergeant had delivered sealed orders to Young from their CO. The ex-fire chief and his two enlisted men were now tasked—alongside their police duties—with monitoring and disrupting this new outlaw offensive.

Captain Frank Young, journaling in the wheelhouse, tried to ignore Booker's crooked course. Colonel Dennis, CO of the Griffins, insisted they write everything down—names, dates, moon phase, and geography. Frank endeavored to do so. But how to document these stars?

Young observed them through bulletproof glass; they dipped right down, spangling the horizon. A landsman all his life, he'd never seen such a thing; it took some looking at. Dark Sky enthusiasts finally got their wish: not just Michigan, but the entire planet was now a starry sanctuary. Frank tracked the undead transit of a zombie satellite through the sky. Like all human clutter, even space junk would eventually decay.

The night was calm. The engine thrummed. Young's thoughts unmoored and he drifted through time. Eyes closed, his mind opened. However briefly, Frank was free.

His wife Terre, the scent of her skin, the love they'd cultivated, her garden in bloom....

Sergeant Anthony Booker knew he was oversteering. Too much rudder and way too often; he could feel his chief's unspoken critique. Booker was grateful to be off the damn roads, the chance of ambush or IEDs on open water was practically nil. He could breathe better too. No MOPP gear, no respirator, no hissing Virals spitting venom.

The drunken compass sobered him. Keeping the needle between the lines took effort, but freed his mind for travel. As always, Booker bought a ticket to the past—his capable wife, his beautiful boy. Anthony knew he'd been oversteering for years, even before collapse. Raising a son, a young Black male in Detroit, had been the scariest shit he'd faced, worse than the Sand, worse than the Suck. He'd shouted too often, pounded the table too loudly. His wife disapproved but bit her tongue, just as Captain Young was doing tonight. Booker took a belly breath and tried to steer the boat—and his brain—on a happier course. The zigs grew smaller as he opened a memory:

Home on leave, teaching his son to ride on a hot, summer night. The cool steel of the crescent wrench as they unbolted training wheels. The oven-blast of concrete, even at dusk. His grinning boy as Booker ran alongside, catching every wobble....

Specialist Alfonzo Cruz, student-athlete from Saginaw, was good-looking. The specialist, wearing night vision goggles, stood watch on the bow. Lacking electronics, Cruz was their GPS, radar, and lookout. An EMT in the civilian world, he'd done his combat tours as a medic. Unlike Booker and Young, Cruz was single. Pre-collapse he'd been Mr. Popular on all the dating apps. Without wife or kid, Cruz had surplus care to give. Along with his big heart, he had the instincts of a first responder.

Now, the specialist left his post for the helm and opened the watertight hatch, cold air flooding the wheelhouse. Cruz cleared his throat and reluctantly woke their napping chief.

"Sir? Captain? We've got land ahead, could be the island."

Young, adrift in the love-bright past, opened his eyes upon a darkened world. The transition from love to loss was a physical hurt. The captain grunted and set his battered boots on the deck. "Shit, Cruz. With Booker steering it might be Chicago."

Frank could feel his men grinning. He toggled on the red light and studied the NOAA chart, 14911. "Looks like the harbor is on the north end. Let's keep our distance, stay in deep water, follow the coast, and look out for lights."

An hour later, Cruz confirmed their position. He'd raised two more islands, chart-labeled: Garden and Hog.

They shut down the engine. Young ordered shut-eye for his men as well. He took Cruz's NVGs and stepped onto the bow. His wristwatch glowed, 0430. He checked their boat, confirmed no lights were showing, and gave some thought to the coming dawn. Beaver Island was terra incognita. Strange lands, strange waters—a fascinating tale if he wasn't in it, but he was. Young rehearsed the action-steps in his mind. What was left of

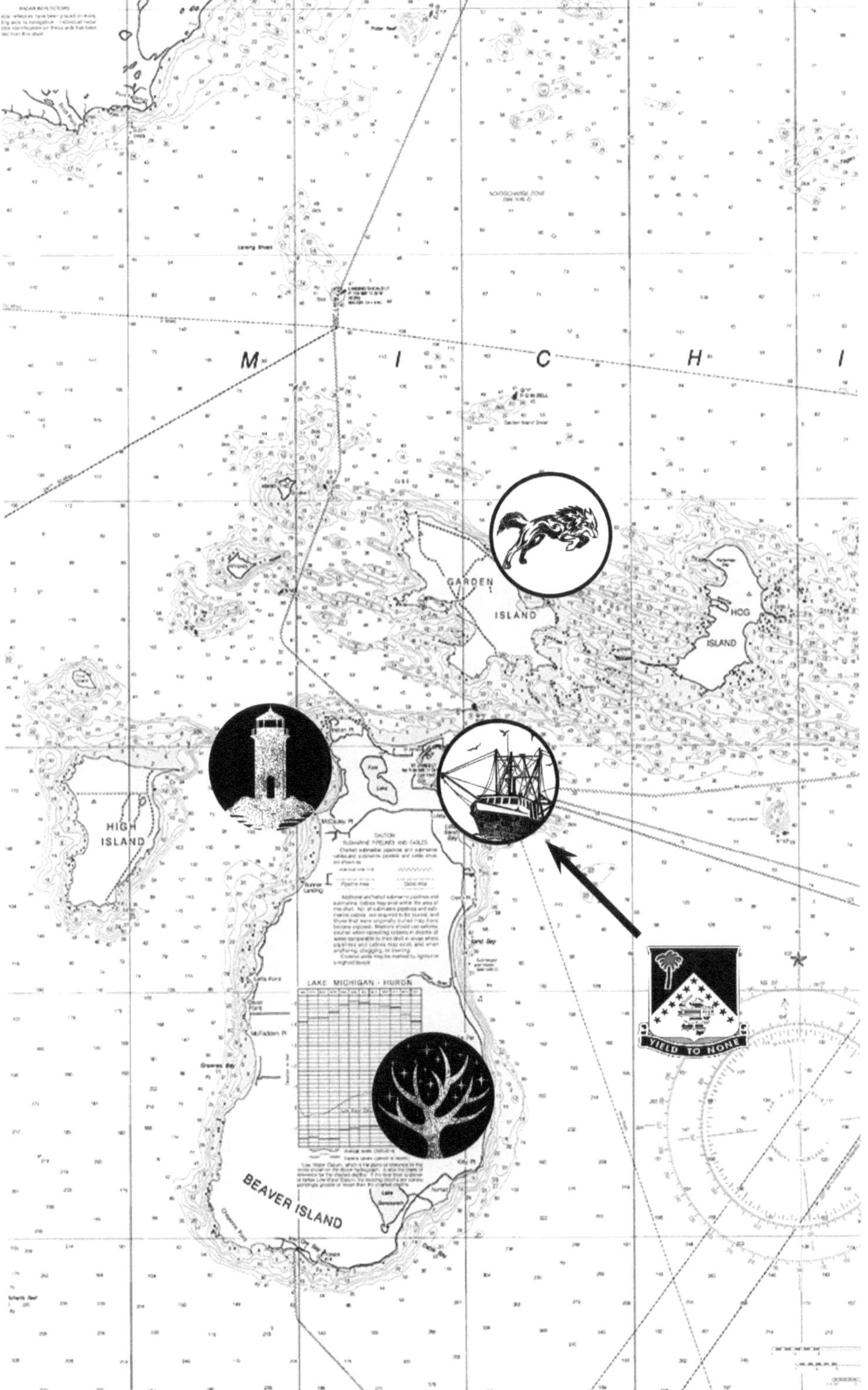

MICHI
GARDEN ISLAND
HOG ISLAND
HIGH ISLAND
BEAVER ISLAND
LAKE MICHIGAN - HURON
YIELD TO NONE

their lives—as always—depended on him not fucking this up: approach-vector, MOPP level, weapons status, unit-pennant, sat-comms....

The captain scrolled through his duties as a bright star—Sirius?—shook water from its fur and began barking, brightly, in the east. The big lake had cooled and the air was chill. A predawn breeze riffled the surface as something eerie echoed between the islands. Young's ears, bruised by battle, were confused by overlapping frequencies. He cupped his hands, capturing sound. A constellation—wolf like—leapt above the horizon as Young's synapses synced. What Frank was hearing, ever so faintly, was howling from a hundred feral throats.

Sunrise

THE RISING SUN ILLUMINATED a banner fluttering from a dune on Garden Island: a loping wolf, hand-painted on deer hide. As the blue planet rolled towards the sun, red light inched down the staff. A woman and a boy stood upon the strand, shading their eyes from the dazzle of dawn. The Earth was at equinox; the two had been up all night, holding vigil.

Their fellow voyageurs were bivouacked off the beach, under trees. Food was ready and a welcome prepared. A sweat lodge had been constructed; its stones—grandfathers to the Indigenous—were still warm, sparkling from last night's visions. Archipelagic birds were astir: gulls, terns, loons, bitterns, herons, plovers. The feathered world, ever-hungry, keening for calories.

The boy said something to his mom. She'd just turned fifty and was named for the season. The mother's gaze shifted as she followed his point. Visitors, as expected, were vectoring their way. She counted six Beaver boats chugging up from the south. Autumn stooped and lifted her copper bowl. She breathed upon its surface, opened herself, and felt anger approaching.

Doyle gnashed his molars, craving a cigarette: *nothing so bad a smoke couldn't soothe.* He carried a cargo of fools on a fool's fucking errand.

Bloody Mary led the way, five Beaver boats following. They'd patrolled all night with no sightings and no shots fired. In the predawn, Doyle had been radioed to return to harbor to take on passengers. He ignored the first call, was angry by the second, and raging by the third. Desperate pleas had pestered his wheelhouse—from Deputy Williams, Doc Newsome, and that fucking professor too. The only call he heeded was Diana's, and only because she threatened to fire up the ferry and steam across herself. She could do it too—damn her. An ex-mariner, the Canadian had salt in her veins and had crossed some deep waters.

Fuming, Doyle returned to St. James. He bumped against the dock, grimacing as they tumbled aboard: the limp-dicked deputy, two doctors, that hippy Brian, and Captain Canada herself. More assholes stood waiting, including crone Samantha. But once Diana stepped aboard he throttled away, leaving the rest behind. Stranded, they shook their fists, giving him an earful, but this wasn't a Carnival cruise.

Doyle squeezed the handset, keying its mic. "All boats, all boats, this is *Mary*. I'm gonna run in close and drop off the Nats. Spread out and watch for surprises. Post shooters but wait for my signal. These paddlers are probably contagious, don't let 'em near you. Doyle, out."

Captain Young glassed the party on the beach. Through binoculars, he saw a banner in the breeze. He adjusted focus. A running wolf was revealed, reddened by the rising sun. Cruz was at the helm now. The specialist kept the sun at their six and steered a straight course. Sergeant Booker manned the Squad Automatic Weapon they'd mounted on the bow.

Young counted five figures—all unarmed—on the beach. Six fishing boats hovered just offshore. The one closest had *Bloody Mary* stenciled on its transom. The boats bristled with men— check that—some were women. He counted ten rifles, at least.

His two enlisted, awakened before dawn, had breakfasted

on MREs, donning MOPP hoods and respirators, following Young's lead. Per SOP, they'd sterilized their gear after Liz, but went through decontamination again just to be sure, "Remember," Young reminded them, masking up, "we assume they're Viral, we assume they're hostile, but we do not shoot first. Our mission is to protect and preserve. These folks might be the ones that need us most."

His men nodded, familiar with protocol. Their unspoken hope was that these islanders were isolated and therefore unexposed. After two years of apocalypse, all three men craved an encounter with normalcy. The sunrise glared behind them, covering their approach. When Young saw they'd been spotted, he hit the Coast Guard siren and began flashing lights.

"Well, Specialist," he shouted to Cruz, already sweating at the helm, "here we go again."

On The Beach

DOYLE MOTORED IN CLOSE. The Nats—Brian, Chow, Diana—plunged overboard into thigh-deep water, unafraid of contagion, confident in their shields. *Bloody Mary,* with the deputy and Doc Newsome still aboard, backed away. O'Donnell, menacing with his rifle, spat phlegm from the bow.

Three Naturals waded ashore. A wolf-banner and two voyageurs—boy and woman—awaited. The shore birds combed the surf for sustenance, dune grass feasted on fresh photons. There was a minute of charged stillness.

The first words were spoken by the stranger. "Good morning," the waiting woman began, "*boozhoo,* my name is Autumn." She placed both hands on her heart. "This is my son. You can call him Loon."

Her boy repeated the hand flutter. The three Naturals, after a moment, proffered names and gestures of their own. Doyle and his boats cast shadows that chilled the five ambassadors. The sun kept climbing, like called to like, and kinship slowly kindled. The boy Loon blinked his old eyes at Brian. "It was you flying last night, with the osprey?" he asked.

The blue-eyed shaman nodded in affirmation, then asked his own question. "I saw your boats. I heard your singing. Where are your companions? Your three canoes?"

Loon gestured towards the tree line. "Didn't want to intimidate." Brian nodded, and he chastised lightly, "Your osprey scared away my loon."

"I'm sorry." Brian smiled, revealing a chipped tooth. "No offense. I never felt you. I have a lot to learn."

"None taken. I bet you could teach me some things too."

Both pilots tipped their wings and grinned. Diana interrupted the two flyboys; the Sentinel was more serious, searching eyes for signs of infection. "Excuse me, but are you *immune* or *unexposed?* And what about your party? Does your group carry weapons? Do you come here in peace?"

A shifting breeze fogged the beach with diesel fumes, Doyle's *Mary* chugging just offshore. Autumn kinked her nose at the combustion of carbon. "We are immune. I believe you are too?"

Diana, ELF warrior, kept her face stony—could neither confirm nor deny.

"And yes, we carry arms," Autumn admitted, "though not against you. We travel in peace, even as war clouds our horizon."

Dr. Chow cleared his throat, diagnostic. "Where do you come from and what's your purpose here?"

Autumn inventoried the man, taking note of his bright eyes, his black satchel, his delicate hands. "You are a healer? A medical man?"

Chow, a lifetime ago, indeed had sworn the oath. "I used to be."

"Then there is much to discuss," Autumn said, and nodded. "I will answer briefly, as our time on this beach grows short."

The Indigenous woman eyed the boats—rusty colonizers—behind Chow. "We passed *Michilimackinac*—the great turtle—then crossed under the bridge at Mackinac. Our crews are Canadian. My boy and I come from Manitoulin Island, far to the east, in Lake Huron. Our purpose is to warn the people of the Straits. Danger approaches from the south—Virals, slavery, and death. We would have a proper council. Are you the leaders? Do you three speak for your people?"

The sun, thermonuclear, mushroomed above the horizon,

radiation in its rays. Diana stood tall, answering for her party, "We speak for only one group—we call ourselves Naturals. We are refugees from the mainland and are indeed immune, which is why we stand here. There are other leaders," she indicated the Beaver boats, "for the islanders. Is it safe for them to join us? They do not have our shields."

Autumn promised safe passage, adding, "No plague paddles with us—"

The Manitoulin woman was interrupted by a sudden revving of engines; plumes blotted the sun. An electronic siren—discordant—shrieked from offshore. Many eyes were shaded, seeking its strident song. A Coast Guard vessel approached at speed, its metallic surface blindingly bright. From its loud-hailer squelched a commanding voice: "This is Captain Young of the National Guard. Boat crews, put down your weapons. I repeat, put *down* your weapons or you will be fired upon!"

Stars and Stripes rippled, muscular, from the mast. Beneath Old Glory, a yellow pennant streamed—a rampant griffin flashing talons. A rising wind stormed the beach, fluttering the handmade banner. The painted wolf was on its feet and running.

A Garden Party

THE SMALL ISLAND—*Minis Gitigaan* to its Anishinaabeg farmers—was no longer inhabited, at least by the living. Its villages were subterranean, their murdered citizens subsumed by soil. The only structures on the island were spirit houses—sunbleached boards strangled by bramble and vine. The insular animus was hostile to humans.

Smallpox had washed ashore here two centuries ago. The "running-face-sickness" had come in waves. The white man's plague depeopled the gardens. Escapees had fled, island to island, but the pox went with them, death on its breath. Europeans and their invasive specie—minted coins—pursued close behind.

Variola evicted the Indigenous. Once blighted, Native villages were burned by carpetbaggers. Their faerie-house *wiigiwaams* were razed and replaced with brick buildings. Teeming waters were soon overfished; the plentitude of pine, slash-cut for profit. The remnant Anishinaabeg were marginalized by addiction, terrorized by trauma. The pattern of displacement was an old one; genocide stains the modern genome. *H. heidelbergensis*, Denisovans, Neanderthals—unrestful ghosts haunting Caucasian DNA.

Sunrise shielded the present from this problematic past. More passengers disembarked from the Coast Guard vessel and *Bloody Mary,* making the *jiibay* of Garden Island burrow deeper, fearing fresh colonization. A strange party soon assembled under the trees; the three voyageur canoes were repurposed for distanced-seating and the serving of food. A cook fire was tended, iron pots keeping breakfast warm.

Representing the Howlers—their nickname wherever they prowled—were Autumn, Loon, and the large Métis man, Baptiste. The rest of the voyageurs kept out of earshot, engaging in camp chores, hammocking, and small talk. Jaded diplomats, they'd seen such gatherings before.

The Beaver Islanders—sitting as far away as they could—were Doyle, Deputy Williams, and Doc Newsome. The trio were masked with N95s from the clinic. O'Donnell—Doyle's grumbling deckhand—had taken *Mary* offshore and patrolled with the other five boats. Sentinel Diana, Dr. Chow, and Brian—unmasked—spoke for the Naturals. Seated separately, protected by Army PPE, were Captain Young and his sergeant, Mr. Booker. Specialist Cruz was offshore in the Coast Guard vessel. He had their rifles with him, and Young's pistol too. The two enlisted were not pleased with their captain's decision to honor the parlay and attend unarmed. Cruz kept the beach covered with their mounted machine gun.

Ten in number, introductions were made, the proper words spoken, and impressions—as varied as the guests—were forming fast. The food proffered by the voyageurs had yet to be touched. Untouched as well were the weighty subjects at hand.

The wolf-painted banner rippled, its beast loping above the beach. The taloned griffin flew from Cruz's mast. Diana's hood was thrown back; embroidered on the ELF parka was the stylized tree of Earth's liberators. The islander men—the only group without a sigil—began the discussion.

Deputy Williams, muffled by his mask, cut to the chase. "Our island doesn't want any trouble. We've survived this far, and we want to keep on surviving. You folks gave us a scare last night with your canoes, and coyotes, and singing and all. Please state your purpose here and let's get on with it."

No one bristled at his bluntness, good manners a casualty of collapse.

Doc Newsome added his support, saying, "I agree with the deputy. None of you appears contagious, and I want to trust your claims of immunity. After all," here he looked at his colleague Dr. Chow, "we've seen such things before. But still, the sooner we go our separate ways, the better."

Big Baptiste sat serene, large hands on his knees. He nodded to Autumn. The matron stood, closed her eyes against the sun, and delivered her stump speech as the trees and shrubs leaned in.

"You are not alone," she said, "nor are you the only ones we've encountered on our journey through the Straits."

The Guard captain straightened; Young was all ears. It was intelligence like this that helped justify his fuel expenditure and the exposure-risk to his men.

Autumn continued, "Almost everyone, as you know, has died. The living—as we've seen them—are divided into three. First are the Hidden, those unexposed to the virus."

She gestured towards the islanders. Doyle rebuffed her, crossing his arms. Williams and Newsome looked concerned.

"Second are the Spreaders, the virulent. Something in their blood protects them. They spread the plague, yet it does them no harm. Their lusts, both violent and sexual, are often increased."

She directed a querying look at the two soldiers wearing MOPP.

"Captain, you've seen such? Sergeant, you've fought against them?"

Young nodded, visage grim beneath his mask. Booker, his subordinate, stayed silent.

Autumn turned next towards the Naturals. Diana nodded too, her ageless face clenched with sorrow. The corpses of her comrades were laid out before her: *Diving Duck, Squirrel, the dog-mauled bodies of Matador and Tigre. Many elves were still missing. Where was Thorn? Where was Bull? The rest of the rearguard? Enslaved? Tortured? Scattered by scavengers?*

The Sentinel choked back her grief as Ambassador Autumn continued.

"All Spreaders are similar, though their backgrounds may vary. We've heard them called Chosen, and Virals, and also XCons. Baptiste, and many of our crew, know them as *Violeurs*." A tremor shook the big man as she spoke, and he lowered his brown-eyed gaze.

"The third group we've encountered are the Protected, and again, there is mystery here. Covee and its variant, Stinger, finds no purchase in them, though the virus may slay close family and friends."

Autumn regarded Brian, Chow, and Diana. "You call yourself Naturals? You believe your bond with the Earth Mother protects you? Perhaps some of you develop strange abilities?"

Brian confirmed. Autumn nodded, then continued, "For us, it is similar. Wolves and coyotes follow our movements. Their packs have killed many Virals, driving them from Michigan's Upper Peninsula and nearby Ontario—a territory some are calling the Free North. We don't know why nature is intervening against the Spreaders, though there are theories.

"And so I've named the living, a tiny fraction of what used to be. The Hidden. The Spreaders. The Protected. There are others, outliers to these three, but this is not the time."

Her audience was restless. Doyle smoldered. Dr. Chow was curious. Captain Young craved a map. The gathered guests were hungry; most had been awake all night. Baptiste stood, rolled his heavy shoulders, and in accented English proposed breakfast and a pause. There was agreement at this, though no one moved towards the food.

Loon took the lead. Keeping socially distanced, he invited the islanders to begin. The Beaver men were reluctant, but he insisted. Soon Newsome, Williams, and even Doyle were loading paper plates with smoked fish, warm porridge, and fruit. An enameled pot cradled coffee, and the bleary men filled mugs, sitting down in stubborn silence to blow on the beany brew.

The Naturals went next, nodding thanks to their hosts. Then the two soldiers scooped food, walking down the beach before removing masks and sampling the non-freeze-dried fare. Captain Young used his handheld radio, updating Cruz on the Response Boat. Their Howler hosts went last, respecting the quiet, endeavoring to keep their eyes to themselves.

The sun climbed higher. Boats chugged offshore, diamonds glittering in their wakes as gulls followed, sharp-eyed for any scraps. Many eyes watched the garden party: the lighthouse on Beaver, binoculars from the boat crews—envious of the fare—and curious looks from the red-capped voyageurs, discreetly distanced under trees, resting from their labors.

The painted wolf was running across its banner. His little brothers on the island, *bashkwaajaash*—the shy coyotes—had secreted themselves downwind. Unseen, they scent-checked the picnic and kept apace of its progress.

When the guests were sated and greasy plates had flamed on the coals, they regathered in the shade. Stomachs full, the primates sat a bit closer, reclining more at ease. N95s now dangled, unused. Baptiste produced tobacco, sifted a pinch to the spirits, and passed the cigarettes around. Doyle imbibed, as did the deputy and Brian. Even Diana and the doctors accepted, puffed once or twice, and then let their sticks smolder. The disciplined soldiers, still fully masked, declined, keeping their distance, following protocol.

Baptiste tossed the rest of the pack to Doyle with a Québécois shrug. The gill-netter kept a poker face, though something inside the Beaver captain loosened. Mother and son didn't inhale but wafted *semaa*, waiting for the fragrant clouds to clear.

When the time was right, Autumn began detailing a map in the dirt. She narrated as she crafted its cartography, a sing-song of creation, using sticks and stones and humps of sand. She gouged the Great Lakes, each hand a mighty glacier, contouring the continent, shaping centuries in seconds. The garden party guests leaned in.

First, she indicated the starting point of the voyageurs, far in the east: Manitoulin Island, lapped by Lake Huron. "After Covee came, its variant, Stinger. In successive waves, the viruses washed away everything, like a flood."

She moved her arm, drowning Canada, the Upper Peninsula, and Great Lakes.

"Everyone died. First Nations, white people, the Métis, livestock, even pets. All were vulnerable. Year 1—not so long ago—was a time of calamity."

The guests grieved over the map, furrowing their faces, remembering how it had been—a lifetime ago, the end of an age. A mere two years had passed, but it felt like forever.

"Those that survived, whether Hidden or Protected, gathered in places where food could be found and settlements defended from Spreaders."

The woman pointed to landforms that fit this criteria: Bruce Peninsula, Manitoulin, Drummond, Les Cheneaux, Bois Blanc, Mackinac. She traced the westward progress of her canoes in the dirt.

"Each of these places still holds people, the beginning of a new beginning—the Free North. Nowhere in this territory have we encountered the virus, though everyone is struggling. Now, the second winter approaches and many settlements won't survive it. The grid is long gone, and unspoiled gasoline is going fast."

She engineered a long piece of bark, suspending it across a sand-scooped strait—the Mackinac Bridge. Five miles in length, its span connected Lower Michigan to its wilder cousin, the U.P.

"We paused our paddling to resupply at St. Ignace. Shadowed by the big bridge, there is a settlement there—some Protected, some Hidden—that is well-organized and well-informed. Mounted on motorcycles, horses, and racing bikes, their irregular cavalry has scouted much of the north."

She scribed a circle around the eastern U.P., from Escanaba to Sault Ste. Marie. "They've begun to send their biker scouts across the bridge to reconnoiter the south."

With twigs, she marked Petoskey, Indian River, and Cheboygan inside her radius of what was known. Everything outside this staked circumference was beyond the pale.

"Everywhere, reports are the same: small pockets of survivors, doing the best they can, preparing for winter. For now, except for skirmishes, most Spreaders have been pushed away, though recent reconnaissance from south of the bridge sounds ominous."

At this, Captain Young, still masked, squatted over the sand map with a stick of his own. He indicated all the territory she'd just described. "So, from Ontario to Escanaba, you're talking about an east-west distance of nearly 400 miles?"

Autumn nodded. Baptiste, burly arms crossed, confirmed as well.

"Then from Indian River in the LP, to the Soo in the Yoop, maybe another hundred miles, south to north?"

Another affirmation from Manitoulin's medicine woman.

"What I don't understand," the Army captain continued, "is the absence of outlaws. Of Spreaders. This same chunk of territory downstate would contain multiple cartels—Chosen, XCons, bandits—you name it. There'd be thousands of scavengers, hundreds of vehicles. Why are there none in your so-called Free North?"

Young, awkward in floppy gear, looked skeptically at Autumn, her boy, and their big-fisted guardian, Baptiste. The guests studied the map and wondered the same. To answer his query, Autumn indicated the lupus painted on their banner. "I can't fully explain it," she began, "but somehow we've been protected. Wolves, coyotes, and other wild creatures—especially predators—will not abide Spreaders. I've heard reports of huge packs hunting down the virulent. I've witnessed this on a smaller scale myself."

This was too much for the Beaver Islanders—a stick-bridge too far. Young and Booker shot each other looks as well, professional skepticism on full display.

"Come on!" Doyle guffawed. "You're telling me that yer four-footed friends have taken it upon their furry fuckin' selves to patrol the U.P. to keep it clear of bad guys? For what reason? So you Indians and some Native wannabees can live in happy, hippy peace? Bullshit!"

Noontide approached and the group's disbelief was at its zenith. Baptiste scowled at Doyle. *Mary's* bloody captain could give two shits about some mixed-blood Canuck objecting to his manners. Tom Doyle grumbled on, profanities plopping like turds upon the beach. Now the other voyageurs were standing, two dozen of them, lounging no longer. No weapons were in evidence, but disapproval wafted from them in waves.

The Naturals—Diana, Chow, and Brian—more open-minded, remained mute, unsure how to clean up the mess. Captain Young shook his helmet. The Army officer reached for his radio; time to call in his boat and evacuate from this picnic.

Doyle thought the same, and switched on his walkie-talkie. The sooner they were clear of these yahoos, the better.

Unnoticed, he Loon stepped to the banner, gathered himself, then released a tremolo howl. His call—amplified by dune and distance—was wildly feral. Something primal pulsed outward from the beach, a rapacious ripple in spacetime. His throaty utterance belayed all bickering. Arguments were dropped in anticipation—would there be a response?

A moment of silence as a hundred ears twitched in the void. Then the resident coyotes on Garden erupted, shockingly close. The beach party was pinned in place by a perimeter of sound.

Guests improvised weapons and edged back-to-back, fearing the assault that surely would follow. Doyle's handheld squawked nervously with a call from Whiskey Light, two miles away on Beaver and clearly visible: "Tower to Doyle, not sure if you can hear this, Tom, but we got a situation here."

Tower kept its transmission open. Doyle's radio went scratchy with sound. Howls exploded from its speaker, a furious response to he's call-to-arms.

Baptiste's canoe crews opened their throats as well, joining the chorus. These long-haired Howlers now strode into the open, canines flashing in a show of force against the stupidly skeptical. Blacks and whites, Indigenous and Métis, men and women of all ages vocalized together the vehemence of their beliefs.

The Coast Guard boat, with siren and flashing lights, cut through the cacophony, its yellow griffin swooping to intervene. Tight to the shore, Cruz idled its engine before manning the machine gun. He readied the weapon, preparing to strafe the beach in defense of his captain. Young shook himself from paralysis and waved his man down. Cruz swore, then safetied the SAW.

Loon removed his small hand from the banner-staff, silencing the would-be saviors. The voyageurs quieted as well, slowly backing off the beach. Doyle's radio resumed its static as Beaver Island's coyotes lay down. The pack on Garden Island stretched, fore-legs and hind, resuming their watchfulness.

Doyle, hiding a tremor, shook out another cigarette, flicked flame, and took a long drag. Baptiste, fists clenched, watched this white man closely, a seeming supplication in Doyle's smoking. Baptiste let it go. It was a lot to ask after all—*Dieu seul le sait!*—especially from an isolated islander. In the eerie silence that followed, the guests gathered again around Autumn's etchings.

"As I was saying—they've protected us before." The Manito-

ulin woman grew menacing. "And they are *merciless* to Spreaders."

Each guest could see this clearly. Those with more imagina-
tion upgraded Garden's stunted coyotes to the U.P.'s heavy-bod-
ied wolves, a hundred per pack, a sentient centuria of violence.
They looked anew at the map and found its Viral-free territory
a bit more believable.

Captain Young adjusted to the new world that was proffered;
ever-practical, he sought solace in data, intel, and the familiar
routine of threat and response. Young looked from the map to
its maker. "Ma'am, you were saying something about the St. Ignace scouts? Their recent reconnaissance to the south?"

The woman, a water-protector of the Wiikwemkoong First
Nation, took a steadying breath and resumed her diplomacy.

Birds of a Feather

THE GARDEN PARTY HAD ENDED. Disturbed by the howling display, the grumbling guests went their separate ways. The guardsmen, Young and Booker, were evacuated by Cruz on the Response Boat. Their yellow griffin—Yield to None—flew as they followed the Beaver boats towards St. James and a grudgingly promised berth. For now, only Diana and Brian remained, voluntarily stranded on Garden Island.

Crashing the party, dour O'Donnell had beached *Bloody Mary*, retrieving his cursing captain along with Deputy Williams and the medical men. Once aboard, doctors Chow and Newsome discussed decontamination and protocols to protect unexposed islanders from the returning partygoers. Unthinkable mere months ago, Beaver Island had dropped its guard, first to the Naturals, now to voyageurs and soldiers, compromising its quarantine. True, none of the newcomers evinced signs of infection. Autumn, Loon, the Howlers, and the three Griffins were all clear-eyed and asymptomatic. Certainly—the doctors concurred—none appeared stung.

Captain Doyle stood hunched at the helm, dragging on a gifted cig, half-listening to their medical chatter. He'd tasked two of his boats to continue blockading the Howlers, ordering shoot-to-kill if any longhairs attempted to cross. He led the rest of the fleet back to harbor; they'd burned too much fuel with too little to show. That damn Coast Guard boat was following too.

The water-protector, Autumn, backed by big Baptiste, had shared a great deal of information. The display of howling, instigated by Loon, had helped focus her guests. The recipients of Autumn's intel—especially Doyle and Young—processed its implications, rearranging her pieces to fit their separate puzzles.

Picnickers learned that St. Ignace scouts—self-named SIS—rode muffled Harleys and specialized in long-range reconnaissance. SIS reported that Michigan's Upper Peninsula—as far west as Marquette, anyway—was clear of Virals. South of the bridge, however, was a different story. Autumn was fresh from a briefing where an SIS messenger had updated the map in St. Ignace—Ignace being the temporary HQ of a hoped-for Free North.

From the map it appeared that Spreaders were on the move, mustering at jumping-off points for a feared assault on the ever-strategic Mackinac Bridge. The industrial parks of Cadillac and West Branch were filling up with vehicles, specifically the tanker-trucks needed to fuel any mechanized push.

Autumn, Baptiste, and their voyageurs were warning the people of the Straits, recruiting volunteers to rally at Ignace. Beaver's archipelago was their western terminus. Soon they would return to help defend the big bridge. Autumn's final words to the party had been a plea: "Will you join us?"

Her guests lowered their eyes. It was all too much, and much too fast. The mind-jerk reaction had been universal: rejection.

After an awkward minute, Captain Young—quid pro quo—bartered intelligence of his own, confirming rumor. The Army officer affirmed that the president was indeed dead, murdered six months ago back in March, apparently by an assassin. What remained of the military—much reduced by Stinger—had fractured on fault lines, racial and regional. Fascist units, enraged at their dear leader's death, had run amok. The last Young had heard, a Confederate flag gloated above the Capitol. Federal buildings had been gutted by fire, their smoke-stained statuary toppled and disfigured.

This news was months old, and Young admitted his worldview had been much reduced. The captain confirmed that a resistance movement in Michigan—a mix of Guard and Old Law—was sabotaging the Spreaders. In the battle for Michigan there'd been heavy losses, and mistakes had been many. No one at the picnic-parlay should underestimate the contagious. There'd even been rumors—Booker shot his captain a look—of a new breed of soldier, undeterred by virus, hairless, skeletal, and not entirely human. Several Guard posts, including Fort Custer downstate, had been decimated. Young knew of survivors, troopers from Custer's 177th, who'd described being utterly outfought by this new form of nightmare.

Young, ever-tactical, closely observed the voyageurs' reaction. Autumn and Baptiste had flinched, sharing a look Young wouldn't forget. Continuing, he confirmed the SIS reports. They matched the latest SITREP from Camp Grayling—massed movements of Virals. West Branch and Cadillac had been named by his CO, Colonel Dennis, as well.

As the guests departed, they promised Autumn to at least convene a council, share her news, and relay her call for bridge volunteers. Soon, the voyageur canoes would return east, rallying U.P. harbor towns—Naubinway, Epoufette, Brevort—along the way. Time was short, and if a stand was to be made, action must be swift. Help from Beaver Island would be looked for: the rally point, St. Ignace.

Naturals Diana and Brian, self-marooned on Garden Island, now stood on the beach with Loon and Autumn. Together, they watched the Beaver boats depart. The bowl of sky was blue. Gentle waves flashed, scattering sunshine.

"Will the island council act?"

Autumn, water-protector from Manitoulin, tried for calm. Beaver Island was their best bet by far. No other community came close to their numbers, and she'd only seen a fraction of their strength. If these islanders could be rallied, and guardsmen too, then their odds at the Straits would be much improved. The big bridge was everything: lose it, and they'd lose any chance to establish the Free North. No pack of wolves, no matter its size, could fend off an armored assault for long. Any attempted crossing must be contested.

Diana shaded her eyes and considered. Most of the Beaver boats had rounded Sucker Point, welcomed home by their harbor. Two remained on station, continuing their quarantine of Garden Island.

"It will be a lot for the council to take in," the Sentinel said. She shook her head. "We Naturals have been here since June and are still strangers to them."

Autumn frowned. Loon and Brian, eyes on the sky, kept quiet.

Diana, an ELF veteran, continued, "I believe you, and many Sentinels will, too. Your diplomacy here was not in vain. As for the islanders, who can tell? These are dark times, and the calculations are complicated. But there's no predicting the council. The right spokesperson just might sway them."

The mariner—schooled in navigation—judged the azimuth angle, calculating the time of day from the sun. "Can a canoe return us to Beaver Island undetected?"

Autumn nodded. "Baptiste will bring you back when you wish. The man's a born blockade runner. Let's go find him; he wants to talk with you anyway."

Brian made to follow as the two women set off towards the canoe cache, but a look from Loon held him back. "Their talk will be a long one, filled with weapons and war," he said. "Let's fly instead. Brother Brian, what do you say?"

The blue-eyed shaman smiled at the wise child. "I thought you'd never ask."

Behind Closed Doors

And when we get behind closed doors
Then she lets her hair hang down
And she makes me glad that I'm a man
Oh, no one knows what goes on behind closed doors

Confined and isolated in his cabin, Bob's quickly callusing fingers remembered the chord progression. Charlie Rich—RIP—had been his wife's favorite. The prisoner ached when he played it, even more if he sang. This heartburn was unfamiliar; Bob hadn't felt such pangs since collapse. Apparently, no amount of pillage had immunized his sorrow. The mayhem of Y1 may have distracted and delayed, but it hadn't healed his broken heart. Dr. Chow had neglected to add a journal entry for crying, but if he had, its box would be overflowing with tearful tallies.

Outside his barred window, dusk was falling. Another day down and nothing gained. Yes, he'd exercised, he'd eaten, he'd pissed and shit; he'd strummed his guitar and leafed through some books. Bob used to enjoy drawing; drafting blueprints was what he'd liked most about building houses. Doctor's orders, he tried sketching the dunescape. But no matter his vista, certain icons kept surfacing: taut ropes, stretched necks, the dangle of human fruit—bruised and rotting in the sun. Hiding from the world, he searched for himself. No luck. Oh well, Campbell doubted he'd be pleased to make his own acquaintance.

A knock on the door and a key in the lock returned Bob to

the present. Bright-eyed and brisk, the doctor entered, making his rounds. Trained in bedside manner, Chow read his patient's mood and remained mute. Clinical, Chow checked the journal, slopped out the bucket, re-provisioned the cupboard, and readied a syringe for his daily blood draw.

Chow's patient prisoner volunteered nothing except his arm. Neither did the doctor. When the vial was full, the two men regarded its contents, the chemical cataclysm it contained. The doctor knew he was slipping. Constant vigilance was exhausting. The lack of screens, the lack of live footage, was lulling them all. Without reminders of virological violence, mistakes would be made; a single lapse could lay them all low. If the IFR of the SARS variant was applied to the 300 unexposed islanders, then only one or two might survive Covee's sting. Chow tucked away the vial, a pocketful of plague.

Campbell ignored his captor and continued playing, attempting to tune himself closer to standard. Chow, weary from Garden Island and the morning's parlay, was out of words as well. With a nod to his patient, the doctor exited, locking the cabin tight.

The skinny moon dipped a silver toe into the purple pool of sunset. The big bell began tolling from St. James, not the wild alarm of last night, but the more cadenced call-to-council. Daniel Chow, homesick for the past, hummed Cowboy's tune as he walked away.

My baby makes me proud. Lord, don't she make me proud.

Chow's eyes welled as melody summoned memory. He blinked through the blur, neglecting to check his back trail before exiting the dunes. Distracted by the past, he missed the predator from the present.

From beneath a gray hood, two sharp eyes—utterly unmisted—pierced twilight's pall, tracking the doctor's every move.

A half mile away, the same call-to-council reverberated through the bulkheads of *Emerald Isle,* tied tight to the ferry dock. Specialist Cruz stood sentry at the gangway, his M4 and MOPP gear projecting authority as he guarded his comrades and their forensic investigation within.

Earlier that day they departed Garden Island, following the Beaver boats to their berth in the harbor. Young had insisted on filling the fuel tanks of their Response Boat; Captain Doyle had god-damned them to hell, but Deputy Williams intervened and their 45' craft had been topped off with diesel. Williams had helped with the hoses, querying the soldiers about Old Law and any surviving sheriffs on the mainland. Tight-lipped, the guardsmen shook their helmets at the deputy's list of names, a roll-call of RIPs—the fraternal order of the fucked.

Scraping free of barnacle Williams, Young and Booker entered the ferry and went below. During interrogation, Red Liz, eager to implicate Campbell, had detailed the location of his improvised brig. Now the two CIS detectives navigated the lower deck by flashlight, passing padlocked compartments that gave Young pause.

Booker undogged a hatch, wrenching it open. Paired beams illuminated the space, a storage area for spare parts. At first glance there was little to see: no body, no blood, no obvious signs of imprisonment. But the men were methodical. Ten minutes later, their hunch was confirmed—a scuff-marked stanchion had been recently scrubbed, but spots had been missed. Blood stains surfaced in the LED lumens. Liz's clues had been confirmed: the game was afoot!

The tolling bell pulled them topside. The guardsmen exited the compartment with care, leaving the scene as it was, minus some evidence they sealed in a bag. The crescent moon flashed its blade above the town. Cruz stood sentry at the rail. "Any luck, Captain?"

Young, in a low voice, affirmed, "Our Liz spoke the truth. Someone was held there. Nothing Campbell-specific, but at least I know our next move."

The two enlisted men side-eyed each other, but their chief

wasn't ready.

"I want you two back on the Response Boat. Take a break from those masks, heat up some chow, and rack out. I need you both rested up. We might see action later tonight."

Alfonso Cruz was fine with that. "What about you, sir?"

Young led them down the ferry's gangway. Dockside, he replied, "I'm attending that council."

His sergeant made noise about protection and protocol. Young waved him off. "I'll be fine. I'm not making any big moves, just keeping my eyes open."

Reaching their vessel, Cruz offered, "How about some grub, sir, before you go? Let me make you something."

Young turned towards town. "Later. And I mean it, get some rest. Could be a long night. Charge up the NVGs and monitor your two-ways."

He pushed the transmit key on his chest radio, beeping the units of his men.

"Sir, your rifle?"

Young didn't turn but patted his holstered pistol in reply. Cruz and Booker watched their captain step smartly toward town, passing through ghosts of the strangely haunted docks. Once safely aboard their Coast Guard vessel, they pulled off helmets and lowered MOPP masks. Unwashed and greasy with sweat, they gulped unfiltered air, unloaded their battered rifles, and racked them.

Booker was always hungry. The Detroiter never stopped craving the calories of the past—Coney Island, square pizza, shawarma, Vernors. He sighed, rummaging instead through their mildewed carton of expired MREs. Cruz badgered his hangry battle-buddy: "Come on man, what'd you guys find in the ferry?"

Booker tossed Alfonzo the least bad MRE, meatballs in marinara, and readied the chili-mac he'd picked for himself. The flameless ration-heaters did their thing, and soon both men were forking hot mouthfuls from steaming pouches. Between bites Booker finally answered, "Like the captain said, not much. But I can tell you what he zipped in the bag."

Cruz paused his plastic fork. Booker, mouthing flavorless macaroni, continued, "A tip-cap from a syringe, an empty bandage packet,"—he gulped a too-hot bite—"and a piece of flex-cuff that had been cut."

Cruz computed, nonplussed. "What's it add up to?"

Booker scraped the pouch corners for a final bite. "You know the chief. He's not ready to share, but apparently someone tried to cover their tracks."

The hungry men, never satisfied, moved on to dessert. Cruz unwrapped his protein bar, asking, "What's the next move? Where's this perp Campbell at? And who the fuck helped him?"

Booker pounded his cake—artificially preserved. "No idea, but Campbell's a confirmed Viral and that makes this shit urgent. You've seen these people. Hidden this whole time, unprotected. Stinger would light this place up."

Bellies technically full, the men policed up their trash. Cruz stretched out in the wheelhouse; per their rotation, the first sleep was his. Booker, reluctant, readied his MOPP hood. The last words to his friend, half asleep already, were a prediction: "Captain's headed to their council. Bet he'll have eyes on those two doctors. Chow? Newsome? They'd better watch their fucking step. It's not the crime but the cover-up, and chief smells a rat."

Cruz, almost napping, nodded in response. The exhausted medic knew that soon enough he'd be busy. Great care was needed with these people. The EMT fell asleep to waves lapping against the hull. Dreaming, he cradled Beaver Island in his arms, shielding its people from harm, including harm from himself.

Booker heard his buddy snoring, shook his head, and geared up: gloves, helmet, and mask. He selected his rifle from the rack, inserted a magazine, and slung it. He unplugged a set of NVGs from their charger and stepped on deck.

The moon's blade had been sheathed by Earth's rotation. Silver blood—the Milky Way—splattered the sky. The harbor was dark. Booker was alive in a world where most had perished. But he never felt lucky. For the duration of his watch he'd have to fight off sleep. He'd be fighting memories as well. In quieter moments, he felt them calling—his beautiful boy and baby mama, too. Tonight, this family felt near. Anthony Booker wasn't strong enough, never would be. He took a last look at the naked stars, slid the goggles in place, and powered up his vision. The tinted world, all too familiar, was his purgatory, a green room in which he abided. His real life was behind him, and any heaven far ahead. For now, he'd keep the watch, minding the minutes till he could tumble home to sleep.

Holy Cross

ERECTED IN 1860 BY IRISH IMMIGRANTS, the wooden structure—washed white by colonizer hands—was the largest venue in St. James. The church had been consecrated as a place of unity just as the loosely united states were dividing. Post collapse, its parking lot held horse-hitched wagons again, along with aging bicycles on balding tires. Island SUVs and pickups were gas-guzzlers, rusting dinosaurs who'd gone extinct. The old church was packed full, with more folks streaming in.

Captain Young—alien-looking in his MOPP suit—loitered outside, monitoring arrivals. Islanders had heard the rumor of outsiders and stared at this invasive species, most keeping their distance. The uniformed soldier represented the mainland and its landscape—a valley of death. Deputy Williams lobbed Young a friendly greeting but went inside, rebuffed. An Old Law wannabe, Young had seen his type before.

The big bell ceased its clang and the council called itself to order. Stragglers hustled in and the dark street emptied. Lanterns and candles illuminated the nave. Biblical figures, stained in glass, pulsed lifelike with refracted light. To Young, outside in the shadows, the very building seemed alive. After two years in the wasteland, this overfull church was surreal. A hundred voices affirmed their allegiance, pledging to a fallen flag.

Young couldn't unsee the super-spreading event. He envisioned the virions—inhalation, exhalation—the humid interior, a great wooden lung of rebreathed air.

"—with liberty and justice for all." A gavel banged and the council began.

A latecomer crept stealthily towards the church along an unused alley that led to the dunes. From shadow, Young observed his prime suspect and made his calculations. The suspect was shielded—allegedly—from the variant. He was well-educated, athletic, a professional in his prime.

Captain Young, trained in artillery, fired a spotting round. "Good evening, Doctor."

Daniel Chow, fresh from the dunes, flinched at the sudden greeting.

"Captain," the doctor nodded, recovering quickly.

Young fired for effect and watched his rounds hit. "Working late at the ferry? Don't want to miss tonight's council."

Chow—clearly impacted—cleared his throat. "Yes, well, so much to do. You know how it is. Shall we go in?"

Suspicion confirmed, Young waved the liar through but remained at his post. A parliamentarian droned from within, detailing topics for council consideration. The captain—keyed up after sighting his quarry—stepped away, thumbing his radio. "Sergeant, you there?"

After a pause, the Detroiter responded from their vessel. The captain gave his orders, named the rally point, waited for confirmation, then ended the call by saying, "And Booker, be sure to bring cuffs, NVGs, and my carbine. Young out."

Frank switched off, checked the seals on his suit, and stepped into the light.

"But this new information changes everything!"

The sheriff's deputy gripped the lectern; an argument was underway. Williams aimed his ire at Doyle and the pew packed with fishermen. Tom Doyle almost spat, "Changes everything, does it? Coyotes? Some damn Indians in canoes? Now you want us to break quarantine, go off questing on the mainland?

Play cops and robbers with your Army friend? Travis Williams, you're off yer fuckin' rocker!"

His fellow boat captains grinned crookedly. Bloody Doyle was speaking their minds. Father Peter stood up by the altar. "Mr. Doyle, please. You are in a house of God."

Doyle still smoldered. "Apologies, Father Peter. You're right, it's a holy place. There should be no damn nonsense here."

Doyle leered at Deputy Williams, his junior by thirty years. Tom's wife Annie blushed from her pew, fanning herself as she was soothed by her friends.

The old church was in schism. Naturals sat sequestered in a private alcove on the left, islanders filled the pews in the main room—a shotgun wedding between two feuding families. The pastor for the Naturals, a mule of a man with a florid face, wore his collar as did the island priest—the charismatic Father Peter. Lutheran and Catholic, they mended in tandem, attempting to knit the divide. Pastor George stood in the private alcove while Father Peter sat in the chancel, his back to the altar and its oversized cross. Together, both men shouldered its weight, modeling for their flocks—cooperation was possible, even necessary, for island survival.

In the alcove sat ELF refugees from the mainland—Elena, Grace, and a nervous Dr. Chow. Nearest to them were the farmers, Rodriguez and White, along with Sentinels Nighthawk and Sparrow. Miin and Mukwa—though fostered on the island— also sat with the Naturals. The folding chairs behind them held fifty more: farmers and fishermen, artists and hunters. Nontraditional families—newly forged by collapse—sat together, parents hushing children overstimulated by the novelty of a nighttime church.

Just outside the alcove, in the main room, island leadership sat nearest the transept: Doyle and his captains, Doc Newsome and the deputy, Shawn Greene and his fellow farmers. Another fifty packed the pews behind them. In the back, near the narthex, elders brooded from Indian Point. Samantha—eldest of the Anishinaabeg—was there. Her silver head was down, but her ears were wide open.

"Captain Young! Will you speak, sir?" Travis Williams, sheriff's deputy, implored from the lectern. Fifty curious Beavers turned in regard. Frank Young stood near the font, its stone-cool water trembling in expectation. The reflected figure, insectoid in his hazmat gear, remained still. Then with slow ceremony, Young unfastened mask and helmet and stood bareheaded and human behind the congregants. Helmet under his arm, eyes-front, the Army captain marched up the aisle, turned neatly, and assumed the lectern vacated by the deputy.

A moment of silence. Candles guttered in a gust of night air. Employing his command voice, Young began his briefing: "Good evening." From both sides—alcove and nave—a reflex of "Good evenings" was returned.

"My name is Frank Young. As a civilian, I was a fire chief downstate. Now I'm a captain in the 125th regiment of Michigan's Guard. I'm here with two men on a reconnaissance mission. Our unit—the Griffins—is stationed at Camp Grayling, though our numbers there, like everywhere, have been much reduced."

One of Doyle's captains—crooked Bill Ferny—jumped up and interrupted, "What's it like then on the main? And what about this bridge? Is Mighty Mac really in danger? Or is young Travy pulling our leg? Or maybe he's pulling something else?"

His clowning crudity got guffaws from his boat crew. Deputy Williams glowered, Father Peter flushed. Captain Young fixed his clear eyes on Ferny, staying silent till the grinning man sat down.

"You ask about the mainland? It's a ruin, sir. Much worse than you can imagine."

For a few seconds Young absorbed the medieval interior, a chiaroscuro of candlelight—glasswork, crowded pews, babes in arms.

"Most of you," with a nod he exempted the Naturals in their side-room, "have no idea how rare such a gathering has become." He stared hard at Ferny. "You ask about the Mackinac Bridge, and if it's threatened? Well, my latest intelligence says yes. Do I believe the voyageurs, these 'Howlers' that arrived last night by canoe?"

The captain cross-haired Ferny with his gaze, could feel the stunted man's snarl, his growing rictus of rage. Young surprised himself as he continued, "Again, I say yes. I believe them. My soldiers and I are bound by oath to defend the Constitution, including, 'We the People.' Our duty is clear: to aid these voyageurs if we can and prevent the plague from spreading. If the U.P. turns Viral, then your island will be surrounded."

At the captain's confirmation, a collective gasp escaped the islanders. Young recalibrated before firing his next salvo. "Our world is not as it was. Never will be again. Accept this, and live. Deny it, and die."

He scanned the room again and stepped down. Young marched smartly down the aisle, a uniformed lodestar pulling both sides of the church together. The captain exited the nave and went out into the night.

Utter darkness outside the church; inside, raised voices defied the gavel. The September evening was chilly, stars brightening with his eyes' dilation. Young took his bearing from the Dipper: Merak-Dubhe-Polaris. He resealed his chem-suit and turned his back on the council, vectoring north to a rendezvous point in the dunes.

A House Divided

CAPTAIN YOUNG DEPARTED and the spell was broken; both sides suddenly erupted. The collared shepherds sprang to their flocks, soothing panic, avoiding stampede. On each side, deliberations began—overhearing each other in snippets, their leadership adjusted in real time.

Pastor George, a dreadnought, left the main room and anchored the ELF in their alcove. The focus of the Naturals moved with him. George raised heavy hands and had silence, though across the aisle, the islanders in their pews kept braying.

"What we've heard here tonight, and earlier from Garden Island, should not surprise us. Unlike our Beaver Island brethren, we've been there, we've seen it. To us, it is real."

The Naturals nodded. So far, they were with him.

"Forewarned is forearmed. Like Captain Young, we are in a position to help, and that we must do. We believe we've been spared, not by chance, but by purpose. *Thy will be done, on earth as it is in heaven.*"

George paused his sermon when he overheard Doyle raise his voice in the main room.

"For most of us," George assured the Naturals, "this news changes nothing. Many of you have children to raise, crops to cultivate, and flocks that need tending. Your duty is clear. Your help has already been given. Without your labors, your assistance, this coming winter might have killed many. Instead, thanks to you, there's a chance, for the islanders and for us."

His honest face kindled their trust.

George saw a few raised hands. "Yes? Elena?"

Acknowledged, the athlete stood. She wore a plaid shirt and jeans. Her gear of war—parka, headband, weapons—for the past few months had been put away.

"My mind is made up, and I'm guessing I speak for many of the Sentinels."

Elena paused. Her ELF warriors, sidelined for a season, nodded grimly—they were with her.

On the other side, in the church nave, Deputy Williams could be heard pleading with Doyle.

Elena continued, a glint in her eyes. "I will fight. But not for the voyageurs and not for the bridge. My fight is against Chosen, against XCons and their devil dogs that hounded us from our home. I have not forgotten our fallen. My fight is for THEM!"

Sentinels stomped on the floor boards—wooden thunder shook the church. The ELF commando sat down.

Pastor George called on the next hand raised. "Doctor Chow?"

The medical man stood. Professorial, he collected his thoughts.

But Nighthawk—staring daggers at Chow—swooped in and struck first. "All these words! This noise! I will fight as well, but not for you!" She shot a look of scorn at Elena. "And not for *them* either!" She sneered contempt at the islander pews outside the alcove. "My fight is for *Gaia!* Have you already forgotten Her? Forgotten why we're alive when the whole world is dead?"

She flashed a look, raptorial, at Pastor George. The good man flinched, a lamb in her shadow. Hawk continued, "Yes, we've been spared. But keep your God-of-patriarchy, his bearded son, and all the penised popes out of it! We've been spared by Gaia! To do *Her* work! To restore *Her* world! Not to protect and repopulate the very filth that polluted this planet in the first place!"

The extremist paused, chest heaving, talons clenched. No thunder, only silence. Mukwa moved to console. Nighthawk strafed him with her eyes and fled, furious in flight. No voice called her back. Radicalized, she ripped open the cage door and departed the church. Seeking prey—her cabin quarry—Nighthawk winged towards the dunes, hunting by starlight.

Mukwa pushed through his row. Stepping on toes, the big man bumbled after her. Blueberry reached for brother's paw but was rebuffed. Mukwa, a force of nature, forced his way to the foyer and out the door. Passing the baptismal font, its holy water reflected a bruin.

In the main room, Father Peter, the island's popular Catholic priest, called for order. Captain Young had just departed, and Peter's church was in riot. Amy Gillespie, the township clerk, banged her gavel, giving cadence to the chaos.

The deputy pleaded, "All of you heard the captain. Deny, and we die!"

"Well we're still livin', ain't we?" Bill Ferny, arms crossed, standing with his crew, sneered at Williams. "I say we're doin' just fine!"

His thorny clan backed him with a parade of profanity.

"Damn right!"

"Fuckin' tell 'em Bill!"

"Mind our own business, that's what we say!"

"Islanders first!"

"Stay out of their bullshit!"

"Nats are rats! Nats are rats! Nats are rats!"

Father Peter, a part-time pugilist, threw in the towel. Clerk Gillespie gave up her gaveling, head in her hands. The island's farmers—the Martins, the Greenes—yelled for order. Families were leaving, reluctant kids in tow.

Tom Doyle compared both groups. Across the aisle, in their private alcove, he saw the Naturals, hands raised, waiting patiently. Frustrated, the fisherman throttled forward, glaring at the priest as he commandeered Peter's lectern. Deck boots planted, Doyle seized the helm, fighting to control the rudder. His fellow captains elbowed the unruly islanders to order.

"Hear! Hear!" from Hannigan, the big man brandishing both his buoy-sized fists.

Tom McCann moved on Bill Ferny, Keith Two-Crow's killer. "Watch yer damn tongue, Cap'n Ferny!"

The smaller man flinched under the veteran's glare.

Captain Sue Keller and her crew called for calm as well. The anti-Nat chanting ceased.

Mutiny averted, Doyle indicated the orderly alcove of refugees, shaming his side to silence. "Now, ain't that better?"

The departing islanders paused. They could overhear the other pastor, George, preaching to the Naturals in their side room: "—in a position to help, and that we must do."

Doyle, regaining steerageway, could see his wife Annie beaming proudly.

He started with the deputy. "Now Travis, no one is 'denying' anything. There's no need to go scaring folks with such talk. We've made it this far now, haven't we?"

The islanders affirmed.

"And we'll keep on making it, that's for *damn* sure!"

Scattered applause. Father Peter was nodding too.

"Now on this island, we're still free." Doyle looked at the deputy, at Doc Newsome, and Shawn Greene. "Any man or woman wantin' to leave can do so. Join Old Law's posse? Go die for a bridge? Catch the Covee and get stung? Well that's your choice, and you're all free to make it."

Led by Pastor George, the Lord's Prayer droned from across the divide.

Doyle continued, "Free to leave? Yes. But don't count on returning. We've let our guard down lately, you know we have. First with these Nats," he pointed as Elena stood in the alcove to speak, "and now with these furball 'Howlers' and the frickin' US Army, too."

His people approved, but Deputy Williams demanded more. "Well, what about our fleet then? And what about you, Captain Doyle? What will *you* do?"

Elena said something they couldn't hear, and thunder boomed from the Naturals as they pounded the floor. A locker room feeling emanated from the visiting team in their alcove. Doyle frowned, then raised his voice to be heard above the pep rally of the Nats.

"The fleet? We'll protect the island, of course. Just like before."

The thunder rolled away as Doyle's personal trauma flashed him back: *Keith Two-Crow, shot in the chest by Ferny. The veteran, the redeemer, his corpse falling, falling, falling … Tom's tortured night in the tower, Judas, the betrayer, alone.*

Doyle drifted a moment, becalmed in this doldrum of dread. Then he shook his head as a fresh breeze luffed his sail. The boat captain's next utterance surprised everyone but Annie.

"And me? Well young Travy, I'll be going to babysit the bridge. Someone has to, after all. Got no kids, no grandkids, plus I don't trust no one else to do it."

Doyle charted it out for them. "Now look here," his thick fist became the island, "we didn't know it at the time, but so far we've been lucky. Say what you will, but these Nats stole that damn ferry, stopping a big threat comin' from Charlevoix." He illustrated with his hands. "But if those Viral bastards get behind us, and take the U.P. as well? Manistique? Naubinway? Epoufette? And their boats and barges too? Well pardon me,

Father Pete, but we're fucked."

A lamentation rose from his crowd. Pre-contact with Naturals, the islander worldview had been narrow. During collapse, threats had only come from one vector—southeast from Charlevoix—with the fleet just barely managing to fend them off. During today's picnic parlay, Autumn from Manitoulin and Captain Young from Camp Grayling had widened their lens. Terrified of the potential threats arrayed against them, islanders looked to their leaders.

"Now, now, it ain't that bad. There's deep water all around, and you can always count on the fleet." His boat captains confirmed. "Plus, there's a good crop in the ground—thanks again to these Nats. Thank God, our cellars are full and the flocks look fat."

Greene and Martin were nodding too. Doyle bowed his head for a moment before acknowledging, "But deputy's right, we can't be blind any—"

The islanders flinched as a furious woman flew out of the church, followed by Sam's big foster, Muck, who bumbled after her.

Doyle resumed. "For now, it sounds like the U.P. is clear of Virals. Folks are even talkin' about settin' up a 'Free North.' Now the only way this works is to defend—or destroy—the big bridge. The mainland, we know, is crawling with Spreaders, but they're bottlenecked by the Straits, cock-blocked by Mighty Mac. We wanna keep on surviving? Raise up our little ones? Then we've got to keep it so." Doyle drew a deep breath before concluding, "In two days I leave on *Bloody Mary*. If you wanna talk, you know where to find me."

The End of Something

"GOD DAMN IT, Hawk, wait up! Let me help!" Muck was breathing hard. "Where are you going?" She'd flown from the church, and he was running after her—of course he was, what else could he do? Bent low to the ground, the big man was a blur, shockingly quick despite his thick limbs.

By starlight, St. James was a clutter of boathouses, net sheds, and castaway gear. In its heyday the little harbor shipped a million pounds of fish a year, making it the freshwater fishing capital of the country, and maybe the world. No one who lived in the town, or near it, could escape the smell of whitefish. But by the 1890s, there were no more fish to be caught. The companies left, boats were hauled out to rot, and the Irish who'd emigrated for the fishing were left stranded on Beaver's sandy shores.

Nighthawk flew through the empty town, arrowing towards Gaia's mission in the dunes. The big brute—part oaf, part circus clown—was definitely not part of *Her* plan. The Sentinel was faster by far, but still, she couldn't have him following.

So the flier dropped her flaps. Reducing speed, Hawk pivoted, challenging her stalker face to face. Muck stumbled to a stop, then stood heaving, heart valves wide open. There she was! Finally, they could talk in peace. He forced his breathing to slow. His throat was so dry! Muck tried swallowing, but couldn't speak. Romeo, panicking, had lost his lines, and there was so much to say.

"Not a word! Not one fucking word! Mukwa, don't. I'm warning you, man. Just back the fuck away!" Nighthawk's eyes were killing-keen. The bird-of-prey didn't blink, just stared right through him as if he were dead already, at the bottom of a tomb.

Seeing this naked truth, that he'd lost her, truly lost her, Mukwa's eyes welled with sudden tears. Damn it! He could feel his chin trembling, too. No way he'd trust his voice. The Muck stood mute, heart bared to her hostility. Curious, the stars peered down upon the sandy stage. Would the lover remember his lines? Would Juliet's rage relent?

Mukwa tried, he really did. But the words wouldn't come because there weren't any. Not for this. Eloquence gone, Muck improvised, arriving at a closer truth: "So, what then, Hawk? It's not fun? Just not fun anymore?"

His questions quivered as he spoke them. His whole body was shaking, his sentences too.

The raptor stared blankly at its pursuer, then finally blinked. A tiny aperture opened, a prick of light came through—but not enough, not nearly enough. "No, Oso. No, it's not fun anymore. Nothing is."

A tremor went through him. She spoke the truth, and he knew it. Sparrow's earlier counsel was spot on. It wasn't him, it was her. The problem was with Hawk, but he couldn't help her, no one could—not the Nats, not shaman Brian or elder Grace, not even her comrades, her fellow commandos. Maybe if Matador was here, he'd know what to say? Or Bull, or Thorn?

But no, they were all dead, or worse, captured. Mukwa knew they haunted her, because they haunted him, too. More harm than healing if he summoned those ghosts. So he didn't.

He didn't know shit about Hawk's former life, her family and friends from before. Had there been a husband? Loving parents? A bestie or two? Most elves wouldn't say, and Nighthawk was no exception.

Mukwa's character sketch of her was blurry, but he'd limned in some lines—ivy-educated, she spoke several languages and had lived abroad. Even in the before, the woman had been hawkish about the environment. Some kind of globetrotting do-gooder, urging First World's elite to give a shit—or money at least—to the Third's hoi polloi.

"There's no good way to do this. Oso, I'm sorry."

Nighthawk stepped back, breaking the bonds of their chemistry, their covalence, their electric connection. Mukwa felt his heart breaking, too. He couldn't survive this, he didn't want to, he wouldn't. She moved to get past him, to continue Gaia's mission. Any love-light left her eyes as the Sentinel's feral mien resurfaced. The ELF extremist was done with talking.

Mukwa saw this clearly and moaned, her arrow of indifference shafting his heart. His life-force ebbed, and the might left his muscles. She was moving, moving away. Done with him, she'd leave him behind. Ol' Muck had been dumped. It had happened before—abandoned by his deadbeats, exiled from the island, cut from the team.

Another move from Hawk, not towards him, but away. Another moan from Mukwa. Then he mucked it up, big time. He reached for her, one last hug, one final farewell. Blindly, the bear groped with its paws. The raptor, screeching in alarm, raked him with flashing talons. Three lines of blood striped his face, and away the bird flew.

His legs turned to jelly, and *thump*, down he went, ass in the sand. Heartstrings cut, cheek lacerated, Mukwa tasted blood— salty, like tears. He squinted in the starlight, but she was gone, flown far away. He'd lost her. His wild thing wouldn't return.

Fuck it. Come death, and welcome, since Nighthawk wills it so. Broken-hearted, he would volunteer to fight. He'd overheard Elena in church, knew she'd be leading the elves to war. If Hawk joined the fight as well, so be it. He wouldn't look at her. He'd never say a word. Instead, he'd kill some more Virals, and hoped to be killed—quickly, if possible—in return.

Damn, his cheek felt like fire though. Did he need stitching? Pawing his wounds, he shuffled back towards town, towards granny and little sis in the church. Samantha had planned a sleepover, a rare family night. He wasn't in the mood, but his face was falling off, so fuck it, Muck was in. They'd be heading home soon, taking King's Highway south to the state forest, then the brambled path to the bog.

Nighthawk altered her flight path, picking flesh from her nails. Shit! She hadn't meant to do that. None of this was his fault, not really. They'd had something once, really had it, the real thing, nothing false. But that was dead now, as she was dead, dead with all the rest—the billions from before, and the handful she'd cared about since. She felt a great sob rise within her but she stifled it. Stifled it for Her. For Gaia, damn it!

Something good must come from this mess, and it would start here tonight. Mother Nature had a plan for Her planet—a great cleansing via Covee. Now Gaia's will was contested by that fucking Dr. Chow, his recovering patient, and Miin's green-shielding, too. The world was changing too fast, leaving too many behind. She needed to get off her ass, get back in the game, and off this fucking island. But where to start?

When in doubt, go back to the beginning, to the night of the XCon attack and their devil dogs back in June. It was there that things had fallen the fuck apart. There they'd lost Bull, and Thorn, and his whole damn squad.

If prisoners had been taken, if any elves were POWs, then Hawk's mission—thank Gaia!—was crystal clear. The only clear thing in this chaotic, fallen world. Clearer than her feelings anyway. And who was she to have feelings, when so many had none? Chow's prisoner/patient was tonight's target—two birds with one stone. She'd thwart the doctor's meddling, plus secure a Chosen hostage for future exchange.

Hawk reached the dune edge, an inflection point: *now or never*. Town was behind her, and the noisy church, too. She looked above at the stars: Gaia's tears.

A shooter streaked across the sky—another teardrop, another fallen? The Sentinel retrieved her gear-of-war from where she'd stashed it. The ELF militant donned her military parka, raised its gray hood, and slung her quiver. Shimmering, Nighthawk merged—Gaia's Guardian—with the nightscape.

Cowboy Has Company

SOLITARY IN HIS CABIN, marooned in the dunes, Bob Campbell read by candlelight, though his shit bucket—a most odorous
roommate—was growing hard to ignore. The stars above were
pulsing. Outside his barred window, the Milky Way flowed like a
living thing.

> *You want to cry aloud for your*
>
> *mistakes. But to tell the truth the world*
>
> *doesn't need anymore of that sound.*

He couldn't agree more with this Mary Oliver, one of the poets
from Chow's stack of books. Bob was all cried out, at least for tonight. He felt sleep descending and welcomed it. Whatever buzz
he'd gotten from the drugged meal had faded, returning him to
his sober self. Disliking the company, he perused the borrowed
book, its worn pages stamped: BIDL, Beaver Island District Library.

> *So if you're going to do it and can't*
>
> *stop yourself, if your pretty mouth can't*
>
> *hold it in, at least go by yourself...*
>
> *...and roar all you want and nothing will be disturbed*

He didn't much feel like roaring, his bunk beckoning instead.
Bob bookmarked the page, stacking the author—another RIP—
on the pile of dead poets. They'd be there in the morning to ac-
cuse him afresh.

Holding his breath, he pissed in the bucket, stretched his push-up-sore muscles, and threw an extra blanket on his bed. Soon he'd be needing fuel for the winter. Bob wondered how Chow would keep the woodstove a secret. Cupping the fragile flame, he blew out the candle. Night-blind, Cowboy groped towards his cot and a too-brief oblivion.

The three-man extraction team was in position—two at the door, one guarding their backs. The soldiers wore MOPP and were armed with automatic rifles. They overheard the recited poetry and their target's gush of urine. They waited for the candle; its snuffing was their cue. A rifle butt smashed through lock and hasp, breaching the door, granting ingress. Two men rushed the room while its occupant, blind and helpless, raised both arms.

"Bob Campbell, this is the US Army! You have the right to remain silent. Anything you say can be used against you. You have the right to a fair trial. You have the right to an advisor. You have the right to know what you're accused of. Do you understand these rights?"

Cowboy blinked in the dark, nodding assent to his alien abductors.

"Turn around, put your hands on your head!"

The voice commanded and Cowboy complied. He felt the familiar bite of flex-cuffs on his newly healed wrists. Bob smelled the staleness of their unwashed gear—Eau de Collapse.

"You're accused of multiple counts of homicide, sexual assault, and human trafficking. Do you have anything to say for yourself?"

Campbell—surprise, surprise—felt mostly relief. His arrestors heard their prisoner recite: "The world doesn't need anymore of that sound."

Apparently, her quarry—the Viral caged in a cabin—was stalked by other predators as well. Nearing the dunes, Nighthawk had overheard the extraction team at their rally point: "Campbell ... Chosen ... Homicide."

The wary Sentinel kept her distance. Contour flying, she beat the soldiers to the cabin, plotted her ambush, and awaited their arrival.

A single flame illuminated the knotty-pine interior. From her perch in a dune fold Hawk observed the Viral—*Murderer!*

The criminal, with ELF blood on his hands, sat reading by candlelight. She gnashed her teeth at the doctor's duplicity—*Chow! That fucking hypocrite!*

The half-elf doctor had deceived them all. Worse, he'd thwarted Gaia! Nighthawk guessed at blood tests, antivirals, and future vaccines.

The night was calm. The big lake was a mirror in which the galaxy gazed at itself—as above, so below. The goggled soldiers approached, insectoid in starlight. Two went to the door, a third— their lookout—positioned himself in the spot she'd predicted. She evaded their green gaze, loading her weapon with a non-lethal missile: a blunted arrow.

Hawk heard Campbell's recitation and the splashing of his piss. When the cabin candle was snuffed, the breach team smashed the lock, kicking in the door.

"Bob Campbell, this is the US Army! You have the right to remain silent—"

The she-elf stood quickly. With avian acuity, Hawk acquired her target. Tensioning her bow, she loosed. The lookout crumpled from the violent blow to his neck. Hawk was on him as he fell. Muscles amped by adrenaline, she heaved the heavy, unwashed body out of sight. Loud voices could be heard from the cabin— the Viral's fucking rights were being read, what a joke!

She flew to the door and readied her next strike.

Campbell complied with his capturers, resignation in his voice:

"The world doesn't need anymore of that sound."

The second soldier exited, leading with his rifle barrel. The Sentinel seized its oily muzzle and leveraged her larger opponent into a vulnerable position. She crunched his goggled face with a single blow. Strings cut, the man dropped onto cold sand. The prisoner, cuffed but still standing, now blocked the entrance, allowing Hawk to regain her balance. The final soldier cursed, backing into the cabin with his rifle raised and ready.

With an urgent prayer to Gaia, Nighthawk dipped low and accelerated. She shouldered Campbell's bulk and, human-shielded, charged the interior. Surprised and unable to fire, the soldier dodged too late. She heaved her shitty-smelling shield and knocked the rifle askew, clawing off the soldier's goggles. Hawk ducked under the swung rifle, swept her opponent's leg, and followed him down as he fell. His helmet bounced off the wooden floor; her elbow-drop finished him, spattering his mask with broken-nosed gore.

Campbell cowered, prone in a corner. The cuffed man struggled to rise. Hawk regained her feet and quickly assessed. The three soldiers were down, but for how long?

She utilized their extra cuffs; in a minute, all three had been trussed, ankles to wrists.

Cringing at the touch—Gaia forgive!—she tossed their metallic rifles in the sand and stood her prisoner up. "Time to go, scumbag." She collected her bow, touched the knives in her belt, and started heading towards town.

Her POW didn't move. Nighthawk turned on him with a hiss: "You'd rather wait here for *them*?"

In a blink she was bladed, starlight keen upon the dagger's edge. Her captive flinched at the display.

"They were gonna *hang* your sorry ass. You know that, right?"

Campbell squinted at the prone figures—large men, combat-vetted. Disbelieving, he peered inside the woman's hood. She kneed him hard in the gonads. He doubled over, grunting from the blow.

She rolled the knife across her knuckles. Seizing his forearm, she sliced him free of their cuffs. "You're being rescued, dumbass. Now let's go!"

She took the path towards St. James and disappeared in the dark. Captive no longer, the wanted man calculated. It only took a second. With a groan, he followed her. Shackled by his past, Cowboy Bob was out of options.

Fueled by Ferns

NIGHTHAWK LED HER PRISONER through the blacked-out town towards the harbor. They skirted the glowing church, parishioners departing from the parking lot. Whiskey Light loomed high above the point. There were eyes in the tower, but she avoided its gaze.

Slinking shadow-to-shadow, Hawk quickly ransacked the wharf for transport. At the third boathouse, she pulled Campbell inside; flicking a lighter, she nodded at the floating motorboat. It looked good—a sixteen-foot aluminum with a fifteen-horse Johnson. Essential to her escape plan were the oarlocks and the two long oars mounted there. She released the flame, the boathouse going dark. They both breathed familiar fumes of boat gas and oil.

"You want off this island, Campbell?"

"How do you know my name?"

"Overheard your arrestors, asshole. Now answer."

The newly freed man grunted his assent.

"Then we're gonna need gasoline, lots of it."

She flicked flame again. The boat's external fuel tank, of course, was empty, but the shed had containers—jerry cans, siphoned dry back in Y1. Hawk checked the bay-side door. It would open. She prayed it was quiet.

"Grab those cans and follow me."

Campbell gathered the red jugs, ten empty gallons per fist.

He trailed after the archer as she navigated the waterfront. The fuel dock was fenced but appeared unguarded. Beaver's Home Fleet—with topped-off tanks—was tethered nearby. The big ferry hulked from its berth, the entire scene unlit save by distant suns and their long-ago light.

"Start pumping."

Her arrow glinted, its broadhead shaving-sharp. Hawk took a covering position as Campbell entered the fuel cage. Ignoring the diesel, he arranged his jugs by the regular. Bob breathed his own silent prayer, and it was answered: the hand-pump didn't squeak, thank fucking Christ. The only sound was the splash of gasoline.

"Gaia, we are grateful." Penitent, the Sentinel gave quiet thanks. Refined petroleum was the plasma of Mother Earth. "Forgive us this carbon, guide us in its use."

Bright-eyed, the ELF warrior hunted shadows, tuning her sharp ears for footsteps. She heard Campbell shift containers; the jugs were filling fast. Their escape would be fueled by fossilized fronds. *Plant Lives Matter!* The Natural pictured these innocents in her prayer—the ferny forests growing 300 million years ago, ripe with sunlight, basking in the utter lack of hominids.

"We're full. Hey lady, need a little help here."

Nighthawk put away her missile and slung its launcher, joining Campbell in the cage. For now, anyway, her trust in the Viral was total. On-island, he was a dead man walking—and he knew it. If they made it to the mainland, then reached Chosen headquarters to barter a hostage exchange, their roles would reverse. She heaved her share of the sloshing load, hoping like hell that stabilizer had been added.

They muled the heavy gallons towards the boathouse; halfway there, she stopped to douse a storage shed. Reaching the darkened boathouse, they added oil to the jerry cans and swished. Together, they laded their vessel, connected the fuel line, squeezed the bulb, checked spark, and readied for departure.

Campbell sat in the stern by the motor. Hawk rummaged the shed by Bic-light, commandeering two PFDs, a stained deck jacket, a coil of line, and some fishing tackle. She untied the boat and slow-rolled the overhead door.

"Not yet," she instructed as he gripped the pull-cord. "Oars first."

He shifted seats as silently as he could. Hawk flitted lightly aboard, perching on the bow. She removed an arrow from her quiver and dipped a rag in gas, tying it tightly just behind the broadhead. Campbell handled the splintery oars with soft hands. She whispered the go-ahead and they eased their small vessel into the harbor.

Following her point, he rowed south by starlight, hugging the cluttered wharf, avoiding tower detection. When the range was right and they were ready to make their dash towards open water, she nocked her arrow and sought for calm.

Above the harbor, constellations glittered; another shooting star lit towards the shore. Far below, Hawk breathed gratitude, ignited the rag, tensioned the bow, and zipped her fiery tracer towards its pre-soaked target. They both heard a *thunk*, then *WHOOSH*!

Their beacon burst brightly into flame.

"Now pull!" she urged her galley slave.

Campbell put his back into it, rowing quickly along the shore until the open water was near. Behind them, the old shed was ablaze, its column of smoke vacuumed vertical by the void. At their most exposed position, an alarm bell clanged from the tower.

"Keep rowing!" the hooded woman hissed. Swiveling his gaze, Bob could barely see her shimmering form. Hawk-eyed, she peered keenly ahead, fitting another missile to her shoulder-fired launcher. Campbell—palms already blistering—kept his pace. Their boat, overladen, progressed slowly. Another bell joined the clamor, the big one from the Holy Cross belfry. Shouts shattered the soundscape; the harbor was garish in the gassy glow.

Then they rounded a point and put St. James behind them. Nighthawk shoved him hard towards the stern. "Start the motor."

Hawk assumed Campbell's position, taking up the oars. His curse cloud mingled with carbon exhaust as the somnolent motor coughed itself awake. Nighthawk rowed till adjustments were made—choke, richness, angle of tilt. Campbell put the outboard in gear and the propeller started pushing. Hawk stowed the oars, folding up their wooden wings. Campbell opened the throttle and made their getaway. Beaver behind, mainland ahead—next stop, Charlevoix!

Sleepover

THE BAY MARE MONTANA was excited. She was up way past barn-time, and her people—the Greenes—were up late too. They'd be sleeping in tomorrow, and she'd have an easier day working their fields. The old church was packed with humans, its parking lot crowded with uneasy horses and keyed-up farm dogs. Her nostrils flared, scenting friends and old rivals from all around the island. Voices rose and fell from the wooden interior. What was going on in there? Every equine was equally curious. Colorful windows pulsed as light refracted through the glass. She gazed at her favorite picture: a bundle of wheat and a scythe. The sight of grains made her hungry. She was ready for home.

"Ready for home, Montana gal?" She caught Shawn's grassy scent before she heard him—Master! And here came the Greenes! Wife Amanda and their kids clambered into the wagon. They were leaving church early—perhaps they'd heard enough? Something cool and green moved through her large mind. She knew this touch—it was Eldest, and young Blueberry too, hooray! The wrinkled woman, sage-scented, proffered an apple; Montana took it with her lips and then crunched. Sweet juice filled her mouth. Elation! When all were aboard, Shawn spoke his words to her and away they went, clip-clopping through the outskirts, then south along King's Highway while a starry path blazed above.

Drawing near the weedy airstrip, the mare picked up her pace. For two years now the polluted field smelled of death. Wrecked planes littered the runway, oozing fluids. Pilots and passengers from the mainland, long desiccated, were still buckled inside.

Her friend, the zig-zagging collie, yipped a warning—danger! The big bay heard a metallic clatter and caught a scent she didn't like at all, an ancient one—musky fur, bloody claws, rotten breath. Old *Ursus* had haunted her ancestors, 30 million years of predation encoding her genome. And here He was again, afresh! Montana laid back her ears, panicky.

Master spoke some words, and Eldest sent a soothing, but still, the horse and dog weren't happy. Soon the bicycle overtook them, pedaled by a monster, face dripping with blood. Shawn Greene greeted the new arrival with a grin, "Mukwa! Kickstand that hog, climb aboard and join our boodle." The young bear lumbered in. Shawn handed back a jar of homebrew.

Crossing the bridge over Jordan, Montana halted without being told. Eldest always stopped here. Shawn helped the old one descend. Blueberry and Bear scrambled down too. Another apple was proffered—an apology for the fright? Montana claimed it, crunched it, and much was forgiven. Master clucked, and she pulled the Greenes away.

The foster family stood in starry silence till the water song ran clear. They listened to its lullaby and felt the peace that was promised. Then, from a long way off, came a clamor of bells. A red glare flared in the north, some beacon of doom.

Samantha shook her head. "There's trouble back in town."

Miin was worried about their sleepover; she'd prepared popcorn, and a jug was cooling in the spring. "But it's not *our* trouble, is it, *nookomis*?"

Samantha squinted at Miin's brother, his blood-smeared face looking ferocious. "No, Miinan, it's not our trouble, not tonight anyway. Is it Mukwa?"

The big man hung his head. "No granny, no trouble, not tonight. I'm done with all that."

"Let's go home then." The trio turned away from the road and took the short cut through ELF Country. They spoke the old passwords, and the paths did their bidding. At Natural checkpoints, hooded Sentinels simply nodded them through.

Finally, nearing the shack in the sugarbush, Sam's familiars picked them up. Escorted by fairies—owl, fox, and feline—they soon arrived home.

Sam's garden was sleeping, processing the day. Miin's maples—sweet blooded—all shared the same green dream. The little family shut out the night and its alarms, kindled a fire in the woodstove, and settled in for their sleepover—sepia-tinted, a scene from before.

When the kettle started steaming, Mukwa's flesh wounds were tended with herbs, needle, and silk. His spirit wounds were more serious—neglect, ostracization, Keith's killing, Hawk's indifference.

Miin and Sam—witch doctors with leafy diplomas hanging from the rafters—did what they could, hoping his soul wouldn't fester. Sister's kettle corn helped. As did the jug of cold, rooty beer. An islander named Dorothy, a recluse, brewed it in eight gallon batches, stirring it with a canoe paddle before bartering it away. Miinan, ever cheerful, read aloud from favorite books, cracking jokes as the woodstove pinged and shadow puppets performed.

In the great green room

There was a telephone

And a red balloon

And a picture of—the cow jumping over the moon

Miin acted it out, making her usual faces. Mukwa started grinning, couldn't help it, though it tugged on his stitches. Laughing hurt even more, but a good hurt.

And there were three little bears, sitting on chairs

And two little kittens and a pair of mittens

Sister Miin was marvelous, the warmth in his belly worth a face full of fire. The hours passed, fast or slow they couldn't say, but no one wanted it to end. Except the owls.

Sam's familiars knew best—of course they did—and so she listened. *Who? Who? Who looks for you? Who looks for you all?* Her feathered sentry scolded them from the treeline. The forest kingdom and all its folk knew there was trouble. Smoke and ash were on the wind. Violence had been done, north of town, in the dunes. There was a growing divide, and division meant danger. Samantha would be busy; her witching hour drew near, and there was dream-work to do.

The quiet old lady whispered, "Hush." Samantha's mirth lines crinkled as both siblings groaned. "Kids, I'm sorry, but it's time for bed."

Goodnight room

Goodnight moon

Goodnight cow jumping over the moon

Rewind the years, and the scene stayed the same. Tonight's sleepover was a throwback, a rare one, and they knew it.

Sam passed around her tea—a dreamcatcher—and prepared the grandkids for sleep.

"Have peace now, until the morning." She tucked Miin into her cot, a bright-eyed mouse under blankets.

"Heed no nightly noises," Sam advised. She hugged Mukwa as the big man shuffled out into the yard, stretching a hammock—ELF style—tree to tree beneath the stars.

Samantha poked around the firebox and sang the old songs. Anishinaabemowin was the language; her fosters caught only snatches before sleep snatched them away. Their granny sang a humble song—like she used to—lulling them both to slumber.

Gdaa dbaadendizimi kido Gizhemanido

Gdaa jiingwanitawaanaa

Gdaa dbaadendizimi kida Gizhemanido
Gdaa gikendanaa gikendamowaad

In Mukwa's dream he was four-footed, strong but clumsy; he'd changed his skin. With a blow from his paw he broke open a cage. Ferocious, a woman flew out, shredding his face with crescent-moon claws. Mukwa's sight grew dim as his eyes filled with blood, but he followed her across a wide water till he remembered—shit! He didn't have wings! Panicking, he fell. The last thing he saw before impact crushed his body—an angry hawk, pecked at by crows, caged again, but this time in a tower, a sort of silo. As he fell, Mukwa twitched with terror, making his hammock shake. Dreaming or awake, he heard Sammy singing: *Gdaa dbaadendizimi*—We should all be humble.

Instead of splatting on the surface, he transformed into a fish and dove. Humbly, he finned himself from the big lake up the Bear River. There he found Keith, his leathery mentor, lounging on a boulder. Together, they fished, sharing one trout dream, or many.

Miinan tiptoed through the garden of brother bear's dream, planting seeds, pruning trauma, figuring out his frequency, storing it away for future contact. He'd be leaving the island soon, off to war, but Miin's place was here. Of course she wanted him to flourish, so separation was necessary. She had other gardens to tend and new students to instruct. The next generation must be shielded, their green skills surpassing her own. But something gnawed towards her—a red-eyed beaver with bloodstained teeth. She felt great pain; her wrists were chafed and her joints felt like breaking. There was a dungeon too, a cellar, dank with urine and masculine lust. She kinked her nose at the smell while her whole body shivered. *Nookomis!*

Gdaa gikendanaa gikendamowaad—We should know what they know. Samantha's song instructed, proffering a key to forgotten knowledge.

Blueberry—a bookworm, even in dreams—unlocked her encyclopedia of green lore, instantly finding the proper passage. Suddenly there was life in the dungeon, a tiny sprout of green. Miin touched it with her toe and was free.

The medicine woman knew the way of the heart, its darkness and its light. The family Sam had fostered would soon be splintered. Mukwa, born for battle, would again be leaving, but this time Miinan, her precious blueberry, would stay. Samantha would not risk her again; many things needed tending. War clouds were gathering: murderous crows stormed a bridge, and mammoths again walked the earth, defying extinction, trumpeting terror. Strong medicine would soon be needed. Samantha wove several summons, shaped them as dreams, and flung them.

Nearby, on Garden Island, a woman caught one, unraveled it and replied. Autumn, the water-protector, would cross over in the morning. From ELF Country, elder Grace RSVP'd as well—*Certainly, Samantha. See you soon!*

Sam's final dream was a nightmare, but there was no song to soothe her. She visioned a dark tower, not above ground, but below. In its turret sat a madman, a monster in a lab coat, white hands dripping blood. Though subterranean, he had far-seeing eyes, and a compound of creatures to command.

PART 2:
Panzerland

Panopticon 2 by Pieter Léon Vermeersch

Where Am I?

I'M STILL HERE.

You haven't heard from me lately, though I continue to dictate to my devices. It's been eighteen months since my variant—without consent, mind you—was loosed upon the world. The first humans to host it were mainland Chinese. The Han ethnic group, per Panzer's design, was quickly decimated. The quarantine vulnerabilities of the People's Republic, exposed during the first wave, were now exploited. The lab variant of SARS-CoV-2 was expressly engineered to wreak havoc on the Asian phenotype. Our creation did so with aplomb, its gain-of-function functioning perfectly. The PRC's zero-Covee script had been flipped. The variant, Covee's Stinger, became the one with no tolerance.

Ever premature, our POTUS preened as China imploded. Meanwhile, I made hasty preparations, knowing full well my creation was uncontainable. I've detailed much of this already, so let's forge ahead shall we? What else would you like to know?

I suppose that depends on who you are? And also on when you are listening? Impossible to predict a future audience; my hope, dear reader, is that you are an inheritor of sorts. A someone, or group of someones, following my footsteps, profiting from the social structure I am endeavoring to create. Is that too much to ask? Another, albeit less pleasant scenario, is that these dictations could be evidenced against me, or my followers, by noose-happy Nurembergers with execution hoods at the ready.

Am I reliable? Can you trust my narrations? What sort of man—pícaro, madman, naïf—empowers this voice? I suppose time will tell, but for now I speak truth; setting the record straight has been my raison d'être all along.

So, where am I?

Using literary license, one answer would be, everywhere. The sting of my variant has now been felt in every peopled part of this planet: from ships at sea, ghost-crewed and rudderless, to Antarctic stations where Mom's care-package, contagious, came coated with cough droplets from her last day in the kitchen.

If you prefer a more prosaic answer, then most of the time my location is in Michigan—Kalamazoo specifically. Yes, there really is a Kalamazoo—a ridiculous name, I know. Of Potawatomi origin I believe? It is the headquarters of my company, Panzer Pharmaceuticals Inc. Though admittedly these days Kalamazoo is more compound than campus; it has become a fortress of iron. Most activity occurs below ground, and there are strange creatures afoot. I've redesigned the logo as well: two medieval towers now flutter from corporate flagpoles. In this throwback age I've created, Panzer has gone all-in for neo feudal.

What else would you like to know?

I'm guessing that who or what is next on your list. You've caught me in a chatty mood, so I'll eschew the cryptic for concrete. Call me Dr. Schark if you prefer formality; my lackeys use "Sharkey," though not to my face. To the rank and file Chosen—frankly, quite foul—I'm nameless, which is fine. They know I'm the Big Boss, and fear me, as they should. I am the cunning mind in the bio-safe tower.

As for the rest—parentage, birth, and education—don't bother. I've deleted my backstory, erasing the arc of my character—or what was left of it. Was there ever a Mrs. Schark? Some great white wifey, or sand tiger princess? Perhaps a nest of shark pups all looking like daddy? Again, don't bother searching. I've scrubbed such data from the files. I wear a cloak of many colors, and all of my choosing.

Dr. Schark, Big Boss, or Sharkey, I use the power of my voice. With a single word I captivated my minions—*Chosen*. I wormed it in their minds. And they were thrilled to be selected. Who wouldn't be, when the alternative to being "chosen," was dead?

Early in collapse, I used every means to amplify my message, fanning the flames and firing up the base. Soon there were Chosen cells in every hive. I tasked my worker bees to spread Stinger's venom and wished my Virals good hunting.

As to what I am doing, that's a bit more complicated. My white hand has many irons in the fire, this dictation being one. On the simplest level, I am trying to survive. The human population, in less than two years, has been reduced from billions to sub-millions. But don't blame this all on me! Yes, my variant did some stinging, but the world, as you know, was ready to implode. I gave a small push and it did so, with aplomb.

Nuclear exchanges of course occurred—Israel v. Iran—India v. Pak—a triumph of tribalism. But most non-viral deaths were from winter, from starvation, from crop failures. Not enough sunlight came through. Growing seasons shrank as mushroom clouds sprouted. Earth's upper atmosphere grew hazy, mass extinctions occurred. The sun, our sole source of life, was blurred, not by volcanoes or asteroid impact, but by polycarbonate plumes from our burning metropoles.

The decline in humans is shocking when you see it charted, completely unprecedented in our millennia-long march towards Malthusian misery. Even that pest *Yersinia*, the Black Death, barely dented our curve. Like most predators, we are difficult to eradicate. Hard times flip a switch and we breed, breed, and breed. But breeding, dear reader, is a chapter for another day.

How Much Do I Know?

EXCELLENT QUESTION. I'm tempted to be flippant here and show off my bonafides, misconstruing your curiosity to indulge in brain-pan braggadocio. Instead, I'll play it straight—how much do I know about the events playing out along the northwest coast of my Michigan?

Well, that begs the question, how much do *you* know about these events, and what are *your* sources? If these dictations are being used to piece together a plot, let me declare for the record that I object to being typecast as the clichéd villain!

If indeed my voice becomes a POV in a larger work, then you, future reader, might be tempted to skip—or skim?—these "Sharkey sections." Fine by me! I like to think I inhabit deep waters, but if you prefer the shallows, then close your eyes to my text, plug your ears against my voice, and swim on! Follow the narrative flow! Pursue your favorite pod of POVs, whoever they might be. But beware! Whether you like it or not, ol' Sharkey is circling. Ignore my white fin at your peril.

I am a truth-teller. If you knew how many hours of recordings I have deleted, fearing the faintest hint of falsity, you would not question me now. Indeed, I hope you'd cast a sterner eye upon the verity of viewpoints you've imbibed thus far. Ask yourself, what are their biases? What agenda are they following? Alas, though far-seeing, even I cannot limn the published product, its contributors, nor its eventual audience. So I will carry on, dictating disaster, doubtlessly speeding my own demise.

My answer to the titular question—"How Much Do I Know?"—is that I know very little of the recent doings along my coastline. Intelligence gathering for Panzer, and other entities, peaked right as we were unsealing the jar of Pandora. Her container, once emptied of Covee, soon became an overfull urn, stuffed with souls awaiting a rebirth that may never come.

But mine isn't the only hand with blood on it. I also blame solar storms! Early in collapse, the dark sky, unpolluted by electric light, blazed with auroras, a heavenly EMP. The circuits of civilization—a global ring of semiconductors, decades in forging—was forever broken, bombarded by ions fired from the sun. It's a strange sort of collapse where our gadgetry remains intact, yet is inaccessible without these electrical switches and without human operators to interpret their data-stream.

Remember Jani Beg, the Mongolian leader from the siege of Kaffa? He and I are separated by a millennium, yet our intelligence sourcing is depressingly the same—human eyes and ears. Like Jani Beg before me, I am mostly deaf and blind except for what my underlings report. Upon this subjective foundation I'm attempting to build a societal sandcastle for the future.

So, what exactly am I aware of?

I know that Michigan, my base of operations, my peninsula-of-plenty, is not yet secure. My annexation of the north has encountered resistance, Old Law and National Guard remnants being the usual suspects. Apparently there's also been a surge of eco-insurgents? Wide-eyed survivors tell tall tales of painted primitives, Native warriors, and even—dare I say it?—elves.

Here's where I'd give a great deal to task a National Reconnaissance Office satellite, hovering its sophisticated sensors over the region—high resolution, digital imagery being the quickest way to dispel rumors of tree spirits and scalping savages. Alas, the NRO, like every other acronymic agency, is now defunct. Apparently, nothing works without people. Oh, how we used to fret about our addiction to apps, to screens. But societal collapse proved—plot twist!—that our vaunted software was hooked on humans instead.

As technology peaked—pride goeth before a fall—rumors grew of a shadow in the east, a whispered menace: A-EYE, an artificial superintelligence, plugged into the Pentagon, training on terabytes. The EYE, never sleeping, could only see so far, dependent on servants—and server farms—to open a way. My guess is that this EYE—like billions of others—will soon close, its electronic lid held down by Charon's obol—a coin for the ferryman.

And so I sit in my positive-pressure command center. Thanks to my technocrats, the compound's CCTV still works, showing me scenes of combat training, crop cultivation, lab experiments, and security, all with the click of a button. I'm in radio communication with local commanders and food producers too. To see farther, my satellite phone—brand-name Palantir—occasionally functions, at least for now, but it takes a kingly mind to wield it well.

I kid you not, in these darkened times most of the intelligence I receive comes from embedded pen-pals. These underlings send me misspelled notes, passed hand to dirty hand, arriving weeks late when they arrive at all. My written orders are sent back the same way. I enjoy sealing them with wax; a lab tech even crafted me a signet—Panzer's double tower. The Big Boss has made his mark.

Reader, you should know, if you don't already, that I am not the only prince staking claim to Michigan's Lower Peninsula. There's another Machiavelli out there, self-named "Mustafa." Like me, Mustafa comes from white collar culture yet has a working class willingness to dirty his hands. The upstart—an ex-convict—has got panache, I'll give him that. Unlike myself, he's been stung by the variant, and isn't afraid to mingle with his minions. My snitches report he hides his infection behind expensive Ray Bans, has been implanted with a metallic halo, and brands his Viral followers with his favorite letter, an X, right between their bloodshot eyes.

I've heard darker rumors as well. He's lobotomized himself, and is—or was?—neurally linked to the Pentagon's supercomputer. If true, what does this make him? A cyborg? Some kind of ghost? An electronic wraith, enslaved by his master, the EYE?

I received a missive recently from this Ponzi scheme princeling. Mustafa didn't use his Palantir—though he has one. Instead the poser sent a scroll sealed with, you guessed it, melted wax embossed with his X.

Dear Dr. Schark,

Michigan's sandbox is big enough for both of us to play in. You take the west, I'll take the east. Let Route 127 be our dividing line, the Bug River between Molotov and Ribbentrop. I suggest our armies push towards the Mackinac Bridge together. I've heard reports that the U.P. is currently uninfected and rich in resources, with enough Lebensraum for both our peoples. But we must move quickly, as apparently there's a resistance movement—the nascent Free North—that needs ripping out before it grows roots.

Mustafa

Do you see what I mean? In these benighted times, the man—if we can still call him that—seems a bit too artificial in his intelligence. Poland's Bug River? V. M. Molotov? Joachim von Ribbentrop?

Mustafa's scroll, rather than a throwback, scans closer to ChatGPT. Did he write the note himself? Or did some neural ghostwriter—linked to his halo—plagiarize the pages of downloaded history?

What Happened to It All?

I CAN HEAR YOUR QUESTIONS, future reader, your fears and frustrations. What about the government? And the mighty US military? What about FEMA, the CDC, and all the alphabet agencies tasked with keeping us safe?

Well, Covee happened, plus some other things.

All told, the federal government, uniformed and civilian, once had a workforce of 9 million. With an IFR (Infection Fatality Ratio) of +99%, 100,000 might have survived the initial scything unscathed, at least physically.

The emotional trauma of total loss rendered most survivors professionally ineffective. So, counting trauma casualties, plus the surplus deaths from collapse—homicide, malnutrition, cholera, typhus and their contagious kin—leaves us with a federal force of 10,000 collapse-hardened soldiers and civilians.

This culling of capabilities played out at the state and local levels too. For an ambitious survivor like me with a blueprint for rebuilding, this fraction of a fraction was a non-factor. Yes, Old Law gives my people some trouble, but arrangements can usually be made, and for the stubborn ones there's always my skeletons, my tattooed Aghori.

SARS-CoV-2 and its STING variant you know about, at least enough for now. But my dictated words were, "Covee happened, plus some other things."

So far, as your narrator, I've kept the details vague. I'm not sure what kind of light these "other things" put me in. Probably not a flattering one, but truth-telling must triumph. Agree?

Of course you do, that's why you're still here, captivated, listening to my voice with every ear—electronic or otherwise—that you possess.

You'll remember that my *totenkopf* terrors, the Aghori, began streaming back in Y1? Their pilot episode was a daylight raid on Merch Biotech's campus. This viral success was followed by a season of destruction—prestige TV at its peak—culminating in the conflagration of the CDC and its annexes. A real apex moment for me, as my pharma-foes were decimated. My creations caused quite a stir. The world's attention pulled away from Covee for a cycle, focusing squarely on my accomplishments. Of course my name was never mentioned, but from the shadows I basked in reflected light.

What does this say about me? Was I not praised enough as a child? Why this craven craving for recognition? Why massacre innocents to put my stamp—Panzer's double tower—on the world?

Good points, I agree. What can I say in defense?

Not much, though I can point to precedents where one man's machinations—questionable out of context, and disparaged by the *Demos*—can survive as statuary, or even as currency of the realm.

"Look kids, the Lincoln Memorial!"

Or remember the old twenty-dollar bill? Wherever my wallet is, you will find legal tender printed with Andrew Jackson's visage.

If you could query Confederate widows, or the blood-shod Cherokee, trailing genocidal tears, they'd be none too pleased with our pantheon of persecutors.

But enough! I'm under no illusions that currency—with or without my mugshot—will make a comeback, nor will we return to the statues of statism.

What I've done, I've done because I could.

Perhaps I've delved too deeply into history, and the hubris of its humans?

Too long I've studied the enemy, the zoonotic pathogens of primates.

I have curb-stomped America's sandcastle. It amused me to do so. Fear not, I'm building back better, and Michigan—neo feudal, my pleasant peninsula—is project number one.

Don't give me too much credit, for good or for ill. Stinger was stolen from me, remember? It was not my order that loosed this leviathan. Like you, I am merely reacting to events, albeit with a larger budget and superior skill set.

So what if I gave a small push? Dumped President Humpty, cheered his flabbergasted fall? Or that I poxed a pandemic upon our *Pluribus Unum?*

Those deeds needed doing. Gravity beckoned. Historians of the future may well agree.

Panzer's Paramilitary

POST COVEE BUT PRE-COLLAPSE, after USAMRIID confiscated my STING variant, I forged an elite force of my own, enticing war-fighters away from their service branches with eye-popping salaries and the promise of asymmetrical action. Applicants with families were rejected; I wanted a monastic vibe for my future Panzers.

Their last step was an interview with me, the Big Boss, their Sharkey. I showed them classified footage of Chinese hospitals and bulldozed mass graves. I alerted them to the inevitability of contagion and promised protection from Stinger. My recruitment success at this final step was 100%. Immediately after signing, they were injected with a first course of virucide. Metamorphosis began, and then they were mine.

Virucides are substances that kill viruses and are different from vaccines. They're also different from antiviral drugs, which prohibit the proliferation of a virus.

And so I injected my Panzers with Cyanovirin-N (CV-N), a protein produced by the cyanobacteria *Nostoc ellipsosporum*. Basically, I used bacteria to fight a virus, two of the oldest lifeforms—or near lifeforms—on the planet, locked in a microscopic battle for the future of humanity.

Side effects? Of course there were.

In the rapidly closing window between my variant's confiscation and Stinger coming to America, there wasn't time for clinical trials. We knew the virucide was effective in fighting SARS-CoV-2 and its engineered ilk. We knew it didn't kill the host—at least not right away—and we knew we could manufacture enough of it to begin dosing our fighting force.

King Mithridates V was assassinated by poison two millennia ago. His son and heir, the sixth of the name, fearing similar death, fled into the wild. There he encountered Scythian shamans who micro-dosed the prince with lethal substances. Over time his body adapted and he was thereafter inured against poisoning.

Mithridatism became the term for building up tolerance to toxins. Rasputin survived eating poisoned cakes and tea with this method. Snake handlers in Burma tattoo themselves with venom to achieve the same end. Panzer's paramilitary—balls-to-bones—morphed monstrous. Great changes were wrought by cyanobacteria, but my fighting-folk, steadily dosed, were shielded now from the variant and its cytokine STING response.

The Scythian shamans who protected the prince?

A Hindu sect known as Aghori.

Transformation

AFTER AN INITIAL COURSE OF INJECTIONS, my minions metamorphosed. They were exposed to the variant, intentionally at first—to monitor results—then haphazardly, as their duties required.

The virucide worked.

Cyanovirin is a protein with a highly complicated structure. Discussing its efficacy, I can't escape the mad-scientist cliché. Hair loss happened first. After several injections, not a single soldier had a hair anywhere on his or her body. Tissue and muscle transformation occurred as well. Again, this is too comic-book for comfort, but my virucide dampened sensitivity to pain.

We're still mapping results, but our medical team—treating the wounded of early operations—reported hyper-healing as well. And these are just the tips of the berg! Who knows what icy truths loom beneath?

Trained in scientific rigor, I flinch at the lack of trials, data collection, double blinds, and placebos. There are too many variables, too many effects to effectively control for.

Physical transformation, while surprising in amplitude, was expected. Our standard dose of CV-N was large, and it was predictable that corporal changes would occur. What was more surprising, and harder to quantify, was the psychological evolution that these soldiers underwent. Again, correlation and causation are sticky, but over time it was undeniable that something strange was happening to their minds.

Remember how I cultivated a monastic vibe for my paramilitary? Selecting applicants of a certain mindset, free from familial obligations? Well, be careful what you wish for! To be honest, this unit has gotten a little away from me. Again, the mad-scientist trope!

Dear reader, have you ever heard of monism?

I hadn't either. I endured the ignominy of being lectured on its tenants by one of my Aghori team leaders, a former Tier-1 special operator with US Army roots.

Master Sergeant Jones reported to my antechamber as ordered. I had a hard time asserting authority through intercom, but my staff of technocrats had been disturbed by the Panzers' new posturing, so I persisted. Apparently, to cover hair loss and emphasize their esprit-de-corps, my ghoulish soldiers had engaged in some radical tattooing.

Jones, one airlock away, kept silent during my tele-questioning. Did the man even blink? Try as I might, I couldn't keep my eyeballs from rolling all over the freshly inked skull that now covered his face and bald head. I struggled to ignore the fact that he was bare-chested and had discarded his Panzer uniform, probably for good.

My master sergeant is of mixed race, and his olive-toned torso had been inked with an anatomically accurate ribcage, sternum, and spine.

When my shallow babble had run its course, Jones shifted attention from "eyes front" and pulled me into deep waters with a direct stare into my video feed. Erudite, he began speaking. I heard words but couldn't grasp their meaning. I was in over my head and floundering. After some time, he released me and I found myself dismissing him. He turned smartly and departed.

That's when I noticed the Sanskrit etched on the back of his neck. I searched the vaults of my downloaded internet till I found the signifier—Aghori, eh Jones? Well, why not?

I played back the video from the end of our meeting, decoding his code-switch of English and Hindi. Jones's final words were a mantra of sorts:

Om namah śivāya hana hana hana bhaksaya bhaksaya bhaksaya....

Om, salutations to Shiva, the stone-cold killer who destroys and devours....

Fort Custer: The Target

SO FAR, DEAR READER FROM THE FUTURE, I've described some of our Year 1 activities, a busy time for many. The many are now the few, and Y2 of collapse is proving just as difficult, if not more so. It is one thing to tear a system down, quite another to rebuild it. My recent setbacks around Petoskey and Charlevoix are proof of that. And yes, I've heard the rumors—elves indeed!

Much of Panzer's original focus was national. As the federal government's card-house collapsed and the country's communications—our ring of fiber optics—frayed, I returned my attention to Michigan. The future was trending feudal; it was time to stake out my freshwater fief.

In November of Y1, the grid gave up its electric ghost and Panzer's paramilitary decapitated state government, mounting the governor's head above a turnpike. Master Sergeant Jones—the Aghori's freshly inked conductor—began orchestrating raids on Detroit's refineries, securing petro-stocks for Panzerland. I conscripted technocrats and the tools needed to illuminate the darkness, at least for a while. Local police were mostly defunct, but National Guard remnants still posed a threat—utterly unacceptable to me and mine!

"Opportunities multiply as they are seized," wrote Sun Tzu, twenty-five centuries ago. I won't claim to be an *Art of War* expert—I'll leave that to Aghori Jones—but the man behind the treatise, Sun Wu, "fugitive-warrior," not only survived, but prospered during China's chaotic Warring States period (481-221 BCE), so perhaps his advice should be heeded. Also, Panzer's strategy of seizing opportunities had worked so far—why stop now?

Michigan's National Guard originated in the US Civil War. Before our Covee-collapse, the War Between the States had been our nation's bloodiest chapter, though its sepia tint sanitized some of the stain. The storied history of these units, however, hadn't saved them from my RNA-strand, my Stinger. The men and women of Michigan's Guard—like most Americans at the start of Year 2—were mostly either dead or dying.

The nearest Guard unit to my Kalamazoo compound was Fort Custer, some twenty miles away. Master Sergeant Jones, the highest ranking Aghori I'd recruited, had been keeping tabs on this installation with an RSTA squadron he'd formed—Reconnaissance, Surveillance, and Target Acquisition. I am not a military man, and their nomenclature can be maddeningly opaque. Forgive me if I don't gloss every term going forward.

Where was I? Oh yes, the Target.

During January of Y2, Jones's skeletal scouts were reporting that Fort Custer had locked itself down. Jones and his other NCOs had formed three Operational Detachment Alpha teams—ODAs—of a dozen soldiers each to conduct an ambush, with an ODB team in support. This was a fighting force of fifty Gories, a sizable fraction of my unit-strength.

Among the Aghori, Jones is much admired for his Delta Force background. Lacking commissioned officers, he insisted on making me company commander. During mission-planning for the Fort Custer Op, I overheard him refer to me, not as "Dr. Schark," or even, "Sharkey," but as "18A," whatever that means. Even virological verbosity is preferable to the acronymic asininity of Milspeak!

Our mission objective was twofold. First, eliminate the National Guard threat to our base of operations in Kalamazoo. Second, capture as much military hardware as possible, especially communication and transportation equipment. Jones had been clamoring for more recruits as well, so if the A-Teams could capture viable candidates, they were free to do so. To achieve our objectives, we needed to lure them out.

Panzer Pharmaceuticals at this point was still a government asset—not that there was much government left. SATCOM and MILSTAR satellites provided limited command-and-control capabilities for those with the expertise—and electricity—to wield them.

Remnant Guard and active-duty units had stitched themselves together, merging with ragtag veterans and local law enforcement. Old Law became the colloquial term for this assortment of white hats. "Old Law." How delicious, with its Wild West roots and tumbleweed-tonality. God bless the American vernacular.

As Y2 began, I was doing my best to keep up appearances. The leadership of our country, including El Presidente, had been duped—by my cunning!—into believing that Panzer Pharma was close to a vaccine breakthrough, a medical miracle.

The commander in chief's standing order was that our research was to be aided, and that our growing stockpile of vaccine—a total fabrication—was to be protected at all costs. Panzer's fictitious pursuit was the Hail Mary that might yet win the game. National leaders, bunkered and blind, had no idea that their clock had run out.

Sun Tzu again: "Know the ground, know the weather; your victory will then be total." Jones finally had the weather window he wanted. The Michigan winter turned cold, wet, and cloudy. Ideal conditions, Jones said, to negate any air assets that Fort Custer might utilize. His teams were trained-up and standing by. On a January night of fog and freezing rain we made the decision to execute the operation.

"The natural formation of the country is the soldier's best ally."

Sun Tzu's rivers were the Yangtze and Zhujiang, but we had the Kalamazoo. This water-obstacle flows between Fort Custer and our compound. There was only one bridge with the load capacity to support Custer's armored vehicles, a perfect pinch-point.

Jones placed two ODA teams near the bridge; they would hit Custer's sortie when it was on the span. The third ODA was to ambush any rescue force the fort might send as backup. He placed the ODB team in reserve, so it could quickly pivot to assist where needed. When all was ready, we flew our false flag, broadcasting a phony distress call. Then we waited.

Aghori Jones, a skull-faced Horatius, stood upon the bridge. The Kalamazoo River, drunk on rain, roared below; sleet spattered the icy pavement. Jones switched off his NVGs. Enhanced by the virucide, his own eyes worked better, even in the dark. The injection sparkled in his veins, the champagne of steroids. His fellow Gories swore it was laced; it amplified their senses, gave them extraordinary abilities. Jones heard his 18E, the comms-sergeant, through his earpiece: Custer's convoy was coming.

Jones lingered a moment in the kill zone—the center of the span—embracing the lethality ranged against him. A murder of crows, impatient, roosted above the river. The black birds felt it too. Come daybreak they'd dip their beaks in blood, and a fleshy feast would follow.

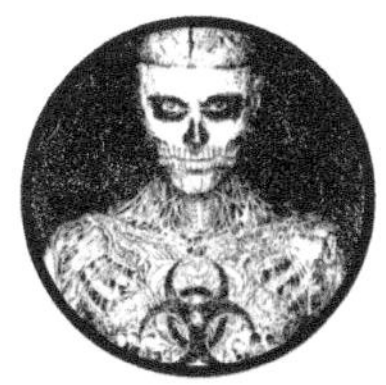

Fort Custer: The Execution

SPECIALIST MCKENZIE, E-4, squinted as the overheads were flicked on by her sergeant. "Rise and shine, motherfuckers! Time to gear up and go play in the rain."

Groans emanated from the barracks until their eyes adjusted and they got a glimpse of Sergeant Willis. Their NCO was wearing Level 2 MOPP gear and had his M4 rifle already slung. Apparently Sergeant "what-you-talkin'-bout" Willis wasn't fucking around.

By 0400 she was gulping down a stale hash brown—cold—from her Humvee's MRE. Her crew was waiting to depart the assembly area. Radio checks had been conducted; weapons, ammunition, and MOPP gear inspected. The CO himself, Lieutenant Colonel Armstrong, briefed the convoy as they mounted up.

"This is it! The Big One!" Colonel proclaimed, standing in front of the open bay door. The country—hell, maybe the world—was counting on the 177th to do their damn job. Panzer Incorporated, as they all knew, was making a vaccine, and now some gang of criminals was laying siege to their lab and threatening its stockpiles. To be expected, really; the 177th had prepared for this contingency. Their approach route had been pre-planned, their order of march was set, and they were in communication with Panzer personnel. Those thieving bandits—cartel wannabes—were in for a world of hurt!

The assembled soldiers gave their CO the "Hooah!" he expected.

"No offense, Garcia." McKenzie winked up at their Latino gunner.

Garcia grinned around a mouthful of crackers and patted his M2 .50 cal in response. "None taken."

Minutes later, they were rolling out, vehicle wipers fending off fog. The forces of Fort Custer sallied forth towards an underestimated foe.

Decimated by Stinger, what remained of Custer's 177th could barely crew two dozen vehicles. LTC Armstrong was the convoy commander. His Humvee would center the eighteen-vehicle column. The column was divided into six march units with a gun-truck for each. The fort's remaining vehicles would be kept in reserve and would deploy only if necessary. Besides the six gun-trucks, there were twelve task-vehicles transporting the troops needed to break the cartel's siege around Panzer.

SOP called for blackout lights and Level 4 MOPP protection when leaving the fort. The column took M-96 southwest towards K-Zoo. Months ago, the grid had gone down; the ice-glazed roadway was dark and empty. McKenzie's mask was already misting— sitting shotgun, she couldn't see shit. Daylight was hours away. She heard snoring behind her and elbowed Garcia. The gunner grunted, then resumed.

They rolled through Galesburg, passing its empty school. Last winter's snowflakes were still taped to the windows. Using safety scissors, each kid had carefully cut one out. Then the variant came, cutting classes to the bone.

The column dog-legged left, descending towards the river valley and its icy bridge below. The CO's voice came over the SINC-GARS net: "Halfway there troopers. Panzer reporting bandits on their perimeter. Maintain virus protocols. SROE status is Weapons-Hold. Repeat, status is Weapons-Hold."

"Fine by me," Garcia mumbled through his mask. "I'm cozy right here, thank you."

McKenzie threw another elbow, trying to maintain situational awareness. Her fogged goggles, the sleet-streaked window, and the murky predawn reduced her SA to level one. A naked tree hooked her gaze, dozens of crows roosting in the rain. Something there tugged, then let her go. Her view-field changed as they drove onto the bridge. She looked down and could see the river below. Their Humvee was a submarine and her window a port-hole, submerged in gloom. Then her optic nerve flinched. Multiple spark-trails seared her retina. A giant hand of air shoved her against the hard seat of the Humvee, deflating her diaphragm with a whoosh. Drowning, McKenzie gulped for air but couldn't get any.

Ka-Rumpf! Ka-Rumpf! Ka-Rumpf!

The concussive force of detonating warheads bruised her eardrums as 66mm rockets crumpled the convoy's lead vehicles.

SINCGARS panicked: "Contact! Contact front!"

McKenzie, still gasping, swiveled her goggle-eyed view.

Fire streaked from the woods, lancing towards the tail of the column.

"Rockets! Rockets! Contact rear!"

The flash from exploding HEAT warheads blinded her.

Ka-Rumpf! Ka-Rumpf!

Blinking, she tried to peer around the afterimage. Both the rear gun-truck and the troop-carrier were upside down and smashed. Strewn on the pavement were burning piles of MOPP. Her neurons needed a second to resolve the input—those flaming piles were people.

The CO was barking, "Gun-trucks engage! Task-vehicles forward! Get the fuck off the bridge—" *Ka-Rumpf!*

McKenzie was blinded again as Colonel Armstrong's command-vehicle tumbled over the guardrail. The colonel and his crew disappeared in the gorge. Her own driver cursed, steering a path through the wreckage. "Garcia, get the fuck up there!" the driver yelled over his shoulder.

McKenzie, awkward, shoved their gunner towards his duty. "Crew that fucking fifty, Garcy!"

Nightmare-slow, the reluctant man popped the hatch and stepped up to the gunner's platform. Their driver had found an opening and snaked them through the burning column. Surviving Humvees and troop-trucks were on the move. McKenzie felt thumps—*Dhak! Dhak! Dhak!*—as soldiers pulled triggers, stitching tracers towards the tree line and its unseen terrors.

Ka-Rumpf! Ka-Rumpf!

Two more spark-trails connected with the convoy.

"Fuuuck!" Their driver braked as a troop-truck pitched over, spewing flaming figures into their path. A muffled voice screamed, "Don't you dare fucking stop!"

The driver obeyed; the terrified voice was her own. They bumped over a body and pushed past another, gas mask melted to its face.

Plink-plink-plink-plink-plink-plink!

McKenzie knew that sound. A Mk 19, on full auto, was firing from the forest. A string of 40mm grenades detonated, pulverizing the people on the bridge.

Plink-plink-plink-plink-plink-plink!

Another pregnant pause as more grenades tumbled inbound, their explosive force ripping the convoy apart. Garcia, KIA, had stopped firing. Their driver sat slumped, windshield shattered, his goggles dripping blood. McKenzie's door wouldn't open, her body weight totally ineffective. Chemical fires burned—white hot—unquenched by intensifying rain. The relief convoy had ceased to function, and the smoking woods had quieted too. McKenzie's ears were buzzing; she was definitely going to puke. The sky, if anything, had darkened. Day broke without its dawn.

Then she saw *them*.

Ghoulish warriors ghosted through the wreckage. Through misty panes, she watched their grim reaping of kills. Cold rain beaded upon their bare flesh as the shirtless skeletons drifted between the bodies. A pile of MOPP gear twitched on the roadway; raising an arm, it pistoled the nearest torso. McKenzie gasped as the monster absorbed the bullet, dipped a bony finger in the entry wound, and tasted itself. The death's-head laughed and kicked away the pistol, embracing its victim. A quick spinal shake snapped the soldier's neck. The corpse, disconnected from itself, flopped fishlike upon the asphalt.

Trembling, McKenzie reached for the radio, then screamed as the creature jumped upon her hood. The Skull raised a rifle butt and smashed out the windshield. With awesome strength it hauled McKenzie from the Humvee and pitched her to the pavement.

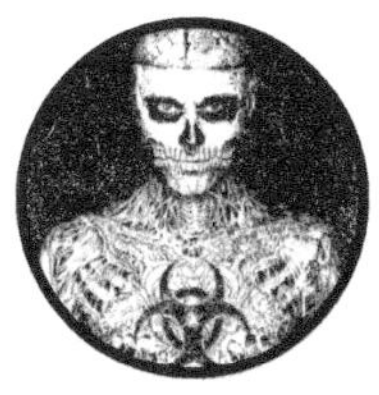

Fort Custer: The Murder

ENGINE NOISE AND THE SCENT CLOUD of humans had evicted the birds from their forest home. It was not a night for flying. The murder re-formed in a roost tree near the river and blinked its black eyes as the hairless ones moved about, preparing their ambush. When stillness resumed, a lone figure stood upon the span. The crows memorized the man's inky markings and filed away the information. The shirtless warrior probed their collective cognizance, offering an acknowledgment of sorts.

Then the figure was gone.

The murder shared a crow-dream as all eyes closed but the lookout's. This sleepless sentry tended its flight feathers, enduring the rain.

Time passed.

A column of vehicles approached; vibration and diesel fumes stirred the feathered forms from slumber. Avian eyes winked open, intelligence perched sharply on every branch. Through millennia, crows had witnessed many such scenes. The current murder remembered.

Generations of battle-birds—feeding well—had encoded their chromosomes. These mitochondrial missives alerted future corvids to caloric opportunities. The rainy night's stimuli fit this primal pattern: primates+stealth=ambush=slaughter=-carrion.

The murder—educated by its ancestors—was keen.

When the clanking column crossed onto the bridge, their avian eyes blinked at the sudden blaze. Lightning forked horizontal from the tree line, thunder followed, and a metallic wind blew, sharp with shards. Their roost tree was tossed by a tantrum of steel. The smell of blood and ruptured gut was dampened by the rain. A stray waft of meaty molecules escaped the downdraft. This tantalizing trickle, scented by one, was transmitted to all. The murder stirred.

The winter day never dawned. The hairless ones worked quickly, clearing the bridge of debris. Most of the machines were driven away. Some captives had been taken; many had been killed. Their corpses cooled quickly in the rain.

A final figure stood upon the span—the skull-face with the memorized markings. Wreckage burned about him; the pavement was slick with blood and oil. His two eyes locked upon their beady hundred. He raised his inky arms, inviting them to feast, then departed. The braver birds went first. When no man-traps were sprung, the famished flock descended.

This confluence of rivers had fed crows for centuries. Twenty feathered generations ago, Potawatomi had skirmished here with encroaching whites. Further back, the corpses had been Iroquois and Kickapoo, each tribe distinct in flavor. A thousand generations, and the crow-mind was blank—an Age of Ice. The grinding glacier had been a mile high before it melted into Michigan.

Ambusher projectiles had seared the corpse-flesh with a chemical taint; armor-plates protected the choicest morsels. Undeterred, the crows gorged in the rain, un-honked at by traffic, un-shooed by pedestrians. Their world as it should be.

Vishkanya

SHARKEY HERE AGAIN to set the record straight. This dictation, dear reader, is by necessity a few months behind. My access to technology, DOD satellites, and the old Palantir network indeed grants me far sight, helping me outline the future. But you should know that I'm also aware of the present, though so far I've mostly narrated the past.

Yes, I'm gathering forces—Chosen, XCons, and Aghori—to consolidate my northern realm, a tree-infested territory rich in resources, with a paucity of defenders.

And yes, there are pockets of resistance. I've heard tall tales from scouts and seen sketches of their sigils—Wolf, Griffin, and Bloody Tree. Duly diligent, I've scrolled through their data files—both digital and paper. Surprise, surprise, in this fallen age there isn't much.

Still, I'm not too worried. My Spreaders—virulent and red-eyed—are coming; soon this rabble will be stung. The future of course is a throwback, neo feudal, and *mishigami*—land of large water—is my freshwater fief. For I am the Prince of Panzer, a man of cunning, and there is power in my voice.

Back in Y1—thanks to my Aghori—state government lost its head and Michigan's Guard units were much reduced. In January of Y2, Fort Custer fell. To me in my tower, the season seemed ripe for settling old scores.

Part of this was ego, I'll admit; mine is large and contains multitudes. But the president—our pompous POTUS—was an

ass, a clown, an imp. He had stolen what was mine—the variant!—then ordered his ham-handed attack on China.

To be clear, I loathed this person. Yes, I could justify his assassination as patriotic, could argue that any successor would
protect Panzer—and its profits—far better. But these reasons
were false. The man irked me, and I wanted him dead.

*Side note: As far as I know, I don't have an agent, editor, or pub-
licist for this narrative opus—my debut in the genre! Without
their feedback, without sensitivity readers, I'm a bit tone deaf to
my own dictations. Am I too shrill when it comes to our lecherous leader, our soon-to-depart POTUS? If his imminent undo-
ing seems too lurid, too on the nose, then skim ahead! Getting
this off my chest has been therapeutic, but if it causes you trauma, dear reader, please send me the bill!*

Once committed to regime change, my Aghori debated strategy.
These men and women—if we can still call them that?—are the
best in the world at what they do. This kind of challenge is exactly what they live—and half-hope to die—for.

Some Gorie operators argued for an assault on the White
House itself. This tactic worked on the governor's mansion,
why not Pennsylvania Avenue? Schematics were studied—the
security fence, the armored limousine, Air Force One. Weapons
were inventoried—sniper rifles, magnetic mines, ground-to-air
missiles. The planning continued.

As a rule, I don't leave my bubble; as far as I know, my cytokine system is susceptible to STING. No virucide has turned me
mutant, no Brunner-like syndrome shields my genes. My tower,
a silo really, is built to Level-4 specs. Biosafety dominates my
days; I am a goldfish in a bowl of my making. Of course, my eyes

are everywhere. A thousand cameras surveil my compound, but Sergeant Jones is the one I watch most.

Jones is an active leader and his days are quite busy. He's efficient in his NCO duties, exercises with vigor, and still makes time for solitude and meditation. I like watching his body steam when he sits *asana* in the snow.

Jones pays particular attention to assimilating new recruits. We acquired half a dozen from Fort Custer, my Gories ambushing their column in the rain. Care was taken to shield these conscripts from transmission until the injections had taken hold.

Did I mention our female Aghori?

We have a few; Jones lobbied for inclusion from the start. His experiences in-theater had shown him their worth. He devotes much time to training McKenzie, a Spec-4 he plucked from a Humvee during the ambush. The virucide of course has changed her, but unlike the others, her skull and torso have yet to be inked.

Jones also insists on daily briefings. "Dr. Schark, regarding our POTUS operation."

Though known for my voice, I was all ears. Screen-to-screen, I bid him continue.

"Sir, have you ever heard the term *Vishkanya*?"

Admittedly, I had not.

By briefing's end, he'd convinced me. I had a hard time sleeping that night; his plan was just too delicious.

Metamorphosis of Specialist McKenzie

DURING CHINA'S WARRING STATES PERIOD, a certain King of Wu, doubting Sun Tzu's abilities, challenged him to train the palace concubines into a fighting force. Master Sun, much like Master Sergeant Jones, succeeded, furthering his reputation and adding a lethal weapon to his employer's arsenal. Sun Tzu used decapitations and fear to transform Wu's tittering concubines. Sergeant Jones, true to form, took a different tack. I observed him daily with McKenzie and other female Aghori, leading them in meditation between bouts of hand-to-hand combat.

The women were attractive, baldness and skull-markings accentuating their allure. My virucide added muscle and they carried it well, femininity intact. There is something sexy in lethality, I'll not deny it. Nor will I deny binge watching their barracks. My Vishkanya bunked separate from the men; Jones insisted on it. If any "fraternizing" occurred, either between the sexes or within them, it was hidden—alas!—from my voyeuristic view.

"Poison-maidens" is the English translation of Sanskrit's *Vishkanya.* Sergeant Jones was furthering my education in the esoteric. I learned more about the term in a book he leant me— leafing through its pages was a respite from swiping at screens.

Once Stinger broke containment, the internet grew iffy. My techies did what they could, but the massive ring of server-farms—power dependent—had been broken. As the filaments of electricity frayed, the world's wide webbing quickly unraveled. The vaunted electrical grid proved the merest of membranes, thinly meshed and vulnerable, a lesser ring of power easily destroyed. The planet would never see peak wattage again; my white hand had turned out the lights. One viral puff from Stinger blew the world's data clouds away; hardcopy-only was the forecast for the future.

As Michigan collapsed, scavengers soon learned that the "Big Boss" had a kink for books and would pay bounties for rare editions and encyclopedic sets. Jones has his own bookish sources, and during a briefing, he presented two translations—looted from universities, no doubt—detailing Vishkanya: Chanakya's *Arthashastra* and *Kalki Purana*.

Tedious reading. Once the tomes were decontaminated, I admit I only skimmed them. Perhaps the daily dose of Cyanovirin—"Shark-juice" they call it—helps Jones to focus? References to Mithridatism and phrases like "poisonous bodily fluids" kept me from nodding, but anything above the waist, frankly, went over my head.

But I digress. Let's return to our maidens!

SPC McKenzie quickly progressed. I'm sure Jones learned her backstory, but I cared only for her present and how to best utilize her unusual assets. McKenzie's sparring sessions quickly became must-see TV; not just for poor Sharkey, alone in his bowl, but for the whole executive team of Panzerland. We marveled at how quickly she absorbed training. I tasked my medical staff to explain what we were seeing. Could injections of cyanobacterium be responsible for her freakish feats?

They reported back in a week. By this point McKenzie was besting all challengers; only multiple opponents could penetrate her defenses. The bruises she suffered—and once a broken collarbone—healed almost overnight. Even without tattoos, she was an alpha Aghori. Her fellow poison-maidens accepted this ascension and protected her.

My researchers—plundering library troves and university stacks—eventually found treasure. Apparently, our genus of cyanobacteria, *Nostoc*, had first been studied in the 1500s by Paracelsus, a wizard-of-sorts from the mountains of Switzerland. His full name, I kid you not, was Philippus Aureolus Theophrastus Bombastus von Hohenheim.

Bombastus indeed!

Nostoc forms symbiotic relationships with plant tissue and is normally invisible. Rain will cause a colony to swell into a jellylike mass, and was once thought to have fallen from the sky, thus the popular name "star jelly." Rich in vitamin C, *Nostoc* was sometimes consumed as a foodstuff, especially in Asia during times of famine; other names were "troll's butter" and "witch's jelly."

Intriguing? Certainly! But ultimately unhelpful in explaining McKenzie's martial-metamorphosis.

Asāsiyyūn

BY MARCH OF YEAR 2, the Stinger variant of SARS-CoV-2 had profoundly altered the human experience, namely by removing all the humans. In just one year, my Michigan fief, along with most of the world, was utterly dark. Washington D.C. surfaced as an island of normalcy in a virus-tossed sea. This Potemkin-on-the-Potomac mirrored the wishes of President Pretend.

I must digress for another moment. Jones's recent lecture—a brief history of assassins—was just too fascinating. The concept of course is older than we are; even chimps have their Oswalds. The word itself goes back a millennium, linguistically tracked to the sands of Arabia.

Asāsiyyūn was the name that Hassan-i Sabbah gave to his disciples, "Those who are faithful to the foundation." They once controlled a string of castles in the Middle East that formed the backbone of an Isma'ili state. First Marco Polo, then returning Crusaders, told grisly tales of their prowess. Not having an army, the "Faithful" relied on a band of trained killers, the Fedayeen, "Those who sacrifice themselves," to eliminate their opponents. For 300 years they excelled, their preferred weapon the lowly dagger. With tiny blades, they murdered giants—caliphs, kings, and generals—by the score.

I could go on! Aghori Jones certainly did, in that monist-monotone of his, maddeningly devoid of judgment or opinion. I admit, the man swims in deep waters. Ah well, let's get on with it, shall we?

Location: 1600 Pennsylvania Ave, Washington D.C.

Timing: March 15th of Year 2

Target: The President of the United States of America

Asset: SPC McKenzie

Armament: None

Support team: MSG Jones

Contingency plans: None

I'm not really building anticipation here, am I? What happened to the sniper rifles, assault teams, and man-portable missiles? I'll admit to feeling underwhelmed as Jones and his NCOs briefed me on the op. I shouldn't have been surprised. The mission was on brand for Jones: simplicity and singular focus. McKenzie, the lone asset, on-screen during the briefing, only spoke two words. I had asked her through the intercom, "Specialist, are you sure you're ready for this?"

She snapped out of whatever trance she was in and stared through the camera. Awkward, unblinking seconds passed.

"I am."

Sergeant Jones stayed silent, though a facial muscle twitched—a sadhu's smile.

The King is Dead

WHOEVER YOU ARE, you can see by my chapter title that we're nearing the end of this narration, Zapruder's frame 313. I've tried your patience—no, don't deny it!—so again, I'm offering an off-ramp from Elm Street, a detour away from Dealey Plaza and the lurid scene to follow. I advise most readers, future editors too, to skip ahead. I murdered the president and mayhem followed. That's all you need to know.

Still here? Dearest rubbernecker, you are one in a million and are most welcome! Sit back and enjoy! I know I certainly did.

By mid-March of Y2, McKenzie was ready. Her CV-N injections had begun in January, immediately after capture. Since then her progress in all arts martial had been exponential. The woman, like all Aghori, was altered, not just physically through baldness and tissue transformation, but mentally as well. But, per Jones's purpose, she remained un-inked, a malleable asset built for specialized missions.

Her training for this operation was intense. She studied films, and even created content—Fans Only—for the president himself. She was thoroughly coached in posture, biography, and regional dialect. McKenzie became a mask—not the death's-head tattoo of Jones and her fellow Vishkanya—but one of makeup, cosmetic surgery, and practiced mannerisms. Her body was weaponized, not for mass destruction, but for the destruction of one.

When ready, the asset and her operator drove across an America in ruin—Michigan, Ohio, Penn's Woods, and the Land of Mary. They traveled at night, speeding in an armored vehicle, self-sufficient with fuel and avoiding all obstacles. She was the driver, while Jones, sitting shotgun, handled navigation and defense.

The entire route was darkened, not a single town or city evincing an electric pulse. No cell towers blinked, no truck stops beckoned with neon eats, no traffic was encountered, and no tolls were paid. Most of their drive was conducted in silence. Above, the Milky Way flowed from sea to shining sea. The moon was new and cast no light. The Lion roared, star-maned, regal from the void.

At the outskirts of the electrified capital, just before the checkpoints began, she was inserted, alone. Jones drove away as the Potomac turned pink with the dawn. The specialist, a doppelganger, took her bearings, then set off to find her unfortunate double.

Later that evening, a government limousine idled outside a townhouse in warm twilight. The chauffeur, with decades of driving dignitaries under his belt, listened to a D.C. radio station, keeping an eye out for his passenger—a journalist, much-favored by the president. The chauffeur had driven her to such rendezvous before.

The FM broadcast—a beltway bulletin—detailed the annual Cherry Blossom Festival. The pageant was hyped as a continuation of tradition, celebrating Japan's gift of trees back in 1912. Of course, no mention was made of deceased diplomats, or that none of the states had sent a Cherry Blossom Princess as tribute. No matter; thousands of trees were in bloom, and all was well along the Potomac.

The driver was about to honk the horn when she finally appeared, late as usual, stylish and poised in designer heels. The chauffeur turned down the volume, put on his cap, and exited to open her door. A glimpse of cleavage and a waft of perfume was his reward. He shut her in and resumed his position.

"Everything OK this evening, ma'am?"

The traffic was light as he steered towards the first bio-checkpoint. He eyed her in the rearview. Her compact was out as she touched up her face.

She caught his probing eye in the mirror. "Sorry, Mike." She snapped the lid and sighed. "Yes, I'm OK, just a bit blue. It's hard not to think of past festivals, that's all."

Impeccable, she continued in her southern accent, "Did you know that, years ago, I was a Blossom Princess myself?"

Mike slowed at the K Street checkpoint. D.C. Guardsmen stopped them; the unit wore the Red Hand badge of the 372nd Infantry Regiment. The soldiers, wearing chem-suits and respirators, were inspecting vehicles before clearing them to proceed.

"A Georgia peach competing for D.C. cherries, eh?" Mike glanced back, powered down his window, handed over his credentials, and exhaled into the diagnostic device. Blowing green, his ID was returned.

"Georgia? Come now, Mike, you know I'm a Carolina girl." The journalist, razor sharp, handed her press badge to a MOPP-suited soldier and blew green herself.

"No offense, Ms. Kelly. How could I forget?"

The Guardsman, wearing gloves, handed her lanyard back. Mike rolled up her window. The limo processioned through the barricade of Humvees and heavy weapons. The journalist, with fresh eyes, noticed that behind every respirator was a white face. Armored vehicles displayed desecrated battle-trophies, captured from the Blues: Black Lives Matter, Pride flags, Abolish ICE. Each trophy had been slapped by the unit's Red Hand. Another stencil, spray-painted red, flew from their guidons—the president's visage, noble in profile.

After clearing several more checkpoints, the journalist sipped her champagne in the East Room waiting for POTUS to make his cannonball splash. Cleared by biosecurity, none of the guests were wearing masks. They mingled nervously—breathing lightly and socially distant—trying to forget the dozens who'd died from events just like this one, for they were in the inner sanctum and their Dear Leader was coming.

The grand old room sported a cherry-tree motif. To the journalist, the scent of cut blossoms was funereal. The sycophants stirred as black-clad Secret Service—his personal SS—entered and swept the room. Then suddenly He was there. Charismatic, the man floated above the crowd, his ego-balloon gassed by their puffery.

The woman, a trained professional, positioned herself perfectly. He winked a wanton eye, proffering his damp hand. Tingling, she took it, then he moved away. Apparently, they'd done this before. Kingly and leering, he jested with his bodyguard, POTUS pointing her way. So far, so good. The actress picked her moment, then exited the stage.

Long Live the King

SPECIALIST MCKENZIE STOOD utterly still. The target's pulse, at full throb seconds ago, had flat-lined now to nothing. His unseeing eyes still stared at the screen. Moving quickly, the asset performed many small tasks. She slipped back into her dress, smoothed it over her hips and rehung Ms. Kelly's press credentials around her neck. She pulled the thumb drive from the TV and reset its channel. She opened his inlaid box, scattering paraphernalia on the table. With a tissue, she wiped down the necessary surfaces, strategically leaving others imprinted. When the stage was set, she secreted herself away, fully prepared to weather the coming storm. The long night waned as the corpus cooled and vented gas.

The butler's morning visit detonated a day of Sturm und Drang. SS agents flooded into the room, followed by a tide of doctors and the chief of staff. The First Lady kept her distance, savoring the surreality of an answered prayer. As the sheeted body was rolled away, the residence grew loud in lamentation.

Lawyers flocked on black wings as king-making commenced. The VP was summoned; soon the limp Mr. Fiske was sworn in.

"Long live the king," the buzzards intoned, knowing full well the kingdom was finished. The press corps swarmed against SS guards. Some reporters fell—tased—but eventually the suited wall was breached and journalists fanned out along forbidden floors, overwhelming White House security and surveillance.

Tyrannous had fallen. Chaos reigned.

The news, utterly unspinnable, quickly spread. Angry Red Hand soldiers balled their white fists. Targets once deemed off-limits were now green-lit by low-level commanders. The Pentagon—purged too often—couldn't stop them. The Joint Chiefs—presidentially partial—were a joke.

A Red Hand tank unit live-streamed blowing MLK's statue to pieces. "I have a dream!" the gunners shouted, giving the peaceful pastor a stiff-armed salute.

Lincoln too lost his head, lynched by a drag-chain hooked to an Abrams. "All Lives Matter" was scrawled on his pedestal. Abe's honest hands were dipped in red.

An emergency session of Congress was gaveled out-of-order by gunfire. Capitol police were slaughtered by Red Hand storm troopers. Minority members were dragged from their seats; Jewish representatives, pogromed on the House floor; objecting lawmakers received jeers and rifle butts. Enemy lists were circulated, offices ransacked, suspects seized. The People's House was depeopled of color.

The Supremely white Court was quickly seated, its marble palace protected by Red rifle platoons. Proclamations ensued; martial law was declared, and President Fiske—pale-faced and trembling—was empowered well beyond his modest means.

It took twenty-four hours for Secret Service to assemble the pieces. Surveillance videos were scrutinized till the faux-journalist, a stowaway, was discovered. Prints of the sly fox were all over the president and his chambers. Mike, the limo driver, was detained, his interrogation enhanced till the chauffeur cracked. FBI agents were dispatched to her residence. Knocking ignored, they breached her townhouse door. Ashleigh Kelly, the prime suspect, was found naked; her slender neck broken by a fall in the tub.

Aghori Jones drove, westward this time. McKenzie, still blonde, stared up at the starscape. They fled a March storm that towered behind them. Its thundering mass overtook the constellations as their blacked-out vehicle sped away through the night. Hercules was swallowed first, then Corona Borealis—the Strong Man, the Crown—both obliterated by lightning bolts from Brahma. Jones's lips were moving. McKenzie stayed mute.

Om namah śivāya hana hana hana bhaksaya bhaksaya bhaksaya....

Om, salutations to Shiva, the stone-cold killer who destroys and devours....

"Beware the Ides of March," the dead kings muttered—Tsar Nicholas, Julius Caesar, Flavius Odoacer. These regicides snubbed the newcomer. The desperate man—once *Colossus Americanus*—was detained at the border of the afterlife, then deported for illegal entry to their Stygian shore.

PART 3:
Troubled Waters

Charlevoix Lighthouse by Ryan Fox

Cleaning Up

THE WHARF REEKED OF CHARRED WOOD and melted plastic. Damaged structures steamed in the sunrise as hand pumps quenched the last of the coals. The night—thankfully windless—had been a long one. By morning, the responders were bleary-eyed and stinking.

The alarm had emptied the church. Naturals and islanders fought the blaze side by side. Most had gone home—some to breakfast, others to bed. Farmers living near the state forest—the friendlier ones anyway—offered wagon rides to Naturals returning to ELF Country. Many had accepted. Handshakes and names had been exchanged.

Captain Doyle, soot-stained, stumped around the docks, cursing the cleanup crews. Last night's fire changed nothing; if anything, it added urgency. He'd take *Bloody Mary* to the bridge the next morning—fire be damned, hell and high water too.

Diana and Dr. Chow consulted charts in the ferry's wheelhouse, plotting their next moves. The good doctor had yet to come clean about his dirty secret—Bob Campbell—or his captive's reduced viral load. The dune cabin was empty. The patient and his journal were gone. Chow prayed Campbell—still shedding virus!—would isolate, or better yet, escape the island altogether.

Father Peter and Pastor George, ecumenical, manned a folding table together, distributing hot drinks and snacks to those still laboring.

The three soldiers—ambushed in the dunes by a force of na-ture—had freed themselves from flex-cuffs in time to save St. James from conflagration. Led by their captain, Fire Chief Frank Young, they'd fought the blaze unmasked, without MOPP. Even in the chaos, their fresh cuts and contusions had been noted—they'd been beaten up by someone, and it wasn't the fire.

On Whiskey Point, high in the tower, eyes scanned the lake in all directions. A loon and an osprey—flying reconnaissance vectors—confirmed it as well. Lake Michigan was empty.

Samantha's shack was also empty, her family's little sleepover over too soon. Eldest and youngest walked the bog, gathering herbs. Sam and Miinan were on a mission; medicine must be made, green lanterns to light the darkness ahead.

Elena, an ELF militant, had called her Sentinels to a weap-on-take at noon. Mukwa—face freshly stitched—took the path to ELF Country. Oso, bruised heart and all, was going to war.

On the Coast Guard Response Boat, EMT Cruz deployed his med kit. All three Griffins were badly battered, their egos not least. Flames finally doused, in daylight they'd investigated both scenes. They were pretty sure their assailant in the dunes had been a woman. Acting alone, she'd kicked their asses, stealing their prisoner.

Cruz had an ugly lump at the base of his skull. He'd found the arrow afterwards—thank Christ it was blunted. Sergeant Book-er had double black eyes from the crushed NVGs. Their chief, Captain Young, looked like shit; his broken nose had been set, but his whole face was roadkill.

On the boat, Booker cleared sand from their rifles. Cruz packed up his gear; he'd need a resupply from the island clini-cian, Doc Newsome. By the grim look on his captain's busted face, Cruz guessed they'd be back in the shit, and soon.

The sheriff's deputy waited on the dock, tail wagging, begging permission to come aboard. Young, annoyed already, waved him inside and made a move towards his MOPP.

Travis Williams, out of breath, began, "Don't bother masking, I trust you guys. Close call last night, could have lost the whole town. Thank you, men, for your help."

The soldiers, bare-faced, kept quiet, hoping he'd leave. All three had headaches.

"I figure it was an accident. A cigarette maybe, from a deckhand poaching fuel?" Looking for confirmation, Williams continued, "All islanders are accounted for, and I think the Nats are too."

Silence again, but the deputy forged ahead. "Anyway, what's your plan? You guys headed to the bridge fight? Or back to the main? Don't suppose you'd need a fourth? I'd be honored to serve."

Captain Young, nose busted, looked him over, shaking his head. "Thanks, Deputy, but I think your place is here. These are your people, and they need you."

Williams, deflated, looked at each guardsman in turn. "Guess you're right."

More silence.

The man, reluctant, at last took his cue. "Well … if there's anything I can do?"

Young spoke up; actually, there was. "What sort of armory has the island got? Your department have anything unusual? Anything special?"

Williams shook his head. "Rifles and shotguns. Nothing too tactical. You've heard of our veteran, Keith Two-Crow?"

The Army captain had not.

"Vietnam vet. Indian. Back in June old Keith led the scout mission that found the Nats—I mean Naturals. Whatever I had,

I gave to him. From what I heard he used it well. Blew a convoy to smithereens with some Army surplus mines."

Young's heart skipped, but he kept his face blank. So this Two-Crow character was behind that ambush on M-31? The one they'd investigated north of Charlevoix while looking for Red Liz and Cowboy Campbell. Well-used indeed.

"Where is Mr. Two-Crow now?"

The deputy's face fell. "Killed. By mistake, I'm afraid. I wish he was here though. Tough old bird for sure."

Fanboy Williams ogled their cargo, hidden under tarpaulin and lashed to the stern of the Response Boat. "What about you guys, anything special?"

Young turned away, dismissive. "Just some extra gear from our Humvee."

The deputy's puppy eyes were ignored. Williams disembarked and made his way down the dock. Call of duty denied, he made house calls, dutifully jotting down details instead.

"Looks like we're not sharing, eh Chief?" Booker, racking the newly oiled rifles, shot a smirk towards his captain.

Young confirmed, "Correct, Sergeant. Not yet anyway."

Cruz, heating their breakfast MREs, tucked a pouch of instant coffee, dip-like, against his gums. "What's our next move then, sir?"

Chef Cruz spooned out the chow—dehydrated biscuits and sausage gravy. Like locals at some dystopian diner, the three battered investigators tucked in, discussing their evidence pile.

One. The blunted arrow had Natural written all over it. In their twenty-four hours on the island, they'd heard about ELF's extremist faction of Sentinels—their skills, their rejection of technology.

Two. The soldiers guessed at what Dr. Chow was up to. They examined Campbell's journal, knew Chow had been hiding—and blood testing—their person of interest. But why? What were the results?

Three. They'd found Campbell's flex-cuffs nearby in the sand. Their prisoner had been freed, most likely by a Sentinel. But for what purpose? Rescue? Revenge?

Four. Investigating the docks, Fire Chief Young played chess to the deputy's checkers. Young had noted the fuel numbers when their own tanks were filled. The captain knew twenty gallons had been pumped—by their escapees?—sometime after that.

Five. The chief knew fire, how it moved. Young found its point of origin: the skeletal remains of a shed. Evidence of accelerant pointed to arson. He'd raked the ashes and found a charred arrow that matched the one that had thumped Specialist Cruz. A getaway then, with arson to distract?

Six. The boathouse. One of many, but this one was unburnt, its bay door wide open. There were dust-shadows on the shelves. An oil can had been recently disturbed, fresh drops unabsorbed by the concrete slab.

Young could picture them—captor and captive—absconding in the night with the harbor ablaze behind them, wild bells clanging alarm.

Sergeant Booker policed up their breakfast and brought over a chart. Last night had been calm, good conditions for boating. That amount of fuel—twenty gallons—could've taken them far. With his sooty finger, Young traced the radii of possible routes. The U.P.? The bridge? Maybe. But Young's best guess was the mainland, back towards Charlevoix for some unfinished business.

"Is our satellite phone charged up, Sergeant? We'd better check in with Ops."

"Yes sir, bled some juice from the boat batteries. Palantir should be good to go."

A minute later, a ring of satellites powered up—a relic, peak technology from before. Geosynchronous, 22,000 miles above the Earth, they received a rare signal from the newly silent planet. Once authenticated, Young's message was relayed to the Operations officer at the Guard post in Grayling.

Young replaced his terminus and awaited a reply.

Weapon-Take

BY NOON OF CLEANUP DAY, the season had turned. September's heat, like the harbor fire, had been extinguished. Deep in Beaver Island's state forest, a grove of hemlocks was astir, the tops of *Tsuga canadensis* tossed by Canadian air. The Sentinels, impervious to the wind, hid their stern faces beneath gray hoods—the cold, steely edge of the ELF.

The elves had mustered and were going to war. Guided by shamans—Brian, Grace, and Pastor George—they volunteered to fight, protecting their Earth Mother from poison, from pollution. If there was a battle at the bridge—good against evil, leafy green against oily black—they'd do what they could. Two dozen fighters, multi-cultured, were clad in camouflage parkas embroidered with their tree—Gaia's Guardians, the Elves Militant of the Liberation Front.

Their gear of war was stacked, long spears forming a tepee. There were quivers of arrows and laminated bows with spare strings. Tactical backpacks were piled as well, filled with rations, trussed with tomahawks and melee weaponry. Gaia forgive, some also carried solar cells, portable power enhancing their electromes, confusing the eyes of their enemy. A few wore body armor under their cloaks: a silver weave, lightweight, with the strength of triple steel.

Grim faces peered out from under hoods. Goodbyes had been said already—to children, to spouses, to friends who'd stay and prepare for winter. Elena was there, with Sparrow perched beside her. Mukwa—his muzzle full of stitches and head full of trauma—had been adopted again by the elves. Ever-changing his skin, he wore his patched parka again, blades tucked in his belt. Many fighters were missing since their last muster—Matador, Tigre, Diving-Duck, Squirrel, Bull, Thorn and his squad. Apparently, sometime last night, Sentinel Nighthawk—radicalized and furious—had winged away too. She'd last been seen cursing at the church; where the extremist was now, only Gaia could guess. Those who knew her best—Elena, Diana, and Sparrow—assumed the angry bird had flown for good.

Elena looked them over. "This mission to the Mackinac Bridge is voluntary. None of you are compelled to join it." Her keen eyes glittered beneath her hood as she spoke. "Your labor is needed here, for the harvest, for the hunt."

The wood elves stood still as the cold wind increased. Hemlocks, summer-soft, bemoaned their fate, an ancient lignin lament.

"If the bridge rumors are true, we'll be outgunned, outnumbered, and disadvantaged in many ways. Your death is quite likely, and any burial uncertain."

Still, they kept quiet.

Sparrow raised her small fist in the air and was acknowledged by Elena. The gymnast pushed her words against the wind: "I fought in the night attack, when the XCons unleashed their hounds. When they murdered our comrades, driving us from our forest home," the assembled elves were nodding, "you were there too. You experienced the same.

"Yes, we were outnumbered, outgunned, and some of us were killed. But that night we witnessed the power of Gaia. We saw how *She* fought for *us!* The trees, the rocks, the river. She saved us! We escaped! No children were killed. Gaia protected us, and now, with Her blessing, we are prospering again, and helping these islanders do the same."

Sparrow closed her eyes, opening herself to the swaying trees and slow-rolling earth. The squad synchronized their electrical fields. They all felt it. Felt *Her*. Gaia's green sap flooded their veins, enzymes and proteins affirming their purpose.

No more words were needed.

Elena made a hand gesture—earth, heart, sky. Sparrow shouldered a pack and selected two light javelins. The she-elf then faced north, a willing martyr for Gaia. The Sentinels, ever orderly, followed her lead. Packs were strapped and weapons hefted, the gear-pile diminishing. Mukwa brooded, suspecting Hawk's arson, her flight off the island and away the fuck from him. Savoring Sam's sleepover, he held dream-Keith—ghost-Keith—close to his heart. The old man always knew his duty, and Mukwa did too. Grunting, he hauled a double load, front-pack and back; Mukwa choked up remembering Matador, his endless teasing of El Oso. Elena went last, taking up the rear-guard. The tall elf whistled, and Earth's liberators set off at a run.

The hemlock grove emptied, its trees signaling slowly, root-tip to twig. Chemically coded, they transmitted the drop in barometric pressure, the diminution of daylight, and the need to reorganize their sucrotic stores. Scant attention was paid to the hasty hominids. If their absence was noted, it was short-lived. For the cold wind was blowing, and winter—the old tree killer—was grinding near. The rooted residents of the realm, as always, had nowhere to run, and so much to do.

The Weird Sisters

MIIN'S MAPLE TREES—*Acer saccharum* to Grace, *aninaati-goog* to Samantha—burned sweetly, red and yellow, just outside the windows of Sam's shack. A cold wind from Canada began to blow. Miin, genuflecting, fed maple fingers to the hungry wood-stove. Its cast iron pinged, expanding as it warmed. A cauldron had been set to boil. Glacial melt filled the island's aquifers; as this meltwater steamed, ice-age ghosts haunted the room.

Samantha—wrinkled by wisdom, silver hair brightly braid-ed—slow-danced around her stove, adding herbs from bundles drying in the rafters. Miinan watched her foster-gran's every move, anticipating many and surprised by some.

Grace was there too, sipping mushroom tea, cataloging its soily contents for flavor and effect. Two elders and an appren-tice—psycho-activated—shared the shack and its vaporous visions. The tossing trees bowed, or appeared to, rooted tight against the gale.

"Miinan, a visitor will be arriving soon."

Their little sleepover was over—Miin's puppet show, Mukwa's laughter, and *Goodnight Moon.* Brother bear, stitched and sto-ic, had shambled off to the Sentinel weapon-take, adopted by his other family—the ELF—embarking for war. Grace informed them of last night's arson, St. James harbor miraculously saved.

The arrival of a morning visitor was news to Miin. The girl looked up from the stove as her teacher continued, "Diana—a re-markable woman—arranged it at the Garden party. One of the voyageurs will join us, a water-protector from Manitoulin Island. Autumn is her name. I sent her a dream and she caught it."

Miin finished loading the firebox. Latching its iron lid, she stood and said, "Would you like me to escort her, *nookomis*?"

Samantha nodded as she unsealed a mason jar, empowering her potion. Miin's eye caught the label: willow bark. A waft of wintergreen triggered the pupil's pneumonic, *minty-green, methyl salicylates means.*

"She'll be coming from the west. Look for her on the Tower Trail."

A gust rattled the windowpanes. Miin took the Mackinaw coat from its peg and pulled a wool cap from its pocket. She worked the stiff zipper, the familiar coat less large than the year before. Grace smiled around her teacup as Samantha tossed an apple from the bushel, a Wagner. Miin caught it and closed the door behind her, stepping out into the weather.

The cold front took her breath away. How exciting!

She pulled the wind into her, tasting Arctic ice far, far away. She leaned into it and put the shack behind her. Her feet knew the way, freeing her mind to roam. As ever, her thoughts quickly found Keith, knowing just where her uncle would be. She smelled him first—tobacco, woodsmoke, gunmetal—a scent-shadow Keith cast from beyond. Then she heard him, the tender leather of his voice.

"What's this now? Miin in the *miinan* again?" Keith rasped his greeting on the wind. They'd walked this path together a season ago, basking in the sunshine of summer, Blueberry and Crow. A sudden welling, and Miin's own aquifers spilled over.

At the old fire tower, Miin ascended the metal stairs. At the top, there was a wide view of the country and a great buffeting of wind. She squinted against it—a mile of forest, then farmland, then dunes. Out on the big lake, whitecaps gnashed the shore. They chewed the beach, foamy molars grinding pebbles to sand.

Was that a canoe out in Greenes' Bay?

Shielded by the surf, it darted towards landfall. She lost it, found it, lost it again. Expertly handled, camouflaged by combers, the rogue canoe slipped through Doyle's blockade, landing their honored guest ashore.

Miin flew down the tower steps, then raced to intercept. A mile later, where the forest faltered and farmland began, she spied a woman on the trail.

Autumn was walking fast with the wild wind behind her. Encountering Miin, she didn't stop, but merely nodded. The girl pivoted, matching the Manitoulin's stride, pace for pace.

"Hello! Call me Miin—Blueberry. Samantha sent me. To show you the way."

The gale guttered the flame of her greeting. The mature woman smiled, saving her breath. The rest of their march was speechless.

Once past the fire tower, she allowed Miin to lead. The bog paths were tricky, ever-changing. The girl, island-fluent, guided them well. They came to Sam's clearing. The leafless maples were moaning, caught in a storm without their coats. The stovepipe's smoke was a weather vane, indicating east. The Manitoulin, strong in spirit, held up a hand, stopping them both as she surveyed Samantha's sanctum.

Miin, ever-hungry, snuck a bite from her apple.

"I've dreamed of this place. This shack. This day."

Miin crunched again, wiping juice from her chin. "Not surprised," she said through a sweet mouthful. "It has that effect on people,"—*crunch*—"I know it does on me."

Autumn paused a moment longer, then followed Miin to the warping door. The girl announced their arrival with a knock, they both entered quickly, shutting out the pushy wind.

Inside, the cauldron steamed. The cabin was fragrant with a ferny smell. They pegged their coats and were welcomed. The

three wise ones joined hands in wordless greeting. The girl busied herself with small chores while the women calibrated. By
the time Miin stoked the stove and pumped the buckets full, the
trio had found their frequency.

"A tincture?" Autumn inquired, eyeing the iron pot. Grace
and Samantha were sagely smiling. The Canadian re-plaited
her wind-teased braid. Sniffing their concoction, she rolled up
her sleeves and recited, "Chamomile, feverfew, St. John's?"

Three guesses, three nods.

Autumn inventoried their apothecary—the bundled herbs,
the labeled jars. She asked permission with a glance, and with a
glance it was granted. She selected a long-handled spoon from
Sam's hand-carved collection. Autumn felt its features, finger-
ing the grain to sense the sunlight still inside this once-leafy
limb. She then began to stir the cauldron's contents counter-
clockwise, freeing more fragrance.

"Willow bark? You'll be sending this with your warriors
then?"

"We will," Sam replied, "and we hope you'll take some as well."

The water-protector nodded. "Honored, though this will not
heal all wounds."

"Nor is it meant to," Grace added, "but what we *can* do, we
shall do. Because, at-the-last, when the hurly-burly at the bridge
is done, a black breath may cloud many minds. This medicine
might help."

Autumn, a woman of strong medicine, followed her heart. "I
don't see *echinacea*. Has your island no daisies?"

Sam smiled knowingly. "A gap in my stores. Have you?"

Autumn pointed Miin to the peg where her coat and bag were
hanging.

"Fetch my pouch, young Blueberry, and thank you—*chi miigwech.*"

The teenager did so and brought forth the bundle.

"Unwrap that now and sniff."

Miin complied, inhaling its parts. "A sweetish smell, with something tingly?" The apprentice looked up from the exam to see her three masters confirm with their smiles. Miin pestled the plant, further empowering their potion.

Autumn stirred on. Grace and Samantha, spoonless, were stirring too. Electricity—green energy—bubbled up from the cauldron. The indoor gale mirrored the outer. The concoction cooled as it was ladled into jars. Blueberry, tipsy from fumes, averted her senses. Miin suddenly wished to get away.

Samantha felt it. "Blueberry, why don't you visit Shawn Greene? Go borrow his bicycle. This batch must reach the harbor before Diana's ferry and your big brother depart for the bridge."

Miin, still spinning, was bundled out the door. Her satchel clinked with Mason jars of medicine, and she carried a salve for Mukwa's freshly stitched face.

A Charlevoix Sunrise

THE TWO FUGITIVES, exposed and hypothermic, arrived with the dawn. The sun's nuclear power slowed their shivering as Campbell throttled down just inside the breakwater. Bob's tiller-hand was a frozen claw. A cold front was massing, pushing up whitecaps; they'd barely beaten the storm.

Charlevoix sat empty, the drawbridge down. M-31, its main road, had been traveled upon, Cowboy's old roadblocks rudely shoved aside.

Nighthawk pulled a knife from her belt, sunlight bouncing off its blade. "Before we touch land, let's be clear about our wants."

Bob agreed. As a couple, they needed therapy; thirty miles of celestial navigation hadn't changed their basic calculus of predator and prey.

"What *I* want," the Sentinel italicized with her knife, "is to exchange you for my comrades—Bull, Thorn, and others. We abandoned them back in June when your XCons attacked, driving us—kids too, you twisted fuck—from our forest home with dogs."

And what I want, Cowboy thought, *is a hot cup of coffee and a break from your eco-bullshit.*

Bob nodded dumbly as he thawed his hands in sunlight, willing his teeth to stop chattering.

Nighthawk continued, "Now, that attack was three months ago, so what I need from *you*, Campbell, is information. If your Chosen buddies took prisoners, where would they be? Who's your leader? What information can you offer me for keeping your infected ass alive?"

Cowboy—feeling half the Viral he used to be—predicted her posture and was ready, "First, the Big Boss is downstate, but you already know that. I've only heard his voice, never seen him; apparently, no one has. Any prisoners, especially any of you immune-types, would be brought south to Sharkey."

Hawk stared, a bird of prey, unblinking.

"It's what we call him."

"*Where* exactly downstate?" She brandished two blades now, flourishing for effect.

"Like I said, never been there, but Panzer's compound—fortress really—is in Kalamazoo."

"That's a long fucking way. How do I get there?"

Bob shook his head, a cowboy without a hat. "Sorry honey. You mean, how do *we* get there. I'm your bargaining chip, remember?"

The sun bathed them both in ionic gold. The outflow from Pine River—crystal clear without pollution—pushed their idle boat backwards. Cowboy closed his red-rimmed eyes, absorbing heat through the lids. Whoever she was, this woman was *pissed*. But the amount of shit he gave about her mood was rapidly decreasing.

"Look," he tried, "you can put those slicers away. Fact is, for now, we need each other. I know what *you* want, but what about *me?* Well, I'll tell you. What I want is some food and warmth and a fucking break from you and your threats."

Bob's feet were soaked: boots, socks, and skin. The boat's rivets had leaked—of course they had—and they'd been bailing all night. His core temperature still cringed from exposure.

Fuck it.

He toggled the motor forward. She glared. They put-putted along the causeway, under the bridge—his rusty nemesis—and into the harbor. He looked up at his old office, sight-checking the other buildings as well. None had been burned, none looked damaged. Bob bumped them to a berth. Nighthawk jumped out and made them fast to the dock. Scanning for threats, she signaled him to unload. He handed up the rope, the fishing gear, and what was left of the gas. They'd burned through three containers, only four sloshy gallons remaining.

Hawk hesitated, then reached down. Bob grasped her calloused hand and was easily hauled up.

Damn, she's strong.

Bob's boots squelched; he wobbled a bit on the too-solid ground. Together, the elopers looked the place over, their dystopian honeymoon. The linden trees on Bridge Street were waking up, yellow leaves stretching towards dawn. At the empty ferry dock, there were still signs of summer's skirmish. Bullet holes pockmarked the landing.

And were those bloodstains on the concrete?

Cowboy paled, pointing at a ticket booth. "And what the hell is *that?*" Traumatized, he flashed back: ambush, River Road, broken glass, broken bodies. He and his fixer, Mikey—RIP?—had seen this sigil before:

Don't Fuck with the ELF!

Hawk, clearly combative, grinned at the graffiti. Above the tag line bloomed a bloody tree. She remembered June, how it had been—their rainy exodus from ELF Country, the moonrise, the night swim, the rafted weapons, fighting beside Mukwa, their intimate dance of death.

She unslung her bow, answering his question with a feral grin. "The ELF?" Hawk nocked an arrow. "Earth-Liberation-Front. Elves, Campbell, we're fucking elves."

She gestured, and Bob picked up their gear.

"You remember? The ones that kicked your ass? Made you piss your pants? Stole your precious ferry? Pushed your infected friends the fuck out of town?"

She had him lead the way. "You want food? Warmth? Well, hop to it! I'm sure you've got some supplies stashed. Make a wrong move though, reach for a weapon, run for it, and I'll feather your ass. Now let's go."

Twenty minutes later they were up in his office. Bob checked all his hidey-holes, scrounging a bit. They made out pretty well— some cans of food, some plastic-tasting pastries. His desk, of course, had been rifled, the entire town thoroughly scavenged. Generators, gasoline, chow hall, armory—all had been gleaned by pickers unknown. The only calling card they found was a runic ᚱ, charcoal-smudged above a jimmied door.

Sunlight beamed through glass, radiating his corner office. They shared a fork, eating corned beef hash, cold from the can. His spare pistol had been pilfered, but he found an emergency bottle behind a ceiling tile. Bob thumped the whiskey on the tabletop, hoping this birdie might wet her beak.

The sight of whiskey brought Lizzy to mind. Damn, that girl could drink though, and after that she'd screw. That was all gone now, lightning in a bottle.

His captor didn't touch the booze. Campbell, three months sober, fought temptation, remembering the mantra: *to thine own self be true.*

Seeking distraction, Bob nodded at the map, marked and pinned as before. He'd lived a whole different life then: gathering for bosses, hunting for Hidden, padding his stats, climbing the Chosen chain.

"So, young lady, where might you be from?"

She gulped her hash and glared, *no fucking way*. Full of food and finally warming, Campbell stretched, standing up as she fingered her knife. Bob had no doubt this chick could fling it. He moseyed to the map, pointing to a southeast burb downstate. "I'm from there. I built houses. I had a wife, a daughter. Spoiler alert—they died."

The map's notations—stats, skulls, and circles—were a timeline of that first year. Societal collapse, the real fucking thing; so much worse than anyone predicted.

No one stayed themselves. You donned a mask or you died. Not an N95, or MOPP, but a persona, a mean, badass persona— bloodthirsty, piratical, rapacious. You merged with your mask or were murdered by one who had. It's not like he'd wanted to become a monster. The only thing that made him Chosen, was choosing—and Christ, he wished he hadn't—to survive.

Bob's back itched. He could feel the blade this bitch would throw, his severed spine, his voided bowels. "Look, whoever you are, wherever you're from, we both want the same thing. We're here," he pointed at the northwest corner, "and we both want to go here." He dragged his dirty finger south, 230 miles to Kalamazoo. "You want to find your friends—if captured, they'd be there. I want to find my friends—if I have any left, they're in K-Zoo as well."

Despite the food and some warmth, Campbell still felt wobbly—withdrawals? If Dr. Chow had been dosing him, the next couple days might really suck. Fighting nausea, he turned from the map and met her angled eyes. Again, that raptor-look, not quite human. Whoever this she-elf was, she wore a mask too.

"What do you say, Tinkerbell? Let's get some rest, then travel together. We've got some gallons left. We'll boost a vehicle. Watch each other's backs, at least for now?"

Sentinel Nighthawk scraped her food can clean, glaring at the bleary-eyed Viral while contemplating his bullshit fucking plan.

Thorn, are you alive?

Bull? Comrades? Where are you?

Gaia, give me guidance.

Headed South

FOR THE LAST HALF MILE their car's engine had sputtered. Now the man at the wheel was sputtering too. "What's wrong?" snapped Nighthawk, tired of Campbell's toxicity and their road trip from hell.

"Steering's gone, honey, hydraulics too." Cowboy mock-wrangled the wheel. "Sweetie, we're done." The driver pumped the brakes and maneuvered their boosted car across the oncoming lane. Satisfied with the roadblock, he took the pulse of the car's gassy heart as it gave a final shudder. Dr. Bob consulted his non-existent wristwatch. "Time of death, 3:30 p.m. Cause, apocalypse."

Unamused, Nighthawk jumped out, slamming her door. "Well, we didn't make it very far!"

They'd taken M-131 south from Charlevoix. She pointed to signage for nearby Cadillac. "We're not even close to halfway!"

The billboard, which once read "Buy Local," had been scrawled over: "NO VIRALS!" The year-old paint was weather-faded. The models' eyes had been daubed bright red—shop till you drop.

"Not a problem, dear. This is a decent crossroads."

Cowboy exited and gave the expired automobile a pat. "If what you say about massing Chosen is true, we should see something eventually."

"Eventually?" Nighthawk spat back. "Well what if we don't? What then, Bob?" She reached into the backseat, hefting out her pack, bow, and quiver. They'd outfitted as best they could from Charlevoix, scrounging food for maybe a week. Obviously the gas was gone already.

Cowboy, bareheaded, stood in the road, shading his eyes, planning the bushwhack. He foresaw a scout-car, motoring up from the south. It could work. He mentally placed a machine gunner, some mines, and an OP on that hill. Get someone up there with binoculars and a radio. The Chosen boss blinked; his phantom assets still itched.

Instead there she was, a pissed off female, shouldering her pack and hiking away. Fuck it. He should let her go. Or run away himself. She'd kill him anyway, as soon as things got dicey. This nameless elf was a fanatic; he'd seen the look before. But, like it or not, this forced marriage, for now, was binding. Bob needed her—captured of course—as a present to Sharkey, a green gift, tied up tight, to regain his Chosen cred. Bob squinted against the sun as she quick-marched off the roadway. Campbell missed his cowboy hat.

Nighthawk didn't turn, but could feel him following. *Chicken shit!* Here was his freedom, why not fucking take it? Because Campbell was a coward, a Viral son of a bitch. Because anyone they'd meet would shoot him on sight and leave his contagious corpse to rot.

She'd done the math—150 miles from here, straight south to Kalamazoo, forty-eight hours of hiking. She could be there in three or four days. But then what? Face the Kalamazoo com- pound alone? Without a Chosen chip to bargain with? Without a hostage to exchange? That was the whole point of nabbing his infected ass in the first place.

Dying for Gaia was acceptable—an earthy end, Hawk's ener- gy recycled. Living was too hard. Too much had been lost, and nothing gained—nothing that worked anyway. But it wasn't time yet. She grit her teeth, picturing Thorn and Bull as guinea pigs in some Panzer lab.

The ELF extremist opened her green apertures. The afternoon felt unsettled. A Canadian cold front gushed across the border. Sugar maples flared from woodlots. A great V of southing geese overtook her, navigating the same concrete river. A lone honk floated down from above. Solidarity? Support? Or utter indifference?

She'd never merged with a migrator, and wouldn't try now. Of course Grace had tested her, but Hawk's anger interfered. How did Brian keep so cool? And that islander girl Miin? Hawk had witnessed enough to know they'd both been blessed by Gaia.

She'd been blessed too, but for battle. Predatory, she strung her bow, felt the notches, the tallied kills. Gaia's gifts took many forms; Hawk's came with a barb—a hardened heart. Admittedly, she missed Mukwa, but at the same time she really didn't.

From monster to moper, the poor dude was a mess. Still, she hadn't meant to hurt him, and raking his face was a real regret. But Oso, that clumsy bear, had tried pinning her down. She fled from him outside the church, going from break-up to break-in. Hawk escaped Muck's cage while freeing a Viral from another—Chow's fucking cabin.

Bob's boots were worn thin. His filthy feet were blistering, atrophied muscles whining for fuel, pleasure receptors screaming for Dr. Chow's missing dose. The woman had disappeared down the road, and so far he hadn't gained any ground. Was she gone for good? Didn't she need him? He definitely needed her, at least for now.

He kept going. At twilight Campbell caught a whiff of woodsmoke. And there, to his left, away from the road, was a flickering orange flame. He whistled as he approached her stand of cedars, hoping to avoid being shot in the dark.

A creek snaked coldly through the sheltered spot. He spied a small fire and her form in a sleeping bag. He knew the lands about were empty, but still, she was too trusting. Not wanting to wake her, he slipped off his pack, took a knee, and began rummaging its contents for a can of well-earned soup.

Bob felt a stir of air, heard the thunk of impact, and a bowstring's *twang!*

An angry arrow quivered in a tree trunk, inches from his face. He controlled his flinch, resuming his shaky whistle, and emerged with a can.

"Since you asked so nicely, yes, I'm happy to share. Chicken noodle, ma'am?"

Dignified, he presented the label to the unseen shooter. Monsieur Campbell, a sommelier of soup; the cedar copse was his Chez Paul.

The woman—apparently *not* in her sleeping bag—swooped down from a branch. Retrieving her missile, she stalked off towards the road. Bob called after her, "I'll take that as a no? You'll take the first watch then?"

No response.

Sighing, he pulled the tab on his soup can and utilized her pot, sacrificing sticks to the fire. She'd filled her water bottle; he guzzled it down to sandy dregs. Bob smacked his lips in case she was watching. "Ahhh, nothing like a cold one." She wasn't.

He stirred the broth with her spoon, savoring steam. The ex-contractor excavated his pack. Bob's fingers found, then fondled, the smooth glass bottle he'd brought from his office. He hefted it, admiring the amber elixir within. He refilled her bottle, drank off half the creek water, then drammed in his poison. Steeped in peak capitalism, commercials defined him, defined them all. He saw a rugged version of himself in a TV ad: "Don't let the End Times end your good times. Enjoy Jack Daniels responsibly. The choice of the Chosen."

Bob burned his tongue on chicken broth, before burning his belly with booze. The fattening crescent wobbled in the west. Instantly tipsy, he was falling fast himself. He unrolled his sleep sack, taken from his go-bag stashed in Charlevoix. He congratulated his past self and zipped himself to bed.

The Sentinel—hawk-eyed and invisible in her parka—observed the road. The moon sank. Cold air filtered down from Canada. The heavens heaved slowly, gravid with stars. Deer hoofed across the now-harmless highway. Owls called, marking their turf, calibrating sonar for midnight murder. Her green senses twitched—menace, tire vibration, engine noise! A blacked-out vehicle raced up from the south. Hawk darted a look towards the cedar copse. Shit! Their fire still flickered.

The song from the dune cabin—his wife's favorite—played in Bob's dream.

And when we get behind closed doors, then she lets her hair hang down.

But instead of Ashley—his sweetheart since high school—it was the she-elf undressing, backlit by firelight. She undid her battle-braids and was bending down to join him in the sack, but instead of a kiss, Bob—half aroused—received a stinging slap and a calloused hand clamped hard over his mouth. Thrashing in his goose-down cocoon, Cowboy couldn't breathe.

A hawkish hiss: "Shut the fuck up!"

Bob was awake and rapidly wilting, his bleary eyes wide with panic. She shoved his face again—hard—then released. Quickly, she packed her sleeping bag and cookware. Cowboy, catching on, did the same. In thirty seconds both packs had been strapped. He followed her, stumbling, away from the copse and towards the road. A vehicle had halted there, ominous on the highway. Screens glowed from its interior, bass notes thumping; a modified engine idled roughly, burning bad gas.

Nighthawk led them, running, to the drainage ditch. She followed the stream to its culvert, stuffing Bob inside. The car drooled fluids above them as the engine shut off. They heard two doors open, then quietly close. There was some whispered planning, then silence. Earth paused its rotation. The stars, interrupted, peered down.

Nighthawk saw it all clearly, a raptor's view of the roadway. The Sentinel hoped to Gaia she was right. Two figures stalked towards their campfire. Was one of them the driver? Fuck! The time was now. So she went.

Cowboy, unconsulted, could only listen. The creek had soaked his boots. He smelled damp concrete and rusting rebar. His muscles cramped from stooping. He heard a door wrench open, then a scuffle. He scrambled up the bank—too late?—and tripped. A body was slumped on the road. Was it the elf?

Blind, he bent down, but felt a bristly mohawk instead of her braids—a Chosen then, an errand boy delivering orders from some boss down south. There was hot blood on his fingers, the feel of it, the smell. He pictured the plasma, platelets plagued with virions. Then the ignition was keyed and the engine came alive. Bass notes resumed their thumping.

"Get in!" came her whisper from the driver's side. A window exploded, sharp glass shaving his face. A second later came the sound—*Crack! Crack! Crack!*—a three-round burst. The air zipped with stinging bees. Bob ducked, flinging the rear door open and diving inside. Awkward with his pack, he couldn't turn to close it.

Hawk put the transmission in gear, floored the gas pedal, and cut the wheel hard. Tires screeched, rubber burning as they spun 180. His soaked boots dangled out the door. Lacerated, his face was on fire. Muzzles flashed from two barking rifles as the remaining Virals—duped no longer—ran back towards the road.

More zips, more bees, *Crack-Crack! Crack-Crack!*

Impacts shook the vehicle as Nighthawk straightened her wheel. They bumped over poor Mohawk, and made their getaway.

Dozer

THE PHARMACY TECHNICIAN, fully garbed in PPE, depressed her plunger, emptying the syringe. The newly muscled man—once known as Mikey, a Chosen, Cowboy's Charlevoix fixer—held the gauze till tape was applied. His mutant blood, altered by injections, clotted quickly.

The technician checked her patient for adverse reactions. "Please remain seated for fifteen—"

"Get the fuck outta here!" Dozer roared. The woman, a Panzer employee, flinched from the bald brute and quickly withdrew. Rewired—body and mind—the man closed his eyes, embracing the virucide, the virility in his veins. Utterly hairless, he leapt from the exam table, swished through a series of airlocks, and quick-marched towards his motor pool. Dozer took huge breaths of cold air; his lungs, forge bellows, firing his furnace. The big day drew near. He'd sent his best scouts—Big Rapids, Cadillac, Traverse City—but so far they hadn't returned. Soon the compound's black gate would open, and Panzer would march north to war.

Last winter, after the sleety slaughter along the Kalamazoo River, Dr. Schark's tattooed Gories had taken Fort Custer. Blood-spattered, they commandeered its equipment and its personnel too. The civilians and guardsmen, scared shitless by the Skulls, had been given a choice by the Aghori leader, Sergeant Jones. Most had joined Panzer, pledging allegiance to its banner—a medieval two-tower design. The remains of the refusers still dangled from their nooses. Dozer passed them now as he pushed through the cold front sent by Canada. The corpses twisted in the first big gale of the season, muted wind chimes of jerked meat and bone.

Then, in June, he'd betrayed Cowboy—a decent dude, really—and was badly wounded while riding shotgun for his new boss, Red Liz. Their column of Raiders had sortied from Charlevoix, chasing a false flag—some old fart's phony transmission. Mikey, a supposed "fixer," had really fucked that one up. Their column had been pinned by treefall, then shredded by well-placed mines. Red Liz had been sheared—mastectomy via shrapnel—ol' girl hadn't made it, none of them had. Lacy, Hammer, the others were pounded to pulp.

Regaining consciousness, Mikey had limped from the carnage as dawn pricked the sky. By the time he made it to Charlevoix, the ferry, *Emerald Isle*, had been stolen and the Chosen garrison either slaughtered or fled. He'd almost given up right then and there.

Dozer cringed remembering his pity party, his puddle of tears, his hunger pains and asthmatic wheeze. The ELF graffiti—another bloody tree—had decided him. Fucking elves always marked their turf with gore. The bright-eyed bastards would be back, and they'd scalp his ass for sure. So Mikey the mechanic had rallied. Scrounging a vehicle and some grub, he coughed his way south on gassy fumes.

Dr. Schark, the CEO, welcomed him to Panzerland via voice message. Mikey hadn't expected this, thinking Big Boss would punish him for Cowboy's blunders up north. Instead, he was assigned to a clinical trial and promptly dosed with Cyanovirin, though anyone could see the asthmatic was no warrior.

Mikey's father, stung with all the others in Y1, had been abusive, an alcoholic, but his son—a gifted mechanic—was mostly harmless. The doctor's dose changed all that. Sharkey had tweaked his juice, boosting Mike's musculature while leaving his IQ alone—unlike the too-cerebral Gories of phase one trials.

Fixer's flab quickly melted. Born again, Dozer was awed by his strength and stamina. Excited by his new chassis, he fondled tight abs, running strong fingers across his newly bald dome.

He'd never met Dr. Schark, not face to face anyway; few had. Mikey was fine with this. He'd gotten too chummy with his old boss, Cowboy Campbell. Red Liz had been right, the dude was a loser, all hat and no cattle. Mike's misplaced loyalty had almost cost him everything. He didn't regret betraying Bob, just wished he'd done it sooner.

Had Campbell escaped the ferry? Had the elves found him? Put him on trial? He'd seen their work; those fanatical fairies were capable of torture. The thought of Cowboy's mutilation didn't bother him much—*better him than me*—the Chosen code.

Freshly juiced, the ex-mechanic pushed into the hangar that served as his motor pool. Dr. Schark's latest order—voiced through his mercenary, Mr. Wermer—put Dozer in charge. A grinding wheel spat sparks, blue light strobing from his team of welders. Ozone and aluminum scented the air, flavoring their flesh. Compressors were running; they guzzled gas, but for now there was plenty. Back in Y1, Gories had secured Detroit's refineries for Panzer.

Their CEO, bio-secure in his silo, had big plans for Michigan, for the region. Via Wermer, Schark voiced his orders. Unlike other bosses, Sharkey provided workers and resources as well. The fall of Fort Custer had doubled Panzer's punching power. Michigan's 177th—*Eye of the Tiger*—had left behind a well-stocked armory. Nothing too heavy, mostly small arms and loads of ammunition. The bulk of Custer's Humvees and APCs were disabled in the Aghori ambush. Panzer salvaged some, scrapping the rest for parts. At the Army airfield, scavengers found a tractor-trailer packed with DOD prototypes and swarms of interesting tech.

September dropped its leafy guards as the cold front gusted through the breach. Arctic air howled into the hanger. Dozer stood in front of his creature, a mechanical mammoth from the Age of Ice. A special project, Sharkey—white hands layered in latex—had sketched the design himself, discussing details with his new fixer through the intercom.

The Big Boss, far-seeing, anticipated battle. Panzer's forces were already in motion—fuel and vehicles, pre-cached at rally points. An unusual alliance had been made with haloed Mustafa and his conned followers of X. He and Sharkey agreed to divide future spoils: the Upper Peninsula and Ontario—two plums, rich in resources—deemed ripe for picking. Local resistance was predictably meager, and the rewards were substantial. Sharkey had shown Dozer schematics of the big bridge up north. The long span of roadway was narrow, and no doubt there would be obstacles to clear, a path to be plowed.

Another Panzer employee, wearing corporate coveralls, peeled a large stencil from the machine, stepping back to view the result. Dozer ogled the massive plow-truck as well—a pre-collapse project by the Pentagon to clear heavy snow from northern runways. The oversize dump truck was now plated in steel. Its blade, tusk-like, had been enlarged, repurposed to push ten-ton roadblocks instead of snow. The beast bristled with machine guns. Desiccated scalps festooned its hairy hide.

Wet paint gleamed from the stencil. Apparently McKenzie, one of the female Gories, drew it herself. Surprise, surprise, it was a huge fucking skull, an elephant's. Delivering her drawing, she said it was a trophy of sorts, a *memento mori* from a mission. Dozer wisely kept his mouth shut. Two rules in Panzerland: You don't say no to Sharkey. You don't say shit to a Skull. So far, he hadn't broken either. Gazing at the scalps, Dozer hoped he never would.

The employee, bleary and paint-spattered, shook two cigarettes from a crush-proof pack, another perk of Panzer. Grimy, with arc-burns on face and hands, the painter offered one to Dozer. Both men lit up, admiring the armored mammoth standing asquat the oily concrete. A similar model—its terrifying twin—had been bartered away, branded with Mustafa's X, traded for slaves.

"A beaut, ain't she boss?" The mechanic squinted a smoky eye at his brawny supervisor.

Dozer, pupils dilated from his dose, responded, "That she is."

Cig dangling, the underling climbed into the cab. Dozer blew clouds in the hanger bay, imagining the battle smoke, the bridge, this monster in motion, cars and trucks tusked aside, guns blazing, lead spewing, shitting hot brass from every gunport. The mechanic hand-signed a warning and Dozer covered his ears. The gearhead pulled a cord, powering the horn of the plated pachyderm. Elephantine, its roar thundered through the hanger—prehistoric, primal. Stimulated by steroids, Dozer's blood roared in reply: "That she is, indeed."

The Gate Opens

THE RAIN, pulled south by a cold front, began before dawn. In their stolen scout car—RIP Mohawk—the wipers and heater were creature comforts. They took turns sleeping. It was trippy, almost a journey from before. Cowboy even tried the radio—fuzz only, no dice.

Approaching K-Zoo in the murky predawn, billboards on 131 were repurposed for Panzer propaganda, each one bearing the corporation's logo. Hypothetical no longer, Bob's thoughts on his next move were growing messy. Climbing the Chosen ranks, he'd always had a plan, or could at least follow Lizzy's. This ability had abandoned him.

Chow's fucking therapy hadn't helped. Lizzy's voice—the red-haired devil on his shoulder—urged him to dupe his abductor. Instead of Hawk exchanging him, he'd pull a switcheroo, exchanging her instead. But for what? Forgiveness from Sharkey? A Panzer promotion? Could he drink that Kool-Aid again?

His stomach flared, a migraine looming. Patient Campbell missed Chow's daily dose. *When in doubt, keep driving.* Cowboy Bob motored on.

On the outskirts of Panzerland, the billboards were polite: "Tired of surviving alone? Join the Panzer team today!" An artist—some Rockwell of Revelations—painted smiling families in warm tones being fed in a cozy cafeteria.

Closer to the city center, Rockwell was replaced by Edvard Munch. "Still in hiding?" screamed a billboard. "Come out, come out, wherever you are!" A family of figures, all wearing nooses, dangled from the catwalk. This was no painting. Children and parents had been hanged together. Cowboy slowed the car to view the art installation, then recoiled, its surrealism all too fucking real. The rain and his fog lights blurred the scene, mixing with his own memory—the street lamps of Petoskey, each pole ripe with human fruit. Bob sped away as his companion stirred.

"What is it?" she asked, curled up in the backseat.

"Nothing, honey. Just a deer in the road."

She raked him for the endearment: "Fucking told you not to call me that."

Approaching Panzer's pharma compound, they pulled off the road and hid the hot rod. They still had some fuel, but Bob worried her with talk of LoJack, AirTags, and GPS tracking. Doubtful, but they were deep in Chosen country; better safe than permanently sorry.

Hawk stared at her captive as they prepared to set out. What were his motives? Bob blinked, innocent, just a good ol' boy trying to help. They waterproofed themselves as best they could, stashed the messenger vehicle, and continued towards Panzer's HQ on foot.

"How much farther?" the ferocious woman snapped.

Cowboy, weary from the trail, ignored his nameless companion.

Hunched against the rain, they wandered through a wasteland of dilapidated box stores—Welcome Shoppers!—Target, Best Buy, Home Depot. Each one had been turned inside out. The dragons of disposability had vomited their bloat, then rolled over and gone extinct. Their plastic hoards had been scavenged, then abandoned to wind and weather. Campbell led them through the labyrinth of rusting carts and soggy cardboard. He looked up frequently, hoping the mall's surveillance system was blind.

By early afternoon they'd hoofed past the parking lots, putting the looted mall behind them. They trudged east in the rain along an access road bordered by once-prosperous farms. It was late September, but there were no crops to harvest. They both wore packs, the elf carrying her bow, removing the bowstring to keep it dry. They'd searched the car, but had found no weapons. Cowboy wished they'd stopped to frisk the body they'd bumped. Oh well. Against the power of Panzer, what good was a pistol?

The landscape was washed with gray. Low clouds dragged rain-heavy bellies across the brambled fields. Visibility was shit, a point in their favor. Topping a rise, Bob raised a hand and stopped them.

"What now?" she snarled.

Bob motioned her up, gesturing to keep her head down. They squinted through the rain at a sudden blaze of light. Panzer's perimeter wall—an iron enclosure—was lit up like a football game, or a supermax prison. Guard towers had been constructed and razor wire unspooled. Sentries could be seen manning their posts.

"Shit. We're way too close. Lady, whoever you are, this place is dangerous."

Hooded by her parka, she surveyed the scene with raptorial resolve. Cowboy wouldn't be surprised if she was counting guards, cataloging their features, noting the right-handed from the left.

"Now what?" he asked. "What's our next fucking move? If you think I'm marching down there, sweetie, you're crazy."

Nighthawk ignored him and the endearment. This pitiful man only had one purpose. He was a Chosen bargaining chip, a live Viral to exchange; that's all he was good for. She could care less about Bob Bullshit Campbell, his incessant jokes, his phallic insecurities.

If there were Sentinels here—Bull, or Thorn, or others—she'd free them somehow, or die trying. Hawk half-hoped for death anyway. Hers had always been a one-way ticket, no there-and-back-again reconnaissance. If there was collateral revenge to be had, then she'd take that too, especially against any Panzer higher-ups. But for right now she just needed to get closer, and to make sure her hostage—what was his plan anyway?—didn't run.

"Did you hear me, Tinkerbell? I said, now what the fuck do we do?"

Bob put a hand on her wet sleeve, trying to pull her off the rise. A sudden move, and she broke his grip. Foolishly, he clutched again, and with the flat of her palm she crunched his nose. The tall man buckled, then dropped. Bob groped his numb face, both hands coming away red with blood—still contagious?

She quick-chopped his neck, the vagus nerve, and he was out—Bob saw white, then stars, then nothing. Some paracord from her pack, and the spineless Cowboy was trussed. Still viable for exchange, she gagged him, dragging soggy Bob under wet brush, caching her captive for future use.

Her avian eyes returned to the wall. The ELF archer scooted over the hill, heading towards Panzer. She hooded herself and disappeared.

Free of the Viral, Nighthawk flew from tree to tree. The odor of wet woods invigorated her; fungi were fruiting in the rain. She inhaled oxygen, ozone, and the good, green smells of Gaia. The hardwoods ran right up to the western wall, oaks and maples frazzled by the high intensity discharge from the buzzing guard towers.

Centuries old, the woodlot—too hilly for cultivation—abided, undisturbed by plowmen. To the trees, Fortress Panzer was an aberration. A fleeting, electrified interruption to the way things should be. The concrete and steel—timid in their temporality—for now were tolerated. But the root mass was brooding. Anger was stirring. From twig to trunk, medullary muscles were flexing—molasses in motion. The woods, ever so slowly, were waking up.

Nighthawk, mission-focused, found a vantage point on the verge. Portage Road, a four lane, ran north-south, separating the woodlot from the wall. An access road, Industrial Drive, intersected and ran east through several gates and into the compound. Each gate had a guardhouse. Each guardhouse had been sandbagged, converted to a bunker. The snouts of gun barrels poked out from the concrete embrasures, their oily nostrils sniffing for targets.

Nighthawk climbed a tree. Once perched, she strung her recurve, nocking a broadhead. She enfiladed the access road—100 yards, maybe less—to the inner sanctum. The gloomy dim of the countryside was banished by 40,000 watts of electrified menace. The trees' photoreceptors flinched from this flameless fire, their shadows springing back from the sunless source.

There were plenty of targets, but Hawk wasn't hunting. She sought instead for ingress. The woman—an athlete of the Ivy League—wished she could fly, always had. In the before, as VP for conservation, she'd circled the globe, a soldier for sustainability. Post-collapse, all that was gone.

The stadium lights buzzed above, cold rain spattering on leafy limbs. A crow called, another answered. A third *caw-cawed*, and was greeted by a fourth, then a fifth. The black birds were hard to see. Nighthawk, blinded by the glare, swiveled her sonar, echo-locating. *Caw-caw!* She adjusted her array. *Caw-caw-caw!* There! The murder massed above the lights. She shaded the bulbs with her hand, attempting to get a glimpse. Sheets of rain came down in watery curtains.

Hawk could see them now, their inky plumage like voids in her vision-field. Portals between worlds, black holes, feathering souls from life to death. Hawk feared them, their mobbing beaks, the malice of their hive-mind. They rode the lights, wielding the wattage like weapons. Corvids raised their young to be adept with tools; nothing man-made that crows couldn't utilize.

This particular murder—well fed—had been fêted by Panzer's paramilitary, not once, but many times over. Their cortices now connected the corporate double tower with caloric reward. They learned that loyalty to this logo led to hot flesh and pungent gut. Thus incentivized, they pledged themselves to Panzer—at least for now—in symbiotic servitude.

If she could see them, they could see her—an avian axiom. Hawk shivered. The wet tree shivered too, raindrops beading upon its bark. From the compound, souped-up engines began roaring just inside the walls. A carbon cloud of exhaust, dampened by the drizzle, wafted over the wall and into the woods. The Sentinel flinched from its foulness.

The conservationist—MBA, PhD—knew the math: a hundred tons of Gaia's greenery to distill a gallon of gasoline. Each revved engine was a sacrilege, each push of the pedal a blaspheme. Internal combustion was the irreverent gas chamber for single-celled souls. There were a billion cars before Covee, the final solution of human transportation. To her, each traffic jam had been a Treblinka. Suburban driveways had dripped with late-model Dachaus, cash back and low APR. Every autobahn was an Auschwitz—*work sets you free*—the commuters' coda. Nighthawk gagged on the reek from carboniferous corpses.

A great horn trumpeted from inside the compound, trees trembling in terror. The electrified gates slid open on rails. The walls were crowded with cheering figures. Modified vehicles began to roll out—Humvees, pickups, troop-transports. Some towed weapons, some were hitched to fuel-trailers instead.

Panzer's paramilitary was a motley bunch. Some were kitted out as professional mercenaries, while others looked like conscripts "chosen" for this crusade. A wedge of motorcycles roared in the vanguard, their leather-clad riders a biker gang on parade. She counted vehicles and was nearing three dozen when a mechanized mammoth lumbered into view. Warriors nested in its armor plating, crewing machine guns, spewing profanity at their cat-calling comrades. The great horn was winded again, its elephantine echo shaking raindrops from Hawk's canopy.

School buses came next, their glossy yellow defiled by crude etchings: skulls, erections, and various slogans, variously spelled. They transported a labor force, unarmed as far as Hawk could tell. A final bus—DEPARTMENT OF CORRECTIONS—left the compound, with blacked out windows and an oversized X marking its hood. A mystery to Hawk, she tallied it and counted on.

Semi-trucks—the convoy's supply train—rumbled through the gates. Gun-trucks formed the rear of the column. The gates began to close as these last vehicles departed. The strike force turned north on Portage Road, vanishing into the wet distance. Hawk shivered in the rain; she'd counted fifty vehicles at least.

The compound, no longer roaring, grew quiet. Spectators shook precipitation from their ponchos and sought shelter. How many could be left inside? Surely the fortress must be empty, at least of fighters. She watched as the final taillights—red eyes peering backwards—submerged in the murk. What could stop that column? Its firepower, its ferocity? Nothing. Her stomach sank. The north had nothing. The big bridge would fall, the Upper Peninsula too. No amount of Howlers, Sentinels, or Old Law wannabes could put a dent in that force.

Fuck! Her plans were changing; hostage Cowboy shrank in importance as the Chosen threat grew. Could she warn them at least? Get a message to Elena, or Captain Diana on the ferry? It pained Hawk to think it, but the ELF should stay on Beaver Island, remain dark, and keep quiet. Resist the urge to meddle on the mainland. Their turn would come, sure, but for now they should trust the thirty-mile moat of deep water.

Could she find a radio then? Make her way back to the car they stashed? Scrounge gas somehow, race these Raiders to the bridge? What about the girl Miin, or Grace, or Brian and his birds? Send a mental message to one of them? An ESP email?

Could she do it? Would they hear her? Fuck again! She could not. They would not. Her green abilities lay elsewhere.

She considered Campbell, half-healed by the half-elf, Dr. Chow. The ex-Chosen was a mystery, his own motives unknown. Maturing slowly perhaps, but no help to her here. She wished she had allies, but her furious flight had been solo. By igniting the town, she'd burned her last bridge. Radios and technology were so not her thing.

What was then? What the fuck was her thing? Rescue? Maybe, but Hawk didn't sense her comrades. Revenge then? That felt more likely. Especially when rescue failed, as she knew it would. Were the MIA Sentinels even here? She doubted it. Had they ever been? Probably not. So, a suicide mission then? Martyrdom? To what purpose? For what possible gain?

She drew a deep breath and closed her bright eyes, pressing her hand upon the tree's damp bole. A degree of comfort came through its cambium. She inhaled again; the fumes had cleared, the spill of carbon sponged up already by a billion leafy scrubbers. The holocaustic horde had departed, one more oily stain upon the overly human Holocene, a gassy last gasp at the end of an epoch. The green smells remained. It was enough, it had to be. In the end, Gaia was enough.

A stirring of air alerted her. Her sharp ears detected a flutter of wings, then another, then another. Raindrops sprinkled down as the murder shifted its roost. The sentry birds had left their lights. Had they scented her somehow? Hawk knew crow olfaction was keen. They could sniff out stress pheromones, sometimes from miles away. Of all the trees in the forest, they'd alighted on hers? Fuck! She was busted! Oh Gaia!

Hawk, capture imminent, sliced the ELF tree patch—Gaia forgive!—from her parka, letting it fall from her fingers. Just another leaf in the woods, but it did not fall idly. Determined now, she slung her bow and climbed down the ladder of wet branches. Her last drop was a far one. The Sentinel landed on her feet in the duff and immediately put hands on her weapons.

She came up ready, but for what?

Not for this.

Certainly not for this.

Blinking through rain, she saw a skeleton backlit by electric blaze. A death's head. A ghoulish grin. The twitch of teeth and inked-on bones. Nighthawk rolled in the loam and came up bladed. She threw. Heard it thunk into flesh. The dark elf rolled again. Threw again. Another thunk. Another laugh. What in the *fuck?*

Strong arms pinioned her from behind. She faked compliance, stalling for time. In front of her the drizzly blur resolved. She was looking at a ghost? No, a man. A tattooed man, morphed monstrous, but nothing more.

A woman's voice flicked her ear: "Now, now. Take it easy, little birdie."

The mutant man straightened. Both blades were buried to the hilt—right shoulder, left shoulder. *Shit!*

The skeleton was bald, shirtless, glistening with cold rain and hot, dripping blood. He locked eyes upon her, unflinching, unblinking. Slowly, he plucked her steel talons from his flesh, licking each of her knives clean, then looked up at the canopy, a black umbrella of crows.

The thing gave a nod. Two inky corvids spiraled down, alighting on his muscled shoulders. Another nod, permission granted. They dipped their beaks, sipping hot blood from their host.

Arms still pinned, the Sentinel felt a sudden injection, her knees weakening as metallic cuffs clicked tight.

They'd caught themselves a hawk, banding it with steel.

Again, a woman's voice purred in her ear: "Time to put birdie in a cage."

Hawk's last thoughts surprised her, flashing to Mukwa in spite of everything. She wasn't a dream-walker, but composed a message anyway and hit send—*a fortress blazing with lumens, Virals spewing from its metallic maw, her urgent need for Oso.*

Forgive me, Bull, forgive me, Thorn.

She dropped into oblivion—*Gaia, you abandoned me. Abandoned us. Why?*

Skewered Rabbit

BRIGHT SEPTEMBER WAS WANING, October's dark drawing near. Thorn hadn't conversed with a human since the XCon attack three full moons ago. He led the rearguard that night, his Sentinels buying time for Naturals to escape. None of his squad had made it. Days later, from cover, he witnessed Bull's execution. Exhausted, Thorn hadn't intervened as his comrade was ravaged by dogs. When Thorn regained consciousness, prone on the battlefield, pitiless stars pricked the sky. The Cons had exited the trap of felled trees. Their vehicles were gone. Their dead—Thorn's too—still rotted on the field, smashed pumpkins, goopy with flies.

He'd had a choice then: follow their tracks and be revenged, or remain in the forest and fight another day. He chose poorly. Add it to the list. The corpses had decided him—Bull, Matador, Tigre. The summer sun had risen quickly, and with it came crows. He just couldn't leave his comrades. Hating himself, gagging at their gastro stink, he rifled their parkas for food. And so he'd eaten, kept crows and vultures from the carrion, and undertook the undertaking.

Once started, there was no stopping. There were dead aplenty. Thorn toiled to sanctify the Natural's sanctuary. When his people fled, an exodus, tools were abandoned. He utilized them— shovel and pick—to gouge the graves. Thorn knew he should depart, but each task tied him tighter. And there was food to be had; not everything could be carried off by the refugees. Dried fish, smoked meat, dehydrated fruit—all served to fuel his fury. XCons, their hounds, and Chosen were easy targets to hate, but Thorn mostly loathed himself. And so he abided, the last elf in ELF Country.

As summer green faded to gold and September tinted towards sepia, he ranged far from his forest home, scouting the edges, pushing frontiers. He needed to know what was out there—friend or foe, or nothing at all?

ELF Country had been cleansed; he buried the dead, tamping earth with his spade. Fairy mounds now filled the woods, barrows for the fallen. Sentinel graves—there were many—he marked by planting spears. He made myths for himself, an audience of one. Someday the exiled elves would return—mothers, fathers, laughing kids with vines in their hair. His duty, once he'd slunk from revenge, was to caretake the encampment, stewarding the forest.

The nameless creek steamed in the cold of early morning, each night a bit longer than the one before. A lonely planet climbed a willow tree, companioning Thorn as he watched a small clearing. The shooter crouched in a bush with barely room to draw. An arrow was nocked, tipped for his purpose. Would a target emerge? Was it thirsty? There were tracks everywhere, a real warren.

From cover, ambush-ready, the sharp-eared Sentinel could hear his prey breathing. A twitch tugged his vision. There! Target acquired, he loosed!

Back broken by his blunted arrow, the rabbit thumped its defiance—anything but death!

No thing intervened, and soon the mammal was dead.

"Gaia, I am grateful." Thorn pouched the warm creature.

The rising sun gilded the clearing: willow, stream, and brambles utterly indifferent to the agony of harvest. The hunter, less so, scrubbed away his tracks and departed.

Thorn was on a reconnaissance, twenty miles northeast from his Bear River home. A crossroads bore a sign—Wildwood—a borderland of state forest, fallow fields, rolling hills, and ridge-tops with views of big water. There were streams and creeks aplenty. Mapless, he named them for his needs—Big Trout, Red Cedar, Sweet Berry.

At each farmstead and cabin he was duly diligent. The results never varied: there were no people here. Not that nature seemed to mind. Her skies—uncluttered by contrails, by conspiracies—were crowded instead with convoys of geese, flying low and carefree past the gunless blinds. Ducks, too, were on the wing, great noisy formations in numbers he'd never seen. Massive flocks of south-bound starlings murmured from the trees. Taking flight, they'd block out the sun, like passenger pigeons of old. Deer were everywhere, fat and sleek. Unshy, they commuted on roads, browsing kitchen gardens for groceries. Two summers of growth, and the green world was fast encroaching. Grape vines ticketed abandoned cars, leafy parking boots grounding them forever. Weeds exploited every crack. Roadways, undermined by roots, were buckling.

Thorn was equipped to travel, kitted for a long scout—probably his last before the snows. Early migrators—a great biomass of southing birds—hinted at a hard winter to come. He wore his gray Sentinel parka over many layers, and was well-shod with waterproof boots. His rucksack was stuffed with dried food and good gear—compass, knife, fire kit, first aid, bedroll, and bivvy tent. He carried a recurve bow, spare strings, and a quiver of carbon-shafted arrows. His game pouch held the rabbit. Thorn's stomach held nothing, and gurgled its complaint.

Thorn found a sheltered place, a pine wood with dry dead-fall and a crick nearby. He unshouldered his heavy pack and laid out cooking gear. He dipped the kettle full and stropped his knife. Removing a turve of loam, he kindled fire in the hollow earth. Soon, his sooty kettle was licked by flame.

Thorn thawed his hands, then busied himself with skinning the coney. His first incision was a circumference cut—belting the rabbit, top half and bottom. Careful not to prick the gut, he inserted strong fingers and stripped the creature, pants first, then sweater. Furless, the carcass steamed in sunlight. Its thermic ghost left the body, warming the air a fractioned degree. Yellow globs of fat were scraped into the boil. Heart, lungs, and liver followed as he scooped its cavity clean. The gourmand sectioned the critter, running green skewers through each portion. When the coals were just right, he set the meat to sizzle.

Waiting, Thorn scrubbed gore from his hands in the icy crick. He filled his canteen and forced himself to hydrate. Returning to camp, he tidied his pack, propped his weapons, and sat against a tree to monitor the meat. A bird whistled nearby—a vireo?—its trilling call welcoming the dawn. Its mate answered; all was well in their avian world. Thorn closed his eyes, and his thoughts walked away.

A minute passed, dripping grease hissing on the flames.

A subconscious fact—vireos had already migrated!—ran back in panic. *Threat!*

Thorn's bright eyes flashed open, fight-or-flight, ready to spring. He quickly scanned his perimeter, then repeated the scan more slowly. The Sentinel noted nothing, felt nothing. Each tree and bush looked exactly as before. He relaxed his threat posture and chastened the too-twitchy sentry—his traumatized self.

Tending the skewers, he felt the beam before he saw it. A laser, red-pointed, played upon his chest. He fought a feline fascination with the darting dot. Seeking the spotter, he saw no one.

Then a deep voice commanded from behind, "Don't move!"

Of course, there were two! His calculations grew complicated.

"Don't even think about it."

Thorn looked down at the laser scribing his heart. Stalling for time, he lifted his hands, seemingly supplicant. He heard forms moving about, in front and behind. He swiveled slowly and saw them. Tall men, both masked against infection, stalked towards him, rifles raised and steady.

One spoke to the other: "Doesn't look Viral."

They pincered Thorn between them.

"I see a bow, some arrows, one pack."

They halted, two dots tap-dancing on his torso. Thorn kept his hands high. The men were clad in green and brown, and they wore long gloves. Green medical masks covered their faces; only their eyes could be seen, bright with challenge in the morning light.

"You infected? Who's with you?"

Thorn offered nothing.

"Speak up, man! It's the last chance you'll get."

They sighted upon him, tightening their triggers.

Thorn watched his rabbit begin to burn.

The Sentinel shrugged, eyes welling suddenly. "I'm not infected. I'm alone."

Robert and Freddy

THE MEN WERE ROUGH but not cruel. They marched Thorn between them, hooded and blind. They confiscated his weapons and bound his hands. The last thing he saw was one of the men, the leaner one, sliding rabbit off the skewers, sealing hot chunks in a steamy pouch. That gesture of frugality had decided him— these were not Chosen, not Cons. Too capable for Hidden, to Thorn they were something new.

Blind, he tried mapping through his feet: deer path, two track, asphalt road. His captors thwarted his cartography with frequent halts, spinning him around, shaking his Etch-A-Sketch, erasing his line of march. Thorn could feel the sun though, mostly from his right—they were heading northeast.

The tall men didn't speak. Thorn intuited their kinship; he guessed brothers, maybe cousins? Simpaticos for sure. They reminded him of Sentinels, moving humbly through the land-scape. Their path meandered, marshy smells seeping through his hood. They made several stops on the way. He heard the clink of metal, the twang of wire, occasional grunts of satisfaction. Thorn's mind pictured a trap-line with baited sets, a harvest of critters, of calories. These two were on their home turf.

An hour passed, maybe more. Thorn's adrenaline evaporated with the dew, leaving him ravenous and wobbly beneath a wearying load. They marched for a while down a long, bumpy stretch of two track.

"Hold it."

Thorn stopped, and the trailing brother stepped closer. A sudden de-hooding. A cool lungful of air. Blind no more, his thirsty eyes gulped detail—a farm gate askew, an abandoned house on a rise, a rusting pole barn behind it, a deflated car in the drive, a scattering of trash, and not much else.

"Home sweet home," the heavy one said.

They avoided the gate, shunning obvious approach. Thorn, curious, followed his captors further up the path before turning off and slanting towards the house. One of the men stopped and brushed away their backtrack. Near the road, graven high on a beech tree, was a crudely hewn ᚱ.

Twice they pointed at trip wires; he mirrored their caution and high-footed over both. The farmhouse porch was trashed— old clothes, sodden cardboard, a stained mattress. The car's windows had been smashed, its interior beshat by nesting creatures. They went around the back. Storm cellar doors yawned wide open, the dangling latch pried off. Tools littered the yard, rusted and broken. The rakes were missing teeth.

Hands still tied, Thorn watched them descend the dank stairs—a false wall, a key in a lock, a steel hatch groaning open. The larger man disappeared through it while the other turned, beckoning. "Come on, friend, it's safer inside."

Thorn crouched through the hatch, bumping his pack on the casing. He stood upright in the interior as an oil lamp was lit. An unused command center, that's what it looked like. Dust covers were twitched aside, revealing shadowy gear and an amateur radio with solar panels and a bank of batteries. Thorn noted the wall-mounted gun rack, a pallet of MREs, another of water, a Honda generator with jerry cans of gas, propane tanks with attachments, a cooking area, a composting toilet, curtained cots, foul weather gear, and paired boots of sundry sizes.

"Let's see those hands."

Thorn, penitent, offered up his wrists. The younger one—his

beard more pepper than salt—stepped close, probing Thorn's eyes with a penlight. He grunted, flicked a blade, and the cords were cut. The larger man—beard mostly gray—was busy at the hatch, replacing false plywood. He shut the inner door, sealing them inside.

"You can drop your pack."

Thorn did so, propping it against a wall next to others. The younger man, thoughtful, lit a burner and set a skillet to heat. He dumped in Thorn's rabbit portions, pinched some salt, and drizzled oil. Savory smells soon flavored their bunker.

The older one, more warlike, tended their carbines, ejecting magazines, clearing actions, and ragging them down. Thorn's bow and quiver were safely stored too. The men unzipped their tactical jackets, pegging them near the hatch. Each man wore a pistol and a belted knife. Lowering their masks, they shared the same look—pale eyes, strong jaws, dark hair flecked with gray.

Thorn was nodded to a sofa; as their guest, he complied. Soon, a greasy plate was passed to him, along with a bottle of water and a fork. Starving, he waited. Permission granted, he began. The rabbit was fucking delicious.

Thorn mentally graced it and was soon sucking bones as the two men looked on. Belly full, plate empty, an apple was tossed his way. He caught it, savoring each crunchy calorie. The older man loomed on the couch across from him, while the younger stepped to a PVC pipe that passed through a hole in the ceiling. He put his eyes to the angle and slowly turned 360 degrees, periscoping their perimeter. Satisfied, the submariner nodded the all clear.

The big man began, "Look, whoever you are, we want you as an ally, which is why you're not dead."

Thorn annihilated his apple—core, stem, and seeds.

"Call me Robert," the older man continued. "Handsome over there is my baby brother, Freddy."

No one was smiling.

"My name is Thorn."

Nods all around, properly acquainted. The rabbit in his belly kick-started Thorn's manners. "How exactly can I help you guys?" he asked.

The two brothers kept quiet. Their shipping container, subterranean, fumed with kerosene. Freddy adjusted the ventilation, freshening the air.

"Well now," Robert replied, finally grinning, "that's just the kind of question we like."

A Gathering of Rangers

THORN, PEDALING ALL DAY in the rain, had been wet for miles. The saddlebags on his loaner bicycle were soaked. His hands were prunes, he was shivering, and his over-taxed muscles were mutinous. The prepper brothers, Robert and Freddy, had given him a mission and a map of the thirty-mile corridor between Indian River and the big bridge at Mackinaw City. The crosses on the sodden road atlas indicated a chain of cell phone towers, deaf and dumb since grid-down a year ago. Brush and logs were stacked under each tower. Thorn's task was to inspect these tinder piles, refreshing their fuel if necessary. They allowed their laborer a handsaw and an ax; the tools had blistered Thorn badly. The spitting rain gave the lie to his mission. He wondered if the brothers simply wanted him away.

"Stay on the roads," they warned, "don't approach buildings, or trespass across fields."

Robert tossed him an NHL stocking cap. "You're in prepper country now."

"Try not to get shot," was Freddy's advice.

Thorn sported the red and blue logo all day—"Rangers" was printed, diagonal, on his hat's shield.

"Where do we meet up?" Thorn asked.

"We've got a thing tonight in Indian River," Robert said, winking.

"Yeah," Freddy added, "you'll have to study the signs."

Both brothers were grinning as the Sentinel pedaled away.

The I-75 corridor proved deserted. Thorn, zig-zagging along the highway, hadn't seen a soul all day. Many of the towers sported nests—eagle and osprey—and Thorn thought he saw a sniper once, or maybe just a spotter? Either way, he was being watched. The nest of branches had been huge; he swore he saw a flash of lens.

Bicycling south towards Indian River, his dubious mission accomplished, Thorn inspected the MDOT signage for gas and lodging. Next to Best Western's icon, a small ᚱ was etched. He coasted down the off-ramp towards the abandoned building, logoed with an oversize crown. Sheltered from rain by its overhang, the Natural dismounted stiffly, shaking the precipitation from his Sentinel parka. He tried the glass door—locked. He shaded his vision and peered into the lobby—deserted, trashed, flooded. Without climate control, without custodians, the boxy temples of consumer culture had collapsed like a soggy house of cards.

There was no sign of Robert or Freddy. He stepped to the portico's edge and slaked his thirst with rainwater cupped from the deluge. Thorn stood behind the waterfall, a window made of rain, facing west. He found himself brimming over, again. Another pity party? Why did this keep happening? The young man flexed his sticky blisters. Shit was just too hard, and even when it wasn't, the survivor felt guilty. Since the slaughter, on rare moments when Thorn was warm and dry with food in his belly, when he caught himself enjoying a sunset or a well-made camp, the dead would rise up—accusatory ghosts amongst the geese.

Surprise, surprise, he was fucking hungry. There was no food, unless he found the brothers and their "thing" in Indian River. They'd confiscated his pack, his provisions, and his weapons too. Returning to their hideout was impossible; they'd blinded him again before setting him on the road with a borrowed bike and its basket of tools.

Shivering, Thorn looked around. He was freezing. Fuck those guys. He found a service door near an old butt-bucket for smokers. Another small R was etched into its lintel. This door was unlocked, and he stepped inside the darkened hallway.

"Hold it!" a voice ordered from the shadows. Thorn raised his hands, looking down. Sure as shit, a laser sight dotted his chest.

"Speak!" the same voice commanded.

Thorn shrugged; he was over it. "I'm a friend. Of Robert and Freddy?" Were those even their names? "I'm not infected. I'm not armed."

He looked down again. The red dot had disappeared.

"Ah, you'll be Rabbit then?" The voice sounded amused. "Won't they be surprised. Come along Thumper, follow me."

The sentry, by headlamp, escorted Thorn to the double doors of a conference room before disappearing to resume his post. Thorn cracked a door and peered inside. The room was dim. A dozen or so figures—men and women, multiracial—sat in the dark, barely illuminated by a lantern on low battery. They were gathered around an amateur radio. The older brother, Robert, sat in front of its microphone. A voice came through the speaker, digitally distorted. The LED lantern briefly flared. Light sprang from the shadows.

"—recent comms with the National Guard confirms your reporting. Fuel convoys, well-protected, are mustering at jump-off locations. We know of two for sure, Cadillac on M-131 and West Branch on I-75. There's been some confused reporting, but it appears that 131 is a Chosen operation, while 75 might be XCon controlled. Apparently these factions are no longer fighting each other, which is bad news for us. Questions? Over."

The room remained quiet.

Then Robert keyed the mic. "Walker, what about Camp Grayling? The Guard post straddles I-75. Will Colonel Dennis fight? If his Griffins can handle the XCons, we could focus on 131 and the Chosen. Over."

Some nods from the listeners, then the distorted voice replied, "Bad news again. The colonel confirmed that his soldiers will be dispersing. They can't hold Grayling, not against what's coming." The distorted voice then became bookish: "Demosthenes once wrote, *He who fights and runs away will live to fight another day.* Over."

The listeners responded with soft cursing and shaking heads.

"Damn it."

"On our own again."

"Come on, Colonel!"

"Time to take a stand."

Freddy noticed Thorn by the door and waved him in, muting him with a motion to his lips. Robert replied to Walker's bad news, "Roger. We'll do what we can. Any idea about timing? Over."

Thorn joined the conference and closed the door behind him. He noted a row of rifles against a wall and a pile of packs on a table. Robert's radio was powered by a battery-bank. Where did these people come from? The town had looked deserted. Water dripped from mildewed tiles; Thorn avoided the puddles and tried to blend in.

The speaker answered, voice still digitized: "Timing? My guess is imminent. A day or two tops. Those tanker-trucks are too valuable to sit idle for long. Prepare for action. Over."

More muttering. No one was satisfied with what they were hearing.

"Roger, imminent action—"

Robert briefly broke transmission, feeling the room's reluctance, then resumed "—Walker, if the Guard is falling back, maybe we should too? If Army can't stop 'em, what chance do we have? Over."

Static from the speaker, earth's atmosphere made audible.

Then Walker replied. His words bounced from antenna to antenna, a rainy relay of 300 miles or more. "What chance? Same as always, not a great one. But we know what happens in territory they control—slavery, rape, murder."

Sentinel Thorn recalled the night attack—the dogs, the slaughter of innocents, the loss of his squad, Bull's execution.

Walker's preaching continued, firming Thorn's resolve: "Downstate, we are fighting in the cities, pushing them hard. We're growing stronger. But the bridge is up to you, to the north. Virals want the U.P.—to plunder its resources, to infect its people, to spread contagion. This must not happen! Colonel Dennis assured me that you don't fight alone. A stand will be made at the Straits. You have allies. Your mission is to slow them down. Weaken them, confuse their plans, draw off their strength. You're Rangers, after all; it's what you do. Godspeed! Walker, out."

Robert keyed his confirmation, then powered down the radio. The room waited. Rain beat upon the blacked-out windows. The drips from the ceiling increased their tempo.

Freddy gave some quiet orders: "Elmer, Ed, relieve the lookouts."

Two bearded men—ex-military?—retrieved their rifles and left the room. Robert gestured at the map-strewn table, and the Rangers got themselves seated.

Relieved from sentry duty, a man and woman entered, racked their weapons, and joined them at the table. Thorn sat too. One of the women—older, with a no-nonsense look—fished batteries from a fanny pack. She tended the lantern, brightening the room. They were seated now, grim-looking, a dirty dozen.

Robert introduced Thorn by saying, "Everyone, this soggy specimen is Rabbit. We snared him, set him free, and yet he returned. Rabbit, say hello."

Thorn kept his face blank and nodded. Some cracked smiles as Robert jested, "And how did your mission go? I see you remain unskinned? Preppers have a taste for coney. I congratulate you on keeping your hide."

Thorn, a collegiate wrestler, was no stranger to hazing. Toothy grins circled the table like sharks.

"Rabbit here was tending the beacons. Did anyone see him today?"

The woman wearing the fanny pack said, "My granddaughter—remember Ella? She's ten—had him sighted at 200 yards. She radios me from the OP, 'Grammy, I've got a bicycle rider, pretty pathetic. Permission to put him out of his misery?'"

The table stifled their laughter.

"I asked Ella if he had a weapon, any markings. First she says no, then describes his hat."

The table looked his way; time for show and tell. Thorn pulled off the NHL cap. Wringing it out, he tossed it to Freddy. Little brother grinned and displayed the logo before tossing it back. "Keep it, Rabbit. You've earned it. You're a Ranger now—if you'll have us."

The gathering—a ragged remnant of before—settled down; maps were consulted, and planning commenced.

The Man in the Tower

IS ME.

Although tunnel, or bunker, would be more accurate, but precision and poetry don't often mix. These days, given the choice, I prefer poésie. Call it my midlife crisis—though with the drugs I'm developing, my "midlife" might be decades away.

My "tower" is entirely subterranean: a bio-safe silo constructed post-Covee, but pre-collapse, while Panzer prepared the variant, envenoming its STING. My only windows are digital, a video vista of flat screens kept working—for now—by my pale technocrats. Without STEM pipelines and the university system, their skill sets will die when they do. All the more incentive to discover *Fons Juventutis*. Which of my lab coats will play Ponce de León? Who will find for me the Fountain of Youth?

For thousands of years, the genii of genus *Homo* have sought the elixir vitae. It has hundreds of names, but they all translate the same—immortality. In Mesopotamia, Gilgamesh came close, but was foiled by a serpent. The emperors of China sipped and sampled but never quite succeeded. Ancient India had Amrita. Their Rigveda praised this concoction, though the secrets of Soma are now silent. In Japan, the moon god tried sharing the "waters-of-rejuvenation," but again, a serpent intervened. Something similar transpired in Eden. So many serpents! What do they signify?

On and on it goes, though I will try not to. But what is Big Pharma if not lab-coated alchemy? At its peak, before the world was stung, a trillion dollars a year was spent extending our allotted threescore years and ten.

Most fascinating to me, as I scroll through my downloaded internet, or page through stacks of scavenged books, is that the literal root of these historic elixirs were all plant-based.

Curiouser and curiouser!

Dear reader, did you know that pre-collapse, 40% of modern pharmaceuticals were derived from plants, including all twenty of the top selling prescriptions? When Panzer eventually unlocks our mausoleum of mortality—and we will!—I predict its key will be a green one.

Speaking of green, you'll never guess what my Aghori just brought me. A Greenie! A live one too! At least that's what Jones called her as he and McKenzie presented their catch to my camera. She's a fierce little thing, ferocious, even when shackled and sodden with rain. She was armed only with arrows, caught spying at the front gate. We're waiting on her blood work, but to me, this bright-eyed beauty looks like a new type, neither Viral nor Hidden. I can hardly wait for the results. My Aghori are interested as well. Somehow, she cloaked herself from their sensors, video and infrared. Panzer's surveillance simply hadn't seen her. Something to do with her electrical field? Apparently, she was caught by their crows.

Onward!

The chess board is northern Michigan. Panzer's pieces are in place, and I've made some big moves. I've held my nose and formed alliances—with Chosen, with Convicts. My white hand has signed contracts with red-eyed killers. I've bartered food from our plantations for fuel refined in Detroit. I've traded one of our mammoths—a plow-truck—for indentured servants, though of course their term of "service" will expire only when they do.

Do I trust my allies? Mustafa, the false prophet with his halo, an implant neurally linked to what's left of A-EYE? Certainly not.

Do I fear my enemies? I'd be a fool not to. We've decoded transmissions sent from "Walker," a resistance leader. His voice, unlike mine, is distorted, but if my guess is right he's a noble challenger from a well-respected family. Still, when combined with the XCons, our side is much stronger—knights and rooks against their scattering of pawns. Does that make Assassin McKenzie our queen then? After the regicide she pulled off—in the White House no less—I'm inclined to say yes.

I've made my opening moves, sending the mechanized might of XCons and Chosen—stiffened by my Aghori—against the rag-tag remnants of National Guard and Old Law. Michigan, my messy freshwater fief, will soon be mopped up. An evocative phrase, used recently by my top sergeant as we went over the battle-map together.

"Mopping up"—Jones pointed at the National Guard post in Grayling.

"Mopping up"—His tattooed finger stabbed Charlevoix, the scene of recent setbacks.

"Mopping up"—The big bridge to the Upper Peninsula, and O' Canada.

Grayling Army Airfield

DATE TIME GROUP: 232200RSEP21
LOCATION: Grayling Army Airfield

Colonel J. R. Dennis, Garrison Commander of what was left of Camp Grayling, stood alone in his control tower. The cold front had drizzled itself dry, and a foggy night had fallen. Generators hummed, the glow of electronics lighting his clean-shaven face as Dennis considered his options. None of them were good.

His Army Combat Uniform was fraying but clean. The unit insignia of the 125th Regiment was visible on his shoulder. A steward of history, he knew each component in its coat of arms. The griffin was for Michigan. Its eleven stars were earned in the Civil War—Vicksburg, Wilderness, Cold Harbor, Appomattox. The palm tree dated from the war against Spain. The 125th fought in the Great War as well—along the Marne, Oise-Aisne, and in the Argonne. Twenty years later, the regiment pushed Hitler's Wehrmacht out of the Rhineland. Since then the Griffs had deployed to Korea, Iraq, and most recently, Afghanistan.

The CO was a realist. There'd be no more ribbons, chevrons, nor streamers. Their deeds since collapse, delaying defeat, would die when they did. And their doom was upon them. The amateur radio calls had started coming in this morning. Local ham operators risked their safety to relay intelligence on the double-column that was belching their way.

Reportedly, the WESTERN FORCE had set out from Kalamazoo this morning in the rain. The operations map tracked its progress, straight north, utilizing the still-decent roadway of M-131.

By 1200 the WF had reached Grand Rapids.

By 1600 it was at Reed City.

The WF had entered Cadillac by nightfall, where they'd pre-cached supplies.

The last transmission described a reunion of forces and the commencement of refueling operations. Dennis had heard nothing since. He guessed the Chosen column would halt there till dawn. By noon tomorrow they'd be at Kalkaska, or beyond. Dennis feared his post at Camp Grayling would soon be outflanked.

His operations sergeant, CSM Amanda Taylor, had sketched the components of this column as it was described in the reports: Humvees, gun-trucks, towed weapons, tractor-trailers, school buses, and a biker gang acting as cavalry. At fifty vehicles, it was the biggest force they'd seen since collapse. More worrisome was its apparent discipline. This wasn't a rally of hooligan Raiders. Each ham operator was reporting the same: bikers were deployed as skirmishers and rearguards, the march-order of the column never varied, ambush precautions were taken at bridges and pinch-points. Unfortunately, someone with convoy experience—probably ex-military—was leading this thrust. As a disturbing side note, spotters reported the WF was shadowed by a huge cloud of crows.

Reporting on the EASTERN FORCE was similar. The EF sortied from Flint this morning. The column appeared to be run by XCons, not Chosen. Their progress up I-75 had been steadily logged by radio operators, observing in the rain.

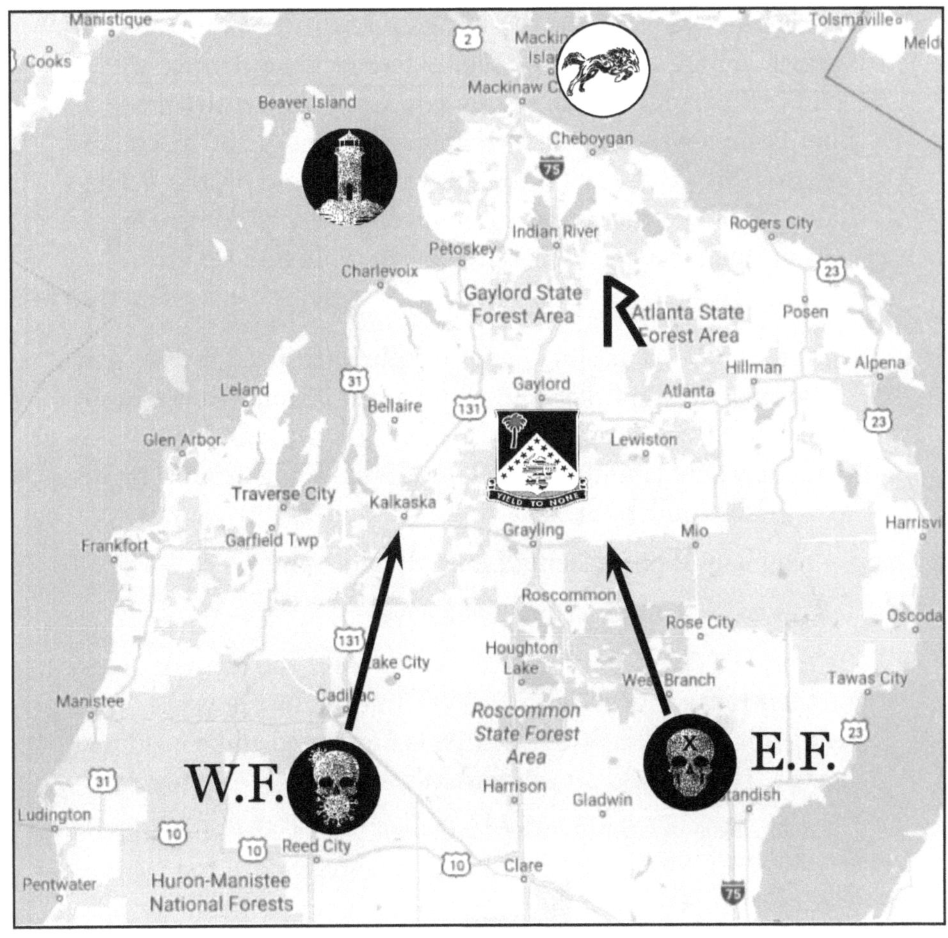

1200 at Saginaw.

1700 near Standish.

Similar in size, less organized, but with plenty of armory hardware, this column made West Branch by nightfall and was refueling. The EF was only two hours away, with no guarantee they'd wait for dawn.

The CO didn't like it, but it was time to give the final evacuation orders. If Grayling got caught in those pincers, the Michigan Guard, after a valiant fight, would cease to exist. It was time to save asses and assets by falling back and redeploying.

"Sergeant Major?" the colonel keyed his two-way radio. The sprawling base was just too big to defend. They'd already consolidated personnel and equipment at the Army Airfield. Colonel Dennis was in the control tower, the nexus of communications. His CSM responded, from somewhere on the tarmac below. Her Detroit accent came through the handset; Dennis had a thing for dialects, classifying hers as Inland North.

"Taylor here. Orders, Colonel?"

The CO didn't hesitate; they'd talked it through. Yes, they could make a stand here, slow down the XCons, inflict heavy losses. But that stand would be their last. He wasn't ready for that. He wanted another shot at these red-eyed bastards, on his terms, on ground of his choosing.

"Sergeant Major, execute Lima Alpha. Over."

"Yes sir. Executing Lima Alpha. Over."

"And Ms. Taylor, our birds need a new nest. Top off their tanks, fill their racks and redeploy to TVC. Inform the pilots they'll be flying blind and that Traverse City is unsecured and considered hostile. They should arm themselves accordingly. Dennis, out."

The Garrison Commander reviewed his checklist. It would be a busy night. By first light they needed to be gone. From Dennis' elevated vantage point, he observed the lights of the motor pool flicker on, the hangar doors beginning to open. Engines were starting up as soldiers were rousted prematurely from their racks. The Spoons were heating up some chow. What remained of the airfield's fuel-farm was siphoned into gas tanks and portable drums. Whether beans, bullets, or Band-Aids—nothing useful would be left behind for the Spreaders.

Colonel Dennis, amateur historian, tasked himself with documenting collapse—at least in Michigan. Dennis had an inkling the 125th would not be returning; he packed up his notebooks, news clippings, and hand-drawn maps. Trained as a Signal Officer, he specialized in languages and intelligence gathering. He'd made a start on the narrative already, fashioning symbols for his different sources—a coat of arms for the Griffs, a runic ᚱ for Rangers, and the corporate double tower for Panzer and its reclusive CEO, the war criminal Dr. Schark.

In quieter moments he tried to get it all down, weaving the disparate POVs into a unified whole. This night, the 23rd of September, was not one of those moments. Frustrated, the would-be writer sighed, focusing instead on his duties. In the red light of the tower he checkmarked names and frequencies as he issued orders: his pilots and their call signs; Captain Young's team, who'd swapped their Humvee for a boat; the prepper group, Rangers, led by two brothers; and the leader of mid-Michigan's resistance, a mysterious pastor with the war-name "Walker."

All his calls were down-chain, orders for subordinates. He had superiors once, but one by one those frequencies stopped responding. Dennis missed taking orders, being a mere link in the DOD chain. He had faith there were still units out there. He believed that somewhere the center still held, though it sure as shit wasn't here. The code phrase, prepared in advance, for this final round of calls was Lima Alpha. The Last Alliance. Grim in his tower, the colonel shook his head. *It very well could be. God save us all.*

Amanda Taylor consulted her own list, mustering Grayling's remaining vehicles into a march-column. She needed to secure their prisoners for relocation, including a high value female, a Viral nicknamed Lizard. The sergeant major supervised the EOD specialists as they mined the approach road. The sappers would destroy all stores, including fuel and ammo, that couldn't be transported with them. The Combat Support Hospital was almost ready to roll. Taylor scanned a checklist of their supplies: surgical equipment, generators, quarantine tents, experimental drugs against Covee's variant and its cytokine sting.

Squads were mustering by their vehicles and checking each other's equipment. Tonight the sergeant major insisted on full battle-rattle. The Griffins groaned as they loaded each other with fifty pounds of gear: flak vest, Kevlar helmet, MOPP, medical pouch, MREs, water, ammunition, weapons.

CSM Taylor barked as she made her rounds: "Where's your MOPP bag, soldier?"

"Get that NBC suit squared away!"

"Beat feet Joes! Find your vehicles!"

"Have your masks ready!"

"We're fighting Virals! Their breath'll kill you quick as a bullet!"

Sergeant Major Taylor patrolled the tarmac. The regiment, what was left of it, was astir. Weapons were being checked, and the fug of fuel hung heavy in the damp night air. The bomb techs were fusing their mines, troops were moving through the chow line, and the column was forming up.

She looked up at the flickering control tower as Colonel Dennis made his final calls. The electronics strobed blue when he used Palantir, the satellite phone; It pulsed green when he operated MARS—the Military Auxiliary Radio System—connecting radio operators and the prepper network on the ground.

Thank God for those guys, Taylor thought for the thousandth time. Maligned and oh so mockable when the lights were on, they'd understood SHTF better than the authorities. When the Shit Hit The Fan for real, they were prepared—better than most—for the grid-down Armageddon that ensued. She hoped to meet them someday. Taylor was dozing on her feet, beginning to drift.

She'd love to see them recognized for valor. Watch the colonel distribute medals while a marching band played and flags fluttered.

The improbable scene was shaken from her sleep-deprived

skull by the thunder of afterburners. The rag-tag regiment looked up, cheering as the tarmac trembled. Their beloved birds were leaving the nest, shoved aloft by 30,000 pounds of thrust from turbofan engines.

They streaked away, winging west through the night, off to find a safer roost. The clouds were lifting and a low moon sank. Taylor watched till their engine glow was out of sight.

"Keep the greasy side down, boys. Till we meet again."

At The Bridge

TOM DOYLE KEYED THE MIC with thick fingers. One eye was on his gauges—RPMs, rudder-indicator, fuel—the other on the approaching bridge, its two towers tipped with cloud. "*Nodin*, this is *Mary*. Cap'n Diana you see that plane? Your 11 o'clock? Over."

Doyle led a screening force of seven islander boats. The passenger ferry, *Emerald Isle*, now *Nodin*—Anishinaabemowin for wind—followed close behind. The Coast Guard Response Boat patrolled their perimeter as an osprey flew ahead. It was a dreary day of drizzle; a cold front had blown through. Two nights ago, back on Beaver Island, they battled the dockside fire. The Army captain—Frank Young, a civilian fire chief—called it arson. Yesterday they readied their squadron, rejected most of the volunteers, and stowed gear and provisions. This morning they'd thrown lines and, three-times-three, the up-armored ships had dieseled away, heading eastward in the rain. Would they return unscathed? Doubtful. Uninfected? Doubtful again. Did Doyle care? He didn't think so, least not for his own skin. Doyle owed a debt—to a ghost. Keith Two-Crow, from his martyr's grave on Kilty's Hill, demanded action. Protect the island. Protect the people.

Sentinel Diana, the squadron's licensed mariner, responded to Doyle's question: "*Mary, Nodin*. Affirmative, looks like a Cessna. Over."

Doyle barked at his deckhand, tossing O'Donnell the binos. His moody man glassed the single-engine plane, cupping lens-

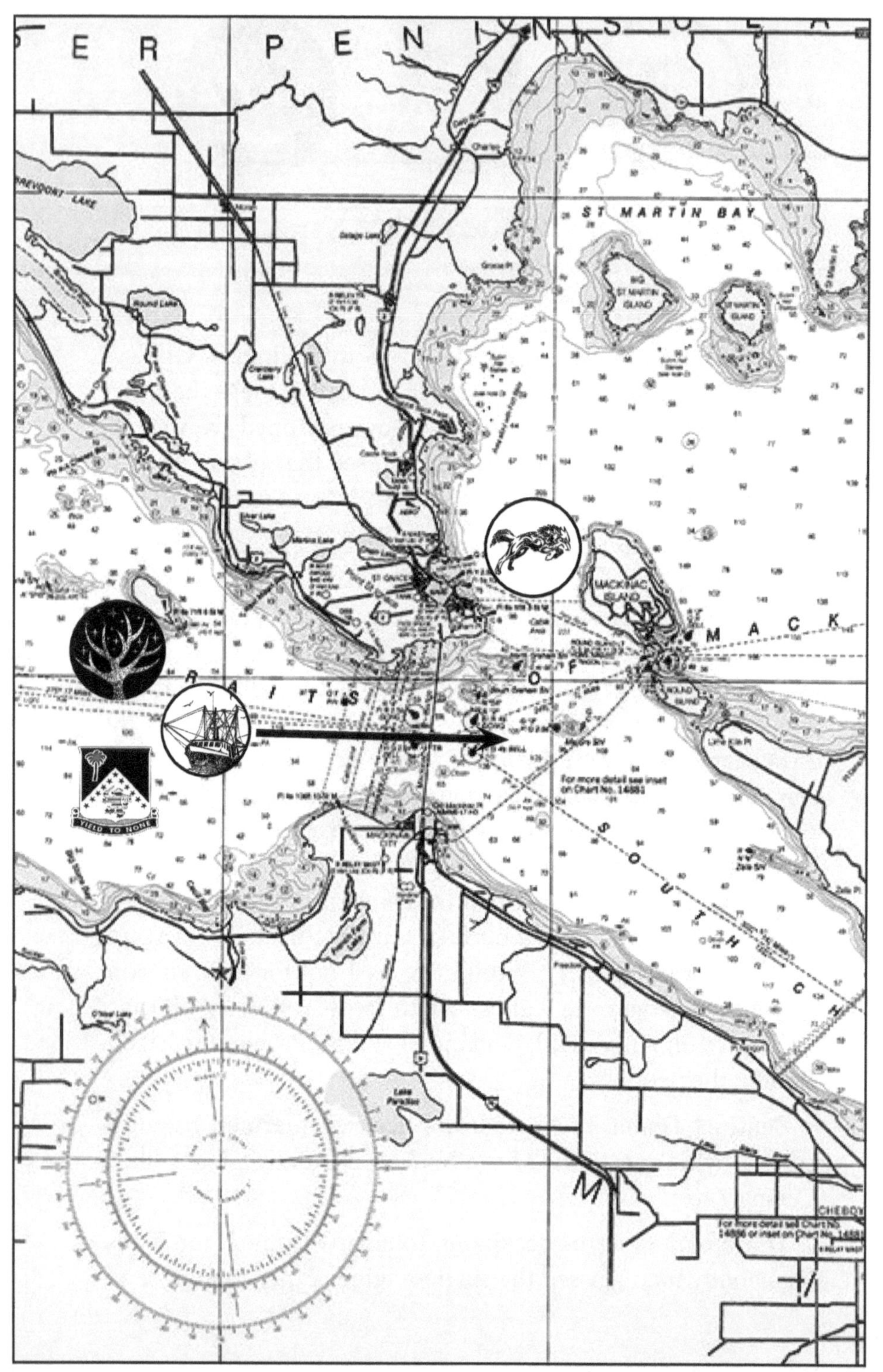
ER PENINS
PREVOOST LAKE
ST MARTIN BAY
BIG ST MARTIN ISLAND
ST MARTIN ISLAND
Round Lake
MACKINAC ISLAND
M A C K
O F
S T R A I T S
ROUND ISLAND
For more detail see inset on Chart No. 14881
MACKINAW CITY
S O U T H
YIELD TO NONE
Lake Paradise
M
CHEBOY
For more detail see Chart No. 14886 or inset on Chart No. 14882

es against the rain. Many eyes watched—some through gun-sights—as the bogey banked low and overflew their formation, diving at *Nodin*. The pilot's window opened and an object—bomb? Grenade?—parachuted ominously towards the ferry's deck.

O'Donnell demanded permission from Doyle: "Can I shoot that fucker down?" Every boat crew was asking the same, fingers itching for triggers. But Doyle stayed silent.

The package hit the ferry—bullseye!—but no explosion followed. Diana radioed her order: "Hold your fire! Hold your fire!"

Red-bearded Brian perched in *Nodin's* wheelhouse while also flying CAP for the squadron. The shaman gave Diana a chip-toothed smile as her ELF crew inspected the unexploded ordinance on deck. The osprey's eyes—eight times sharper than his blues—ID'd the wolf painted on the Cessna's fuselage. The bogey was no bandit, but a wolf-headed friendly. The ELF missileers stood down. Diana thumbed the PTT, reporting on the parachute-package, "It's not a bomb. I repeat, not a bomb."

The brown and white box—*Murdick's*—was cautiously opened, its contents sampled by smiling Sentinels. Diana read the inscription, wryly broadcasting to the fleet: "It says, 'Welcome fudgies! What took you trolls so long?'"

O'Donnell scowled beneath the binoculars. "I see it now, Cap'n. A mangy wolf, just like their fuckin' flag, the one from the beach on Garden."

Doyle's RPMs were revving, aircraft being his particular nightmare. "Bastard's lucky we don't shoot his furry ass down." When the variant started stinging, Beaver's airspace had been loud with their whine. Desperate, flying grossly overloaded, the pilots—probably infected—sought sanctuary for themselves and their families. The island's two airstrips, its grassy fields, and many roadways were barricaded. Planes had crashed trying. Mangled bodies, plausibly Viral, were left to rot. They'd swollen in the summer sun of Year 1. Still seat-belted, they eventually ruptured. For all of Y1 Doyle lived in constant fear of Cessna scouts, till eventually, just like the boats—RIP—they simply stopped coming.

The Howler pilot, showboating for the new arrivals, flew beneath the bridge before banking left, guiding the Beaver boats toward St. Ignace and its sheltered harbor. Doyle, cursing in the vanguard, followed reluctantly. His da—a crusty Irish fisherman—claimed he'd seen an Air Force bomber, a B-47, once do the same. The pilot, a combat veteran named Lappo, of course was court-martialed, losing his wings. Doyle wished for the Stratojet's cannons and 25,000-pound payload of bombs.

Tom had fished these waters, man and boy; he knew its currents and the landmarked shore. Doyle scanned it now. Wind turbines along the Straits had been stilled; could they be restarted? Harnessed somehow for energy? The cell towers stood sentry, unblinking in the murk. The two pump stations for the oil pipeline—Line 5—appeared intact, unmolested on both shores.

Doyle observed his sonar display, their depth approaching 300 feet. He could see the ancient pipeline snaking along the bottom. Was there petroleum in it? Would it ever flow again? Could it somehow be tapped, then refined? Dwindling diesel stocks were ever on his mind. He also marked huge clouds of fish feasting in the confluence of current. Two years without gillnets, without charter boats, and fish stocks were booming.

O'Donnell stepped in from wet weather. Dripping, the deckhand nodded at the biomass on the monitor. "Shoulda' brought our gear, Cap'n. Imagine the haul."

Doyle grumbled agreement, his pitch matching his motor—both needles pointed red. He'd stripped *Mary* of her nets, cordage, and rollers months ago. The other captains, reluctantly, had done the same. They were men-o'-war now, and had been since collapse. Diesel, being precious, was hoarded for defense.

Captain Diana had boosted the Beaver fleet's armament. Back in St. James, during the work-up for deployment, Doyle's captains were surprised by carrying parties of Naturals. The unsmiling porters—oathbound to Gaia and Her Green New Deal— were relieved to be rid of the modern munitions they toted.

In the chaos of collapse, gangs of Spreaders looted state armories, committing mass murder with taxpayer weapons. Charlevoix's Chosen stashed some of this DOD arsenal aboard the ferry, the forbidden firearms unwittingly hijacked by Diana's ELF commandos.

"You Nats sure you don't wanna keep some of this stuff?" Doyle had asked.

The porters only shook their heads, flinching from the firepower they handed carefully aboard. Islander boat crews, wide-eyed, had accepted Squad Automatic Weapons, boxes of 5.56 ammunition, canisters of grenades, and assorted small arms.

The town now came into view. Doyle thumbed his radio. "All boats, keep your eyes open. We're headed into Ignace. Gonna tie up. No visitors. Everyone stays aboard till we see what's what. Doyle, out."

"—Doyle, out."

Specialist Cruz, at the helm of the Response Boat, was itching for intel. His shipmates, Captain Young and Sergeant Booker, had been glassing steadily since they'd entered the Straits— shoreline, bridge, the Cessna, other boats. "Anything, Captain?"

His CO shook his head; Young's flapping mustache was way out of regs.

"Booker, what about you?"

The likeable Detroiter, family man from before, indicated negative as well.

Cruz channeled the thoughts of all nine boat-crews, saying, "Sir, I don't like this. Aren't there forces here? A mustering?

Whole place looks abandoned. What exactly are we doing?"

"Steady, Specialist. Did you expect Patton's Third Army?" Young took a break from the binoculars, rubbing bleary eyes. "If there's units here—Howler, Old Law, or otherwise—then I'm glad they're hiding. Not much good out in the open, in this rain. Who knows what's coming, or who the hell might be watching."

Young relieved his man at the wheel, handing him the binos. "Take a gander, Mr. Cruz."

He admitted that Cruz, his medic, had a point. The empty bridge, the desolate shore, were indeed a letdown. Frank had been half-hoping for Patton too. Add it to the list. Young increased RPMs, circling the task force. The Response Boat's 1,650 horses were his to command. Young could get used to this nautical life, the liberation from roads, from the fear of IED-ambush and fiery death.

The two days they spent tied up in St. James had been put to good use. Captain Doyle, the island's top fisherman, had lent them his mechanic. Mr. O'Donnell, dour like his captain, had come aboard with his tool chest and single-syllable vocabulary.

Utilizing wrenches and voltmeters, fucks and cunts, in an hour of cursing the man upgraded their boat. The electronics were now working, including radar and the FLIR. Forward-Looking-Infra-Red might come in handy; Young would rather have it than not.

Earlier this morning, before throwing lines, each vessel had girded for battle. The Coast Guard Response Boat sported two gun-mounts. Booker and Cruz gruntingly installed a pair of M2 .50s. The machine guns bulged beneath their weather-covers, bow and stern, lumpy with lethality.

Young's men debated their ammunition options. Cruz lobbied for API, armor-piercing-incendiary, Booker for APIT. He anticipated a night fight, arguing that tracer rounds would help guide their gunnery. The decision became unanimous once they uncovered the boxes of SLAP—saboted light armor penetrator ammunition—the Army's favorite. Both fifties would begin any firing with that.

"Hang on, gentlemen!" Young opened the throttle, letting the horses run. The RB-M handled beautifully. The three Army ground-pounders braced themselves, fighting down smiles as their eager craft leapt forward. The drizzly Straits were flat calm as they scribed their circle around the convoy.

"—Doyle, out."

Nodin's wheelhouse maintained nautical discipline. Captain Diana had the conn, Sentinel lookouts were posted on both bridge-wings, and a runner was standing by for orders. The Canadian mariner—no stranger to the shifting Straits—monitored depth, course, gauges, and radar.

Leaving Beaver Island, she'd organized working parties, making sure every hand was gainfully employed. Elena, her executive officer, supervised commando teams on the main deck. Nearly two dozen Sentinels were splicing lines and wielding paintbrushes under the dubious shelter of the ferry's dripping overhang.

An older man—war-named Fletcher—was inspecting arrows: the warship's Gaia-guided missiles. Fletcher filled quivers and sharpened broadheads, rejecting imperfect shafts or too-tattered fins.

Another Sentinel—scar-faced, Lily—utilized a rasp and file to keen their stainless spearheads. Many tips had been blooded in previous battles.

The ferry's officers, Diana and Elena, had purged *Nodin* of modern firearms. The arsenal-looted weaponry of the Chosen—anathema to purists—was redistributed to Doyle's trigger-happy captains instead.

But every faith has exceptions. A rack of parkas was plugged in and charging, powered by petroleum—Gaia forgive! The paint cans—forgive!—were DOD as well, scrounged by Dr. Chow from the same defunct defense contractor south of Charlevoix.

Beaver Island's kayaks had been collected, their collage of colors painted black. The little boats—once rented to tourists—were repurposed for night assault, their stealthy coating supposedly invisible to thermal and infrared sensors.

Mukwa and Sparrow were working together. They'd been squadmates in ELF Country till XCons drove them out. The bear-sized man was speckled with paint.

"Hold it still, you big oaf!" Sparrow pecked at him. "We missed a whole section on that one." Mukwa huffed, rotating the little boat back towards her brush. Sparrow snapped at his annoyance, "You couldn't wait to get off-island, see some action, give Hawk some space. Now she's flown, you get your wish, and it's more fucking moping?"

The big man opened his trap, then shut it with a clack of canines. His lacerated face still burned. When Sparrow blacked out the last of the color, Mukwa hauled the assault craft to the drying rack, fetching back a yellow one. Sparrow gave the spattered man a look.

That morning she'd witnessed the farewell between foster siblings at the St. James ferry dock. Little Miin had gripped both his paws, pulling him down till they were forehead to forehead. Miinan whispered something, but Mukwa was distracted. Sparrow knew he was looking for Hawk. They all were—the extremist hadn't shown, and would miss the ship's movement.

The tiny Sentinel dipped her brush in black and began anew.

Diana had tasked Dr. Chow—medical officer and fellow Natural—with setting up a sick bay on *Nodin*. The tall woman had handed him a parcel, saying, "Miin tells me this is medicine, I'll leave it with you." Doc Newsome and his two island nurses were allowed to join their crew as well. All others, Natural or islander, were turned away. Some of the rejected grumbled about "extremists" and "Sentinel pride."

Chow and Newsome—Michigan alums, though decades apart—readied their operating tables. They sterilized equipment, laying out doses of morphine, antibiotics, and topical anesthetic. The registered nurses—Mathew and Sean, nervous islanders—prepared bandages and saline drips.

"Treated many gunshot wounds, Doctor Chow?"

The Natural, once the suit-wearing president of the region's hospitals, had treated very few. Chow shook his head. Doc Newsome nodded and said, "Well, Beaver can be a strange place. I've done plenty." Newsome then surveyed their surgery, depressed at its simplicity. "This could get ugly."

Chow visualized a Civil War scene. A few wounded, and this compartment could turn garish. He felt like puking.

Newsome was frowning. "Sean, how are you guys doing?"

The RN looked a bit green. "Almost ready, doctor."

"Mathew, better rig up some lighting. Scrounge us more lanterns with fresh batteries."

Their sick bay would have electricity only if Diana could keep *Nodin's* generators going.

"Sean, find us a mop bucket and some bleach, and maybe some sand? It's gonna get slippery in here." Newsome brought forth an old black bag. "Stuff's almost vintage." He coaxed the reluctant zipper open and, one by one, removed the bag's contents, bathing its toothy tools in iodine solution—bone saws, trephines, retractors, gougers, lancets.

Chow looked it over. Nausea stirred his guts. He could already hear the screams, could smell the frictious heat of bone dust. This was not going to be pretty.

"—Doyle, out."

Their radio scanner found the frequency of the incoming

Beaver boats. The men and women in the Wawatam Lighthouse looked to Baptiste. Channeling his Gallic grandfathers, the stoic voyageur hid his relief—*they came!*—and gave the merest nod, confirming, "That's them."

His three large canoes had shoved off from Garden Island—with Autumn and Loon aboard—well before Doyle and Diana finished assembling their fleet. Until this moment, he hadn't been sure they'd come. Not at all.

One of the Howlers aimed binoculars southwest, beyond the big bridge. At fifty-two feet, the St. Ignace tower commanded a horizon-line of ten miles, farther if the ship was tall. The cold front's cloud and drizzle reduced this range considerably. After a minute, the lookout gave a wolf whistle and said, "I've got 'em."

They followed his pointing. "Looks like Sheila found 'em too." The tower watched her Cessna dip its wings and fly under the bridge. Every lookout was counting. Their arithmetic agreed—seven fishing boats, one red and white Coastie, plus the Beaver Island ferry. Despite the flotilla, their spirits sank. It was not enough, not nearly enough.

"Raise the flag!" Baptiste rallied them. A woman stepped out of the fumy lantern room onto the foggy catwalk to handle the halyard. Soon, a painted wolf ran above the harbor, above the Straits. Down at the docks, the Howler's ready-boat plumed exhaust as its crew responded to the signal hoist. Lines were thrown and the steel craft slipped its berth, steaming past the breakwater to intercept—and welcome—the new arrivals.

Baptiste would have to warn the newcomers off the radio. Too many ears were listening. The Virals were coming. Chosen scouts, or worse, were probably spying already. Had their canoe diplomacy paid off?

Beaver Island mustered nine vessels, maybe a hundred fighters? Better than nothing, which is what most settlements, stretched too thin, had sent. The muscular Métis disguised his disappointment. Be grateful—*Dieu merci*—they'd come at all.

But the voyageur didn't like how close they'd approached undetected—unacceptable. Of course, weather was a factor and surely would be again. But they'd need to see farther. Baptiste looked up at the running wolf and considered his options.

Three Fires: The White Bear

MUKWA, BARE CHESTED, stood at *Nodin's* gangplank. They were tied up at the St. Ignace Marina. Night had fallen, and various intentions clashed in his brain—*Should I stay or should I go?*

The kayaks were all coated, work parties dismissed. Henpecked by Sparrow, he'd clawed off his spattered shirt, black paint speckling his hide. It was the only shirt he had; of course he'd forgotten his duffel back on Beaver. Should he go ashore? Yes, he'd be granted liberty, but not from himself. The ferry's gangplank was intimidating, a bridge between worlds. Was he ready to explore something new? Or hunker down instead, lick his wounds, saving his strength for a possible fight tomorrow? His fucking face still burned, and the sticky paint was itchy as hell.

Back on Beaver, he'd said goodbye to Miin. Blueberry—his sister from another mister—was staying behind with Samantha and the noncombatants of the Naturals. Muck had been moping around St. James Harbor—still reeking of smoke from the fire—hoping for Nighthawk, thinking she'd come to say farewell at least. Miin, delivering a batch of medicine, found him instead. Little sis pulled him down, forehead to forehead, the siblings' quiet exchange.

"I'm sorry, big brother. I know you wish she was here."

"It's OK. I'm OK. Just take care of our *nookomis*."

"Samantha? Yeah right, but I'll try."

"And sis, watch out for these islanders. Stranger things—"

"I know, I will. You watch out too."

Then Mukwa had felt a tingle of energy, of protection. Miin's parting green gift? He'd caught a whiff of Cranberry Bog.

Doyle's fishermen, stowing gear, began a bawdy song. The siblings finished their farewell and Miin bicycled away. Muck's heart was a stone, a fucking boulder. He focused on the positive, remembering their little sleepover, though his dreams had been haunted ever since—a fortress afire, an undead army, and Nighthawk, shackled, flightless in the rain. In spite of everything, whether Hawk knew it or not, Mukwa knew he was needed.

Fuck it, he'd decided, he was going ashore. Elena and Diana were already gone; Sparrow said the ELF leaders had a rendezvous with a woman, some water-protector from Manitoulin. Scratching his painted pelt, Muck walked the plank, feeling his way in the dark. Crossing the parking lot, depressed and distracted, he was almost bowled over by a muffled motorcycle driven by a werewolf.

Mukwa growled, hackles up: "The FUCK man?"

The Harley fishtailed, spraying Mukwa with puddled rain and gravel. The bear roared his challenge, ursine senses flooded with detail—sights, sounds, smells—everything sharpened. The biker dismounted, flashing a feral smile. Muck promptly shut the fuck up, dropping his dukes. Dude had golden fucking eyes.

After a long minute, muzzle to muzzle, they reluctantly bumped fists, sizing each other up as likely equals. No time now for measuring dicks. Didn't Captain Diana say they had a common enemy? He hoped so. Mukwa's rage suddenly flared, but not at this dude. Diving-Duck, Squirrel, Matador, Tigre—Mukwa fucking hated Virals.

"Name's Shaggy Wolf. I'm Lakota, a Howler. I ride with the SIS. *Haú khólá!*"

"I'm Mukwa, Beaver Island." He tried the new language: "*Haú kĥolá?*"

Shaggy nodded at the stitches. "Spreader?"

Mukwa shook his blunt head. "Girlfriend. Ex-girlfriend I guess."

The wolfman let out a whistle but held his tongue. "Smoke?"

Mukwa patted his pockets; he was out.

"Nah, man, it's on me." Shaggy loaded a wooden bowl—scents of tobacco and canna—then sifted *semaa* before passing his pipe to the big man.

Mukwa looked back at the ferry. No Sentinels, no cops. He took a toke—why fuckin' not? Diana could throw his ass in the brig, what the fuck did he care? The two warriors, battle imminent, smoked together, sharing a moment of peace. Mukwa inspected Shaggy's rig; he itched seeing a scabbarded rifle. It looked like an M4, reminding him of Keith's. He swallowed the lump in his throat, then asked gruffly, "You SIS guys open carry?"

"Damn right." Shaggy patted the carbine's sheath, dozens of tallies etched the leather.

"Teach me?" Mukwa didn't trust his own voice. "I had an uncle, Keith Two-Crow, Vietnam vet." He coughed away a quaver, adding, "We never had a chance to practice."

"Uncle Crow, huh?" Shaggy's golden eyes glinted in the dark. "Sure man, I'll show you. I'm a vet too. Hop the fuck on. Let's go."

And away they went. They roared out from town, riding High Street to the fairground where the football field was crowded with campfires, a gathering of warriors. Shaggy braked the bike, and they took in the scene. "*Oyate*, The People," Shaggy said, nodding. "Lakota means 'allies,' or 'friends.'" To Mukwa it sounded like *La-kho-ta*. The biker continued, "We're from all over, man. Defending our families, our community, from the

Spreaders—colonizers, slavers, fuckin' *wasicu*."

Scattered drumming could be heard from the encampment—the heartbeat of The People. Tethered horses nickered from the paddock. Motorcycles from various clubs were parked on the pavement—Redrum Nomads, Reguladores, Warriors, RedSpirit Women. A battery-powered boombox thumped an anthem for the gang of riders smoking there. Mukwa knew the tune, "Electric Pow Wow Drum." Through his cannabis calm, he smiled. Fuck yeah.

He answered his new friend, "That's why I'm here too. For my sister, my gran, our island."

"Cool." Shaggy saw the big man eyeing his rifle again. "Let's have a sweat first, meet some of the guys. Welcome you properly to our group."

And they did, for hours. The starry night was a long one, and for Mukwa, a rebirth. His mockable nickname, Muck, and shame about his uncertain ancestry, were both banished. Renamed in the sweat ceremony, he was *Waabi-Mukwa* now, White Bear, Wabi Muk.

Big Ben, one of the elders, said it best: "It's not the blood that matters, Mukwa, but the heart. Welcome brother." Without tobacco to gift, Mukwa tried imparting some of Miin's protection instead: her bubble, a green shield for his new warrior friends.

In just one night with these men—Howlers, bikers, and veterans—something essential clicked. He was a Sentinel no longer, perhaps never was. He remembered the ELF brothers, Miguel and Tomas—"Matador" and "Tigre"—their endless teasing of "El Oso." Much had changed with the deaths of his friends. And then Nighthawk flew away—from him, from her Sentinel sisters, and the whole island too. Mukwa's bond with her, and his stupid heart, were both broken. Since then, he'd been lonely, he'd been lost. During the lodge ceremony—sage and smoke, sweat and steam—he felt less so. There were good people gathered here. Most were resigned to death, and had been since collapse. Their end was near. With few days remaining, why not seek fellowship?

Mukwa's bare chest steamed in the predawn air. His furnace was stoked from the sweat lodge, and the big man felt no chill. The cold front had rolled away in the night, pulling the cloud cover with it. Exposed, the Earth lay naked under glittering stars. The warrior felt a calm settle on his shoulders, in his belly, and between his eyes. A bright star was rising over the Straits—part of a backwards question mark? A symbolic start to their uncertain day?

A thin, red line rimmed the east. Mukwa looked around him. Tipis and tents, wigwams and campers mushroomed on the St. Ignace fairground. This dawn, this day, might be the last for many who gathered here. So be it. Fresh from the sweat lodge, he'd found his center, at least for now.

The frosty field, pre-sunrise, winked with campfires, embers burning low. The lodge-flap opened behind him and a shorter, older man stepped out, sweat dripping from braids that hung thin and gray. His sagging chest bore markings: a faded Airborne tattoo—*Death From Above*—and his motorcycle club: the badge and pistols of the Reguladores. Standing with Mukwa, sage-scented, Big Ben contemplated the smoldering fires of his people.

Present in the past, the braided elder pictured the valley of Little Bighorn, 1876, dawn of the Greasy Grass Battle. In one rusty camper could be the Hunkpapa and Sitting Bull. In that cluster of trailers over there could be Crazy Horse and his Oglala. Female laughter from a glowing lodge might be Pretty Nose and Moving Robe Woman—Arapaho and Sioux, united against uniting with the States.

Elevated on their hillside, Mukwa and the elder watched the Straits brighten with the dawn. Mentally, Big Ben swapped the approaching Virals for Yellow-Hair's 7th Cavalry, the ancestral enemy—Custer and his troopers, blue-eyed and blue-coated.

Mukwa saw differently—red-eyed slavers, Chosen sociopaths, and gas-guzzling gun-trucks.

The flap opened again, portal between worlds. Waabi-Mukwa scented hot stones and cannabis as a wiry man ducked through. Dark-skinned and dreadlocked, Shaggy Wolf punched him hard on the shoulder. Mukwa faked a grimace, coaxing a grin from his new friend. In their long night of tale-telling, this Shaggy character had shared a few. The mixed-race man did an Army tour in Kandahar before being discharged on a medical. He told how his squad had counted bodies once after a drone strike, or tried to. The bug-splat count was at least a dozen. The bride and groom, local Pashtuns, had been wearing their best. Uninvited, the MQ-1 Predator and its plus-one—a hellfire missile—had crashed their wedding by mistake.

Post traumatic, Shaggy had gone months without sleep, collecting Article 15s and psychiatric prescriptions. He was discharged—Other than Honorable—after teasing buddies with a live grenade. "Along with some other shit," the Two Spirit said with a wink as Shaggy's voice and manner shifted. "You know how the Army is, big man. If they don't ask, I won't tell."

In the tent, Mukwa had seen a flash of Shaggy's second spirit—a womanly one. Beneath his new friend's masculine mask was a sassy female alpha for sure. Discharged, disgraced, and confused, Shaggy had returned to his reservation with invisible wounds. When Covee's variant started stinging he enlisted with the biker gang, Nomads, leaving the Dakotas in the dust.

"There's no one left there, Mukwa," Shaggy shared in their lodge last night. "The Black Hills are empty again. *Pahá Sápa*—the heart of everything, the womb for all animals—is quiet, just wind."

Big Ben, their elder, had nodded sagely, saying, "Strong medicine." Shaggy, irreverent, broke wind with an armpit fart, lolling his red tongue, Wile E. Coyote. The stern-faced warriors cracked up as the whole lodge started farting.

Night over, new day beginning, the three men shaded their eyes from the sunrise glare off the Straits. Despite wild rumors, there was no sign yet of the enemy.

"Gonna be a day today, big man! You ready to rock and roll?" Shaggy nudged his super-sized friend. The White Bear nodded. Mukwa's face was striped with eyeblack—part linebacker, part Two-Crow. The mask helped him feel fierce. Sentinel no longer, he was swapping his spear for an assault rifle. The bridge defenders had set up some targets, and a percussion of plinking had already begun.

Mukwa grinned at his new comrades, Big Ben and Shaggy Wolf. "Hooah!"

Shaggy flashed his canines in response. "Time to send some rounds downrange!"

Big Ben gave Waabi-Mukwa a push. Still high from the ceremony, the three warriors floated downhill.

Crack-Crack-Crack! Ping-Ping-Ping!

The iron target spun on its axis, the carbine kicking his shoulder. Mukwa, senses enhanced, blew through a box of ammo and never missed a shot. Ben and Shaggy fed him magazines, thumping him on the back for his prowess. Elated, Mukwa placed the smoking rifle on the bench. Ever envious of Keith's battered M4, he wished the old timer could see him now. Mukwa scanned the trees for crows. Who knows, maybe Keith could?

Shaggy punched his shoulder again, directing Mukwa's attention uphill. Golden beams from the rising sun bathed three figures outside the women's lodge. Two of them were topless, bare-chested in the dawn. Shaggy and Ben wolf-whistled while poor Mukwa flushed fire—he knew them! Elena and Diana were his superiors, or had been. The Sentinels each raised a toned arm in greeting. The women wore smiles and very little else.

Three Fires: Elena and Diana

IN THE DRIZZLE, Autumn met *Nodin* at the pier, inviting Elena and Diana to join her at the fairgrounds after sunset. But first, as XO and captain, they inspected their Sentinels, the kayak flotilla, and the engine room. St. Ignace had a diesel station, and with Autumn's help, Elena reluctantly—Gaia forgive—filled *Nodin's* tanks with fossil fuel.

Dockside, Elena's handsome Diana had an altercation with red-faced Doyle, the angry male abating only when fuel hoses were fed to his thirsty fleet as well. Doyle knew some of the St. Ignace mariners—competitors for whitefish and bragging rights. Boat crews traded profanities. Hard to tell—hostility or harmony? Elena hoped the latter, feeling a gut-dump of anxiety. They needed each other to face what was coming.

Once ashore, the rain finally stopped. Many factions were gathered at Ignace, united by purpose—*defeat the invaders*. An old motivation, Elena thought, maybe the oldest. Mesopotamian granaries—*these are ours. You can't have them.*

The officers walked, hand in hand, to their rendezvous with Autumn. Gaia's Guardians stared at the horsemen, the motorcycle gangs, the modern weaponry so openly carried. If there were traditionalists here, like-minded to Naturals, they were not in evidence. War banners were everywhere, signage from before: Stop Dakota Access Pipeline, Honor Treaty Rights, Water is Sacred, Shut Down Line 5!

No one was masked or wore PPE. Were they all protected? By Gaia? By inoculation? Or were they Hidden? Unexposed yet to

Spreaders, to the contagion they carried? At the entrance to the fairgrounds, the Manitoulin was waiting. There was a powwow vibe to the encampment. Music was heard, and drumming—the life force of Mother Earth pulsing from stretched skins and bent cedar.

Woodsmoke flavored the air, mixing with sage, horse manure, and cooking smells. Gunshots cracked from the rifle range. Dogs were everywhere, huskies and malamutes the most numerous. Notably absent were children. This was a gathering of warriors. If they failed at the bridge, their kids would eventually be found, exposed, and enslaved. Colonization—guns, germs, and steel— was an old story, written anew by carriers of Covee.

Autumn, powerful in the milieu she had made, took both women by the hand. "Tonight, you two are water-protectors and are most welcome at my fire."

Elena and Diana acknowledged with thanks, "*Chi-miig-wech*," and gifted her tobacco, garden-grown on Beaver Island. The gray-haired hostess, a Wiikwemkoong from Manitoulin, smiled, admiring them both—what a pair of Amazons!

Dusk descended upon the fairgrounds as they followed Autumn up the rise. A low, hut-like dwelling had been constructed by bending branches and stretching fabric. Its flap opened east, and a campfire was tended just outside the dome. Stones heated in the coals. Elena observed the twilit camp—the Wawatam Lighthouse, the bannered wolf, boats in the harbor, and the dark straits beyond. She could just make out the far shore in the gloaming. The ELF leader, far-sighted, tried to picture the mechanized menace. These Straits were a good place to defend, always had been. If they couldn't stand here, then what did they stand for? Unpersuaded, her guts again clenched with fear.

Elena and Diana exchanged greetings with other women who'd gathered. All told, they numbered a dozen—older, younger, and in between; dark skinned and fair; long haired and shaved. Autumn instructed them to remove piercings and jewelry, as any metal would burn. Their shoes must come off, and underwire bras as well. Shirts were optional. The women, some nervously, complied.

A bundle of sage was passed, clockwise, left hand to left hand. Green protection was invisibly passed via molecules as well; their fields merged, bioelectric. Autumn let them know she'd be the water-pourer and would join them inside. Hot rocks—the grandfather stones—would be brought into the lodge seven at a time.

Were they ready to begin?

The dozen women took a steadying breath. They were.

Autumn nodded first to Diana. The athlete crouched low, ducking inside. Elena, barefoot, followed her partner into the earth. In the dark, they scooched clockwise around the pit that would hold the stones. The other women filed in, and soon the subterranean chamber was full.

When all was ready, the grandfathers were ushered in.

Each glowing stone was handled with care. Autumn used antlers, tonging each hot rock into place. Words of welcome were spoken. Soon, the first seven stones were arranged, turtle-shaped, in the center of the cavern. The air began to heat. Stones were sprinkled with cedar and brushed by a braid of sweet-grass. Each red-hot surface sparkled with stars. A rich aroma permeated the space, their skin, their hair. Anxiety faded. Focus was heightened. Earth had a heartbeat, fairground drums pulsing through the soil. Autumn closed the flap, enwombing them in primordial dark.

After a time, she began to speak, painting pictures in the cave—English, Anishinaabemowin, and Lakota—each language a brush. Blending them, she traced her visions. Autumn's affinity was water, her talents aqueous. She shared what she'd seen: creeks and rivers, lakes and seas, the lifeblood of Mother Earth gurgling through the Garden. Sunlight, soil, and water, the primeval pyramid of kingdom Plantae. She sang of origins, bringing them back to the beginning, to a watery planet and its first houseguests, dressed in green. More stones were added, flashing, sparking in the Hadean dark. The women, riding brooms of red cedar, flew backwards through the eras of the Earth—Protero, Paleo, Meso, Ceno.

Gaseous and green, the young planet spun through space and time—not another like it, not one, in a galaxy of galaxies. Eventually came The People, each tribe claiming the name. Most lived in harmony, symbionts with the system. Some did not. The rapacious prospered, at least for a while; extractive, they refined fuels from fossilized ferns. Harnessing death, they brought death to others. Petro wars followed, the Earth choking on its own black blood. Yoked to destruction, the masters were soon enslaved. The pillaged planet was electrocuted, sleep-deprived, blinded by incandescent bulbs. Earth, the solar system's squeaky wheel, complained to the cosmos, broadcasting banalities into the ether.

Then came Covee, Earth's last chance to cleanse. God-Gaia-Gichimanidoo had sent it, a virus to kill a virus—a zoonotic disease, primed by primates to target their zookeeper.

Millions died in the first wave. Then the variant morphed, gained function, and billions more were stung. The grid crashed down, the cages were opened. The little planet went dark, went silent, a nuisance no longer to the quietude of space.

But there was a price to be paid—in pollution. With the grid down and its engineers extinct, oil spills occurred and radiation plumed—an apocalypse of poison. Pipelines ruptured; fuel rods overheated; offshore platforms hemorrhaged, spewing crude into oceanic currents, the circulatory system of the Earth. A Great Flood of petroleum, Noah's dove too sticky to fly.

More stones were brought in. Linear time spiraled. The women sweated in the uterine underworld. Autumn painted darker pictures, dipping her brush in the language of oil—*pollution* in English, *oníya yušíčapi* in Lakota, *maji-mashkiki* in Anishinaabemowin. No matter the accent, the vision stayed the same. A black tide was rising, flooding their way. These very Straits were in danger, the pulmonary-piston for the entire Great Lakes. Human lives were small, the sum of their deaths quite inconsequential. Every second, 80,000 cubic meters of water pulsed under the bridge—ten Niagaras per blink.

Autumn prophesied, the coming battle wasn't about a bridge or territory. They fought to protect the pumping heart of the entire Midwest. Spreaders were indeed coming, and soon would be upon them. A cloud of carbon hovered over their clanking columns. An oil slick spoored their line of march. But it wasn't their virions that Autumn feared, nor their machine guns— more terrifying were the wrenches and blueprints of Chosen mechanics.

Behold a pipeline! Rusting beneath the Straits, Line 5 is its name. Parallel to the bridge, 200 feet beneath the surface, it lies lethal on the lake bed. If this thin-skinned artery ruptured, or was reprogrammed, black blood would gush. The oily snake would bleed out, all 300,000 square miles of the Great Lakes Basin choking on its bile. This tar-sand terrorism was the bigger threat by far. Autumn made them see it, and the sweating women writhed in agony.

The long night waned. Daybreak neared. Elena, soaked and disheartened, heard the first shots from the rifle range: *Crack! Crack! Crack!*

Autumn's warning twisted her guts. She'd never felt less prepared for a battle. The ELF fighters should not have come. Then the flap opened. The women—glistening, trembling—emerged from the earth, bodies cooling quickly in the predawn chill. Autumn pointed to a constellation—fading fast—a question mark in reverse. "The underwater panther, *Mishibizhiw*, will help us guard the Straits."

Gourds holding crystalline water were passed. They imbibed, grateful Autumn's oily painting had not yet been brushed. They wrung the sweat from their clothing, from their hair. Every eye found the bridge, graceful and elegant in its spiderweb span.

Each woman envisioned the pipeline beneath—*the snake on the lakebed, belly full of poison, shedding its skin in rusty flakes.*

Jewelry was reclaimed, and clothing. Few words were spoken before the women began dispersing. Autumn remained with the two Sentinels, a statuesque trio standing on the hillside. The fairgrounds were waking, fry-bread and coffee tickling their nostrils. Horses whinnied with the dawn. A motorcycle cleared its throaty engine.

Crack! Crack! Crack! The rifle range was busy.

Diana nudged her partner. The light was strengthening. A large man with a bearish tattoo stood at the firing line shouldering a carbine. They watched as the ex-Sentinel fired a three-round burst at the iron target.

Crack-Crack-Crack! Ping-Ping-Ping!

The men with Mukwa cheered his proficiency as he performed a quick mag-change, repeating his performance: *Crack-Crack-Crack! Ping-Ping-Ping!*

The man-shaped target spun on its axis. Mukwa's broad back was thumped by friends. The two women could see the big man was smiling. A wolf-whistle floated up from the range. Diana grinned as she said, "Looks like our Oso has found some new bears."

Mukwa looked up and saw them both standing on the rise. The women, bare-skinned, raised strong arms in greeting. After a few sheepish seconds, the blushing bear lifted a paw in return.

Three Fires: Brian and Loon

BAPTISTE, BLACK BEARD CURLING in the wet weather, descended from the Wawatam Light. "Go with Loon," he instructed Brian after *Nodin* docked and the bookish ELF shaman came ashore. "We must see farther. I need both of you to fly."

Brian was doubtful. Their passage under the bridge had been damp and drizzly. The cloud ceiling was low; few birds were aloft. Captain Diana agreed with the Howler leader. Distracted by many tasks, she released him into Loon's care. When Brian hesitated, she barked, "Fine! Grab a brush and join a work party!"

No contest. The hippie mock-saluted his captain and went off with his fellow flier. Loon brought Brian first to his mother. Busy with sweat lodge preparations, Autumn had no time for them either. "Do you both have what you need?" she inquired.

Brian patted his beaded pouch, his shamanic supplies ample for their mission. Autumn kissed her boy on the forehead, pushing them both down the hill. "Happy flying!"

A cold rain spattered as Brian, low-spirited, donned the poncho from his pack. Loon's feathers were ruffled as well. St. Ignace, rally-point for resistance, was way too crowded; its cacophony depressed them. Neither cared much for engines, or weaponry, or small talk with strangers. Their skill set required tranquility and access to wild things.

Loon led them south towards the headlands. They disappeared in mist, leaving the human clutter behind. A neglected cemetery, an old one, suited their needs. The rain finally stopped, and they shook themselves dry. Loon introduced Brian to his friend, an ancient white pine. The boy pointed at a wooden platform, high up near its cone-heavy crown. From the ground, the contraption looked like a nest.

"No *way!*" Brian, fan of all things Tolkien, was awed. "A real flet!" Freshly inspired, the bookworm felt a fantastical urge to fly.

The pilots sniffed the wind. Sensitive to pressure, both sensed a barometric change. The cold front from Canada was lifting. The skies, by sunset, would be clear. Too soon to climb, they toured the tombstones instead—*Londraville, Maloney, Sheldon, Johnson, Brown.*

The birth years were various; their expiration dates identical. 1887, anno Domini, had been a scourge-year for diphtheria, the "strangling angel" of children. Many headstones were tiny: *Infant, Beloved Daughter, Child of_______.*

Nothing new about disease, save only in scale.

As the low clouds began lifting, the two friends bowered beneath the pine. It was time to make themselves ready; soon they'd ascend. From his pack, Brian produced a small, blackened kettle. Loon went to fill it from a rusty hand-pump. Brian found dry tinder, snapping twigs as he kindled fire. They both cupped its smoke as the cold water heated.

The bearded man plundered his pouch, arranging its totems: bird carving, bundle of sage, packet of fungi—spindly and dry. Symmetrical, his mind arranged itself as well, going over its preflight list—safety, set, setting?—check, check, and check.

When his kettle steamed, Brian sifted in the caps and stems. An earthy smell arose: worms and soil, the flavor profile of decay. He nodded as Loon smudged sage, he proffering protection to the pine and to themselves. While his tea cooled and chemically activated, Brian stirred in Grace's honey, his thoughts bee-lining back to her garden. Wistfully, he remembered original ELF Country and the seasons they'd shared. Elder Grace remained on Beaver Island, swapping herb lore with young Miin and silver-haired Samantha.

The tea's aroma loosened the tethers of his mind. He pictured the three wise women, master educators, green-training the next generation. He felt his face. It was tingling already. Despite the loom of battle, he found himself smiling. They'd better start their climb while they could. He poured the potion into his battered thermos. Brian tightened its lid clockwise—sunwise, deosil. The neo Druid knew the old words, the power of circumambulation. He would only imbibe upon reaching the platform. "Ready, my friend?" Loon nodded. Now or never.

They tamped dirt on their fire. The boy went first, Brian following after. The tall tree wanted to be climbed, arranging its branches just so. High up, they passed through the lubber's hole in the center of the flet's floorboards, closing the wooden hatch beneath them. The two birds were in the nest. Loon showed him the coiled life-lines. They harnessed themselves to the pine and sat comfortably, back to back against its broad bole.

The vista took away their breath. They faced south, with a wide view of the Straits. Long ago, the Anishinaabeg ancients had named this fertile waterway after its spirit-shaped island, *Michinnimakinong*, Big Turtle. The French, upon arrival, parsed what they heard; *Mish-inni-maki-nong* became *Michilimackinac* as they fortified their position. Their fort was soon lost to the British in a greedy grab for resources. The Indigenous reclaimed their land using lacrosse, *baaga'adowe*, as a ruse. Female spectators smuggled weapons into the stockade, slaughtering the garrison as it bet on the ball game. The next year, the British returned, evicting the Indigenous again, moving the fort to the island. They shortened both names to *Mackinac* before relinquishing the region to the land-hungry States.

All this topography could be seen from their perch—the Straits, the nearby islands, Michigan's mainland, and the suspension bridge too. The Mighty Mac was five miles long, emerging from a lakebed 200 feet deep and soaring 500 feet above the surface. She was indeed a graceful thing, though two years without paint, without cosmetics, left her red-streaked with rust.

Brian charged his mug with tea, merging his motion—metronomic—with the swaying pine. He sipped the soily brew and waited for some silliness to pass—*a sailor needs sea-legs; a flier needs tree-legs.* Self-attuned, he felt the cybin circulating—belly, then blood, then brain. Everywhere it went, the complex chemical opened doors, removed blinders, and derailed neural pathways from too-habitual tracks. His load was lightened, his thoughts floated free. All he needed now was a strong pair of wings.

Loon watched his friend, felt the flier reaching out, preparing to soar. Loon's own technique was different: no tinctures, no tea. He was raised for this, had been connecting since birth. His mind—all minds—were malleable machines, doing what they were expected to do. Growing up on Manitoulin Island, near *Manidoowaaling,* the "Cave of the Spirit," Loon was fluent with familiars and could merge before most kids learned their colors. His *red, yellow, blue* were *cardinal, finch,* and *jay.* With a water-protector for a mother and Wiikwemkoong elders to guide him, Loon was retro and avant-garde both.

A massive osprey, *biijigigwane,* flew a circuit around their tree. Golden-eyed, she regarded them. The red sun, nuclear, dropped from the cloud bank like a bomb, firing her feathers as it sank. A breeze pushed Brian's beard, stirring its beads and bangles. The shaman gave a shiver and was gone—he asked, she accepted. The bird, with Brian now aboard, pumped her wings once, twice, and was far over water, headed south towards the main.

Loon checked his friend's tether, then his own. Tied tight to the tree, he loosened his mind. His namesake, the *maang,* was common in these waters. Breeding pairs, as they had for millennia, claimed every bay. He'd merged with many of them already, sharing their sorrows as they lost chicks—to raptors, to fish, to sharp-toothed mammals, nocturnal and nasty.

The boy scouted nearby waters first—St. Ignace, Mackinaw City—and nothing seemed amiss. Mind-to-mind he made his rounds, scanning the surrounding islands next—Mackinac, Round, Bois Blanc—nothing to report. Twilight darkened, the moon brightened, waxing towards first quarter. Each time he jumped, changing skins, a tremolo cry erupted, sometimes from the mate, sometimes the familiar. A listening ear could track he's yodeled progression.

With the near-waters secure, Loon shifted his reconnaissance further southeast. The boy, bird-to-bird, skipped like a stone down the Huron coast—Cadottes Point, Freedom, Grand View, Point Nipigon. The brighter stars assumed their positions, emerging through the moon-wash. Little Dipper poured starlight till Big Dipper overflowed. The boy knew them as Fisher and Loon, *Ojiig* and *Maang*, celestial symbionts circling the centuries.

A final skip landed he in Cheboygan, twenty miles from their platform in the pine. His nose rankled immediately, smelling diesel as soon as he emerged. The breeding pair he utilized was recently displaced, and were nervous for their nearly grown chick. The boy felt engine vibration through their feathers. Propellers churned and crude shouts were heard; profanity pooled around each craft. Loon-eyed, he saw the scene in ultraviolet. Boats and barges were moving, bioluminescent bacteria sparkling in their wakes. Unknown vessels motored up from the south, gathering in the harbor. Refueling was underway from storage tanks along the shore. The reek of decaying diesel clogged Loon's olfaction, the algae in the rotting fuel flashing green as it sprayed from fuel hoses.

Stranger still were the humans, a new kind of invasive species. In the UV light, every face was flecked with blue. The virus was glowing. Billions of virions were shed by the boat crews.

Violet clouds puffed from corrupted lungs as they cursed each other, jockeying for fuel. The bird, Loon's familiar, was uneasy, eager to be away. The boy's connection was fraying fast.

Loon took a last look, counting the craft, two dozen all told—barges, tugs, and armored yachts. His UV vision found the leaders ordering the chaos, faces untainted by virus-glow. The infected crews appeared to cringe in their presence, scurrying to obey. Teams of Virals worked in pairs, lugging bodies to the seawall and dumping them over. Through the bird, he could read the regalia on the corpses—Nomads and Reguladores—bikers then, SIS captured on patrol? Each forehead had a hole, a black flower blooming with blood.

The leaders of this fleet—so far he counted four—appeared to be bald and uninfected. Their skeletal torsos were terrifying. To Loon, their tattoo ink glowed. On one of their bony shoulders perched a large crow, its plumage iridescent in the high frequency light. Cloaked in black, a wraith-like figure emerged, wearing sunglasses even at night. The apparition threw back its hood to reveal a pale face, crowned by a metal halo—some sort of implant? The perched crow sensed surveillance and shifted its regard. Loon's familiar screamed with alarm, and their tenuous merge was broken. The last thing he saw as his bird and mate winged to safety were four inky skulls and the haloed ghost turning his way.

The clouds were lifting, the moon riding low in the west. The osprey, with Brian aboard, neared Grayling, a three-hour flight from the pine. They followed I-75, winging south from the bridge. Her eyes, hyper-acute, tracked many targets: schools of fish in the Straits, fawns on the highway. Geese—celestial navigators—flew beneath them in ragged Vs. Of humans and their machines, there'd been no sign—no sign till now. The Grayling Army Airfield showed lights!

Brian nudged and the reluctant osprey complied, the data-stream continuing, brain-to-brain, through their neural link. Brian soothed her anxiety, directing her suite of sensors towards the tower. She focused her foveae, sending his occipital lobe a live-feed of the figure she found there—a uniformed man paced inside, pushing buttons. The tower strobed blue, then green.

Despite being tethered to a tree ninety miles north of her position, Brian's olfactory cortex tingled with her next sending—the osprey scented fuel, lots of it, foul and fumy. The bearded man, still entranced, wrinkled his nose from afar. The bird, alarmed, banked away. Brian's temporal lobe flashed fear as a great THUNDER assaulted her eardrums. She panic-climbed to safety as he fought to repurpose her sensors. He caught a brief glimpse of afterburners as a pair of aircraft, each with twin engines, roared aloft.

Follow them! the man urged. *Fly from them!* she responded.

Together, they slipped and slid till rudder control was restored. He convinced her to follow their exhaust, a greasy slick of oxides, sulfur, and soot. The two machines, human-piloted, streaked westwards towards the moon. The osprey, piloted as well, pumped her wings and followed.

Twenty miles later, the red-bearded operator turned her around. The escaping aircraft, far too fast, vanished over the horizon. It wasn't happening, and his magnificent female was tiring. Brian banked them back to Grayling, winging north, returning to the Straits.

The nightscape below them was utterly dark. Not a single light could be seen—no campfire, no cabin-glow, no improvised grid from electric pioneers. Few landmarks were visible save an occasional road or river, pale in the moonlight. Embedded in her mind, he was awed by the osprey's elemental elegance. Her navigational array pointed skyward; the chart she followed was celestial, utilizing Polaris, the fixed star. He felt her mind calculating, so many wing beats on such and such a heading. She automatically adjusted for wind, for earth-spin, even the rotation of stars. Having no such mechanism, he marveled at her computations. Could this be learned? Transferred somehow?

Each earthly organism, alas, is a stranger to the next, with no two species wired the same. Comparing people to birds, Brian felt the hugeness of human speech, the naming of things. She had no comprehension of this. Devoting calories to this cortex had not been her path, nor should it be now. But what a conversation they could have! If he could just give her the words—the Edenic urge, Adam and Eve, labeling their garden, loneliness increasing with each creature they cataloged.

For now, Brian let it go. Her hyper-keen sensors registered a great concussion of air. The man's neurosis for naming immediately found the signifier—Explosion! He urged investigation. Just beyond Grayling's airfield, a great fire was burning. But her steering was unresponsive, the controls wouldn't answer. The bird took a fix on the North Star and vectored them home. Brian sighed, exhausted; it had been a long night. Resigned to auto-pilot, he looked out her windows.

The moon set beneath their portside wing.

Leo, rampant, rose to starboard.

The Lion's bright star Regulus pulsed in the predawn.

Parallel to their flight path and keeping apace, signal fires sprang up from defunct cell-towers. Brian's simian brain sequenced the beacons—one dozen, two dozen, three. By the time they reached the Straits, the dark night was fading to gray. Huron was on their right, Michigan on their left, with Mighty Mac gracefully bridging the between. The osprey found their pine, buzzing the tower once before her pilot ejected.

Still seated on his flet, Brian thanked the great bird. "Happy landings!"

Earth, a blue marble, kept rolling as a celestial shift-change occurred, stars dimming as the daylight came on.

Crack-Crack-Crack!

From their flet, the fairground's target practice was faintly heard. Much louder were the pine needles soughing in the on-shore breeze. The great tree stood rooted in the lakeside cemetery, more ancient by far than the oldest tombstone-tenant.

The boy Loon and blue-eyed Brian had spent the night high in its branches. Both fliers felt the white pine, heliotropic, stretching towards the rising sun, eager to process its photonic fire. Though exhausted, they needed to report on what they'd just seen, but first they must rest a minute. What good was their intel if they broke their necks while descending?

Loon wished he'd brought snacks. His red-bearded friend looked wan in the daylight. Brian's bright eyes were closed, his osprey-connection broken. Like their solar-powered host tree, the shaman recharged in sunlight.

Loon had urgent news for Baptiste about the Viral fleet mustering at Cheboygan, but first he needed his friend to recover. Brian's osprey had been an apex female, matriarch of Mackinac. It was thanks to her tenacity that their reconnaissance had paid off. The osprey shared their same tree—higher up, eyes also closed, utterly depleted.

Morning Meetings

DOYLE SLURPED HIS BLACK BREW, eyes grainy from lack of sleep. *Mary's* coffee, for once, wasn't half bad. One of the guardsmen—Cruz? Booker? Doyle couldn't keep them straight—had gifted some MRE coffee rations as thanks for O'Donnell squaring away their boat's electronics. The sun was up, and already the St. Ignace docks were busy. Doyle supervised new welds to his stern stanchion. Hannigan's boat was tied next to *Mary*, and the big man nodded to Tom while watching his own welder at work. The two Beaver captains—competitors no longer—had sketched out a plan.

Crack-Crack-Crack!

A staccato of shots sounded from the rifle range, but the compressors, grinding-wheels, and chipping hammers deafened Doyle to their din. The cold rain had stopped; the clouds cleared up, the Straits were calm, and he wished he was out fishing. *Oh fucking well.* The good ol' days were behind him, Tom had known plenty. In the days—or hours?—he had left, he'd do his best to wreak havoc on the Spreaders, represent his island, and try to make a good end. If he didn't return, his Annie would understand. So would niece Maggie. Beyond them, he could give a flying fuck.

Doyle's belly warmed with caffeine and crankiness. An osprey flew low over the harbor. Squinting against the glare, Doyle tracked the bird, a fellow-fisher, till she rounded the point. The big female seemed weary.

Raging, O'Donnell threw down his welding-gun and goggles. "Flaming cunt!" He booted the machine, glaring at his captain. "Third fuckin' time this shit-box shocked me!"

Doyle grinned at his man. "I feel the same about yer java juice." He inspected O'Donnell's stanchion, spat, and powered down the unit. "Welds look like shit, but they'll do."

A bell clanged from Ignace. "I got a meeting. Square away the stern, have a mug-up with Hanny, and be ready to throw lines. I got a feelin' today's the day." Doyle stepped away from *Mary*, stomping towards town.

The Municipal Building on State Street was filling up; a plaque proclaimed its WPA roots. Since 1941 its big bell had tolled the citizenry to order. Today was no different, save it might be the last.

The largest room was cleared of tables and chairs. It stank of burnt coffee, ripe bodies, and woodsmoke. After a year or more of social distancing, attendees were uncomfortable, too many breathers sharing too little air. Was Covee in the room? Had anyone here been stung? An SIS granny, clad in leather, was opening windows, folks nodding their thanks.

Representatives from all factions mingled uneasily, eyeing the stage. Autumn was standing there, waiting for the room to fill. The water-protector, cleansed from her sweat lodge, was glowing.

Sheila—the Cessna pilot and fudge bomber—stalked towards Elena and Diana, an angry wolf on the prowl. The ELF leaders were dressed in civvies and holding hands. "I've been asking around," the woman said with a glare. "They're calling you 'Naturals.' But I know you by a different name."

The Sentinels dropped hands, standing their ground. The Howler pilot eyed them angrily. "You're fucking Greenies, aren't you?" Sheila spat the term, daring they deny it. The two women guessed what was coming, and here it came. "You're *murderers!* You know that, right? Pilot-killers! How fucking *dare* you show up here!"

Both Sentinels bristled, but Sheila wasn't wrong. Who among them was blameless? Those gathered here today all had blood on their hands, the stain of survival. Simply put, aircraft had been a threat. In the early days of collapse, when there was still fuel and pilots to fly, Naturals had been followed, their sylvan sanctuaries surveilled. Had some ELF fighters gone too far—sabotaging planes, spiking runways, disabling pilots? Yes, that had happened, and other things too. The two women—Greenies indeed—acknowledged Sheila's wrath, bowing respectfully while backing away. This wasn't the time, wasn't the place, to settle that score.

Captain Young, bruised and unmasked, stood stiffly, talking with Big Ben. The diminutive elder, gray-braided, was a leader of the St. Ignace Scouts. The two men traded intelligence as the nervous hall buzzed about them. "You haven't heard from Cheboygan in how long?"

Young eyed the map by the stage. Ben responded, "The SIS we sent—Nomads and Reguladores—called yesterday with nothing to report. But they missed their next radio check at midnight."

"What gear are they using? How unusual is it to miss comms?"

"They've got UHF. Range should be no problem. Unusual to miss a call though, especially with trouble brewing." Captain Young tried to hide his concern; Cheboygan was way too close. Twenty-four miles by the coast road, maybe twenty by boat. Young checked his watch. *Shit.*

"Who else do you have out there? Any other SIS deployed?"

The room was filling up, so Ben leaned in closer. "Got a team in Indian River, liaising with those Rangers. We've got women scouting too—RedSpirit—in Alanson. Both teams called at midnight. They were nervous, but nothing new to report."

Young thanked the veteran and stepped closer to the map. Autumn glanced his way, attending the room. It was almost time to begin. Young studied the three approach roads to the bridge. As of midnight, M-31 through Alanson and I-75 through Indian River were quiet.

Cheboygan's harbor and M-23 along the coast were unknown. His tactical mind calculated distances and fuel consumption.

Last night, his CO, Colonel Dennis, had broadcast Lima Alpha on the sat-phone. For now, the DOD's Palantir system still functioned. Young—per standing orders—kept his handset charged. Lima Alpha—"Last Alliance"—indicated an evacuation from Camp Grayling and a fallback to a stronger position. The assault, long-expected from Panzer, had indeed commenced. Young fought a flood of anxiety, looking at his wrist again. *Let's fucking go.*

Dr. Chow, waiting for Autumn to begin, edged closer to the guardsman whose name-tape read, *CRUZ*. Chow nodded at the Combat Medical Badge sewn to the man's uniform, the twinned snakes of a healer. "Medic?"

Specialist Cruz shifted his caffeine pouch, lip-to-lip, and grunted affirmative. His neck still ached from the blunted arrow in the dunes. Cruz's trust level for this Chow character was near zero. Cruz knew the doctor had hidden their Person of Interest, Bob Campbell. This Greenie doctor had been rehabbing the Viral somehow, putting everyone at risk, and for what? Fucking glory? Cruz almost spat.

"Doc Newsome and I could use your skills, Specialist. We're setting up a surgery on Diana's ferry. Honestly, we haven't done much of this. If you're ever free, and if things get messy, you know where to find us, maybe lend a hand?"

The nervous doctor was babbling. Cruz steadied him with a look. Chow forced his feet to move away; he had so many questions for this soldier, but most of them, Chow knew, were incriminating. *Did these guardsmen know where Campbell was? Did they know Chow had harbored a Viral? Who beat up the three soldiers? What about the arsonist from the docks? What was it like to fight Spreaders? Did the Army have a backup plan to defend the bridge? Were reinforcements coming, or was this all they had?*

Cruz kept his cool as the doctor scuttled away. He hoped Chow was better at surgery than interrogation. An EMT during collapse, Cruz had seen enough blood and wanted nothing to do with their quack clinic on *Nodin*. Medic or no, he'd rather fight, and Captain Young knew it. Young had tasked Cruz to train the defenders and operate the mortar with Booker instead. Cruz was fine with this; easier to blow things apart than patch them up any day.

Sergeant Booker, still sporting two black eyes, was approached by a skinny, dreadlocked man and his bear-sized companion. The pair smelled of cannabis, sage, and nitro from the rifle range. "Sergeant? Call me Shaggy. This big boy is my man, Mukwa."

Anthony Booker looked them over and nodded; this Shaggy character's eyes were flecked with amber. The dreadlock dude continued, "Afghanistan I'll bet? Me too, man. Kandahar. Discharged on a medical, long story."

Another nod from Booker, warmer by a degree. He'd deployed to KAF with his chief, and he'd stopped judging discharges years ago.

"Anyway, Sergeant, we're hoping you've got some information to share. More units on the way? Maybe some airpower? Come on, soldier, from one Buffalo to another, you got something special to push these Viral fucks off our bridge?"

"Hate to disappoint." Booker shook his head, pitching his voice low as he continued, "What about you guys? What kind of force is mustered here? I saw motorcycles, horses, a bunch of civilians. Tell me you've got more than that?"

Shaggy was grinning; the big bear was not. "Don't underestimate us," the wiry Howler said with a wink, "there's more than meets the eye. Lotta Indians here—Apache, Lakota, Ojibwe, Odawa—strong survivors. Covee cleared our lands of the colonizer. Wovoka's ol' Ghost Dance comin' true. We know our history, won't be pushed again. Seen our wolf banner yet?"

Booker nodded warily, remembering the beach party.

"Heard some howling, have you?"

Booker recalled the keening between Garden Island and Beaver. He nodded again.

"You've no idea, man—no idea, what hundreds, thousands, of wolves can do. I've been running with this pack since the Dakotas. Those infected fuckers better not step foot in the U.P. You don't notice in town, but the woods are filling up. Our four-footed brothers and some *really* big sisters are gathering. They've got our backs too. Can't stand these fuckin' Spreaders."

A year ago—hell, a few *months* ago—Booker would've dismissed this Shaggy as just another PTSD pothead. Since then, the Detroiter had seen some shit, so Booker held his tongue. Like their Viral, Red Liz, somehow surviving her wounds. Or that boy Loon and the bearded hippie flying with birds. The howling party on the beach. The supposed immunity of the Naturals. That freakish woman, the she-elf who'd stolen their prisoner and kicked their asses, blackening both his eyes. Booker guessed he'd be adding to this list soon, maybe today.

The sergeant saw Captain Young checking his watch. "Good luck to you boys." Booker separated himself and stood by his chief.

Mukwa frowned, watching the soldier step away. He knew exactly who'd beaten them up. He'd sparred against Nighthawk, fought back-to-back with her against Chosen and Cons. Hawk had flown from him though, flown from them all, raking Mukwa's muzzle along the way. Apparently, she'd done damage to these guys too. Had the soldiers tried to stop her? Had she been the arsonist? Would he ever see her again? His sleepover dream said he was needed, Hawk in trouble—not that she'd ever admit it. Damn the Sentinel was stubborn!

Shaggy elbowed Mukwa's attention away from the bruised sergeant and towards the stage. Autumn was raising both hands for quiet. "I dig this chick," Shaggy said. His golden eyes were shining. "Strong medicine, man. Strong medicine."

The room quieted as the Manitoulin began to speak.

Water Protectors

"AANIIN! MINOGIZHEBAAWAGAD. Autumn nindizhinikaaz, Manitoulin nindonjibaa." Autumn welcomed them all, gesturing towards the windows and her homeland far to the east.

She paused. The room, packed with people of color, responded, *"Aaniin!"*

Autumn smiled at the assembly, then continued, "We are strong here, stronger than we've been. And the *manidoog* are with us. Spirits of the Wolf, spirits of the Water, spirits of the Air, all have gathered to make a stand."

At "Wolf," her eyes sought Big Ben, Shaggy, and the long-haired Howlers.

At "Water" she nodded at the boat captains, Doyle, Baptiste, and Diana.

At "Air" she pantomimed flight, looking towards Brian—beyond weary—leaning on her son, the young loon.

The Manitoulin continued, "In the past, our ancestors fled from disease and the colonizers that spread it. We failed that test, and the land became poisoned. Generations came and went. The poison spread, in our veins, in the waters. Much knowledge was lost. Many elders died, their wisdom unheeded, warnings scorned. And yet, enough was passed on. The language lives! The People survive! Nature is strong, and the Great Spirit endures. All of this is a victory, and for this we give thanks. *Miigwech manidoog iyaajig noodinong, iyaajig nibiing, iyaajig shkodeng miinwa iyaajig akiing."*

When she finished the prayer, many in the room responded, "*Miigwech!*"

Her face and tone turned sorrowful. "But we have lost much. Our families, our friends, our familiar habits of living, all gone. Gone and not returning. Not in this life. Not as we know it."

The morning meeting had started late. A cloud smothered the climbing sun. The room dimmed, and the defenders felt a chill. Traumatized, they grieved loved ones—improperly buried, improperly mourned. The variant had hit them hard. Stinger flooded their reservations, their ranches, their townships and rural counties. Even after the first wave crested, many died—from starvation or lack of health care, from the dimming of the sun and the cold, dead hand of winter. Human predation culled them further—traffickers, rapists, Spreaders in their various guises.

A shudder passed through the room. This remnant of remnants fought tears, steeling themselves to persevere, at least for one more day. Autumn sensed their resolve and said, "For most of us, a battle death would be welcome, would be easy. Making it count is the hard part."

With eyes closed, she reached out to the gathered warriors, finding their hearts just where they should be. The cloud passed, sunlight beaming into the old room; for a moment they stood in silence. Autumn breathed in and out slowly, the room breathing with her. There was a crackling exchange of molecules and energy. After a time, she called for their reports, starting with her son.

Loon checked with Brian, who nodded limply, before making his way to the stage. The boy stood next to the wall map. Pointing to a nearby harbor, he said, "They've taken Cheboygan."

His mother, frowning, stood behind him, hands on his slim shoulders.

Loon continued, "They've got boats there, two dozen, barges

too, and fuel. There are many Virals, well armed, along with something else."

The boy paused. Looking up to Baptiste, then to Autumn, he went on, "I've heard the rumors, we all have. At the start of collapse, there were even videos. The news called them 'Gories.' The elders on Manitoulin, before they died, used a different term, one from the past—*bakaak*, or *baykok*—skeleton spirits. They slay warriors with invisible arrows. They eat their dead. Last night I saw them through the eyes of a loon. I'm so sorry, but I believe our scouts in Cheboygan were killed. I counted four *bakaak* at least."

The room moaned. The boy felt his mother squeeze his shoulder. He went on, "There were no vehicles there, it looked like boats only." Loon looked at Brian. "My friend here, a Natural, flew further. Osprey-connected, he witnessed a great fire in Grayling. Winging home, he saw signal-fires leaping from hilltops—Gaylord, Vanderbilt, Indian River, Riggsville—the last one was Carp Lake, right before dawn. I believe we have friends on the ground, and they are warning us. Invasion is coming."

Shaggy flashed canines in a wolfish response. "Let the fuckers come! The pack is hungry!" Amber eyes glowing, he threw back his dreadlocks and howled. Others in the room did the same. Outside the windows, more voices joined the chorus. Autumn steered her small son off the stage. The next one she called upon was Captain Young.

All too familiar with briefings, Young stepped smartly to the stage. Smoothing his too-long mustache, Frank got right to the point: "Last night my CO, Colonel Dennis, broadcast Lima Alpha over the net. 'Last Alliance' is the evacuation order for the Guard post at Grayling." His gaze, incredulous no longer, found Brian slumped in the back. "The fire you witnessed was probably the fuel and ammunition the retreating Guard couldn't carry."

Young's mind skipped over the fact that a *bird* had seen this, not a drone or a satellite.

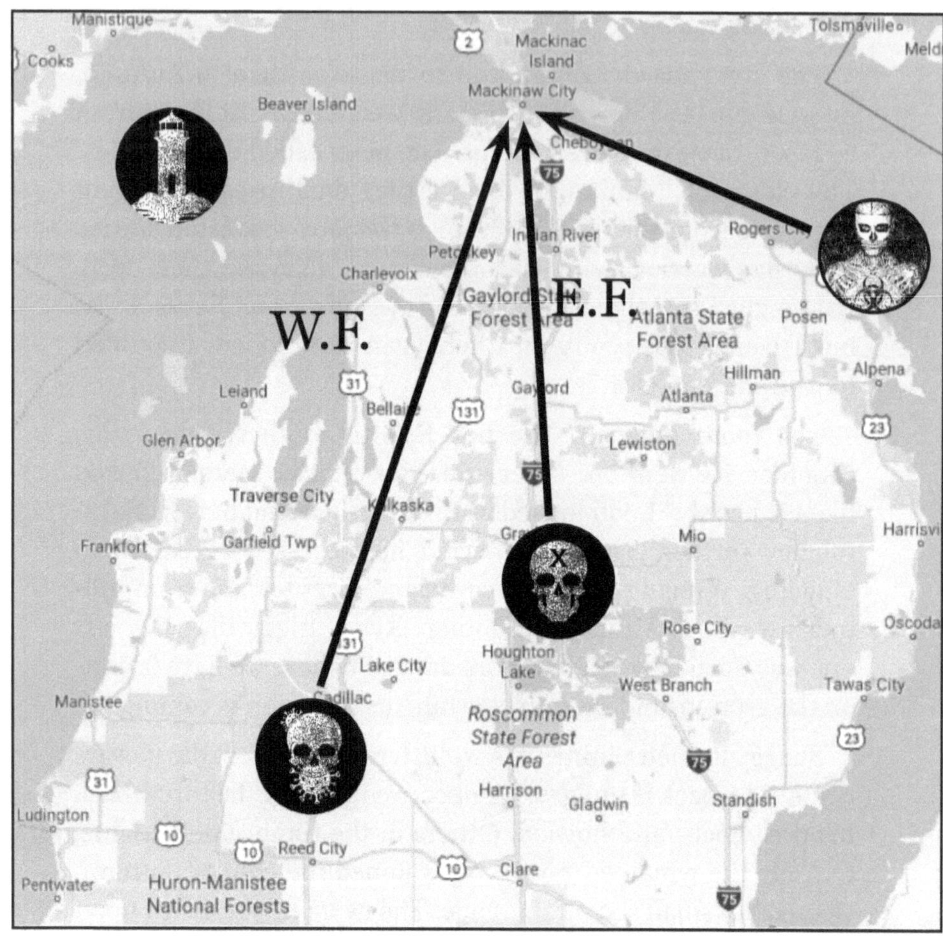

Frank was at the map now, in his element. "Camp Grayling became untenable. A Western Force of fifty vehicles reached Cadillac, threatening their flank." He traced its path up M-131. "This force, mostly Chosen, could be at Petoskey now, or beyond." His trigger finger inched towards the Straits.

"An Eastern Force, mostly XCons, is pushing up I-75. They're probably past Grayling. Hopefully the Griffin bomb techs did them some damage?" He looked to Loon, to Brian, unsure of their abilities. Neither flier could confirm any secondary explosions or IED booby traps. The captain checked his watch again and continued, "Either of these forces could attack us today. One at a time would be better, but we need to prepare for both."

The nervous room began lamenting. Young forged ahead, fueling their fear: "This new fleet at Cheboygan is the third pincer. They won't be bottlenecked by the bridge like the others. They'll attempt to cross the Straits and land a force behind us." He illustrated the envelopment on the map. "This must be prevented. The narrowness of the bridge gives us a chance, our only chance. It negates their numbers, constricts their mobility. If they get behind us, we're in trouble."

There was a rumble from the audience as Mount Doyle, red faced and volcanic, blew his lid. "I hope they fucking try! Sweet Jesus, let them try. We'll DROWN those Viral scumbags!"

The room loved it, responding in kind. "Fifty fathoms deep!" yelled a tattooed deckhand.

"Fatten the fishes!" cried a woman in coveralls.

Captain Young, professional, waited them out, appraising Doyle with a look. Frank hoped this fisherman was more than just bluster. He'd better be. The Guard captain concluded his briefing, then received reports on the assets of the defenders: number of motorcycles, caliber of weaponry, roadblocks they could employ.

A live wire introduced himself as Shaggy, giving an over-excited speech about a "wolf pack" supposedly protecting their flank. Frank listened to the golden-eyed veteran, but tuned him out once the dude started barking. The September sun ascended. The enemy drew nearer. Young pictured the Western Force chugging north on M-31: Brutus, Pellston, Levering....

A Kiowa woman gave her name and details about their available cavalry. Again, Young's mind flinched. He saw the Eastern Force rolling north on I-75: Grayling, Vanderbilt, Indian River....

Baptiste climbed onto the stage, Young making room for the black-bearded voyageur. The Army captain fielded questions about reinforcements and any support they might receive: "Support? Hard to tell. Could be happening now—ambushes, delaying tactics, IEDs—we might never know. Colonel Dennis and the Griffins from Grayling can still pack a punch. There's other friendlies too—Rangers, Old Law—doing what they can. We're not in this alone, though right now it might feel that way."

A female biker interrupted from the back, "Why not blow the bridge? Wait till Spreaders are on it, detonate some TNT, dump 'em all in the drink?"

"I wish we could," Young said, meeting the woman's angry eye. "My CO studied schematics, talked it over with his bomb techs. But there's a million tons of reinforced concrete, and layers and layers of steel—gratings, cross beams, stringers, floor beams. All the ordinance we've got couldn't do it. Instead, we'll use our firepower to slow 'em down; they'll pay a heavy toll to cross this bridge. Mighty Mac was built to last. No doubt she'll outlast us all."

With that, Young exited the stage—no applause—and stood by his two men.

Baptiste, in two languages, spoke quickly: English for most, Michif for his voyageurs. Most pressing was the state of St. Ignace's fuel reserves. No matter the octane—avgas, DFM, unleaded—they had none. Every storage tank had been emptied. Baptiste looked at Doyle, at Diana, at the other Beaver captains. "*Merci* for coming. Your boats have been refueled, but you should know that's all there is."

His eye found Big Ben and other SIS leaders. "The motorcycles are topped off too. You won't be going far, unless we retreat. If that happens, fuel's the least of our worries."

He nodded to the Howler pilot. "Sheila, you have what you need?"

Affirmative. With a full tank her little Skyhawk could travel 800 miles. Once aloft, she could fly anywhere, if there was anywhere worth flying to. In Sheila's experience there wasn't, not anymore, and so she stayed—probably for good.

Baptiste's last look was to Autumn, and much was conveyed. After a moment, she touched her heart and cleared her throat to conclude the meeting, but was interrupted by the Natural, Dr. Chow.

"May I say a word?"

To the room, Autumn's nod seemed tight and took a second too long. But the doctor pressed his case. "I'm a medical man," he said, surveying the room. "I've studied this virus and its pathology. None of us here are masked. We've been living in a bubble. I need to remind everyone, including myself, that this bubble can burst."

The room was antsy; no one needed this reminder. Chow's vibe was corporate and cover-your-ass, just one more safety lecture they had to endure. "Remember, the Chosen, the XCons, whoever else is coming, we know they're highly virulent. They're called Spreaders for a reason."

The lecturer had lost his students, and the assembly hall was stirring. Chow looked at Diana, at Autumn, at the SIS now talking tactics amongst themselves. "Listen! You may *think* you're protected, through antibodies or shielding. But we know nothing about immunity, how long it lasts, what exposure levels it can handle. Look!" He put up his hands, making a final plea. "The variant is a weapon, and they're sure to use it against us. Some of this fighting will be face to face. We don't have enough PPE—"

"I'll pee-pee on YOU!" A hairy biker fake-sprayed the doctor with his zippered hose.

Many laughed. Autumn did not.

Flustered, Chow limped through the rest of his lecture. "If you're exposed, do NOT return to your friends, to the town. Find me on the ferry, find *Nodin*. Its crew is protected; we follow protocol. We can quarantine you there and test you. Don't help our enemies. Don't be a Spreader!"

The biker's friends kept laughing as the red-faced doctor was flushed from the stage. Elena and Diana, knowing the man's worth, offered solace. Daniel Chow accepted with a sigh and stood with the tall Sentinels in solidarity. The tranquility of ELF Country, their sylvan sanctuary along Petoskey's Bear River, seemed a million miles—and years—away.

Autumn and Baptiste were quietly conferring. A man and a woman, faces painted yellow, approached the worried doctor and waited. Chow quietly acknowledged them, "Yes?"

"Apologies for the teasing, doctor. We wanted you to know that we've heeded your warning and have a system that works. We'll be using it again, maybe today."

Chow appreciated this. "Thank you. Why the yellow paint? What's your system?"

"It marks us, prepares us. We're Seekers; it's our death-face."

They moved on before he could respond. Elena and Diana exchanged a glance but kept quiet. Had they recognized the yellow-daubed woman?

Chow attended the stage, where Autumn now stood alone. The room was chatty, chaotic, its attendees ready to be released. Yet she did not dismiss them, waiting them out instead.

Eventually, it worked. The room quieted for her. It took effort, and they wouldn't do so again.

"The dangers we face today are real," Autumn said when she had their full attention. "We thank those who have brought us warning. Captain Young, for your information on the Western and Eastern Forces, *miigwech!*" She gave a small bow. The bruised captain, surprised, returned it. In a career of briefings— as fire chief, as Army captain—this solemn bow was his first. Frank felt like a samurai.

"Maang and Biijigigwane, please thank your feathered friends for us—the loon, the osprey." Her boy and Brian acknowledged Autumn and said that they would.

"Doctor Chow, forgive our crudeness; your medical expertise is appreciated. I predict your skilled hands will save many lives, including those who mock you now. *Chi miigwech!*

"And to all of you, and your comrades outside, who have gathered here to make a stand, you have my thanks: Sentinels from the greenwood, bikers and their clubs, Beaver Islanders, Howlers, voyageurs, soldiers, fishermen, pilots, riders and the horses that carry them, yellow-faced Seekers, medicine men and women, and of course, the wild wolves in the forest.

"Each of you has walked your own path. Each has suffered singular sorrows. I am grateful to God, to Gaia, to the *manidoog*—great and small—that have united us today. We know all too well what we are fighting *against....*"

Autumn's audience filled her ellipsis with a flood of trauma-memories, the electrons in the room charged with remembered violence. Autumn acknowledged their red rage, then dispelled it with her hands. "The anger part is easy. But what are we fighting *for?*"

This question was met with silence, though many answered with private thoughts—family, food, security, the future, nature, peace. Autumn nodded as the ambient energy cooled. She put a name to it all: "The Free North. That's the idea anyway. A place free from violence, hunger, disease, and despair. Farms and fishing co-ops are just getting started, and there's hydro power, or the potential anyway. Upper Michigan must be defended—our peninsula of plenty."

She looked to Captain Young. "You say we can't destroy the bridge?" Frank confirmed with a nod. She sighed and said, "So be it." Autumn waxed philosophic: "Did you know that five workers died during construction? Giving their lives to bridge our divide? For seventy years this steel fabric has woven north and south—Yooper and Troll—together. If it can't be demolished, let's use our weapons to win! Once and for all, here and now, defeat the Spreaders! We fight to keep this welded artery open. The Free North must be reachable, for refugees, for resettlement. No matter what happens on the bridge, this gathering, by itself, is a sort of victory. A Last Alliance indeed, it fills my heart to—"

Bahruuuuuuhhhhaaaaa!

Autumn's warm speech was interrupted by an Arctic blast, a reverberation from the Age of Ice. Its sound waves rattled the panes and shook a dusty light bulb from its socket. The shatter of glass panicked the room.

Elephantine, the roar trumpeted again across the Straits. Many covered their ears from its ferocious frequency.

Bahruuuuuuhhhhaaaaa!

The mammoth horn sounded: deep and toned with doom.

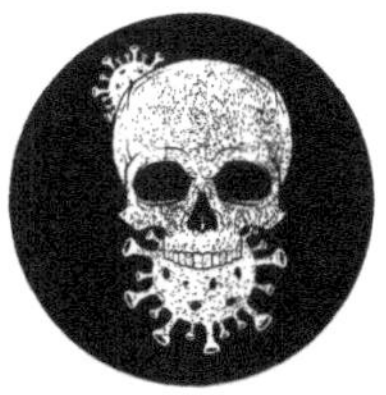

First Come, First Serve

DOZER, TURBOCHARGED BY INJECTIONS, got there first, pushing his Chosen hard, refusing them sleep in Cadillac. Instead they refueled quickly, drove through the night, and now here they were, at the foot of this long, skinny ass bridge. The Straits were empty. His column had beaten the XCons and Mustafa's Cheboygan fleet too. Dozer's command post was going up in the old lighthouse on the southern shore. Electrical cables snaked through the compound, generators chugging, pushing juice through his portable grid.

The newly muscled man—once Mikey, Cowboy's fixer from the Charlevoix days—took a minute for himself. He felt the creep of exhaustion, but there was no way he was giving in. Not now, not when they were so fucking close. He stepped out of the tower's lens room and onto the iron catwalk, forty-five feet above the ground. He began rolling up a sleeve; time to refuel.

The view was a good one.

The big bridge—his objective, per Sharkey's orders—was a graceful thing. Not two years since collapse, and already such architecture seemed impossible, an artifact from the not-so-long ago. He hoped to splash its rusty steel with blood. He loved how high it rose above the surface—200 feet? Maybe more? How many seconds would it take a body to fall, to splat? Dozer would soon find out—he'd make 'em all walk the plank. He'd use a stopwatch, take notes, a Galileo of gore.

The needle found its vein. Dr. Schark's dose of Cyanovirin lit him up. Dozer's fatigue fell away and he was briefly philosophic, a side effect he was adjusting to. Did the Aghori feel this way too? He floated above the catwalk for a minute—*the pulsing clouds, the all-knowing gulls, the impossible blue of this fresh-water sea—*

"Uh, Dozer, we might need you at the drone-trailer?"

Reluctantly, the fix-it-man descended from the clouds and spiraled down the tower stairs, following the nervous errand boy. He shoved aside a red-eyed Raider who was on her way up. The woman, with battle-spiked hair, was carrying a bundled banner to deploy; no detail too small for Prince Sharkey. Spikes saved her curse till the boss was out of earshot. "Well, fuck you too, baldy!" she grumbled, then clipped the flag to the halyard and hauled it aloft. A breeze fluttered the fabric—Panzer's double tower hulked above the Straits.

Dozer fixed the drone problem—an issue with a circuit board. The pilot/controller—an ex-gamer Candidate—was now giving him the thumbs up: laptop and joystick were responding. The tractor-trailer was being unloaded by slaves. XCons had bartered a busload of laborers for a mammoth-machine of their own, a plow-truck mate of the one McKenzie—artist and assassin—had stenciled with her elephant skull.

The drones were being assembled in the yard, each DOD crate bore a stencil: SKTR-10. The slaves worked hard, garbed in orange MDOC jumpsuits. All of them were white, and when they spoke, which was rare, they had an accent—some sort of German gabble?

Dozer admitted the Cons had the right idea. The Candidate system used by Chosen was a poor one, in desperate need of overhaul. There were only so many Hidden, and fewer all the time. Only a handful—like this gamer geek, like Dozer/Mikey himself—survived their trial. And if they did, then they'd been "chosen." Once free, they lost value as labor. But how did the Cons do it? What shielded their slaves from Stinger, from cytokine storms and a choking death? A question for the Big Boss—yeah right, Dr. Schark rarely left his silo.

A Chosen messenger found him. "the Skull calling on the sat-phone, Mikey—I mean Dozer." The Raider only half-hid her smile. This one sported a buzz cut and a face full of piercings; chick looked like a tackle box. Dozer didn't recognize her. Still, word about the bosses—and their backstories—got around. He glared, and her smile fled, as she thought of somewhere else to be. Dozer watched her ass bounce as she strode away; too bad the doses dulled his drive—he was missing out on half the fun.

He ascended the spiral stairs again, re-entering his command center. Picking up the Palantir handset, he acknowledged, "Dozer here."

He listened to Jones's monotone instructions. Sharkey and Mustafa—hotshot CEOs of Panzerland and XCon Inc.— planned a hostile takeover of the Straits. Jones and his Gories had completed step one, capturing Cheboygan last night with their improvised fleet. Apparently, it had been guarded by just a handful of bikers. The promised fuel had been there—diesel and gasoline—mostly unspoiled. Dozer nodded along as Jones detailed the coming assault. He checked his watch, looked down at the drone-yard, then up to the crowded roadway leading to the bridge. He was almost ready, and told Jones the same. Dozer powered down his receiver after the Skull ended the call.

From the lens room, he watched a black cloud of birds— crows? ravens?—fly up from the south. They circled the lighthouse and its two-towered banner, then the murder roosted nearby and shit-claimed their new keep. His walkie-talkie beeped with an incoming call: "Dozer, we got an issue at the stockade, some problem with the prisoners."

The ex-mechanic tried for calm; he failed. "Well? Fucking solve it then!"

"Hey, I'm outnumbered here, you said call if there was any trouble. Well, there's trouble!"

Dozer swore at the Viral, then stomped down the stairs again—maybe a tower wasn't the best spot for HQ? He quick-marched to the shipping container where they'd stashed some biker POWs. Rounding the corner, he saw the problem—utterly predictable. Three big Raiders were bullying his guard, determined to get at the prisoners—especially the woman—handcuffed inside. No weapons had yet been drawn.

"HEY!" Dozer roared as adrenaline surged, delicious, through his veins. "What the FUCK is going on here? Killa, your crew is supposed to be up on that road. You were TOLD to stay in your fucking vehicle!"

Killa, a skinhead with a heavy viral load, sneered his response. "Just checkin' these Candidates, boss man. Heard there's a hottie in there. Time to start her trial, am I right?"

The skinhead pushed past the guard while his two big buddies moved to cock-block Dozer. There was a scream from inside as Killa dragged the biker out by her hair. She looked Indian, her RedSpirit patch confirming it. Arms cuffed behind her, she could only glare. Killa's buddies cheered him on as he crowed, "First come, first serve!"

Killa felt her up, running big hands over her body. "Gotta frisk 'em, right boss? Can't be takin' no chances." The Nazi leaned in close and coughed, coating her with droplets. Dozer visioned the virions. His rage began to build.

Killa flicked his tongue at the RedSpirit. "A true trial needs some penetration!" He threw the bound woman roughly to the ground, where she landed awkwardly on a shoulder. Killa grabbed his swelling crotch, unbuckling his gun belt. The audience gawked, red-eyed, from the roadway above. Crews were leaving their vehicles, leering at the scene, voyeuristic vultures.

"Save a piece for me, Killa!" Truck horns honked impatiently.

"My crew calls dibs!"

Dozer checked his watch.

"We get her next!"

There was no time for this shit. "ENOUGH!" Dozer roared, neck veins throbbing. Cobra-quick from the CV-N, he smashed

Killa's crony in the face, the wingman crumpling. A roundhouse to the head, and the next Raider was down. Mikey had never been a fighter, but Sharkey's juice did all the work.

Killa forgot his crotch and turned to face his boss. Taller and heavier, the skinhead liked his odds. He blew a kiss at the biker POW, prone on the ground. "Be right back, baby. Daddy's gotta work."

He bluffed a charge, but Dozer didn't flinch. The radio beeped from Mikey's belt; so many things needed doing! Out of time, he let the virucide take over. He found himself floating serenely towards Killa. Then the big brute charged for real, a swastika swine with angry pig-eyes. Dozer watched it all play out from afar. He pivoted in slow motion, tripping Killa, then was on him in a flash. Dozer's left hand—it seemed like someone else's?—wrenched the man's chin, exposing the throat. Mikey felt curious—was this really happening? His right hand became a claw. It shot forward, seized Killa's trachea, and ripped. Dozer was misted by a spray of red.

There was a stunned moment of silence from the crowd, eyes and brains reassembling reality. Dozer stood up. Was Killa's windpipe in his fist? The man on the ground, suddenly voiceless, gasped his last, drowning in a froth of blood. The coliseum roared its approval with a great honking of horns.

The controller's voice sounded triumphant over the radio: "Drones are ready, boss! I repeat, the drones are ready!"

The bloody boss, furious with delay, glared up at his Raiders cheering from the guardrail. "Do-ZER! Do-ZER! Do-ZER!" they chanted.

He flung the tubular appendage at them. "Get in your FUCK-ING vehicles. It's TIME!"

The Virals scrambled, laughing, to obey. Engines were started, pluming the causeway with particulates.

"What are YOU assholes waiting for?" He kicked at Killa's cronies till they were up and running too. Dozer checked the time; the column was ready and rumbling. He looked towards the rear and found The Machine, tusked and skulled, his mighty mammoth. He arm-pumped towards its driver. The gearhead acknowledged, yanking the pull-cord for the horn.

Bahruuuuuuuhhhhaaaaa!

Black crows exploded from their roost trees.

The plated pachyderm trumpeted again: *Bahruuuuuuuhhh-haaaaa!*

The invaders—barbarians at the bridge—stuffed fists in ears, grinning like fools. The crows circled them once, then took up the vanguard. Black wings led the sortie as their armored column advanced.

Operation Overlord

CAPTAIN JUAN, the X-branded tug captain, was nervous. Juan was pushing a barge loaded with vehicles and gunmen. The ex-convict had earned his sea legs in the narco navy of the cartels. A decade ago, approaching Florida, his Sinaloa submarine, malfunctioning, was intercepted by the Coast Guard. Juan had been serving time in federal prison when Covee—upstaged by its variant—paroled the survivors still penned inside.

It wasn't today's mission that made him nervous. Compared to dodging FARC off Columbia, this Great Lake Op was a breeze. No, it was these *pinche calaveras*—these fucking Skulls—that made him sweat. Captain Juan steered his course, WNW, on the compass. For now, the green island of Bois Blanc screened his fleet from any watchers in St. Ignace. He could feel the Skull looming behind him; they reminded him of *sicarios*, tattooed hitmen, reapers of souls. *Segadores de almas*. There was something dead inside them.

One of these creatures was meditating in his wheelhouse, though the other passenger might be even worse. Juan couldn't see through the other dude's Ray-Bans—some sort of smart-glass?—to check for infection. This pale creeper had removed his hood, revealing a sort of metal halo implanted in his head, and was muttering—something about "H-hour" and "D-day?"

Goaded by Skulls, they'd captured Cheboygan last night, securing its fuel supply. The fleet—a mixed flotilla of tugs, barges, and repurposed pleasure craft—had been motoring up the Huron coast for a week. Arriving after dark, X-branded crews were pleased with the fuel, less so with the Gories in command. There'd been plenty of grumbling, but no open mutiny; not against Skulls, no fucking way.

The gritty river port of Saginaw had been their initial assembly area. The XCon leader—this Mustafa dude with the halo—tasked his wrench-men with rehabbing engine rooms, pumping bilges, and modifying barges for amphibious assault. Wearing aviators and headphones, the *genio gringo*, a supposed genius, was generous with fuel, salvage, and weapons. A labor force of slaves—mostly healthy—had been provided as well. The X-convoy had surpassed expectations.

Juan rechecked their position and gulped; he had to say something. "Uh, boss ?" He had no idea who was in charge, the Skull or Mustafa. "Bosses, if we don't slow down, they'll see us." As the lead tug, they were about to break cover. Mackinac Island loomed ahead, a fire-gutted hotel haunting its bluff. They'd soon be in the open and vulnerable to attack, if any was coming. Juan hadn't been told shit. Another reason to be nervous.

"Uh, sirs?"

No response from either man, if that's what they even were. The tug pushed its barge closer to open water. The captain stole a look over his shoulder. The Skull had its eyes closed—in prayer?

The other one, with the glasses and the implant, smiled at Juan's anxiety. "Hold your course, *Capitán*. We're right on time." The captain's stomach sank—*pinche loco*. His tug and barge were slow as shit. He kept a bloodshot eye on the compass, on the gauges. He overheard chanting and crossed himself; Skull sounded like a holy man, *un santo monje*.

The halo man pushed a button on his Ray-Bans, and after a minute began reciting. Sounded like dude was reading a quote: "Soldiers, Sailors, and Airmen. You are about to embark upon the Great Crusade, toward which we have striven these many months. The eyes of the world are upon you."

Juan's bad feeling just got worse. *Eyes of the world?* What fucking world? Whose fucking eyes? The only eyes that mattered were the ones in St. Ignace, the ones about to spot his slow-ass barge and wallowing fleet. *Great Crusade?* Fucking please. Juan had earned his X a year ago and had yet to see anything great. Same old rape and pillage—in the beginning anyway. Lately it had been guard duty, supervising slaves, counting inventory. The inmates were the wardens now—*cierra el círculo.* The Cons had become corrections officers. Ironic, yes, but boring as hell.

"Captain, halt your engines."

Juan obeyed the *calavera,* throttling down. Would they stop in time? The Mexican *marinero* reached for the handset—"Stay off the radio." His hand flinched, burned. Juan glanced over his shoulder again. The big Skull, Jones, terrifying to look at, still had his eyes closed. Come on man, did he guide the fleet by feel? *Un brujo? Un mago?*

Juan looked at the other boats. Their bow waves diminished, they were taking their cue. *Gracias a Dios.* Absent engine noise, Juan heard gulls above them. They were still screened by Bois Blanc, but barely. He looked southwest, towards Mackinaw City and the base of the bridge. Also screened. Supposedly they had friends there—a supporting attack? His fleet was only part of it. Fine by him. He inspected the wheelhouse glass—too thin. No way it would stop a bullet. *Mierda.*

Mustafa, was instructing: "Captain Juan, when you receive the call, lead the fleet around the island. You will land north of Ignace and offload your vehicles. *¿Entiendes?*"

Juan got it. "Yes, sir. *Entiendo.*"

Mustafa checked an internal clock and nodded. "Sergeant Jones? It's almost time."

The big baldy finally opened his eyes. Alert now, his aspect filled Juan's wheelhouse with an alien vibe. Fucking creepy. The skeletal sergeant claimed his battle rifle from the rack and stepped out of the wheelhouse and into September's sunlight. The XCons packing the barge elbowed each other.

The tall Skull, backlit by the sun, appeared aflame. The Gorie gripped his military T-shirt. With one bony hand, he ripped it off, flinging it overboard. His tattooed torso was revealed—ribcage, spine, inner organs—anatomically accurate. Halloween had come early, *el Día de Muertos*.

Mustafa plagiarized again, crying out, "Soldiers and Sailors!" Through impenetrable Ray-Bans, he addressed the grinning crew: "The eyes of the world are upon you!"

The muscled Skull brandished his rifle, ordering, "Take your positions! Prepare for battle!"

The Viral assault force cheered. Drivers jumped into vehicles. Gunners loaded weapons. Riflemen lined the rails. A minute of anticipation, then another. The Straits of Mackinac were still.

And then the horn, *Bahruuuuuuhhhhaaaaa!*

Primal. Prehistoric.

A second sound wave pushed through them, balls to bones.

Bahruuuuuuhhhhaaaaa!

Heart of the Turtle by Hadassah GreenSky

On Station

THE BIG HORN ADJOURNED THEM, the municipal building emptying as its bell clanged the defenders to arms. Leadership held a final strategy session and then dispersed, exchanging looks and some meaningful handshakes: "See you on the other side."

Young, Big Ben, and the yellow-faced Seekers were organizing their assets near the toll plaza on the Free North side—the U.P. side—of the bridge.

Big Ben was lining up his bikers; each motorcycle club would fight as a unit. Captain Young liked the look of these scouts and their modified battle-bikes. He tasked Sergeant Booker with distributing extra firepower: M72 LAWS, a light, anti-armor weapon. No sense in saving them. Use the rockets now, or use them never. Young watched Booker instruct the riders—Nomads, Warriors, RedSpirit Women. "Remove the pull pin. Extend the launcher. Check your backblast. Depress the trigger bar."

Satisfied with his sergeant, Young shifted attention to the Seekers, another mixed unit. Some drove trucks and SUVs, some arrived on horseback with slung weapons and bullet-heavy bandoliers. Every horse, every vehicle, every face was daubed with yellow paint; apparently what unified these irregulars was their desire for death, to make an end, and to take some Virals with them.

Autumn, speaking Michif with Baptiste, had parted earlier with her man at the docks: "*Mína ka wapamitin.*" I will see you again. Baptiste jumped aboard the RB-M and blew a final kiss. Autumn hitched a ride to the plaza from Ignace, the gas-tanker that brought her was in the parking lot.

Young nodded to the rig as she approached. "Thought you guys were all out?"

The water-protector shrugged, à la Baptiste. "That's the last of it. Emergencies only. Baptiste wanted you to have it."

Young added the tanker to his list of assets—Seekers, SIS, M72s, deer hunters, Beaver boats, *Nodin*—the list was way too short. Frank wished the Grayling garrison were here instead of stuck on the wrong side—the south side—of the bridge. The Griffs' 105mm howitzers could even the odds.

Camp followers trickled in from the fairgrounds. They brought hot stew and coffee, making their rounds, feeding the fighters, lighting last cigarettes. The Harley engines were chugging, various anthems booming from biker stereos. Captain Young spotted a big man—Mukwa?—and his dreadlocked friend—Shaggy? The wiry wolf-man tried to cajole the reluctant bear into his sidecar. Mukwa was not having it—Shaggy was swearing. Young would have laughed if he hadn't felt like puking.

A mile behind the toll plaza, moated by the Straits, St. Ignace's harbor was busy as well. The morning meeting over, Elena and Diana rejoined *Nodin*. ELF Sentinels were all aboard, doctors too, still anxious from the dreadful horn. Exhaust plumed from twin stacks as the ferry's engines were fired. Deckhands stood by dock lines as Captain Diana barked orders over the loud-hailer. They were underway!

Nodin breezed past Wawatam Lighthouse, the tower's lookouts howling at the vessel. Diana, professional at the helm, ignored them as she kept track of the squadron around her. Baptiste and some voyageurs crewed Young's Response Boat. They exchanged their paddles for pistons and soon overtook *Nodin*, chugging for open water. Several oversized canoes with snipers aboard were spread along the coastline to harass any landings.

Doyle's *Bloody Mary* led the Beaver boats out of the harbor. Big Hannigan came second, the other five following. Younger volunteers, like Hanny's son Nick or Doyle's niece Maggie, had been denied, stranded ashore on Beaver Island. Instead, the captains and crews were gray-hairs, old salts and lakers whose best years were astern. There'd been some shouting about this. Furious at the refusal, Nick cussed out his old man. But in the end, the old-timers held fast. "Son, you and your Maggie are needed here," Hannigan had said to Nick once the young man calmed down. "Nothin' at the bridge but bullets and blood. Even if we dodge 'em all—which we won't—we'll still catch their Cov-ee, and be stung for our troubles."

Captains McCann, Miller, Redding, and Susan Keller relayed the same to their greenhorns. Doyle's parting words had been fewer. His farewell to tearful wife Annie and adopted niece Maggie were his typical bluster: "Adieu Annie lass. Maggie, see you when I see you."

Tom had slung his sea-bag and turned away, both portholes leaking, port and starboard. Doyle thumbed his bleary eyes, dogging down his emotional hatches. He'd scraped barnacles from his throat and tried to whistle—*Farewell and adieu to you fair Spanish ladies*—but nothing worked. Doyle strode away, unballasted.

The Beaver Island boats, outward bound in line-of-battle, were long familiar with the wrecks and reefs hazarding these waters. The Straits, if they cared, would have found the boats strange—gone were their rollers, nets, and cordage; gone were their hauls of fish, and the harrying gulls. Now each boat mounted a machine gun. Dour O'Donnell, busy with *Mary's* bow-mounted Browning, was astounded by the heft of each fif-ty-caliber round. The deckhand, now gunner's mate, readied the weapon and stood by its sights. O'Donnell lit a hoarded cig in the hollow of his jacket and nodded to Doyle, frowning behind the wheelhouse glass. Hannigan had a fifty as well; the other Beavers were armed with SAWs. Untrained in gunnery, Doyle hoped their rate of fire would compensate. At sixteen bullets a second, each boat could throw some serious lead.

Binoculars ogled the horizon, undressing each island with big, eager eyes—no sign yet of invaders, or the rumored fleet from Cheboygan. Each captain felt relief upon making it out of the harbor. No matter what was coming, they now had room to maneuver. Once on station, the boats idled their engines, saving diesel. Radios forbidden, they drifted silently through the doldrums. Earth rolled eastward, lifting the sun to its zenith. The September sky was cloudless, deeply blue and infinitely fathomed. As above, so below—the Straits mirrored the same.

Up on the bridge, the bus-barricade was almost in place. Medieval minded, they welded their wall beneath the north tower, closest to the Upper Peninsula, the Free North. "Make the Virals run the gauntlet," was their thinking. Once committed, any attack would have to traverse three miles of narrow roadway between the south shore and the north tower's barricade. From the toll plaza, defenders could reach their wall quickly, either to reinforce it or to sally forth upon the span. School buses, siphoned dry, were immobilized, then banded together with welded steel. The bus-wall was an art installation, a post-collapse Alamo. "Come and take it," dared its defenders—survivalists wearing yellow paint and body armor. A single sally port angled through the maze. Too narrow for trucks, only bikers could thread it. Seekers tagged their yellow buses with graffiti: "Defend the Sacred!" "#Landback." "Hey Virals, Fuck Off!"

Directly above the bus-wall, the north tower had been scaled and fortified. Snipers nested there, scopes zeroed on the approach road, awaiting targets of opportunity. Glass jugs—wicked and stoppered, contents viscous and volatile—were stockpiled above the barricade, a Molotov menace to any would-be attackers.

Down below, the fleet was on station. The barricade bristled with determined defenders. Captain Young, sheltered in the plaza, marshaled his reserves: SIS bikers and yellow-painted cavalry, well-armed and highly motivated. North of St. Ignace, packed along the forested shore, amber eyes watched: low-slung, hungry, and unblinking.

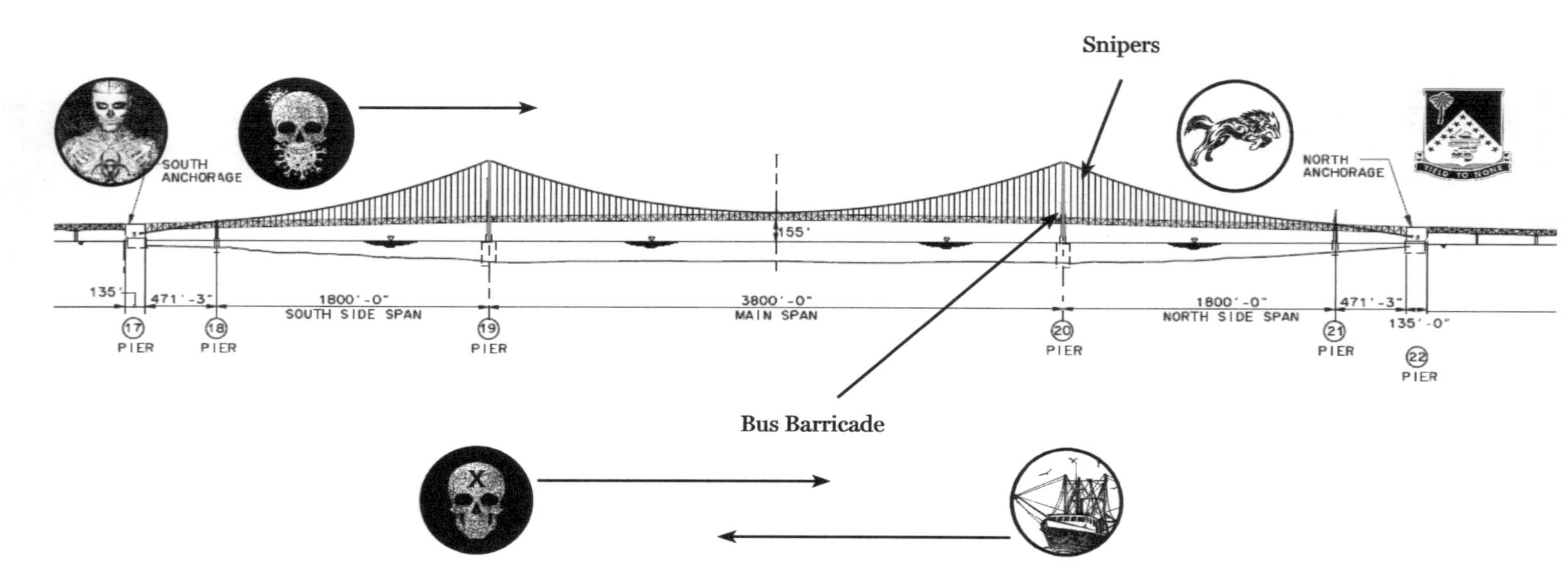

Snipers
Bus Barricade
SOUTH ANCHORAGE
NORTH ANCHORAGE
YIELD TO NONE
135'
471'-3"
1800'-0"
SOUTH SIDE SPAN
3800'-0"
MAIN SPAN
155'
1800'-0"
NORTH SIDE SPAN
471'-3"
135'-0"
17
PIER
18
PIER
19
PIER
20
PIER
21
PIER
22
PIER
X

The Battle of Mackinac

"HERE THEY COME!"

Air horns blared from spotters, bunkered aloft in the north tower. From their crenelated perch, hundreds of feet above sparkling blue water, the yellow-painted Seekers observed the dark cloud approach. There were crows in that cloud, a massed murder of beaks and beady eyes winging north towards the bridge. Exhaust coughed from Raider engines, imperfectly combusting rotten fuel. The light winds shifted north; defenders masked themselves against the greasy fog.

"Hold your fire!" Corvids mobbed their lofty position. "Save your ammo for the Spreaders!" The carrion birds, finding no corpses, bypassed the barbican, continuing their rookish reconnaissance. Sniper teams spun their dials as the first wave of Raiders raced each other up the roadway. The approach was three miles, time enough for the cold calculus of ballistics. The pavement had been pre-painted with range markings; windage flags were closely observed.

The defenders—lifelong deer hunters—chambered cartridges, slowing pulse rates as each spotter counted down the range: "Two miles out. Steady now...."

The approach road was congested with sputtering vehicles, shrouded in soot. By the time they reached the south tower, the assault force began to separate. Faster trucks, better driven, took the vanguard, weaving through the contagious commuters.

"One mile out. Shooters, safeties off...."

Halfway between the towers, where the steel stringers were shortest, a kill-line had been scribed on the pavement, each lane numbered, 1-4. Passing this point of no return, the ten fastest Raiders jockeyed towards the school bus barricade.

"Six hundred yards, weapons free..."

The defenders cloistered in the north tower were monastic in their focus. Spotter, shooter, target—their holy trinity. Ten teams on the tower, each team on a target. Ten scripted conversations, sacrosanct and simple. Amy from Escanaba had lost all her sons to Stinger. Brokenhearted, she spotted for Duane, an old-timer from Ishpeming who'd survived grid-down in his off-grid cabin. Both wore the yellow, seeking an end—a noble one—to their loneliness. They'd rehearsed this scenario, memorizing their mantra.

Amy: "Target, lane 1, Toyota truck, dial up 2.2."

Duane: "Roger, up 2.2 ... on target." The old man was indexed and in shooting position.

Amy: "Spotter ready." She had her wind-call prepared and her reticle was on the hold.

Duane: "Shooter ready." The hunter, at respiratory pause, took the slack from his trigger.

Amy: "Wind, left to right. Dial left 1 MOA, engage!" Her optic was on the Toyota's windshield.

Duane adjusted for wind. Manifesting a hit, he squeezed. At 2,700 feet per second, the .303 bullet flew from his barrel. The conical projectile, weighing 180 grains, impacted with 4,000 joules of energy. The Toyota's windshield exploded in a glassy red spray. The sound followed after, *Crack!*

The driver, hit, dragged his wheel to the left. The speeding truck hit the curb, jumped the low guardrail, and was falling....

Falling....

Falling....

Amy and Duane, locked to their optics, ignored the Toyota, deaf to the cheering barricade below. Soon, all ten vehicles were stopped—windshields, tires, and engine blocks shot out. Surviving passengers, wild-eyed, scattered among the wreckage. Withering fire from bus windows kept them pinned, shredding their metallic cover. Viral blood pooled in potholes, dripping through the grating to thirsty gulls below.

Amy to Duane, as the next wave approached: "Target, lane 1, Suburban, dial up 1.5...."

Dozer observed through binoculars, tending his bank of radios. His probe was successful; the defenders were clearly revealed. Clever bastards, they had snipers on the far tower and gunners in the barricade below. Per design, his first wave was filled with fools, aggressive assholes like Killa carrying heavy viral loads. Panzer was better off without them. Through 10x magnification, Dozer observed the next assault cresting towards the wall.

Black smoke billowed from vehicles afire. Bodies, split open, spilled hot viscera upon the pavement. Cruz and Booker, scenting bile through MOPP filters, flashed back to Afghanistan. The two soldiers were positioned a half mile behind the barricade on the concrete platform of the north anchorage. "Drop it!" Booker called out when the moment was right.

Specialist Cruz, following his sergeant's orders, released the 60mm round into its mortar tube. Gravity-fired, they heard a loud, hollow *Tunk!*

The bomb lobbed slowly above the bridge cables, coming down upon the tightly bunched Chosen. A bright flash, a puff of white, metallic shards shredding flesh, and then the concussion, *Ka-whump!*

Booker observed through binoculars. "Range is good, set for proximity, fire for effect."

Cruz pulled another round from its casing, rotated the fuse—PRX—then dropped it down the tube. *Tunk!* He kept his head down. *Ka-whump!* He repeated the process.

Tunk! Another slow lob as he readied the next. *Ka-Whump!*

Cruz ignored the huzzahs from defenders.

Tunk! Synchronized, their deadly dance continued. *Ka-Whump!*

The attack slowed as wreckage piled up. The mortars were set for airburst; Mighty Mac, despite concussions, remained structurally sound. Sniper teams plied their mortal math. The yellow bus-wall, unbreached, had yet to be bloodied. High explosives rained from cloudless skies. The afternoon sun gilt the smoky scene. The bridge, so far, was holding.

Dozer set down his optics, muttering, "I'll be damned." The ex-mechanic picked up the handset tape-labeled "Jones." The southern causeway leading to the span was gridlocked with his road-raging Raiders. Impatient, they burned precious fuel awaiting their turn. Every few seconds his observation post was concussed—*Fucking mortars?*

Far to the south, in his Kalamazoo compound, Sharkey, micro-managing, demanded regular updates. The bulk of Panzer's assets were committed to this assault. No way Dozer was reporting just yet.

Ka-whump! Another explosion bloomed on the bridge. Even without binos he saw the Raider truck flip. Direct hit. Another flaming obstacle—fuck!—that would have to be cleared.

Dozer counted muzzle flashes from the north tower as elevated snipers culled his milling herd—*Shit! How much ammo do they have up there?*

Ka-whump! Another round detonated, shock wave rattling his cage. He keyed his radio: "Sergeant Jones? This is Dozer."

He waited for confirmation from the Gorie guru, then gave

his order. "Sergeant, begin your landing. Get some fuckin' fire-power ashore and let's pinch these bastards between us. Over."

A moment of static, another detonation—*Ka-whump!*—then some creepy-ass chanting through the radio. The frequency fizzled.

Oily smoke obscured the north tower, nitro-lightning flashing through clouds of carbon.

Dozer assessed his dwindling reserves, idling on the causeway. His gaze lingered on the military column of Humvees and their pennants, signifying Skulls. Was it time for the Aghori?

Ka-whump! Again, he was rattled. Fuck it, these resistors needed killing. Dozer muttered a mantra of his own, "Where we go one, we go all...."

He grabbed the handset marked "McKenzie," depressing its PTT. "Specialist? This is Dozer. How do you read, McKenzie?"

Diana pushed *Nodin* full ahead, her bridge-wing lookout spotting emerging threats. A fleet of X-marked boats rounded the north end of Mackinac Island, heading towards the forested shore of Horseshoe Bay. The ferry revved up as Captain Diana used her loud-hailer: "Sentinels! The enemy is in sight. We must prevent their landing. Boarding parties, stand by your grapples! Kayaks, prepare to launch!"

Diana selected her target, the nearest tug-and-barge, X-marked with drippy paint. She adjusted *Nodin's* course for intercept, steadying her rudder to bear 045. She sight-checked the Beaver Islanders—Doyle steered *Mary*, following her lead. Big Hannigan kept station with his buddy, while the other five Beaver boats followed astern. Baptiste angled the Response Boat; his voyageur canoes would need support. The Viral landing craft vectored their way.

Elena, braided for battle and parka-clad, stood shimmering beside her tall partner. The women put their heads together—hard-bodied athletes exchanging soft words. Elena departed to

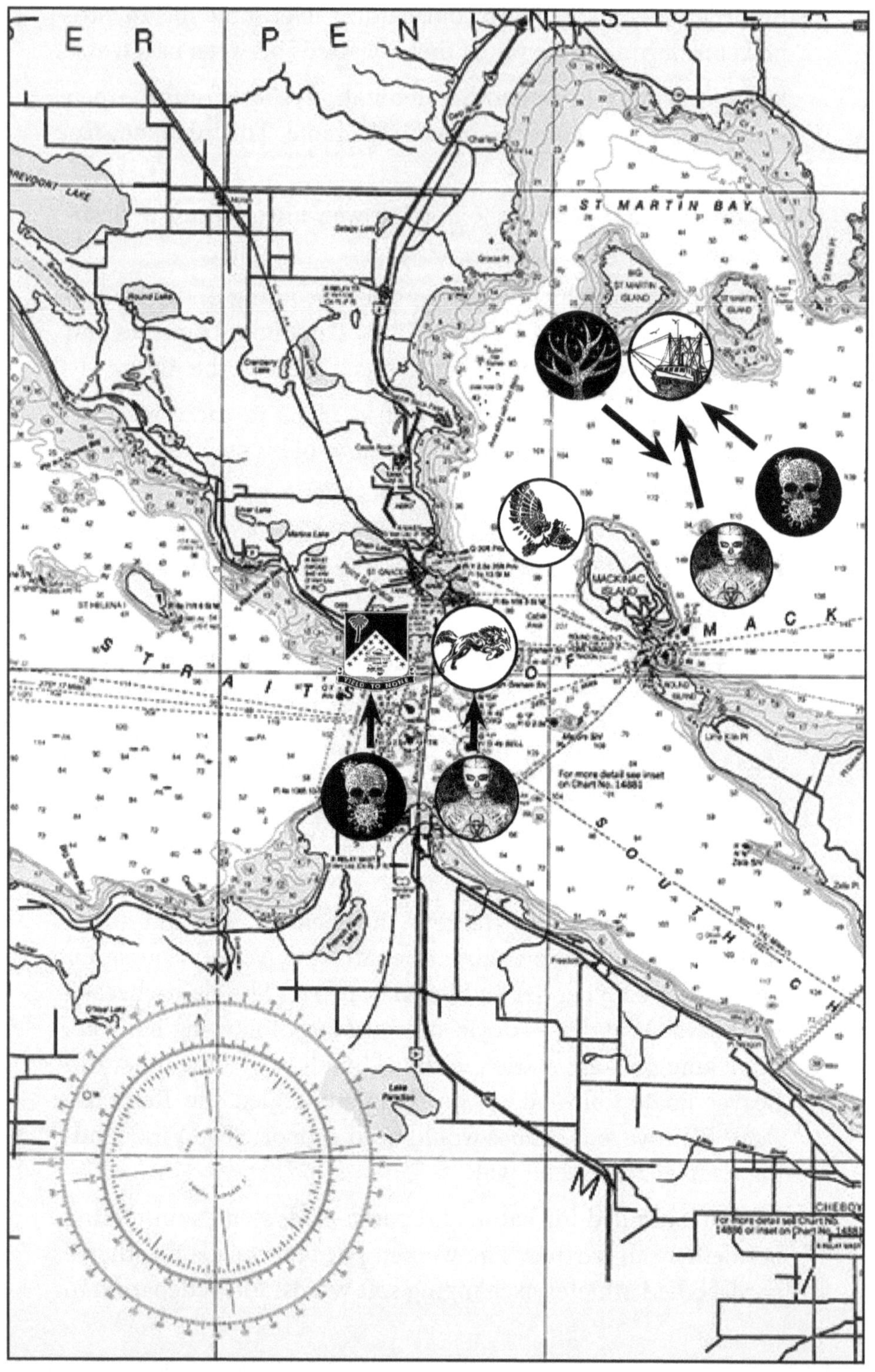
ST MARTIN BAY
BIG ST MARTIN ISLAND
ST MARTIN ISLAND
MACKINAC ISLAND
YIELD TO NONE
STRAITS
For more detail see inset on Chart No. 14881

lead her commandos. Diana, scanning the sky, maintained situational awareness. Blinking through tears, she saw nothing but blue.

Doyle red-lined his RPMs to keep pace with the ferry; Captain Diana would engage the biggest threat. A squadron of armored yachts veered towards them, attempting to screen their largest tug—Diana's target—from defenders. Rail-to-rail with Hannigan, Tom signaled his salty shipmate, then radioed *Nodin,* "Diana, Doyle here. Throttle down, let me and Hanny go first. We'll clear you a path through these yachties. Doyle out."

The two Beaver fishermen were in the lead, *Nodin* following astern. The Viral screening force—X-marked and piratical—quickly narrowed the distance. At 500 yards, the XCons opened fire. Doyle blinked through the flashes as bullets, supersonic, zipped above his wheelhouse. A second after that, gunshots thumped his ear drums.

Neither Beaver boat was damaged, the first volley—aimed by amateurs—too high. Captain Hannigan was roaring as he flashed the Cons the bird. O'Donnell, exposed on the bow, opened up with his big fifty. *Mary's* deck-plates shook as the heavy weapon hammered the fiberglass flotilla. The deckhand's aim was good. Doyle grinned at his man's creative cursing as a million-dollar Sea Ray was shot to shit.

More flashes from the X-boats, more supersonic zips. *Mary* shuddered as bullets, better-aimed, whanged against her hull. Doyle pounded the wheelhouse glass till O'Donnell turned his way: "Get the fuck in here!" The deckhand hunched into the wheelhouse, dogging the hatch behind him. "Get aft to the stanchion and throw Hanny that wire!"

Wide-eyed with adrenaline, O'Donnell ducked his way to the stern. Hannigan's man caught his toss, shackling the steel cable to their own post as well. When both deckhands were clear, Doyle nodded at Hannigan—a lifetime of respect exchanged in a glance. Wired together, the two captains veered apart, unspooling the cable, a galvanized guillotine. At 100 yards the garrote was taut; Doyle could feel Hanny's boat tugging on *Mary*. Tom adjusted his rudder and eyed the fuckers still firing his way. He could see their faces now, ugly bastards, each branded with an X. At this range many bullets hit home, smashing his windshield in several places. *Mary* shook from impacts, but her eager engine still revved, undamaged. The squadron of X-yachts saw their peril too late. Mutant crews ceased firing, some leapt overboard; three of the six boats, tried turning around.

"Too fuckin' late, assholes." Doyle braced for impact as the cable scythed through their lead boat. *Bloody Mary* didn't flinch. He sight-checked his buddy; Hanny's big boat was fine too. Doyle glanced astern at their first victim—a Four Winns Cruiser—neatly decapitated. Its splintered hull was splashed with red, lopped bodies bobbing in the waves.

Doyle growled. Shifting his rudder, he re-tensioned their cable and buzz-sawed the next.

McKenzie led her Aghori team—undetected—along the underside of the bridge. Crisscrossing the girders, they scuttled their way north. The skull-faced sappers carried C-4 and were strapped with Panzer weaponry—M4s, MK 18s, M79s. Encountering gaps in the girders, McKenzie free-soloed the openings, attaching life-lines and throwing them back. One at a time, the skeletons spidered their way across.

Concussions from the battle shook the steel superstructure. Rusty flakes fell like leaves, fluttering 200 feet to tarnish the water below. Above McKenzie's skeletal operators, the roadway was strewn with disabled vehicles, petro-fluids dripping through the grating. Dead bodies—still contagious—leaked as well, oily plasma and gassy gore.

Topside, Dozer's Humvee column steadily advanced. The crews, hand-picked, included the most capable Chosen, stiffened by Skulls. Better disciplined than Raiders, the Humvees utilized smokescreens, covering each other as they dodged disabled vehicles and bumped over bodies—the rotten fruit of the roadway. Surviving Spreaders joined the advance; the swelling strike force approached the north tower.

Amy's yellow face-paint was smeared with soot, and her eyes ached from the pull of optics. Duane's barrel had overheated, his shots flying wild. Their ammunition was almost gone. The ten teams were still intact, and did what they could. Their barbican, and the bus-wall beneath them, had yet to be breached.

Amy tapped the old deer hunter, lying prone with his rifle on the elevated platform.

"Target, lane 1, Humvee, dial up 3." They were holding high; his barrel was hot.

Duane wearily replied, "Roger, up 3 … on target."

Amy: "Spotter ready." She placed her reticle on the driver, a skull-faced nightmare.

Duane: "Shooter ready."

Amy: "No wind, engage!"

Duane—thankless, prayerless—squeezed the trigger and felt his old Remington kick.

Amy: "Shit!" The bullet, slightly off target, was deflected by the Humvee's laminate windshield. She heard cursing from other teams, their fire ineffective. The grenades they'd cached had already been thrown, pockmarking the pavement, but the I-beams were sound. The only option left—jugs of Molotovs— were wicked and ready, but these could only be dropped. The Humvees with the skull-pennants would have to come closer.

Through her spotting scope, the smoke parted and Amy watched in horror as a skeleton crawled from a Humvee hatch, crewing the stubby weapon mounted in the turret.

"Target, lane 1, skeleton on the roof! Up 3…."

She watched Duane's bullet knock the creature down. "Hit! Hell yeah!"

Amy increased magnification, studying the tattooed terror. She gasped: the creature—undead!—was female. Amy gasped again, it was *up!* And moving towards the weapon!

"Target! Target! She's still alive! Duane, HIT HER! Hit that bitch again!"

The Vishkanya—a Gorie name-taped, *KALI*—opened her eyes upon a hellscape of battle-smoke, muzzle-flash, and carnage. Ears ringing and surprised to be alive, she resigned herself to more life—too soon for *moksha*, for release. Shiva, the destroyer, had sent her back. So be it. Kali's right arm wasn't responding, a sniper's bullet having smashed her shoulder. The virucide blocked pain as she crawled out on the Humvee's turret and elevated the Mk 19. Kali sighted upon the north tower, could see the snipers nested there, their crosshairs caressing her tattooed torso. "*Om namah śivāya....*"

Left-handed, Kali thumbed the butterfly trigger—*plink-plink-plink-plink-plink-plink-plink!* A spray of 40mm grenades impacted the tower. A string of explosions followed, and then—*Ka-WHOOSH!* A massive fireball bloomed as the platform's stash of flammables ignited. The entire structure was engulfed in flames. Kali watched the burning blobs tumble off the tower. She bowed to them, envying their flight, their release from *Samsāra*.

Captain Frank Young, standing in the truck bed, felt the heat through his MOPP suit as the north tower erupted. He tore his eyes from the platform, from the drippy fall of burning bodies, as a new threat scuttled up from the girders below—a squad of skull-faced soldiers emerging from *behind* the bus-wall. Shit!

Young thumped the truck roof. "Go, Sergeant! GO!"

Booker hit the gas. Beside him, Cruz chambered a round in

his M4, frowning beneath his mask. Out of mortar rounds, they rallied to their chief. The skeletons—stacking like special operators—were assaulting their wall from the rear; the ghoulish grenadiers punched holes in strong points as they leap-frogged towards the buses under covering fire. Any Seekers shooting back were quickly suppressed.

Speeding to defend the wall, Booker saw a tattooed Goliath gathering suicide vests from its comrades. Loaded down, the thing sprinted towards the open sally port. In range, Booker fishtailed the truck to give Cruz a shot: "Stop!—That!—Dude!"

The oversize Skull, loaded down with C-4, was running in the open. If it reached the wall-tunnel, any detonation would clear a path for attackers. Cruz, sitting shotgun, rested his rifle on the window frame and banged away. The skeletons—aware now of the truck—pivoted and returned fire, protecting their giant.

From the truck bed, Young shouldered his carbine to cover his men. Their truck shook from impacts, but Cruz held steady and knocked the big brute down, pinning the creature to the pavement with a stitchery of bullets. Booker watched the thing twitch; too late he saw the detonator in its bony hand.

"Chief!" Muted by his MOPP mask, Booker screamed—"Fire in the HOLE!"

A half-tick later, and their world went WHITE.

When reality reassembled, nothing looked familiar.

Their toy truck had been flipped, then shoved against the rail by a massive hand of air. Booker, the driver, blinked at the lake's surface far below, slicked with blood and oil, bobbing with body parts. His nose was gushing, a pink paste spackling his mask. Cruz's bulk crushed against him. He shook his buddy— alive, thank God. He checked Cruz's extremities—intact. Upside down, they egressed through shattered windows. Booker, kneeling on the pavement, tore off his mask, vomiting over the rail.

Cruz, brain-injured, struggled for situational awareness. His buddy Booker seemed OK. Puking and bloody, but OK. The suicide bomber had cratered the roadway, but the bus-wall remained intact, and the bridge was structurally sound. Inside the blast radius lay a squad of skeletons, disassembled. Compound fractures marred their tattoos, shards of white bone giving the lie to black ink. Glassy diamonds sparkled in the sun. On the defender side of the wall—the north side—nothing moved. The sniper tower burned, a pillar of fire.

Cruz was fading. He saw Booker puking, way too close to the edge. Cruz couldn't hear, but felt thumping as the determined assault continued—fucking Spreaders.

Something was missing—Booker? Bomber? Bus-wall?

Oh shit—where was their chief?

Cruz groaned as he tore off his MOPP hood, scanning the haze. Where in the fuck was Frank Francis Young?

A string of *plinks*, then explosions, crumped from the battle-side of the wall. Cruz guessed at the source, an automatic grenade launcher—damn. Shards of bus-steel spun through the air like jagged yellow Frisbees—no way the wall could hold. The combat medic crawled towards Booker, rolling his friend from the rail. Strength ebbing, Cruz closed his eyes and lay down—O captain my captain? The roadway began to rumble. With a last effort, Cruz unlidded a blood-filled eye. What the—?

An armed cavalcade thundered past him, last reserves from the toll plaza—horses, smeared with paint; gray-haired veterans wearing camo; 1st Cav pennants, yellow shields slashed with black. Then Cruz saw the Harleys, the jackets, the patches. Each motorbike carried two—a driver, with an operator behind. Each operator shouldered a heavy tube—the LAWS rockets Booker had delivered and demonstrated. This mixed unit wove its way south through the wall, vanishing in the smoke of battle.

Mukwa growled as they sallied forth from the bus-wall, a gritty haze scouring his throat. Shaggy almost spilled him as the motorcycle jumped a dead horse. The sidecar—too small for Muk's bulk—hadn't worked, so they rigged a standing platform instead. Mukwa held tight to the grip-bar as they entered the fray. His vision came in flashes: the oil-slick roadway littered with lopped limbs and vehicles afire.

Skull-painted Humvees pressed towards the wall. Behind this advancing armor, a honking mass of Raiders blared. Each Humvee had a gun turret; in each turret stood a skeleton. Professional, disciplined, the punishers fired controlled bursts, shredding the SIS sortie emerging from the sally port. Many horses were down, thin skins flayed by firepower. Dismounted, their riders returned fire, bunkered behind the big equine bodies. The modified Harleys wove through this carnage—ride or die motherfuckers!

Then the first LAWS rocket *whooshed* from its tube. Riding pillion, the shooter, a Nomad, missed his primary target, but the invaders were too closely packed. His 66mm warhead hit another Humvee instead, tearing its gunner in half. The tattooed torso—sans legs—soared over the rail, a fleshy kite with entrails streaming.

More *whooshes* from the bikers, more fire-balled armor. Overwhelmed by leather-clad rocketeers, the Skull attack stalled. More horses emerged from the bus-wall. Bikers found blind spots and wielded their weapons. Shaggy, war-whooping, throttled towards a grenade-spewing Humvee. He squeezed his brakes; fishtailing, he launched Mukwa aboard.

A death's head, point-blank, greeted Mukwa with her pistol. One of her shoulders was shattered, her grip left-handed. Carbine still slung, Mukwa clawed out his blades. Ripping through her ribcage, he hurled her lifeless body to the pavement, then dove through the turret-hatch headfirst. Shaggy, wolfishly circling on his Harley, watched the Humvee bounce on heavy springs. There was a violent blur from inside, then arterial spurting upon the glass. White Bear emerged, face-painted with gore.

Shaggy approached for pickup, but Mukwa waved him off. The big man crewed the stubby weapon instead, spinning it south against the gridlocked Raiders. Curious, the bear pawed its trigger—*plink-plink-plink-plink-plink-plink-plink!*

Explosions popcorned amidst the undispersed Raiders. Panic was spreading as their road-rage petered out. Just like that, fight turned to flight. The Viral retreat was messy, yellow-striped cavalry mopping them up. Single shots cracked from the battlefield as Spreaders were euthanized and their skull-faced overlords put down, one by one.

Big Ben, blistered by the backblast from his LAWS, re-ordered their defenses. Surviving Seekers and gas-masked SIS salvaged weapons and ammo from the roadway. Would there be another assault?

Camp followers hustled through the bus-wall carrying stretchers, water, and extra bandoliers. Masked and gloved, they probed the wreckage for wounded. Had any been exposed? Had any been stung? Casualties suspected of close contact with Virals were daubed with yellow and treated in place. Some were twitching already. The walking wounded—freshly striped— joined surviving Seekers in limbo and remained upon the span. Those stung were quickly seizing; any purgatory would be brief.

It was late afternoon.

Dusk Swarm

NO FUCKING WAY THIS WAS HAPPENING.

Dozer stood on the elevated catwalk. He pulled his eyes from the binoculars he clutched. Unmagnified, the scene was worse. Oily fires plumed between the two towers, but none from the far side where he'd hoped to be already. Their goddamn bus-wall remained unbreached. His shock-troops had been shocked.

Dozer expected to lose some Raiders, he was fine with that, a dime a dozen. What was un-fucking-acceptable was losing the Humvees. He gasped seeing the damage wreaked by their rockets. Where in the fuck had they scrounged all those LAWS? And then Kali's Mk 19 had been turned against them? How the hell had that happened? Panzer's heavier weapons, per his plan, were crewed by Gories!

With no room to turn around, surviving Chosen abandoned their vehicles, streaming backwards, ants from an inferno. Desperate, these deserters were mingling with his reserves. The chaos they were causing would have to be stopped.

McKenzie and her squad of sappers had briefly given him hope. Dozer knew her plan and had tracked its progress. The flaming north tower was awesome, his staff cheering each burning blob. Then, after the C-4 detonated on the far side of their wall, he'd waited, but the resulting breach—if there even was one?—had gone unexploited.

And where the *fuck* was Aghori Jones, Mustafa, and their "Overlord" Operation? A naval battle was taking place behind

Mackinac Island. Dozer heard explosions, but couldn't see shit. He'd lost comms with Jones and narco-Juan too. Their landing zone—designated "Omaha" by Mustafa's digital master, A-EYE—had yet to be assaulted. Damn that haloed bastard and his neural implant!

Fuck it. Now or never.

Dozer ducked inside the lens room and grabbed the mic labeled, "Mammoth." He gave orders, then picked up another—"Skeeters"—and did the same. Still furious about the LAWS and those outlaw bikers, he remembered his prisoners. Too delicious to delegate, Dozer descended from the tower, raging towards the stockade.

The bloody sun hemorrhaged toward the horizon. The Straits were slick with oil and choked with flotsam from the XCon flotilla. The gill-netters, Doyle and Hannigan, still wielded their wire. Lifelong harvesters, their haul today was human. Baptiste in the Response Boat covered their clotheslining. Supporting Beaver boats sniped the shipwrecked Spreaders—fish in a barrel, if every fish was viral.

Captain Diana was neutralizing X-barges—two out of three had been disabled so far. Her big ferry wasn't pretty; *Nodin* had been shot at, scorched, and some crew were wounded. Disdaining modern firepower—Gaia protect!—they'd taken a beating. But broadside to the barges, Elena's commandos—hard to see in their parkas—grappled their way aboard. ELF archers covered their crossing. Hand-to-hand, Sentinels fought their way into wheelhouses. Two invasion barges had been intentionally run aground. Their X-branded crews—for now—were marooned and harmless on the nearby shoals.

Captain Diana recovered the ELF commandos. Wounded warriors went below to be treated by doctors. Diana's final target, the biggest barge-and-tug, was at full power, making its run towards Ignace's flank, the forested shore. If beached, the modified barge would open its jaws, vomiting Virals behind the un-defended town. Diana arrowed *Nodin* toward intercept. Doyle and Hannigan cleared a path with their cable, their delta of death. Elena and her team were rearming by the rail, preparing to neutralize this final threat, when they heard an approaching aircraft.

Danger!

Elena shaded her eyes against the westering sun, seeking the silhouette that might turn the tide. Sentinels were pointing—a wolfish Cessna wagged its wings, commencing a bombing run against the final barge. No fudge this time: Sheila's co-pilot was pulling pins, dropping grenades on the crowded Cons. Explosions peppered the parked vehicles. Sheila howled, circling for another run. Sentinels were cheering. Diana, closing fast on the blasted barge, fought down her grin.

But as the sun set, another swarm was rising. Clouds of mosquitoes gathered in the gloom. Elena felt a prick and slapped one on her neck. She raised her hood against their whine, contemplating the broken bits in her palm—her blood or theirs? Could they vector the virus? All her Sentinels were swatting. And then the other swarm appeared.

A dozen drones, insectoid, buzzed towards the battle. Controlled remotely, each SKTR-10 was a flying bomb. Elena, alarmed, sent a runner to warn Diana at the helm, then watched in horror as the drone-swarm divided.

Pilot Sheila, too late, tried to shake herself free. A SKTR, heat-seeking, splatted against her windshield, detonating its ten kilo warhead. The cartwheeling plane, in two chunks, hit the waves hard.

Two more drones chased the gill-netters. One locked on Hannigan, one on Doyle. Elena watched, nauseous, as Hannigan's wheelhouse exploded. Cable-connected, *Mary* was immobilized as well. The remaining SKTR zoomed in, proboscis extended. Doyle's man on the bow fired short bursts from the Browning.

Tracer-rounds, like fireflies, darted in the dusk—a hit! A spray of plastic parts! Splash one drone!

The whole fleet was swatting now, driven to distraction by the mechanical swarm. The remaining X-barge plowed on, its landing zone drawing near. A smaller X-craft crewed by Viral yachties sped towards the immobilized *Mary*, tethered to the wreck and Hanny's charred remains.

Sentinel Sparrow shrieked a warning, and Elena followed her frantic point. Several SKTRs, skimming low, were buzzing their way. Archers nocked arrows—Gaia guide us!—and loosed when in range. Ineffective, their light shafts were deflected, doing no damage. Synchronized, the SKTRs kamikazied into the ferry's superstructure—three separate explosions as each warhead hit home. The whole ship shook as the wheelhouse was ripped apart—*Ka-BOOM!*

Elena hid her face from the heat, then looked up, aghast. A ferocious fireball ballooned in the twilight. The entire wheelhouse was gone. Diana was gone. The ferry was burning, dead in the water. The X-marked tugboat, now clear, shoved its barge—a loaded bioweapon—towards the undefended shore.

Dhak! Dhak! Dhak! Dhak! His deckhand was firing, but the final X-yacht kept coming. Doyle tracked O'Donnell's tracers; no effect could be seen. *Mary* strained against her wire leash—Hanny's burning boat was too damn heavy. Doyle idled his engine and, cursing, stomped aft to cut them free. He had only seconds.

Tom sparked acetylene, trimmed its flame, and began cutting the cable. His deckhand shouted a warning as the X-yacht rammed *Mary*, knocking Doyle off his feet. Spreaders thumped aboard as their X-yacht backed away. From the bow came sounds of a scuffle, and O'Donnell's curses, then *bang!*—a pistol shot. His man of few words, silenced forever.

A red rage took him. Bloody Doyle charged forward, battle smoke and twilight confusing his enemies. Tom stayed low and exploded into the closest body. Doyle heard ribs crunch and continued his charge. The next X—O'Donnell's killer?—pointed a pistol. Doyle broke the fucker's arm, then pivoted, hurling the branded bastard off his boat. A rifle butt knocked Tom to the deck. Dazed, Doyle flung a thick leg, tripping his attacker. They wrestled face to face. Hanny's pyre lit the Con's puckered X. The spitting Spreader coated the captain's face with live virions. Doyle's thick fingers gripped its throat, squeezing the windpipe till blood vessels burst and the creature's eyes bled red.

Concussed, Tom cleared the bodies from his boat, including—God damn it!—his shipmate.

Yea, though the tempest rages—Doyle shackled a heavy block to O'Donnell's belt.

I shall not be afraid—Tom rolled his man, a biohazard, gently over the side.

For He knoweth the ways of the sea. The iron pulled him down, fifty fathoms to the lightless deep.

Tom blinked his eyes clear and took his bearings. *Nodin* was on fire; drones pestered what remained of his fleet. Looking back at the bridge, the north tower—blackened but structurally sound—still burned. Doyle squinted through the dusk—was their bus-wall holding? The remaining tug shoved its lethal load closer to shore. If those X-vehicles flanked Ignace, then the bridge and the undefended north were fucked.

Tom's eyes watered, and his throat itched. Envenomed, he could feel Covee crawling inside him—great, a fucking Spreader. Well, that was that. Doyle limped his way aft; at least he wouldn't die ashore. Tom re-sparked his torch and finished the job, severing ties with the burning hulk of his buddy's boat. Big Hannigan was dead along with his crew. Diana, dead. O'Donnell too. Tom, infected, blamed himself. He would never go home again.

Back in his wheelhouse, he geared *Mary's* transmission, brought her around, aimed her at the final tug and throttled forward. Cytokine chills shook Tom's body as visions flashed, tripped by a flood of DMT.

Old Keith rolling cigs on their first trip across. Boosting niece Maggie so she could steer in the harbor. Honeymooning with Annie, champagne in the wheelhouse. His tipsy bride taking his hand, pulling him below. How they'd rocked his new boat, skinny-dipping in the lee of nameless islands.

Doyle's lungs filled with froth as his respiratory system crashed. Tracers from the tug began stitching his way. His RPMs redlined as he vectored *Mary* right at the fuckers.

A hundred yards—bullets busted out his remaining glass.

Fifty yards—*Mary* weathered her final squall, this one of lead.

Thirty yards—an X-yacht tried to intervene, shielding the last tug and barge.

Doyle snarled as the fatal geometry clicked. He shifted his rudder and buried the throttle, exalting as the angle of impact ramped his blessed *Mary* suddenly skyward. His beautiful boat was briefly airborne. Tom's final vision was a glimpse inside the tug—a wraith with a halo and a goddamn ghoul! Halo flinched, emitting a soundless scream. The skeleton meditated in seeming relief. Doyle's blue eyes were shining—mission accomplished, and a martyr's death too. Sins forgiven, St. Tom's final smile was serene.

Mary's keel knifed into the tug—*Ka-Runch!*—rupturing its fuel tanks—*Ka-BOOM!*

The dark straits bloomed, briefly red. Both vessels were blown apart, and fragile bodies too. A rain of steel—and softer parts—pattered upon the oily surface. Pools of diesel ignited, limning the scene a garish orange. Tug and fish-boat were fused by fire. The nautical sculpture listed as it burned, quickly taking on water. The impact severed the tug-barge connection. As the tug sank, the barge—now untethered—coasted towards the empty shore. Its heavy hull plowed sand. Its iron ramp clanged down. The X-marked vehicles, two by two, drove ashore uncontested. A dozen battlewagons, bristling with gun barrels, probed Evergreen Shores with their headlights, seeking the back door to Ignace and the envelopment endgame.

From the Nest

THIS PARTICULAR *PINUS*, solemn with centuries, had witnessed such battles before. The white pine's stomata sniffed gun smoke and recalled past combatants—French, British, Anishinaabeg, American. The pine's woody organs, bioacoustic, remembered past cannonades and added the day's bridge battle to their mycorrhizal memory. As a sapling, its bark had felt the heat from colonial forts aflame, absorbing the atomized flesh of charred defenders. Colonial corpses fortified the cambium of the massive pine, oldest resident of the ancient Straits.

The two tiny humans, platformed in its piney crown, had no such experience. They'd been positioned there—out of harm's way—by Baptiste and Autumn. Brian and Loon were badly shaken by the battle below. Their flet faced south towards the burning bridge. Eastward, to their left, miniature boats still battled in the bay. Behind them, to the north, lay St. Ignace, undefended.

Their bird familiars—loons and raptors—had flown, fleeing cacophony as fast as wings could carry them. The two friends, horrified, saw the north tower erupt in flame. They felt the C-4 detonate, then cheered to see the bus-wall unbreached. They followed the wheeling boats, swatted mosquitoes at dusk while cursing the drone swarm and its terrible damage. Brian wept at the death of Diana, blinded by tears as *Nodin* burned, becalmed, dead in the water. Doyle had been killed along with Hannigan, pilot Sheila, and so many others.

Despite Doyle's sacrifice, the X-barge had beached, vomiting its Viral vehicles ashore. The two friends watched as headlights probed their way towards St. Ignace and inevitable victory. The remaining drones were now regrouping. Once in formation, they left the burning bay, buzzing towards the bridge. Loon and Brian tracked the tracer-fire as defenders, blinded by twilight, sought to slap away the stinging swarm.

Brian's medicine pouch was empty, his battered thermos too. Mosquitoes whined in his ears. The evening was windless, the big water, flat calm. The moon, at first quarter, was smudged by smoke. Muzzles flashed less frequently now from the bus-wall as the Seekers there ran low on everything. A seething mass of Raiders still waited, packing the causeway for a final assault while hundreds of crows flocked above, their inky cloud forecasting a fleshy feast to come. Brian's third eye was dimming; he foresaw the breakthrough, the encirclement, the slavery and slaughter.

Loon and Brian, aloft and alone, bore witness to woe. Tasked towards the bridge, the drones, artificially intelligent, locked onto targets with infrared eyes—the fuel-tanker, the toll plaza, the SIS bikes. Then a final doom, double-toned, boomed across the Straits. First the primal horn, the same one from before— *Bahruuuuuuuhhhhaaaaa!* Moments later a mechanized mammoth emerged from the mass of cheering Raiders.

Then came the fog signal—*DOOOOOOOuuuuuuuum!* Scraping metal, throwing sparks, the plated pachyderm plowed its way towards the bus-wall. SIS prisoners, still alive, festooned the fell beast. The bridge defenders weren't firing—how could they, with their friends in the crosshairs?

Impact! *Ka-RUNCH!* The bus-wall crumpled as the tusked terror broke through. Its fleshy armor had been gashed, its hide of prisoners smeared like red paint. Triumphant, the Raiders flooded through the breach. They faced an open mile of roadway, then the toll plaza, and the Free North beyond. There was nothing left to stop them—some horses, some wounded. The drones arrived, swarming their targets.

A puff of wind stirred the branches and Brian's beads. Both fliers, ever-hopeful, looked to the west. The breeze shifted the pall of battle, the first stars emerging. Brian stared at Antares, the red eye of Scorpio. Loon knew the constellation as Sleeping Giant—*Nanabozho* drawing back his celestial bow. They watched a formation of fast-flying raptors, the big-bodied birds arrowing towards the bridge. Man and boy followed the feathered fliers, hearing faint cries from voices below—"Eagles! The eagles are coming!"

Captain Young—barely alive—had been found. The suicide bomber, strapped with C-4, had blown Frank far from the truck bed. The catwalk caught him as he rolled under the guardrail. His men brought him to Autumn at the plaza's aid station. No-nonsense, she asked first about exposure—how close had they gotten to Virals?

The soldiers assured her they were clean, so they'd gone, unstriped by quarantine yellow, and were allowed to remain. EMT Cruz and big-hearted Booker fetched their med kits, helping out where they could. At dusk, the double-horn blew. Young, dosed and dopey, ordered his men to scrounge weapons and night-vision and prepare a defense. They established a perimeter around the toll plaza, circling their wagons for a final stand. Older veterans and non-combatants were pressed into fireteams. Rifles and ammunition were quickly distributed.

Then the mammoth broke through the bus-wall.

Glowing green in their night vision, the skull-stenciled plow continued its charge. Trucks and SUVs loaded with Virals followed close behind, ignoring the SIS and yellow-faced Seekers harrying their flanks. The open mile between the breached wall and Autumn's aid station quickly shrank. SKTR-10s dominated the airspace, forcing defenders to shelter in place.

"Hold your fire!" Alfonso Cruz, goggle-eyed, steadied the nervy survivors. Booker adjusted his lenses, focusing on the armored beast, the pulped prisoners, and their motorcycle jackets. LAWs couldn't stop it, nor could their mortar. Out of rockets, out of rounds, Booker's thoughts fled towards family. His wife and boy were smiling, waving—they seemed very near. The range narrowed. Anthony Booker prepared to make an end.

But then the SKTRs wavered. Booker saw one ripped from the sky; crashing into the concrete, it detonated. A Raider truck swerved away from the blast and tipped over, smearing its Spreaders on the pavement. Another SKTR tumbled, and detonated. Then another.

Zooming out with his NVGs, Booker witnessed a fury of feathers and grasping talons.

The plaza's defenders were shouting, "Ospreys!" "Hawks!" "And eagles too!"

The mechanized swarm was shredded, biomimicry mocked by the real thing. There was a moment of hope as the last drones were destroyed, but then the defenders ceased cheering. The mammoth machine, undeterred, plowed ever nearer, its cloud of corvids providing close-air support. The crows—far too many—hit the marshaled raptors, murdering the aerie. Black beaks gouged golden eyes, a four-to-one ratio; every fight was unfair. And still, the mammoth kept coming—*God damn it!*

Booker shouldered his battle rifle, flicking on the laser pointer. Awkward with his goggles, he put his beam on the beast, probing for a weak point. There was none.

"Weapons free!" At Cruz's command Booker squeezed off a burst, *Pop! Pop! Pop!* He heard others do the same. Their puny projectiles bounced off its hide, sticks and stones—*shit!*

Then Booker heard a far-off ROAR, and felt a RUMBLE that his body remembered. The very air was jellied by 30,000 lbs. of turbo thrust. The pavement shook. But it wasn't the beast? This was something new, something else!

The source pounded nearer. Unbearable, it rattled the world. He heard Cruz's voice, cool and incredulous: "Eagles? Oh hell yeah! Our fuckin' Eagles *are* coming!"

Booker tore off his goggles. He saw stars, and the two towers, and twin afterburners thundering from the west.

Colonel Dennis was almost at the bridge, and almost out of options. Desperate, he radioed the order, scrambling his last aircraft from their nest in Traverse City. Designated *Arrow-1* and *Arrow-2*, the F-15Es reached the Straits in five minutes flat. Ten miles out, the pilots switched to VFR, vectoring towards the glow from multiple fires.

In their talons, the Strike Eagles clutched assorted munitions. Approaching the bridge, both WSOs toggled to bombs and flicked on their LANTIRNS, painting the target with infrared.

Once released, the pair of GBU-27s, each weighing 2,000 pounds, finned their way towards impact. Detonating together, they completely destroyed the roadway. The big bridge was severed. Suspension wires dangled empty, the watery chasm gaping below.

The Eagles circled once, confirming their hit. Then the pilots dipped their wings, returning—reluctant—to the nest. Both birds were flying on fumes.

"Take cover!" Booker screamed as the defenders dove behind barricades.

Ka-BOOM!

Ka-BOOM!

Mighty Mac shook as its roadway was ripped asunder. Compressed air crushed horses, both dead and alive. Shock waves whipped the cables into a frenzy of steel. The intense heat ignited secondary explosions. Raider vehicles popped off, gas tanks combusting. The blast wind created a vacuum; as it refilled, people and their parts were sucked into the void.

Booker, nose gushing again, looked up to see the red-eyed mammoth trumpet over the edge to extinction. The burning beast fell 200 feet, then shattered upon the surface, its primal fire quenched by meltwater from the Age of Ice.

Back on Beaver

NICK HANNIGAN—college bound before being grounded by Covee—was on watch duty. Diligent in his father's absence, he logged each visitor to the Whiskey Point Light.

September 24th, Year 2

Maggie Doyle, brought dinner, 1700-1800

Samantha, observer, 1900–

Miin, observer, 1900–

Grace (a Natural), observer, 1900–

Nick monitored the tower radios, collecting NTRs—Nothing to Report—from other watchers around the island. Through the gloom of nautical twilight, he glassed the horizon with binoculars, trying to ignore the three women on the catwalk and the goosebumps they gave him.

They arrived together just before sunset, dropped off by Shawn Greene and his clopping mare Montana. The women ascended, a weird trio, nodding hello in the lens room before ducking onto the platform. They hadn't moved since, fixated on the darkening east.

The mosquitoes came at dusk. Samantha flicked flame and lit a smudge. Nick caught a whiff of sage, spicy even through the glass. His dad—Big Hanny—and Doyle's small fleet had gone to the bridge. Lake Michigan was calm and mirrored the quarter moon. Nick sighed, thinking of Maggie Doyle and the kiss she'd delivered with his dinner. The watery world was waiting for something. Weren't they all?

Far to the east, lightning flashed in the dark. Strange considering the cloudless sky? Another flash! Then another! No way was that a storm. A *battle* was being fought in the Straits! Of course his dad and Bloody Doyle were in it. Nick cleared his choking throat, damming back a sudden tear. After a moment he stepped outside, joining the women at the rail. "Hello, ladies."

"*Aanii*, Nick."

"*Boozhoo*, young Hannigan."

A freshening breeze banished the pesky skeeters. Early stars were shining bright. An extra sharp FLASH! FLASH! yanked four pairs of eyes to the eastern horizon. Nick counted under his breath, "One, one thousand. Two, one thousand. Three, one thousand...."

When the sound wave finally found them, the double *Ka-BOOM* mimicked thunder. The wise women gasped. He heard Miin say something—Samantha's foster, a Native girl he sort of knew—"*Aah-nah-mee-kee.*"

Some Indian word? Probably, Nick wasn't sure. Samantha—eldest on the island—smiled slyly, like a fox. The old woman repeated Miin's syllables, spread her arms wide and stood tall with Grace, all three women beseeching.

Nick heard the word more clearly.

"*Animikii*," Samantha repeated, embracing the dunes, the stars, and the entire planet too.

Sick Bay

DANIEL CHOW FELT the drone-damaged ferry bump back to its berth. He heard shouted orders from deck as dock-lines were thrown. Multiple fires had been extinguished by the crew. Baptiste, in the Coast Guard Response Boat, towed them back to harbor. Chow checked his engraved wristwatch: "Happy Father's Day," a message from before. Daniel wiped a smear from the dial. It was after midnight; they'd been in surgery for ten hours straight.

He looked at Doc Newsome; the Beaver Islander looked OK. Newsome's RNs, Mathew and Sean, were champs, their PPE and masks spattered with blood. *Nodin's* sick bay, for the first time, was empty. Patients, stabilized and dosed, recovered in the ferry's crowded cabin. Those they'd lost—way too many— were buried at sea, deep-sixed in Lake Huron.

Newsome stood straight, the old practitioner knuckling his back. Mathew leaned against Sean—was there chemistry there? With the respite, reality reared—Diana was dead, many Sentinels too. When the wheelhouse exploded, the boat lost electricity, forcing Chow to finish an amputation by feel. Then Mathew had lit the lantern, and the sawbones continued by its glow. In sepia and shadow, the centuries compressed—moaning wounded, the pitching deck, the gimballed flame.

Nodin's generators were quickly restored, providing power for the pumps, for the patients. During battle, burn victims were carried down, and shipwrecked sailors too. Most of the Beaver boats had been destroyed. To Chow's knowledge, no contaminated were aboard. *There'd better not be.*

The fires were doused but the carnage continued. Stretchers kept coming, bearing news with each body—the drone swarm, the eagle attack, the deaths of Hannigan, Doyle, and their crews, the loss of many elves. A barge of Virals had broken free, beaching itself behind St. Ignace, a contaminated whale, Moby-X. They all heard the ROAR of fighter jets, the airstrike; the whole ferry had shaken. Cries of joy instead of pain, until the next patient, without anesthetic, went under their knives.

Tie-up completed, many boots thumped aboard. Chow looked up, bleary eyed, as two sooty soldiers dragged someone in. Propped between Booker and Cruz was their chief, their captain, Frank Young. Chow couldn't help but feel guilty—how close had Young gotten to pinning Bob Campbell on him? Chow remembered their confrontation—an accusation really—outside the Beaver church. The doctor gulped—too close.

"He's got a blast injury, Doc," Cruz said. "Maybe bleeding in the brain?"

Chow threw his arms up to stop them. "Wait! Were any of you exposed?"

The soldiers pushed past him, easing their captain to a chair. "Wouldn't be here if we were."

The medic, Cruz, was glaring—still suspicious about Campbell. "What about you, Chow? Who exactly have *you* been treating?"

Dr. Chow shrugged, beginning Young's triage. "No Virals today, if that's what you mean. As far as I know we're unexposed."

Sergeant Booker, still black-eyed, sniffed back a nosebleed. Chow beckoned to Mathew, and the nurse guided the other two out. Carefully, Chow removed Young's helmet, checking his skull. But what if we *were* exposed? What if Covee is here?

Daniel Chow—a founding father of the Naturals—kept thinking of Diana. Her death wasn't real, not yet. She'd delivered him a tincture before they left Beaver Island. Two days ago? Three? A golden liquid sealed in a canning jar, it had a masking-tape label—*At-the-last.*

What had the ELF leader said about the medicine?

"This will help you treat the wounded. *At the last resort,* use it, a light against darkness."

Nonsense at the time. Far too busy, Chow had stashed her jar away. The doctor made a mental note to ask Diana. He choked as sudden grief caught him by the throat. Newsome shot his fellow Wolverine a look—You OK? Chow coughed it away. It was becoming real now. All too fucking real.

Another Fucking Horn

MUKWA, HEAD POUNDING, pulled himself upright, watching two jets roar away. Shaggy, wild-eyed, did the same. Dusting himself off, the Howler shook his fists at the pilots. "Where the fuck are you guys going?"

The elder, Big Ben, fishtailed his Harley, chiding them both. They were stranded on the wrong side—the *south* side—of the bomb-severed bridge. There was shit to do!

The SIS leader shouted orders and roared towards the bus-wall, gray braids streaming behind him. In the low light, Mukwa saw dazed defenders gathering at the breach. The roadway still connected them to the Viral shore, but they were severed— by an airstrike!—from the Free North.

"And where the fuck is my hog?" Shaggy searched the fire-lit wreckage in vain. They were dismounted, blown off their motor-cycle by bunker-busting bombs. Shaggy's bike had cartwheeled over the rail and quickly sank, adding a dash of chrome to the underwater wreckage, a sculpture of collapse.

Shaggy snapped his jaws again. "Ben said to rally at the wall. Big man, let's go!"

Mukwa—limping, bleeding—shambled towards what was left of the school buses. Shaggy, a pissed-off pedestrian, stubbornly scanned the gloom. He gave a wolfish grin, then a whistle.

An Indian pony, yellow-painted and riderless, responded with a neigh. The Cayuse clopped over and Shaggy swung himself up, bareback. Decently mounted, he whooped, kicked his heels, and galloped past his bipedal companion.

The wall was a fucking mess; glass windows all shot out. The mammoth had plowed a jagged breach through the buses. Yellow-faces and surviving SIS pointed overheated gun barrels both ways.

To the north, behind them, where the bridge was now severed, some remaining Raiders were turning around—with Ignace out of reach, they sought return.

To the south, still connected to the shore, the causeway was crawling with infected. The Chosen were shaken by the strikes, but soon would be goaded to attack again.

Big Ben inventoried their assets—six horses, three motorcycles, a couple dozen defenders, and assorted small arms. The Mk 19 Mukwa captured was out of grenades, and belt-fed weapons had eaten all their ammo.

The bridge fires dimmed, and the stars brightened. The quarter moon, reflective, lit the scene in silver. The Free North defenders were marooned upon the span. The raptors were gone, fighter planes too. They were on their own. Then the roadway began to vibrate. Again.

Shaggy threw back his head and howled. "Come on you fuckers!" In the dark, horse-high, his rifle barrel flashed defiance, *Pop! Pop! Pop!*

Big Ben, a Saigon survivor, checked the young warrior: "Shaggy! Hold your damn fire!"

Wolfman bared his fangs, bit back the "Fuck off!" tipping his tongue. Their micro-bickering was subsumed by a macro-sound.

Rolling up from the south, another horn was blown, *Bahruuuuuuuhhhhaaaaa!*

"No fucking way." Traumatized, they disbelieved their aching ears.

Bahruuuuuuhhhhaaaaa!

A second mammoth plow—twin to the one that fell—clanked closer, the oily elephant trumpeting as it charged.

Captain Young, flat on his back and dulled by opiates, felt the ferry floating. *Fairy floating.* Frank envisioned green wings. He fought for control. The captain knew he was in trouble—TBI, micro-bleeding, fractured and fucked. Darkness dimmed his sight, a black breath fogged his brain. Underneath the morphine, Frank was a mess. *That fucking skeleton. The huge one, the suicide bomber.*

Cruz, always cool under fire, had knocked Goliath down, saving the bus-wall with a bullet-stone. Booker had yelled a warning, then it all went WHITE....

Young recalled only splinters, a frag-grenade of reality. He knew Chow had doctored him. But hadn't Chow treated the fugitive too? Where in the world was Bob fucking Campbell?

Young's head was pounding. He'd lost Anthony Booker, lost Alfonzo Cruz too. Where were his men? His little band of brothers? He knew he'd been asking, but he'd forgotten the answers. Had his boys been exposed? How close had they gotten? Frank stopped himself from shouting. His throat was raw—had he been yelling? One thing he knew, the nurses were marvelous. God bless Mathew, God bless Sean. Frank watched them on their rounds. They must have carried him to the ferry's lounge. The large compartment was crowded with casualties.

The RNs checked IVs and pulse rates. Despite masks, they were all at risk. A single cough and the virions, aerosolized, would spread, lung-to-lung, a mortal mist. Young's thoughts, airborne, were drifting too—memories made of molecules: *his wife Terre, their suburban home, the smell of cut grass, cold beers on the patio....*

Feeling a commotion, Frank forced his crusty lids to open. Elena was there; out of breath, she'd been scouting the town. The

ELF warrior threw back her hood, sight-checking the compartment for able-bodies. Elena tapped two Sentinels. Despite bloody bandages, both commandos stood. Young overheard them as they limped out together, "One barge got ashore—X-marked vehicles—enveloping Ignace—Virals—no one to stop them—"

Nodin's generators drowned out the rest, but Captain Young heard enough. Trading the fairy realm for the ferry's reality, Frank stood from the pleasant patio, kissing his wife Terre goodbye. He pulled out the saline drip and gave it to Nurse Mathew—someone else could have it.

Dizzy, drugged, he checked his hip. Heavy in its holster, the lethal 9mm was there. Frank followed the fighters out on deck. Floating no longer, he stumbled, disoriented in the dark. A heavy hand halted him, pushing his chest. "Sir, you better stay inside."

Booker!

Another voice concurred: "Chief, I'm with the sergeant on this one."

Cruz!

Elena gave an order, and someone descended to the engine room. A minute later and the drone-damaged boat went quiet, went dark. Nothing to see here. Hide-and-seek in the harbor. Spreader versus Hidden—*Come out, come out, wherever you are!*

Standing at the rail, three and three, Sentinels and soldiers. Together, they watched headlights beaming through the town. Following State Street, the paired lights were probing towards the harbor. Elena led her wounded elves down the gangway and onto the pier, Frank and his two enlisted following close behind. The bandaged Sentinels both hefted spears. Elena, an instinctive shooter, carried her bow. Somehow, Cruz had kept his carbine. Young unholstered his pistol; Booker, a blade. They fanned out in ambush, preparing their stand.

Cruz inventoried ammo. "Captain," he hissed, "I'm down to

half a mag."

The bombed-out ferry was dark, no light trickling from its sick bay. A couple miles south, the severed bridge still glowed. In the harbor, the partial moon cast impartial light. Invasive, the column clanked closer, X-marked hoods clearly seen. Cruz quietly racked a round, sighting on the lead vehicle. Elena raised a hand. Shimmering in the moonlight, her Sentinels made ready.

Terrifying, a bestial trumpet boomed from the bridge— *Bahruuuuuuuhhhhaaaaa!*

Another fucking horn?

Ears aching from the foulness of the frequency, the defenders flinched, gripping their weapons tighter. They were not alone in their rictus of repulsion; a wild chorus howled in defiance. Bright-eyed, Elena saw feral forms darting furtively through the shadows. St. Ignace was crawling with wolves.

The X-column halted. Hatches clanged open, armed figures exited the doors.

"Hold!" Elena hissed at her ELF comrades.

Elephantine, from the bridge the great horn blew again— *Bahruuuuuuuhhhhaaaaa!*

Snarling, the urban wolves hurled their hate skyward. More hatches opened. The emerging figures—none branded?—threw back their hairy heads, adding howls of their own.

"Friendlies!" Elena stepped into the clear, arms wide, tokening peace.

The lupine leader, a Howler female, did the same. The allies met in the moonlight, clasping arms. A quick exchange of news. The amphibious assault—much feared—hadn't gone far. Howlers, two-legged and four, had shredded the X-column just north of town. Evergreen Shores no longer, Free Northers renamed it the Wolf Wood.

Indian River

COLONEL DENNIS—ink-stained from endless notes—had shaken the wrestler's hand, singling him out for bravery. Sentinel Thorn, aka Rabbit, still felt thrilled. Had that just been this morning? Thorn supposed it had. Rolling north now with the Rangers, they approached the burning bridge. Midnight was near—were they too late?

Yesterday, after finalizing their battle plan, the gathering of Rangers had dispersed from their soggy hotel conference room. Later that night, signal fires flared from the south. Thorn's refurbished beacons were set ablaze by their minders—prepper country, always prepared.

Then this morning, in the gray light before dawn, the convict-convoy drove into their trap. The I-75 corridor bottlenecked at the town of Indian River. The highway narrowed as it crossed the wetlands and then the river itself—no on/off ramps, no parallel roads, no chance for detour. The convicts had entered death row.

Colonel Dennis and his Guard unit—Yield to None—had joined forces with the Rangers. The Griffins of the 125th had retreated north from Camp Grayling after igniting their stores of surplus fuel and ammunition. At Indian River, their Humvee-towed howitzers did most of the damage. Holy hell! The hitting power of those 105mm shells!

Firing from cover, walked onto targets by spotters, the artillery annihilated most vehicles, pulping the pit bulls and their red-eyed handlers. Ranger skirmishers deployed. Thorn, elusive in his Sentinel parka, was the tip of their spear. Gray-cloaked in the gray dawn he wielded his borrowed rifle well—Gaia forgive! The Spreaders couldn't see him; their dogs couldn't smell him. Thorn lost track of his kills, canine and Con.

The colonel's handshake recognized his bravery with the bus. Civilians—slaves actually—had been cuffed to the convoy as human shields. Spared by artillery, their contagious captors had to be killed face-to-face. The Sentinel, an MSU Spartan, had excelled. Thorn, ticketless, boarded the bus, leaving his rifle outside. Grappling, he wrestled door guards. The seated slaves didn't move. Thorn ran the Viral gauntlet as the civilians prayed. He advanced up the aisle, fired upon by Xs in the rear. Unscathed, Thorn somehow closed the distance, finishing the job.

The slaves were clad in MDOC orange or plain clothing and looked much alike. The men wore beards, their accents sounded strange. Amish, he supposed, or some similar sect?

In minutes the Griff ambush was over, only the plow-truck remaining. The oversize machine was stenciled with a mammoth skull, X-branded with fiery eyes. The Cons shielded their beast with a hide of live humans. Captive women were tied to its tusks. Slaves of another sort, they'd been stripped of their homespun and dolled up as whores. Army spotters spared them, keeping the howitzers away. The Rangers, from concealment, laser-dotted the remaining combatants. One by one, Virals were euthanized. Muzzles flashed back from the endangered mammoth as, enraged, it fought for survival. Bullets spewed from every orifice; the beast shat hot brass, desperate to escape.

Brothers Robert and Freddy, wearing MOPP gear from the Guard, led the grenade assault that finished off the tusked terror. Screened by smoke, they boosted their Rabbit to a gun-port. The wrestler, unmasked, wormed through its smoking innards, then knifed its red-eyed driver, booting his infected body from the cab. Exposed, Thorn placed himself in quarantine, watching as the mixed unit mopped up the mess. Sitting on the roof of the commandeered machine, he cleaned his weapons, cleansing his mind. The day dawned red. A battle day, it would end at the bridge.

The 125th's medics, wearing full PPE, got busy. The slaves were freed; the trafficked women, made decent. They stood in orderly rows awaiting their turn—first, a rapid-test for antigens; then, hot food from MRE pouches. Single shots cracked from the wreckage, per the CO's orders; no Geneva for Virals.

Uniformly testing negative, the Amish pitched in. The Griffin's CSM, Sergeant Amanda Taylor, watched as the newly freed farmers stacked contagious corpses, splashed diesel, and ignited the fleshy pyramid, a pharaonic pyre.

"They should all be infected," Taylor, disbelieving, debriefed her CO, Colonel Dennis. "They should all be dead." Sergeant Taylor nodded to the newest Ranger, Thorn, sequestered atop the mammoth. "Him too." The two Griffins shook their heads. No time for that. For now, infection-free was good enough.

It took all day to hunt down the stragglers. Many XCons—fleeing the havoc of howitzers—had jumped over the rail. Rangers tracked them, bog and briar slowing their search. The colonel took to the airwaves, broadcasting in the open. Prepper country must be warned. Calls started coming in, and branded corpses too—Afton, Wolverine, Topinabee, Riggsville. Slowly, one Viral at a time, contagion was scrubbed from Cheboygan County.

Now, nearing midnight, their column—too late?—approached the southern causeway of the recently bombed bridge. Deformed and half melted, the north tower flickered with flame. Disabled vehicles, spattered with blood, clotted the severed artery of the roadway. Flotsam, afire, spiraled upon the oil-slick waters far below. It didn't look good. So Colonel Dennis, an artful dodger, disguised their force, painting fake Xs on Griffin Humvees. When all was ready, Dennis pulled the horn-cord of the plow truck himself—*Bahruuuuuuuhhhhaaaaa!*

The ruse worked! The guardsmen hid their faces and were granted passage through the remaining Raiders. Cheered on as fellow Virals, they wove through the wreckage. Using night vision goggles, the advancing Griffins saw dead horses, shattered Harleys, and the bus-wall, still under siege. Colonel Dennis gave another order, and the oversize plow was deployed to clear the gridlock. The Guard's Humvees, disguised as Viral, followed close behind, their face-masked gunners laying down suppressing fire. The confused Raiders, too late, saw through the subterfuge.

The stenciled plow truck, a Trojan horse, accelerated through the breach in the bus-wall, slamming its brakes close to the edge where the roadway disappeared. A great scoop of polluted filth was pushed overboard—a four second freefall, then *splat* upon the surface, two hundred fatal feet below. Forward and reverse, forward and reverse, scoop after scoop, until the Viral snow was cleared. The mammoth bellowed as it scraped the bridge clean. Satisfied, Colonel Dennis eventually called a halt. Griffins idled their engines and emerged to cheering defenders.

Ranger Rabbit, astride the mammoth plow, recognized a bear-sized figure in the crowd. It couldn't be? *Mukwa?* "Hey, Oso, you hairy oaf!" The beast turned at the nickname. It was!

The big bruin looked up, incredulous. *No fucking way? Thorn?* Mukwa shook his bare head and roared, "Long time, amigo! So glad you're not dead!"

Manic with adrenaline and grimy from battle, both men were laughing. Ex-ELF, the blasphemers raised their forbidden rifles high. The pair of fallen Sentinels acknowledged the change in each other. Whatever they were now—dark elves?—they were in this shit together.

Thorn invited, and Mukwa scrambled up. Sitting atop the mechanical mammoth, lit by the moon and petroleum fires,

Bear summarized the scene for Rabbit, starting with a group of fighters in self-quarantine. These Free North martyrs, seeking surcease from their sorrows, had striped themselves and their horses with yellow. All day they'd fought face-to-face with Spreaders—a suicide mission. Every man and woman was probably infected.

Mukwa continued. His unit, SIS bikers—those without close contact anyway—mingled with the soldiers that saved them. Handshakes and hugs were exchanged as combat medics and first responders made their rounds, performing triage. The ex-elves overheard Dennis as the Griffin CO strategized with Big Ben, the Lakota elder, while Ben's burns were bandaged by a guardswoman.

"On the causeway, disguised, we passed through their ranks," Dennis said. "Too many for us to attack, plus they're all infected. Price is too damn high."

Big Ben, blackened by fire, counted the plow, the Griffs, the Humvees. "This everything you got?"

"Negative." The colonel clarified, "We left a bus of civilians—freed slaves actually—with my top sergeant, Amanda Taylor, and our howitzers, south of Mackinaw City. They've got their hands full and won't be joining us tonight."

Ben took it in; both his gray braids were singed. "So, we're stuck here? On the wrong side of the moat made by your own flyboy pilots?"

"Looks like it." Dennis studied Ben's jacket, noting his patches—VFW, 1st Cavalry, Vietnam. "Bravo Zulu by the way. You held the bridge. Well done trooper. Well done, indeed." The colonel offered his inky hand to the ex-cavalryman. Big Ben frowned—the burning tower, kamikaze drones, *Nodin* aflame, the bloody bus-wall, the yellow Seekers crawling with Covee....

Ben squeezed the historian's soft hand. "The price was too high."

The colonel waited a minute, then had to ask, "Captain Young? His two enlisted men, Booker and Cruz?"

Ben sympathized; he'd lost people too. "Last I saw, Colonel, their truck had flipped. They stopped a Skull though, a huge one, some kind of suicide bomber. I'm sorry, sir, I don't think they made it."

The White Hand

I'M AN IMPATIENT MAN, as no doubt you've gathered. At last check, my pieces were in position and ready to strike—Dozer with his drones, Jones and Mustafa with the fleet, XCons and their slaves. A three-pronged attack, with Mighty Mac as prize morsel. "Mopping up," Jones maddeningly intoned. The wait is intolerable. Still, there's nothing worse than a micro-manager. I must leave them alone.

So let's talk about my captive, the green gift my Aghori brought me the day Dozer deployed. Assassin McKenzie—aided by her crows—banded this birdie outside Panzer's walls. Feathers bedraggled, spying in the rain, the little Greenie fought back, sharp talons raking flesh. I admit there's something new about her—avant-garde, art nouveau. Intrigued, I ordered blood work and caged my newest pet in Panzer's underground lab. I must say, after analyzing the test results and interviewing my patient, I am not disappointed. She calls herself Nighthawk by the way. Isn't that delightful?

Since collapse—almost two years now—"Greenies," at least in Michigan, have proved quite a nuisance. In the early days, these misguided hippies conducted terrorist operations against airfields, planes, fuel depots, and pilots. As a man of ambition, I was eager to acquire such assets; all the warlords were. Their neo-Luddite campaign of ecotage irked me.

More recently, I've endured wild reporting from my regional managers—Bob Campbell, Red Liz, even Dozer né Mikey—blaming these "elves" for setbacks and quota failures.

There was hyperbolic mention of primitive weapons (spears!), green-shielding (impervious to Sting!), and tree graffiti ("inked with blood"). Now, with Ms. Hawk in hand, and more importantly, her lab results, I regret not taking these reports more seriously.

Susceptibility to Covee and its Stinger has paved the way for my corporate success. Therefore, any immunity—physio or pharmacological—is an existential threat to Panzerland that must be combated. The tests we ran were extensive, and for a healthy woman of reproductive age, most results were quite normal. In only one category did we see a drastic departure from the range: three molecular proteins associated with immune response—perforine, granulysine and granzyme—were quite literally off the charts. The quickest way seemed best, so I ordered immediate exposure. It was time for my birdie to be envenomed by Sting.

Now remember, dear reader, my variant (Order: *Nidovirales*, Family: *Coronaviridae*, Subfamily: *Orthocoronavirinae*, Genera: *Beta*, SARS-CoV-2) was designed—per the order of our POTUS—as an extinction-level bioweapon specifically targeting Asian phenotypes.

V-2's real world performance surpassed all expectations, proving to have an R-naught (RO) factor of twenty and an Infection Fatality Rate (IFR) of +99%—more contagious than the measles and deadlier than Ebola. One person infected twenty others, and Stinger killed 99% of its hosts. Of course, there were some design flaws, some unexpected mutations, but make no mistake—the variant we hatched was a stone-cold killer.

So far, Nighthawk, despite exposure, remains uninfected. Microscopic analysis shows that my variant, the veritable crowned king of contagion, cannot gain access to her cells. Something— perhaps one of those elevated immune proteins?—inhibits the entry of my virus.

Needless to say, these results are disturbing, and with the bridge battle about to begin—a battle whose strategy relies on super-spreading disease!—I quickly enhanced her interrogation. My technicians injected her with sodium thiopental, a truth serum with a record of Cold War service.

The barbiturate relaxed my barbarian, making her chatty. I live-streamed the interview for as long as I could take it. "Gaia," "Earth Liberation," "Elf Country," and "biophilia," were some of the terms Ms. Hawk—high as a kite—chirped ad nauseam at her handlers.

Nighthawk—a ghastly nom de guerre, so on the nose!—left me underwhelmed. She seems a naïf, a misguided militant, disciple of Ludd. Alas, she's mere caricature, a stereotype. Of course she's sincere, fanatical even. In the history of lost causes, there's been no shortage of fools. Still, she remains uninfected, completely undiseased. Indeed, per her claims, this eco nut may be shielded. We haven't seen this before. It is irksome. The 1% who've survived, sub 1% actually, so far have all fit a pattern.

Ms. Hawk is a rare bird. She's been stung by the variant yet remains uninfected; indeed, unaltered. The patient is testing negative for antigens (no sign of current infection) and positive for antibodies (she's been exposed in the past and has developed defenses). But again, what is most alarming for me and my plans is that she appears, indeed, to be "shielded." And this shielding, per her panacean faith, might indeed be linked to certain "green" proteins abundant in nature.

Remember her high levels of inhibitors? The perforine, granulysine, and granzyme levels that were off the charts? Well, I've rushed the research, and my access to information isn't what it was, but you'll never guess the possible source of these inhibitors—TREES! Specifically the chemical compound, terpene, $(C_5H_8)n$, produced by Michigan conifers such as pines. Greenie indeed! Perhaps a wise man should know better, but I've never given trees much thought. My erstwhile neutrality towards nature is fading fast!

Full disclosure: I've been dictating to distract myself from the day's battle. My three prongs must have reached the bridge by now, and I'm dying for results. I've given them long enough, so excuse me a moment while I confer with my captains....

I'm back.

That certainly could have gone better. Did I just dictate, "neutrality towards nature?" Strike that from the record! Hostility is where I'm at. Hatred, even, after what I've just heard.

How did my drug-addled Greenie describe herself? A biophiliac? Well, two can play with language. Apparently, the bridge attack has stalled. Aghori Jones's "mopping up" operation has been stymied by MOPP-protected guardsmen and their "ELF" allies. The word that suits my current mood? Biophobic!

Just now, as I power down my Palantir satellite phone—why should *I* be afraid to use it?—the sight of my own hand, pale and palsied, gives me a fright. I feel suddenly frail. Fearing for the future of my freshwater fief, I issue new orders:

Terpenoids from trees? Rip them all down!

Green-shields against my Stinger? Remove those who oppose us!

Primitive elves? I activate my Aghori: "You do not know pain, you do not know fear!"

If nature is the source of their success, their shield, then nature must be denied to them. Luckily, Dozer, far from defeated, has presented just such a plan—pipelines, petroleum, and pollution. I liked it immediately. My Shark-juice appears to have sped up his mind. I've created a monster. If Dozer pulls this off, I'll be one proud papa; call me father Frankenstein.

Line 5

DOZER AND MCKENZIE—fixer and assassin—unrolled the schematics for the Line 5 pipeline. There was something satisfying about using a non-digital chart. Bald heads together, they planned their raid, their pithy act of petro-pollution. The satellite call with the Big Boss could have gone worse—though it could have gone better, too. Dozer's pipeline plan is what saved them. Dr. Schark, successful CEO, wanted solutions, not excuses. No sense in hiding the truth; Sharkey's snitches saw it all.

Dozer, after midnight, was summoned by a limping McKenzie to the Palantir terminal. The ex-mechanic gave Schark, his employer, the bad news—if Dozer buried the lead, he'd be buried himself.

Both plows had failed to secure the bridge. The first—stricken by Eagles—went trumpeting over the edge in flames. The second was captured by remnants of Michigan's Guard.

The XCon column had been ambushed at Indian River and destroyed. Its laborers—Amish farmers—were confiscated along with the vehicles.

Sergeant Jones, Sharkey's favorite Skull, was dead, along with Captain Juan and Mustafa, whose A-EYE halo hadn't saved him. Their X-tug had been rammed and fire-balled by a kamikaze fishing boat.

McKenzie's special-ops Gories had taken a beating as well. Their C-4 bomber had detonated too early, killing their own.

McKenzie, wounded, had skittered back beneath the span—a petulant spider, plotting her revenge.

Many Chosen were killed by those SIS bikers and their damn LAWS rockets.

The airstrike—F-15s? Really?—was a most unpleasant surprise. That one was on Sharkey, though Dozer hadn't said so. How was he to know Old Law had access to such assets?

During the briefing, Big Boss kept quiet, digesting details. A sprinkling of good news had helped:

The north tower was in flames. The defenders' bus-wall was breached. Dozer's drones annihilated the enemy fleet. At least one X-barge had beached, offloading its vehicles behind St. Ignace. A majority of the bridge defenders had been killed, while survivors were no doubt infected and would super-spread on their own. At last check, any remaining resistors were trapped on the roadway. Marooned by their own moat—the bomb-severed bridge—they wouldn't last long.

The battle's prognosis still looked good; Dozer held a force of Raiders in reserve. He would personally lead them against the south shore's Mackinaw Station, opening the pipeline's oily valves. McKenzie and her surviving Aghori would cross the severed bridge—she hadn't said how?—and sabotage the North Straits Facility on the far shore.

Dozer and McKenzie, shoulder-to-shoulder, decoded the chart together. CV-N enhanced, they quickly sequenced valves, figuring flow rate to optimize the oily Armageddon that would ensue. Half a million barrels of crude—that's what they calculated. Dozer's portable generators would power up the southern pumps, build pressure, and force the rusty ring to rupture. McKenzie, on the north shore, would disable its check valves, draining the northern pipe as well. A shame to waste the petroleum, but Boss Sharkey agreed—desperate times, desperate measures.

Hard to tell how much crude was in the system. When the grid went dark and its engineers all went under, auto-safeties had shut down Line 5. It wouldn't take much though. The currents here were strong, so any spillage would bubble up from the bottom and circulate quickly. Dr. Schark seemed satisfied with their plan of pollution. The Great Lakes—source of life, source of green power—would now be flammable. Dozer had a vision of fresh water on fire.

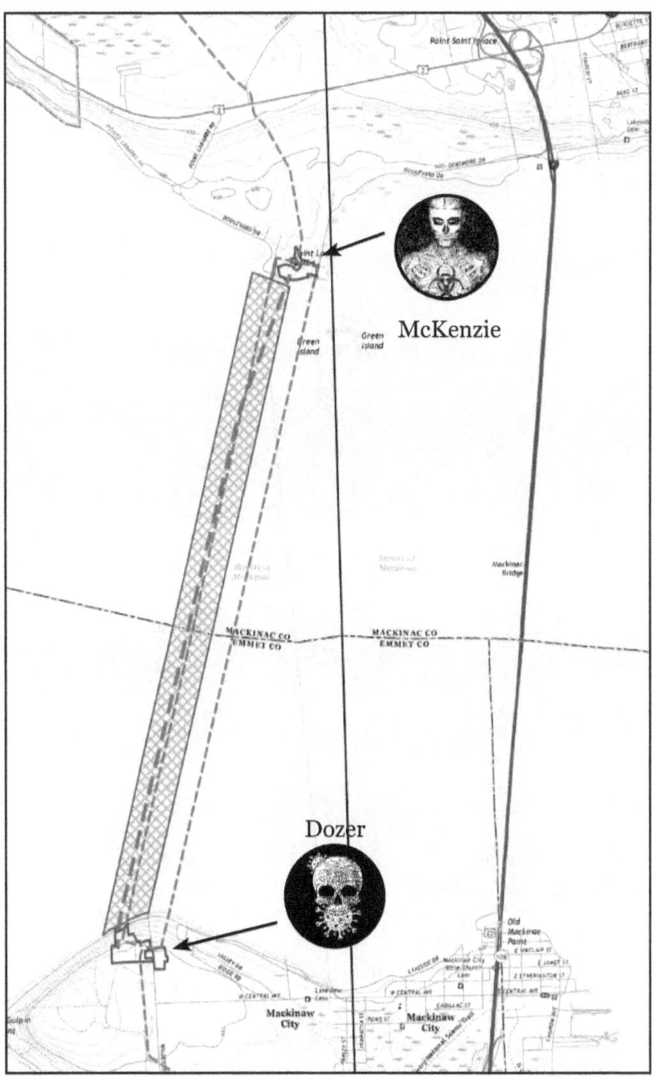

Ozhigwan

IN ALL HER DREAMS, Autumn had seen it—the black tail of a snake oozing oil upon the lakebed. Two nights ago, sharing visions, her sweat lodge saw it too. The water-protector hadn't slept since; none of them had. After the airstrike—*mizgi mi-igwechiwi'!*—and the second horn—a false alarm!—Autumn gathered wounded at the plaza, bussing them north to Ignace and the crippled *Nodin*, rudderless now with Captain Diana dead.

"No contaminated!" Dr. Chow had shouted from the gangway. She assured him that Seekers and other exposed were self-quarantined back at the bridge. She oversaw the offload; stretchers were carried aboard. The nurses and doctors got busy. Many of the wounded would not survive till morning.

Now, in the witching hour, Autumn called a council, spreading the word. Fires were kindled at the fairgrounds. Food was heated. Drums started up. Horses, still traumatized, were tended as leadership gathered.

Baptiste—*oo-tîhî*, her heart—was there, on leave from captaining the Response Boat. Elena and her Sentinels sat on the grass, hiding their sorrow under parka hoods. Howler alphas—men and women—were wild-eyed from their victory in the Wolf Wood. Her boy Loon sat with his bearded friend, Brian. They'd descended from their nest in the Old One, *biisaandago-zhingwaak*.

Status reports were given, rumors confirmed, and sorrows shared. The list of dead, wounded, and exposed was a long one: Captains Diana, Doyle, and Hannigan; their boat crews; Sheila and her co-pilot; the sniper teams on the tower. Captain Young and his men were alive but brain-injured, confined in sick bay.

Big Ben, some SIS, and the surviving yellow-faces were still stranded on the south side—the wrong side—of the severed bridge. Hard to tell in the dark, but they'd been reinforced by Dennis' guardsmen and for now were holding their own. Many boats and canoes were missing, their shipwrecked sailors yet to wash ashore.

Against a backdrop of glittering stars, Autumn stood, warning them once again of her petro-vision. Elena confirmed—she'd been in the sweat lodge. Diana, now dead, had been there too and had witnessed the same: *the rusty snake, its ruptured belly, the spew of oil, the Straits of Mackinac aflame.*

The sacred drums added urgency. Tonight, they were all water-protectors. The quarter moon had set. Stars were turning. The long night waned. There was work to be done.

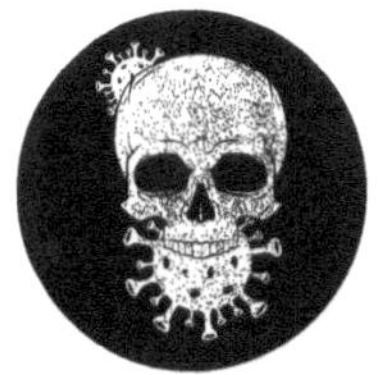 

Zero Dark

"SIR, YOU'D BETTER TAKE THIS."

Colonel Dennis stepped away from Big Ben and picked up the Humvee handset. Pressing the key, he said, "Dennis here." The Griffin's commanding officer listened for thirty seconds, clarified, and then replaced the handset. Returning to the battered bus-wall, he shook his head at the Vietnam veteran. "Ben, you're not gonna like the evac plan your friends just came up with."

Turning to the waiting guardsmen, Dennis ordered, "Search the vehicles! Collect all tow straps!" His soldiers sprang to comply.

Specialist McKenzie checked her team. The Aghori, a tattooed mix of males and Vishkanya, were standing by. She conferred with Virals crewing the lead vehicles. Gunners fondled their weapons, each Chosen crew eager for spoils. She looked at her watch—zero dark thirty. Some things never changed.

Dozer's force stood ready to assault the southern pump station. McKenzie's team of skeletal operators would cross the severed roadway and secure the pumps on the north shore. At the first sign of dawn they'd align their valves, flood the Straits with petroleum, and set fire to the ensuing slick.

McKenzie signaled the advance. Drivers put their trucks in gear as emotionless Gories jumped aboard. Their column pulled away from the staging area, weaving through the wreckage that cluttered the road.

Baptiste eased his Response Boat out of Ignace's harbor. He towed a string of blackened kayaks crewed by bright-eyed Sentinels, faces painted for the night-op. Assorted craft—all little ships—followed in their wake. The mission, dubbed "Dynamo" by bookish Colonel Dennis, was to evacuate their comrades, now high above them, stranded upon the bridge. Against overwhelming odds, they hoped to achieve a miracle, a vertical Dunkirk.

Smoking, severed, but still standing, the Mighty Mac swayed above. Baptiste idled their flotilla beneath its star-spangled span. The Métis man shook his tow cable and felt the kayak commandos cast off. "*Bonn shaans*," he muttered as the stealthy squadron divided.

Sentinel Sparrow led her boats towards the southern pump station on McGulpin Point.

Sentinel Elena paddled north towards Point LaBarbe and the energy station there. Heeding Autumn's vision, the ELF commandos were highly motivated, determined to forestall an apocalypse of oil.

Holding his position beneath the twisted rebar and bomb-severed steel, Baptiste flashed his nav-lights: once, twice, three times. Seconds later, tow straps unspooled from above and were secured by boat crews waiting below. A minute after that, and the first boots—Army issue—hit the deck. Giddy with descent, the soldier clasped arms with his rescuer and pitched in. The vertical evacuation had begun.

Dozer sat shotgun in the lead truck, like he had with Cowboy back in their scavenger days. Map on his knee, Dozer navigated his three-vehicle team towards McGulpin Point and its petroleum pumps. They towed a generator and showed no lights as they rolled along Lakeside Drive. The ex-mechanic started humming, couldn't help it—the past, the "before," just wasn't that long ago.

Running south on Lake Shore Drive, heading into town

Window down, Dozer flashed back to his time as Bob's fix-it man: their fucked up Fox Hunt, his midnight terror of primitive elves. Since then he'd traded junk food for a needle, soft flesh for virucide virility. Sadness stabbed him as the woods rolled darkly by. The song soothed him, Bob Campbell would approve—1971, "an oldie but goodie."

Ain't no finer place to be, than running Lake Shore Drive

Those days were long gone. And where was his old boss now? Dead probably. Mikey had snitched him out, betraying, then tasing his one-time friend. Red Liz, triumphant, dusted off Bob's hat, then led Cowboy's outfit straight into hell. She'd got hers though. Last he'd seen, ol' Liz had been shorn—sliced and diced by old Crow's ambush. A fucking tree had thrown itself in the road. When Mikey—the only survivor—dragged his ass back to Charlevoix, the ferry, with Bob in its brig, was gone. Chosen corpses, pin-cushioned by arrows, littered the sidewalks.

Dozer, depressed by memory, fumbled the plunger till Cyano-virin iced his veins. He breathed from his belly, and accessed— via Sharkey's elixir—the galaxy above.

Just slippin' on by on LSD, Friday night trouble bound.

The Straits were flat calm. The Milky Way met its mirror. Nei-ther good nor evil, the bald man played his part, nothing more.

"No fucking way." Mukwa peered down at the abyss, searching in vain for the Coast Guard Response Boat, 200 fucking feet below.

The Guard soldiers had already gone over. Most of the St. Ignace Scouts had descended as well. The Death Seekers, yel-low-striped and solemn, held themselves apart and would remain upon the span. The damaged roadway began to vibrate again. Raiders were coming; it was now or never.

"Nope, never." Mukwa backed away from the straps.

"Bullshit!" Shaggy's eyes flashed.

Thorn was there too, encouraging but urgent. "Come on Oso, let's go!"

His handlers hemmed him in, bumping the big bear towards the brink.

"Assholes!" Mukwa grabbed a strap just before he fell. Committed by gravity, he commenced his descent. Hand under hand, he eased himself down. Golden-eyed in the dark, Shaggy followed. Thorn evacuated as well, hooded and shimmering in his parka. They each experienced an eternity of emptiness before their boots hit the deck.

Big Ben and Colonel Dennis gave a final salute to the Seekers that would stay. The yellow-faces, a contaminated rear-guard, would cover their retreat, forcing attackers to pay a heavy toll. Seekers would prevent the stolen plow-truck and Humvees from being used against them.

Side by side, Big Ben and Dennis, Indigenous and ally, descended, encouraging each other as they slipped through the stars. Reaching a boat deck at last, they shook the straps to signify, "All clear!" Baptiste pulled his boat away while lifelines were hauled up by those seeking death.

"Keep going." McKenzie steadied her nervy driver, a Gorie-wannabe with amateur ink. A firefight had begun. Advancing Raiders wove through a labyrinth of wreckage. Passing beneath the burnt barbican, they breached the bus-wall. Her driver dodged the C-4 crater, McKenzie cringing to see it. She crawled out the window to operate the heavy gun—an M2 Browning—bolted to the truck bed. Freshly dosed, she fired controlled bursts at remaining defenders. Ice-cold, McKenzie couldn't miss, each fiery tracer perfectly trajected. A line of yellow cavalry stood arrayed against them.

Whap! Whap! Whap! Her big bullets bit flesh, busted bone, horse and human alike. The defenders appeared much reduced—the stolen plow-truck, some Humvees, and a few horses were all that remained. Her Aghori, passionless, pushed this rear-guard to the brink of the bomb-severed roadway. Undisciplined, Chosen exited their vehicles, sexually hyper and lusting for spoils.

She keyed her megaphone, addressing both sides: "Chosen, hold your fire! Defenders, lay down your weapons!" She had them now. Dr. Schark would be pleased: more rats for Panzer's cages. McKenzie heard the enemy rev their engines and repeated her order, "Step away from your vehicles: YOU—WILL—BE—SHOT!"

She sighted on the stolen plow. Picking a crease in its mammoth hide, McKenzie prepared her heavy projectiles. In a surprise move, the defending machines—horses too—lurched towards the Virals, enveloping them, unafraid of close contact. Chosen surged forward, yellow-faced Seekers pulled back, then their stolen plow started pushing—attackers and defenders both disappeared over the brink. McKenzie observed without passion as the mammoth she'd stenciled tumbled over the cliff towards extinction.

Sentinel Sparrow stopped her paddle, hearing the gassy generator fire up. Lights began to show from McGulpin Point. The southern pump station was occupied by Chosen. Elena had been right—Autumn's petro-vision was confirmed.

"Gaia guide me," Sparrow whispered to the waves, to the water, to the stars above. She led her commandos ashore. The Sentinels beached their kayaks, hiding them in the scrub, preparing for assault. The pump station squatted near the old lighthouse. If Nighthawk were here, she'd be up in that tower. Sparrow tasked her two best archers with overwatch. Silently, the pair ascended, found a shooting platform, and arrayed their arrows. Soon, an owl hooted from their position. Her overwatch was ready.

"Let's go."

Hooded, Gaia's guardians shimmered towards the light.

Up on the bridge, cock-blocked and horny, Raiders ravaged the roadway in vain. "No loot, no captives! No booty, no booties!"

"Did you fuckin' see that?" they asked each other. "Rolled right off the damn plank!"

They'd been traveling for days, goaded by Dozer. They'd been promised a lot, with nothing delivered. They idled for hours on the causeway, awaiting their chance, shit on by crows. Slaves tended cook fires, but no chow had been served. They grumbled against bosses, against Skulls. Even the Amish were off limits—untouchable, and unfuckable too.

The roadway had been scrubbed of anything valuable. Scorched-earth tactics denied them their fun. The defenders tossed it all overboard—weapons, food, and finally themselves. Even Panzer's plow-truck, X-marked and massive, had turned against them.

McKenzie could care less about their bitching—Dozer's problem; she had her own. Unlike the Virals, her Aghori sat in silence as she made calculations. A sixty-foot chunk had been blasted from the road. There was no way across, and a long way down.

Campfires winked from St. Ignace; the sound of drumming beat upon Chosen ears. Savory cooking smells mocked them as well. Teased and tempted, they grew agitated. Spoiled by easy spoils, this frustration was new and un-fucking cool. Viral talk began to spread, grumbles of "fair share" and "what was promised." Amish women were "back there," "ripe for plucking," and "under-guarded."

Boss Dozer was away with most of the Gories, but McKenzie remained, and that "bald bitch" was worse. Where was she, anyway?

Then, silhouetted against a smear of stars, they saw her. The Vishkanya, freshened by virucide, was ascending an untethered cable. She computed distance, arc, and radii, then swung herself into space. With pendulum perfection, she released one wire and caught the next, and the next, and the next. The Chosen, red-eyed and lusty, elbowed each other. "There she goes! The Amazing Spider-Cunt!"

Crossing the chasm, McKenzie's boots hit the pavement and the open road north. Her skeletons followed in bony file, weapons strapped to their backs, tattooed faces serene in the starlight.

Underwater Panther

ON THE SOUTHERN SHORE, Sparrow's Sentinels were ready. Her overwatch nocked their arrows; the ELF assault team carried naked steel. From St. Ignace, five miles away, the sacred drumming reached them. Heartbeat of the people, each commando felt its pulse. Something foul was happening inside the Line 5 compound. A generator hummed, electric lights blazing as Virals moved about the pump station. Others, bald and brawny, skulked the perimeter, skeletal sentries for the elves to deal with.

Sparrow filled herself with a lake-flavored breath, tasting cold water and dune grass. She looked to the northern shore. Point LaBarbe was still dark. Was Elena in position yet? The sending she received was: YES—all elements of the Front stood ready.

Eyes closed, senses wide, she merged with the night, a nocturnal predator: *"Who-ho-o-o', whoo-hoo-o-o'!"* Her archers loosed in tandem. Two sentries went down, choking on fletchings.

Little Sparrow grew horns, vast wings, and a beak. Owloid, she glided towards the power generator. A steely talon flashed, cutting its sparking cord; the southern pump station went dark. Curses from inside as more stealthy shadows advanced, breaching the perimeter. Tires were slashed, gushing air. Deadly arrows darted in the night: for Diana, for *Nodin.*

Soon, the deed was done. Furtive figures fled the scene. Sentinels followed, starry-eyed stalkers. Sparrow remained, Autumn had made clear the building—its control panels, its circuitry—

must be destroyed.

Keep the pipeline closed and the oily snake asleep. The generator had a gas tank. The Sentinel communicated her plan.

On the northern shore, blackened kayaks beached undetected. Elena and her team came ashore near Boulevard Drive, the coast road connecting Point LaBarbe to the bridge. Elena felt her enemy approaching at a run. There was something wrong with this foe, something rank. Other muzzles sniffed it too. From the forest, wolves stirred. Elena, an alpha female, bristled at the pack—*these are mine, I claim them.*

The timing would be tight. Elena arranged her Sentinels in ambush. With a minute to spare, she ordered her mind as well—the dreaming trees, the saltless sea, Diana, atomized and all around her. The atmosphere, now articulate, urged patience. Elena obeyed and focused on her breathing. Then she saw them, felt them.

The skeletons, lightly armed but lethal, ran the road in tactical column. The big lake was on their left, the darkling woods upon their right. Professional, they had flankers on both sides, and a skull-scout running point. There was no carbon-cough of engines, and the drone swarm had dissipated hours ago. Each side had a dozen fighters—ELF vs. Aghori, evenly matched. What advantage, then, besides surprise?

It wasn't enough. Elena had only seconds to consider; Sentinel lives were on the line. Too many had been killed already. In her mind, *Nodin's* wheelhouse exploded for the hundredth time. Elena hesitated, balking at the merge. Then Diana's hand, invisible, reached for hers, a caress of coolness. Her lover led her backwards, subterranean, to the sweat lodge of the night before. Topless, they'd sat together, writhing in Gaia's womb. Autumn's vision, her song, became animate again. Elena, from ambush position, watched the stars watching her. Curious, a constellation—a backwards question mark—punctuated the east. Last night, emerging sweaty from the lodge, Autumn pointed to it. What had the water-protector said?

Diana remembered, whispering it on the wind: "The underwater panther, *Mishibizhiw*, will help us guard these straits."

That was it!

Elena felt the panther, bright-eyed, on the prowl. A set of waves clawed the stony beach as this dripping guardian emerged.

It felt good to run, to outpace her sorrow: the fiery death of her guru, Aghori Jones. McKenzie had dosed her squad with Shark-juice. High on Cyanovirin, they flew along the coast road. SPC-4 no longer, McKenzie specialized in darker arts. Jones had trained her well. She'd begun to slip the eight nooses—*Astamahāpāśa*, he called them in their sessions together. Fear, greed, lust, shame....

Jones helped unkink the knots.

Dr. Schark, kinky and curious, surveilled them round the clock—sparring, their seated *sādhanā*, the contemplation of corpses, their detachment from possessions, clothing included. The Big Boss got his kicks as Jones and McKenzie kicked their too-human habits. Of course there'd been intercourse, but of a different type. Transcendent, they left their lusty bodies while Sharkey watched on his screens—their only fan.

During the battle, Jones's soul had been freed from rebirth. She heard about the collision, the burst of light that marked his *moksha*. Hard not to grieve though—that noose still chafed. McKenzie cleared the choke from her throat, seeking serenity.

Her boots pounded the pavement, her disciples following in file. Mission focus was her tantra, her text. She'd memorized Dozer's blueprint, the chambers and valves of the metallic myocardium—Line 5's main pump. Touring Panzer's morgue, Jones once handed her a human heart. They practiced yoga together, naked on a cooling board. Both of them were hairless—her skin remained unmarked, his inner anatomy etched in ink. They contemplated the fleshy pump without passion. Without passion, they merged. Two bodies became one. Properly focused, that one became none. Together, they dissolved.

McKenzie wanted this again. Knew such want was weakness. So be it. Without Jones, she wasn't strong enough. Without his strength, what was she? A bald freak. An assassin. A zombie of zoonosis? Superhuman, Jones had plucked her from a Humvee—her past life too—during the Fort Custer ambush. She'd been chosen to lead, but had anyone asked?

They approached the pump station. Her point-man signaled a halt, and the Aghori went silent. At the first sign of dawn they'd open the valves, tarring the Straits with oil squeezed from Canadian sands. Schark loved the plan; so did Dozer, his fool. Little boys drowning ants. Was she playing too? A red star eyed her from the east, questioning everything.

Hearing enhanced, waves scratched the shore. Her squad unslung their weapons. Something stirred, prowling the dark. Alerted, the Aghori varied their vision. Some donned NVGs, painting the coast road green. Others went thermal, viewing the world through vented heat. McKenzie closed her lids, opening herself to stranger signatures. No matter the lens, the whole team was blindsided.

Her two flankers, seeing a flash of green, were arrowed first. Feathered from the forest, both Gories went down. Her pointman, thermal-visioned, found himself impaled upon a spear. Too late, he'd seen its hurler—the attackers were somehow hooding their signatures? Cold arrows enfiladed their column. No muzzle-flash, no magnesium, to trace them to their source. McKenzie blinked her eyes open; she'd led her squad to slaughter. Fern-clad forms emerged, knifing her comrades, ripping rib cages and throats till every Gorie was down.

Her squad's sole survivor, she tried filling herself—*prana*, life force, *chi*. The forest hedged against her, no chance for escape.

Invisible, the leafy ambushers waited, patient as trees. McKenzie tossed away her rifle, drawing a blade from its sheath. Her first slice was to her own vest. She shrugged free from the Kevlar, found balance, and awaited release.

Something feline confronted her, elemental, in the road. The figure lowered its hood, revealing blonde hair, braided for battle. The day's first photons began filtering from the east. The red-eyed star was still watching. McKenzie felt its curious gaze. *Guru Jones, my love, is that you?*

Cat-like, the braided woman pounced. Too slow, the Vishkanya parried, knifing one of the panther's paws while the other paw raked her side—McKenzie had been opened. Hot blood slicked her bare torso as she tried to recover. The braided panther, with one arm wounded, pounced again. Again McKenzie was clawed, her ribcage opened up, leaving her own pump horribly exposed.

She was on her knees. The gray light increased. She sought Jones's eye, but his fire was out. Suddenly cold, McKenzie died in the road.

Across the Straits, Dozer, on foot and stalked by sharp-eared Greenies, fled from the fiasco of the southern pump station. Line 5's oily valves had not been opened; his bridge defeat was total. The failed invasion was utterly unfixable, even for Mikey, the one-time mechanic. His first rule was *survival* and he wouldn't break it now. His second rule was *have an exit plan,* and he did. Dozer slunk to his getaway vehicle. Prepositioned, the hot rod held extra doses, food, and a weapon. He'd be needing them all. Dozer started up the engine and kept his lights off. *Fuck everyone else* was Dozer's rule number three.

As he shifted and started to roll, all four tires bumped flatly. Dozer had been slashed. Behind him, a massive fireball *whooshed* its way skyward. A second later Dozer felt its heat. The southern pump station had exploded. In the flickering light

Dozer saw Panzer's skeletons—unsmiling—hemming him in.

The Aghori, elite warfighters, demanded the same from their leaders. His doses couldn't save him from the bullet in his brain. Dozer, in more ways than one, was relieved of command. The mechanic's last sigh was one of relief.

PART 5:
The Road Ahead

Full Moon Ceremony by Jackie Traverse

The Wheels on the Bus

RANGERS ROBERT AND FREDDY missed their new friend. The two brothers had been ordered to stay behind and protect the newly freed labor force, while Thorn continued north to the Straits with Colonel Dennis and the Griffins. After his accolades at Indian River, apparently Thorn was Rabbit no longer. All the preppers were talking—the slave bus, the mammoth, dude's prowess hand-to-hand. Good to see their boy recognized by the colonel. Thorn was one of them now. Alone no longer, the ex-ELF was now a Ranger.

Late that night, battle-thunder rumbled from the bridge; rainless lightning had flashed. Robert and Freddy monitored the radio, hoping for good news. Finally, after midnight, the colonel's call came through—the Straits were secure! The bridge, a vector for Virals, was severed by an airstrike—huzzah to their Eagles! The Free North, infection-free, would now have a chance! Chosen and XCons had scattered, most of their equipment captured or destroyed—Bravo Zulu to the Last Alliance! But Dennis warned them that prepper country should prepare for deserting Spreaders; the red-eyes were still contagious and heavily armed.

With her CO at the bridge, Sergeant Amanda Taylor was in command. Her mixed unit of Rangers, Griffs, and civilians had peeled off from the attacking force, hunkering down near a church two miles south of the Straits. The Agape Lighthouse was its name, a rundown place, but well-positioned for her purpose. Taylor's orders were to protect the busload of freed slaves, prepare the unit's howitzers for fire-support, liaise with the Rangers, and stand by either to attack or displace, depending on events.

Sergeant Taylor had been duly diligent. Her 105s were dug in and sighted towards the enemy. She'd established a perimeter, a cook-tent, and a watchlist. Her two Viral prisoners—Red Liz and Lazy Boy—were cuffed inside a Humvee ambulance.

"Uh, Sergeant Major?"

Taylor pulled her eyes from the map. "It's Robert, right? You're a Ranger?" Amanda hadn't slept; none of them had.

"Freddy, actually." She grudged him a weary look, ordering her eyes not to roll.

"I just came from bus duty. There's an Amish woman onboard with something to say."

Dawn's gray light scattered upon the X-marked bus, DEPARTMENT OF CORRECTIONS stenciled on its side. For the first time all night, the Straits were quiet. The sergeant major pulled herself up the steep steps. An accented elder was reading from his bible. A Detroit Second Baptist, Amanda Taylor—Sunday school savant—knew her chapter and verse.

"Servants, be obedient to them that are your masters according to the flesh, with fear and trembling, in singleness of your heart, as unto Christ."

The crowded bus was ripe with body odor and the acrid tang of urine. Sergeant Taylor added another item to her endless list—bathe the civilians.

The interior of the bus was dim in the early morning. The men wore orange MDOC jumpsuits along with their beards and brimmed hats. The trafficked women, dolled up by XCons, had been issued Army ponchos by the Griffs and wore improvised bonnets. Twenty white faces attended the Black sergeant major. Amanda addressed them, "Good morning, I'm Command Sergeant Major Taylor, but you can call me Amanda. Coffee and breakfast are being prepared. When it's safe to do so, you'll have a chance to exercise and to wash. It appears we've won a battle, but it's still very dangerous. Many of your captors have escaped."

She watched their reaction. Some were translating. They comforted each other, resilient.

"Does anyone have a question?"

The bible reader raised a rough hand, ropy with veins, and Taylor nodded. His question came from Corinthians, which he quoted. She had to decipher his dialect:

"Be ye not unequally yoked together with unbelievers: for what fellowship hath righteousness with unrighteousness?"

The phrasing was King James and familiar. Was this grandpa calling her Griffins "unrighteous?"

Taylor had no time for this. Quickly, she answered, a question for a question, same chapter, different verse.

"And what concord hath Christ with Belial? Or what part hath he that believeth with an infidel?"

Amanda's quote caused a stir; gramps wasn't happy. Taylor could give two shits. The Detroit deacon stood tall in her Army Combat Uniform, adding bite to her bark. "Listen up! We soldiers are *far* from righteous, and we *certainly* aren't Christ-like. But friend, if you think we're the Devil, we're gonna have problems."

The old man was muttering in a language that sounded like German. The menfolk around him stirred. Taylor didn't wait for Freddy to ID the informant; she ordered all the women off the bus. "Ladies first now. Time to wash up and get some chow. Move it!"

She stood by the steering wheel, watching them disembark. These women were in bad shape—bruised necks, puffy lips, and the trauma-stares of the trafficked. They limped, bare-footed, down the steps, swishing in their plastic ponchos. She'd have to see about boots and clothing. Amanda knew they preferred simple dresses, no colors—add it to the list.

Ranger Freddy nodded to indicate his informant—a middle-aged woman, much like the rest. Taylor glared at the seated elders with their shaved upper lips. She ordered Freddy to remain, then climbed down and led the women towards the Griffins' mobile kitchen. She'd authorized its generator, trading gasoline for hot coffee—a fuel-for-fuel exchange.

The soldier on duty handed her a cup. She took two and led the Amish woman out of earshot. The little church had a garden and a few wooden crosses. Its gardeners, stung back in Y1, had been planted here, fertilizing the sandy soil. Amanda kicked a clump of weeds with her combat boots, wondering when she'd last had them off.

Side by side, they sat on a bench. At first the two women sipped in silence. The treetops were tipped with fire. October approached, and the birches all wore yellow. The day dawned fresh, a few birds singing; black coffee did its thing. Amanda sighed and loosened up, hoping her companion felt the same.

"My name is Amanda," she said after several quiet minutes, hoping to draw her out.

"I am Hannah. Hannah Hochstettler. *Danke für den Kaffee.*"

They sipped again. "Do you have a husband? Is he on the bus? Any kids?"

"Jah, I have *zwei kinder*, but my *Mann* is dead. The children stay at the farm."

"The farm?"

"Where they work us, the *Englisch*, with the *iks*." Hannah tapped her forehead to indicate the X-brand.

"Where is that place?"

Hannah held up her right hand, the map-hand of Michigan. She pointed towards the middle. "Clare. *Die Grosse Plantage—* The Plantation—*ist nah* Clare. We grow the food for the *iks*."

Sergeant Taylor was wide awake now. Intel plus caffeine— Amanda wanted more. How many farmers? How many guards?

Defenses? Distribution network? Cooperation with Chosen? How many fighters had gone north? How many still remained? Would the slaves rebel? What if they had help? Were there weapons? What about the variant? Were they protected from Stinger? If yes, how so?

Hannah did her best, but it took time. Taylor, delayed by dialect, slowly pieced it together. It sounded like "The Plantation" was a food production center overseen by XCons and Chosen. It was surrounded by a ring of feeder-farms worked primarily by Old Order Amish, rounded up from across Michigan. Yes, the Amish had some resistance to Stinger, though many still died. Non-combative, they were easy targets for Virals. Many died in that violence as well.

There was an opportunity here to disrupt Panzerland. The Griffs had a window, a small one. Could she chance it? She'd better call the colonel. Amanda sighed and stood up, and Hannah stood too. The plain woman, one eye blackened, pointed at the church sign—Agape.

"Frau Amanda, you know this word? This kind of love?"

Taylor knew it—church picnics along the Detroit Riverfront, bible study with her youth group, the teachings of her beloved mentor, their quotation competitions. "Agape-love is universal. It makes the world a better place."

The "Plantation" opportunity felt urgent. Amanda updated her checklist: comms with Dennis, get the 105s ready to roll, pack up the kitchen, secure the perimeter, fuel status, ammo status, march order. Hannah touched the CSM's shoulder with a work-hardened hand. "Amanda, I believe in agape. I believe in you. *Gott segen eich.*" The battered woman took her leave. Proud in her poncho, she limped back towards the kitchen where other women waited in line.

Commanded by their CSM, the Griffins hopped to it. Taylor, tornadic, was everywhere at once. The howitzers were hitched to their Humvees. Radio contact was made with the CO at his new HQ in St. Ignace. Maps were consulted, call signs established. Rangers were questioned about the country they'd traverse. Fuel reports were tallied.

With any luck, they'd make it to Clare, putting the bread-basket of Panzerland out of business. There was no sign yet of Spreaders, but Taylor knew they'd be coming. Any deserters from the bridge battle would be desperate. The detachment's diesel engines started up. Yellow Griffin pennants, unyielding, streamed from antennas. The sun cleared the trees, gilding the once-quiet churchyard and its denizens of dirt.

Robert and Freddy were assigned to chaperone the DOC bus.

"I call shotgun!"

"Fuck you, Freddy, you're just gonna nap!"

The younger brother winked but stood his ground; he'd called it first. Robert buckled up behind the wheel, checked his mirrors, and waited their turn. Freddy stood by the bus doors, flashing a grin at the un-grinning Amish. He adjusted his rifle sling and racked a round, double-checking the safety.

Their turn came. Robert put the bus in gear and took his place in the convoy. Freddy cleared his voice theatrically.

Robert groaned—anticipating a performance—and watched the road. As the convoy accessed the ramp for I-75 south, all the vehicles started honking. Someone approached them from the north, from the direction of the broken bridge. A figure on a bicycle worked furiously to catch them.

"Well I'll be damned." Freddy, finger off the trigger, scoped this bogie with his rifle. The convoy's brake lights were all tapping red. "Open the doors, Robert!"

His big brother braked the bus, handled its lever; the accordion doors folded open. Freddy leaned out, urging the bicyclist to hurry. He gave a thumbs up to his brother at the wheel. "Bobby, you're not gonna *believe* this!"

Robert dropped his window, stuck his head out, and looked back—their Rabbit had returned! Thorn, puffing and pedaling, caught up with them. He wore his Sentinel parka with a rifle slung behind. His face was sooty with battle grime, but his teeth showed white as he dismounted to receive Freddy's hug. The two men secured his bike to the bus bumper. Thorn waved at all the rear-view mirrors, the uniformed Griffins waving in return. The two men climbed the stairs and came aboard.

Robert overheard some of Thorn's breathless explanation—"They were gonna quarantine me!—borrowed a bike—Elena—badly wounded—gave me a kayak too—paddled across—didn't want to miss the fun!"

The hilarity of the reunion was frowned upon by Amish fathers. The three Rangers, boys at heart, could care less. Freddy winked at his brother behind the wheel. "You probably want a song, don't you?"

Then Freddy began it, elbowing Thorn to join. Brother Bobby rolled his eyes before jumping in too. The longbeards wagged in disapproval as they took the highway south towards Clare.

"Oh, the wheels on the bus go round and round, round and round...."

Mackinac Straits Health System

THE HOSPITAL AT ST. IGNACE was new, though its ribbon-cutting had been cut short by Covee. Overwhelmed like all the rest, its modern facilities had morphed medieval. When the U.P. got stung early in Year 1, its morgue quickly filled. Refrigerated trucks were borrowed and stocked—not with produce, but with people, the by-products of plague. And the sick kept coming, their STING systems hijacked by Stinger. Stormed by their own cytokines, there was nowhere for them to go. Tarry pits were excavated in the newly paved parking lot, the mass graves of systemic failure.

Then the grid went down, hard. Smart phones, deaf and dumb, were demoted. No fuel could be found, and the morgue-trucks soon overheated. The drippy stench that summer was overwhelming. Volunteers went in with kerosene and torches. The logoed containers—McDonald's, "I'm Lovin' It"—and their organic occupants were flame-broiled, a crematorium of corpses.

Survivors of the bridge battle called it the Healing House. The hospital was cleaned and scrubbed, Army generators providing occasional power. Colonel Dennis followed the doctors on their rounds, shaking hands, collecting stories for the record. The bookish man had an ear for language and a taste for tobacco. Post-rounds, Dennis would fill a pipe with scrounged leaf, filling pages with unusual words—*fairing, farkle, frisco*—from conversing with SIS bikers; *ahsayma, ahnung, animikii*—from overhearing the Indigenous.

All the wards were full; triage, burn unit, post-op, and quarantine. Other healers, non-traditional, made their rounds as well. Autumn smudged sage and her boy Loon assisted. Patients brightened in their presence, recovery times shortened; those who healed quickly were discharged, joining the volunteers.

There was much to do on the north side of the bridge—the "safe side," they called it—though that had taken some doing. Mopping up cost them plenty, in casualties, in time. During the battle, invasion barges, X-marked, had run aground on the shoals. Stranded there, ex-convicts were once again confined. Colonel Dennis consulted with Big Ben and Baptiste. Autumn's voice was also heard, along with the wounded ELF leader, Elena. There were no easy fixes. What to do with the shipwrecked Spreaders? Marooned on the sandy shoal, they were too big a threat. The sun set without solution, though Shaggy, a Howler, had winked an amber eye.

The first night after the battle, wolves swam to the shoal, crossing the open mile that quarantined their coast. No one saw it save red-eyed Spreaders, and they were soon silenced. Panicked gunshots were heard, then howls, then screams. A burial detail, clad in hazmat, investigated the next morning. They gathered up the remains of wolves and men and lit the pyre, a smoky beacon of U.P. freedom.

XCon weapons were collected and disinfected, their barges—tugged free from the sand—brought to harbor. Their vehicles were decontaminated, decaying fuel siphoned off. On the south side of the severed bridge, the Raiders had run. Brian and Loon, once recovered, flew reconnaissance. Both fliers confirmed that the enemy had fled; the north, for now, was contagion free.

Colonel Dennis, historian and steward, flew flags from both stockades—Fort Mackinac on its island and Fort Michilimackinac on the southern shore. Lightly garrisoned with spotters and radios, the forts served as observation posts, the eyes and ears of the again-strategic Straits.

Four centuries of officers had done the same, Dennis annotated his appendix. The French were the first to fortify—Durantaye in 1683, Lignery in 1712. Then came the British—brave Captain Roberts in 1812. Half a century later, an American from the Union Army, Sergeant Marshall, commanded the fort from 1861–1867, a civil man in an uncivil war.

Panzer's double tower banner—bullet holed and singed—had been hauled down as a battle-trophy. Dennis replaced it with the Stars and Stripes, 125th's yellow Griffin roaring just below.

The hospital's quarantine ward was coed, with large windows and an enclosed garden. Suspected close-contacts were confined there for observation and testing. Full PPE was mandatory for doctors and nurses. Visitors were banned to reduce risk of transmission. Aside from daily rounds, the patients were mostly left alone. The room was a large one, each group staking their turf.

Booker and Cruz, reunited with their regiment, played cards, bet large, talked trash, and encouraged all comers. Their bloodstained cammies were laundered and folded away. The men wore hospital scrubs over dog tags and tried too hard to take it easy. Besides potential infection, both soldiers had suffered head wounds. Their TBI caused headaches and darkened their vision; Booker's nose still bled.

Their captain, meanwhile, was even worse. For the first time, Frank Young felt fragile. Sudden moves hurt him. Bright lights caused pain. Young slept most of the day. When his dreams found him, Frank found them disturbing.

Howlers who'd survived the Wolf Wood gave the medical staff hell. Wild-eyed even in peacetime, recent close combat had amped them up. They distilled their own booze and were generous with it, but they played rough and were raucous at all the wrong times. One hothead pulled a knife on EMT Cruz after losing a poker hand; the longhair almost lost his own, as Cruz crushed his grip. Grinning, the Griff flicked the confiscated blade, raking the pot while the dagger quivered in the wall.

The watchful pack had flashed their canines and roared with approval. The knife-decor remained, a memento to their madness.

SIS bikers also bunked with this group, Shaggy Wolf being an exemplar of Scout-Howler overlap. Their Covee tests remained negative, Mukwa's as well. Most of the bikers suffered from burns, needed stitches, and carried shrapnel souvenirs. The fray had been a sharp one, and their MC membership was much reduced.

Mukwa stole glances at the Sentinels, wishing Thorn had remained on the north side. Fallen from Gaia's grace, ex-ELF, the two men had much in common. They'd evacuated together from the broken bridge, dropping through darkness surrounded by stars. Tying up in the harbor, Thorn commenced his scrounge. Before dawn he'd commandeered a kayak, a bicycle, and a rifle. Mukwa brushed off Thorn's invitation to range south. Instead, El Oso gave his comrade's kayak a shove, raising a reluctant paw in farewell.

Had Mukwa made the wrong choice? Probably. Story of his life. And where the fuck was Nighthawk? The she-elf hadn't been seen since the arson back on Beaver. She'd missed the weapon-take and *Nodin's* movement too. Did anyone even care? Ever-divided, for now, Mukwa would stick with Shaggy. Surviving bikers—even one-percenters, the outlaws—were brothers now. Ride or die motherfucker.

Elena and her ELF commandos were sequestered as well. Securing both pump stations had required hand-to-hand fighting. Their parkas were cleaned of gore and hung in a storeroom with other gear of war. The Sentinels stuck together, lounging in their scrubs, aloof. They claimed the courtyard garden as their own and could be found there at all hours, forest-bathing or reading in the slanting light of late September. Their books bore the stamp of the St. Ignace Library. Requests were given to nurses. RNs Mathew and Sean were diligent, but many titles were missing or wrongly shelved during collapse. The bored

Sentinels weren't picky, claiming that the books, bored as well, enjoyed being thumbed.

Elena, bereaved of her partner Diana, might lose her arm in surgery. Dr. Chow was urging amputation. The Aghori leader—dog-tagged McKenzie—had slashed Elena badly with a poisoned blade. The infected wound suppurated; antibiotics didn't work, and the patient was negligent in self-care. Elena tolerated her comrades but showed no spark of leadership. In a garden talk with Sparrow, Elena owned up to depression, describing a darkness in her mind. Each day she tested negative for Covee, but her arm remained inflamed. Dr. Chow, during rounds, reluctantly planned its removal.

At the Last

PATIENT YOUNG REQUESTED A MAP. Frank hung it in the Healing House, then busied himself with markers. He neglected the garden view for the cartographic, preferring to window the world through mileage and terrain. His CO, Colonel Dennis, passed him notes through the nurses, keeping Young's map up to date.

The enemy had abandoned Mackinaw City. Material was left behind—some vehicles, some fuel. The Chosen rout had been hurly-burly, deserters spreading through the rural north. Metastatic, the red-eyes plagued prepper country. The origin of this cancer was known: Kalamazoo, the hardened headquarters of Panzer Pharma. On his map, Young doodled a double tower floating above the riverine fortress. Unconfirmed, its commander was Dr. Schark, Panzer's eccentric founder and CEO.

Interrogating Chosen POWs produced questionable intelligence. For two years, Young had done his share and was familiar with its follies. The Chosen chain of command was opaque. The typical foot-soldier knew the name—nickname usually—of their immediate boss and not much more. Still, Griffin interrogators heard the term "Sharkey" often enough to guess its source. Spreaders lived in fear of their Big Boss and his death-headed demons. After facing these faceless on the bridge, Young understood their terror. If Frank fell asleep at night, the same dream always found him: *the bus-wall, the breach, the skittering skeletons.*

Frank's rhythms, circadian no longer, had been ravaged. He

couldn't sleep. The captain, concussed, spent the dark hours alone. Wearing a headlamp, Young studied his map, sound-tracked by the snores—and sometimes screams—of the traumatized ward. Headache rumbling, Frank tallied their assets. The F-15s were removed from Traverse City. TVC was on the wrong side of the bridge. The paired Eagles now nested in Sault Ste. Marie. "Better safe-side than sorry-side," the colonel had quipped. Dennis dispatched a two-truck convoy to the Soo—mechanics and security, rations and radio parts. With no jet fuel to be had, his two birds had lost their wings.

The unit's other heavy weapons, its howitzers, had been wrong-sided as well and would remain in the south. Command Sergeant Taylor was in charge of the Griffin cannons. Young penciled "105s?" at their last known position—an abandoned church, Agape, three klicks south of the bridge.

Pain thundered through his thoughts. Frank fought back by listing unknowns. Where was his perp, his POI, Cowboy Campbell? And what about the ELF Sentinel, "Nighthawk," who'd sprung him—and kicked their asses—with her ambush in the dunes? What about the islanders, unprotected back on Beaver? Or Red Liz, the Viral they'd transferred to Sergeant Taylor? And how many fighters could Dr. Schark still field? What new devilry was brewing in Panzer's labs? What was the latest intel on the XCons and their leader, Mustafa? Was he really dead? Or those skeletons? What about oil refineries and farms downstate?

Frank adjusted his lamp as lightning forked his skull. He shrank from the national picture, unconfirmed and rife with rumor. After the White House assassination last March, the president's Red Hands had choked all resistance. Post-purge. Their recruitment soared; one fist was now many. United by rage, they squeezed the eastern states dry—of people, of petroleum. Concerning the global situation, Young shrugged. Anything international was the dark side of the moon.

And there it was, waxing gibbous through the garden glass. And *she* was out there too, pale-faced and beautiful, her bandaged arm in a sling. Young switched off his headlamp. The lunar light brightened, reflecting its source. The moon silvered Elena's tears as Diana beamed down from beyond the veil.

Dr. Daniel Chow considered the Mason jar he was holding. Earlier, during morning rounds, he was accompanied by Autumn. The Manitoulin medicine woman had been blunt: "When their quarantine is over, will they all be discharged?"

Chow shook his head, no. Disapproving, she'd shaken her own, *tsk-tsk*. Every fighter was needed, Chow knew that. Too many had died. The mass suicide of Seekers—had they all been infected?—hit especially hard. Chow wished the yellow-striped patients were here to observe. So much still to learn about the pathology of SARS-CoV-2 and its venomous variant.

Free North numbers were few, surviving Spreaders too many. The Last Alliance had fought hard to keep the north contagion-free: the U.P., Canada, the Great Lakes, and all the islands too. The colonel's Eagle-strike forestalled Panzer's motorized invasion, but without able-bodies, their shield wall was thin. So why not discharge them? Chow's healing ward housed the core of their strength—Scouts, Howlers, Sentinels, Griffins—all veterans of combat, the spirited nucleus of their fighting force.

It wasn't the virus detaining them, as Chow predicted the negative tests would continue. Not Stinger, but some other darkness diseased them. His medical staff—Doc Newsome, the nurses, National Guard medics—had no shortage of diagnoses: PTSD, TBI, major depressive disorder, complicated grief, post-traumatic epilepsy, and generalized anxiety. But where was the commonality? If these ailments could be linked, then so could their cure. And cure them Daniel must. Autumn made that quite clear.

"Have you used it yet?" she'd asked him, as morning light flooded his office.

"Used what exactly? We've tried them all."

And indeed they had. His team had scrounged, bartered, and bought—sertraline, escitalopram, lorazepam, trazodone, zopiclone, clonidine, guanfacine, risperidone, aripiprazole ... their list was long, but positive outcomes were few.

"The tincture we made you on Beaver Island," Autumn replied. "Remember the label, *At-the-last*?"

Chow reached behind him, taking the jar from its shelf and holding it to the sun. The liquid beamed upon the woman's face, refracting pure gold. Autumn smiled, elusive. "I suggest it in tea. Brew it in the ward; even its vapors have potency." She stood to leave. "But the stuff is precious, a *little dab'll do ya.*"

The water-protector then winked her way out.

The ward knew its routine and was killing time before lunch. Morning rounds were over; blood pressures and vitals had been recorded. Dressings had been changed, pills swallowed, and the first cards were being dealt. Bleary Howlers sipped from secreted sources. Masked and gowned, Nurse Sean prevented the Sentinels from going out to their garden. "Sorry guys, but the doctors want everyone in the ward today."

Nurse Mathew, wearing full PPE, ignited propane, setting an oversize kettle to boil. Dr. Chow, protected as well, stood by with an eye dropper and unsealed the Mason jar. He tried not to think about how far he'd fallen. Tried not to compare the high-definition past with this unfocused present. Mathew gave a nod; the water was roiling. Chow, without dosage guidelines or FDA approval, filled his pipette with the prescribed potion. One drop at a time, the liquid gold was dispensed.

Mukwa, olfaction-enhanced, was the first to feel its effects. His nostrils quivered, scenting honeycombs and the clover that filled them. The big man closed his eyes and it was summer on Beaver Island. Four-footed, he basked in fields of flowers and felt himself renewed.

In her mind, Sparrow flitted from tree to tree in a deeply-shadowed forest. The ELF fighter scented wet moss and lichens and the outbreath of trees. A river burbled on the rocks, telling endless tales to its rooted audience.

For amber-eyed Shaggy, it was tumbleweed, sage, and the endless plains. He tasted the tang of rubber and engine exhaust. The Lakota veteran was transported to the Black Hills. The scents of *Pahá Sápa* slowly displaced his sensory nightmares of the bridge.

The pungent fragrance steamed. Healing House was refreshed, the staff feeling it too. They were wounded as well—patients they'd lost, the grit of blades on bone, unanesthetized screams, and, of course, their own loved ones, gone for good.

The elixir was portioned into paper cups. Time for tea; soon all the patients were sipping. Dr. Chow observed his ward. Imbibed in liquid form, the pharmacon's effects appeared fantastical. The Howlers, undrunk, were all agrin. Even disciplined guardsmen were goofing, Griffins raising British pinkies above their cups. Mathew and Sean held hands openly. The ward exhaled its grief as hope—bioactivated—filled their chests.

Pain clouds, cumulus, cleared from Young's mind. The dispelling breeze was scented with lawn clippings, BBQ sauce, and his wife's preferred sunblock. Frank felt his face with his fingers, found that he was smiling. His forehead, pain-free for once, began to unfurrow.

Daniel Chow scented blossoms and the gloss of new textbooks, remembering med school, picnics in the arboretum, blanket-time with his future wife. Data driven, Chow ordered another round of vitals. His heart skipped as results came in: blood pressures were down, heart rates too, and oximeter readings had improved. Inspired, he visited his most critical patient.

Dr. Chow gently removed Elena's bandages. Her arm, gashed by a Gorie, was badly inflamed. Their dwindling supply of antibiotics were ineffectual. Angry red streaks arrowed up the archer's forearm, emphatically pointing to lymphangitis. The Sentinel ran a fever, had chills; her life was in danger. Chow dampened a cloth in the tincture, applying the compress. He bathed the wound and watched her face. Did her pain lessen? Did her shallow breathing just grow deeper?

Check and check. They did! *At-fucking-last!* About time something worked.

Out of Aces

THE GODDAMN ROOSTER WOKE HIM. Every morning had been the same for two weeks now—or was it three? Cowboy, rousted from a dream—bobber fishing with his daughter—blinked back tears, waking to his hayloft instead. Pale light seeped through chinks in the old barn. His nest of cut grass was warm. Bob rolled over, found the dream lake, picked up his fishing pole, then that fowl fucker woke him. Again.

No snooze button on that bird; Bob Campbell, bleary-eyed, plotted its death. Thank God it was Sunday. He flexed his blistered hands. Church day, prayer day, when bosses—the *iks*—left them alone. Services would be at Yoder's, just a mile down Tobacco Road, each Amish house taking its turn.

His fucking beard itched. Bob gave his whiskers a two-handed scratch. He creaked to his feet—farm labor was *hard!*—filled the pee bottle with his warm gush, and looked out the loft's window. His reluctant hosts, the Hochstettlers, were already up and at it. The kids, Sarah and Samuel, tended chickens, while grumpy grandpa milked cows. Did they ever sleep? The last slice of moon climbed in the east. The sun would be next. He welcomed it. Without electricity, October was cold. Each morning he woke fucking freezing.

After Sunday services—a Germanic garble—Bob would be free for the rest of their Sabbath. But by sunrise tomorrow they'd be back in the fields. The bosses, hung-over and oversexed, would be back too, whip hands rested and ready to rip.

The Hochstettlers, homesteading near Clare, had taken him in. The Amish were field labor for The Farm, a Chosen plantation. These longbeards and bonnet-ladies were not typical Candidates, not as Cowboy knew them. When exposed to Stinger, most Amish would sicken but not die. Some did, though; Cowboy had the blisters from grave-digging to prove it. Partial immunity made them ideal slaves. Having been "chosen" himself—thus immune—Bob supposed he was an ideal slave too.

Back in September—two weeks ago, three?—Cowboy Campbell had reached the end of his rope. No gas, no car, no weapon, no will. He'd left her, or rather, the nameless elf had left him—bloody-nosed, gagged, and hog-tied under bushes on the rainy road near Panzer. Why hadn't she returned? He was valuable to her; she'd said so herself. A bargaining chip, a red-eyed Chosen to exchange for her bright-eyed elves.

It took forever, but Bob eventually pulled a Houdini and freed himself—just another rope trick for ol' Cowboy. Would he follow her? Knock on the gate? Snitch the elf out? Find a Panzer bus to throw her under? Nope. Apparently, Bob was done with all that. "Fuck off then. See if I care."

He'd picked himself up, sniffing back his nosebleed. Cowboy Bob retreated down the rainy road, turning his back on Panzer's Friday Night Lights. He returned to the car they'd hijacked, the Chosen hot rod starting right up. He'd driven north in the rain, away from Panzer and the more populated southlands, blinking back tears as he drove.

His pity party was not well attended. Wife? Dead. Daughter? Dead. Lizzy? Dead. Why the fuck wasn't he? A perfect cowboy song, if he had the heart to sing it.

Gas gauge busted, he'd run out near Mt. Pleasant, an unpleasant surprise that turned him pedestrian. The cold rain eventually stopped. Bob hadn't. Nightfall found him footsore on Loomis Road, two miles from Clare. *Move or die*, Campbell's mantra since collapse. Especially when your ass was out of assets—no food, no hat, no pistol, not even a damn blanket. He kept on keeping on—one boot, then another. The stars came out, the temperature plunging. No warmth in those suns; they glittered with malice.

He hiked past an old biker bar, The Loomis Lounge, long abandoned. Bob pictured the place packed—smokers in the parking lot, choppers on kickstands, southern anthems blaring from the jukebox, endless pitchers of beer. How good they'd all had it. And no one had known.

Of course, the Lounge had been looted, turned inside-out, just another picked pocket like all the rest. Bob, the battler, kept going, fighting greasy memories of hot ham and eggs. His road crossed US Highway 10. He paused on the overpass. No movement, no sound—the nightscape was a void. He kept at it. Loomis became Tobacco Road at the Clare county line.

Move or die. Hard to freeze to death while walking, but man, he'd come close. When Bob saw lights at last, he could care less about their source. XCons, Chosen, even fucking elves, he would run to them as long as death was warm.

Hypothermic, he cased the joint—an unlooted farmhouse, tidy outbuildings, lantern-glow. No trucks in the yard, no generator-hum, no armed men, at least none he could see. Too good to be true, too cold to care. Fuck it. Bob made his approach. If he had a white flag, he'd wave it.

Grandpa Hochstettler opened at his knock. The old Scrooge had not looked pleased, but when had he ever? A century ago? His *rumspringa* teens maybe, drinking and dancing, peach fuzz for a beard. Probably not. Bob just couldn't see it. At least the old man opened for him. More than most would do, even before.

"I'm infected. I'm a Spreader." Cowboy, out of aces, laid his shitty cards on the table.

The old man didn't blink.

"I'm freezing. I'm hungry."

Grumpy gramps didn't move.

"Can I sleep here? Come on man, in your barn maybe?" Cowboy pointed, Old Hocher just stared.

"Dawdy was afraid. He thought it was a trap," young Samuel had explained to their guest the next day. Cowboy awoke to see he's fresh face peering at him from the loft ladder. The freckled kid had smiled. Bob, smelling the bacon Sammy brought, smiled back. He fucking meant it too.

"The bosses," he tapped Bob's dirty forehead, "with the *iks*, have tricked us before. Set traps for us Plain. Took the rule-breakers away."

Cowboy didn't doubt it. Fucking Virals. He'd have done the same.

After that first bacon-bright morning, Samuel was his friend. Sometimes sister Sarah was too. Not Dawdy though, fat chance. Cowboy never ran out of questions for the kids. "Why aren't you afraid of my Covee? I'm contagious, you know."

"Most of us don't catch it. *Gott* protects us from Sting."

"Protects you, huh? How come you're slaves then?"

Samuel didn't flinch at the S-word. No shame in it, just another burden for these Amish to bear. "Moses was a slave."

Mic drop from DJ Sammy. Cowboy let it go.

"Please, you put these on." The kid had brought some clothes: a dark suit, wide pants, suspenders, black shoes. Bob sniffed them, catching the faded stink of another man.

"Whose were they?" If they were Dawdy's, he'd puke.

Samuel blinked. "They were *mei daett's.*"

Cowboy thought about that blink, the past tense. Shit.

Daett meant dad? Sammy's father was dead? Again, Bob let it go.

Old Hochstettler practiced what he preached; the damn man was a deacon. *Love thy neighbor,* said his book. Dawdy took it as an order, though he skimped a bit on "love."

Samuel laid it out, along with the outfit. "You stay with us, *Englischer*, and eat our food, get strong." Sammy fixed him with the old Hocher stare. "But Dawdy says you must work at *Die Plantage*, The Farm. And join our *gmay*, our community. Follow our *Ordnung*. To blend in, to avoid the *iks*, you must become Plain."

What choice did Bob have? Mock solemn, Cowboy put his hands together. "Amen, little brother. Amen."

Crossing the Jordan

EARLY THAT MORNING they'd steamed away from St. Ignace. The waning crescent rose astern as they passed beneath the broken bridge. Above them loomed the shattered span, the melted tower. Below, fathoms deep, sprawled a neo necropolis. The twin mammoths were down there, SIS bikes, and Humvees too. Corpses, caged by wreckage, were slowly nibbled free by lake trout, whitefish, and cisco—salmonid first responders, the jaws of life.

Nine Beaver boats had set out to defend the bridge. Only five returned, their crews much reduced. *Nodin*, drone-damaged, was under repair in St. Ignace. New masts—fore and aft—would help her harness the wind. The Coast Guard Response Boat had been commandeered by the colonel. Doyle and his *Mary* were gone, Big Hannigan and his fishing boat too.

On Beaver Island, lookouts spotted the returnees offshore, an island reception quickly forming. No marching band or confetti; the dockside reunion was solemn. Too many had died, with no coffins to cry over. The butcher's bill was steep, the battle's cost quickly known to all. House to house and farm to farm, their hallowed names were recited—Tom Doyle and dour O'Donnell; Big Hannigan, his crew; so many others. The tale of their chain-scythe and of kamikaze *Mary* grew with each telling.

The Naturals, hearing the return-bell and then the news, grieved as well—Gaia save us! Diana, killed? Six Sentinels too? Elena, condition critical, remained in the hospital. At least

Thorn was no longer dead. The ex-wrestler had swapped his acronyms: feared KIA, the missing man was now AWOL. Any disbelief the Naturals felt was soon dispelled by the sight of sad Sparrow. Songless, the gymnast kept her eyes down as they processioned towards ELF Country.

In the fortnight they'd been gone, Beaver Island's crops had ripened. Most of the Naturals—minus their militant Sentinels—had remained behind. The partnership they cultivated with locals was finally bearing fruit. Back from the bridge, the homecoming procession, traveling south from the harbor, noted the bounty in the fields, the fattened flocks, and the apple-heavy orchards.

A hasty ceremony had been arranged; a mutual affair, both sides agreed. Together, they would cross the river Jordan and gather in the state forest. The whole island was invited, though not everyone came. Bill Ferny and his ilk had been busy. Some ears, ever-eager for poison, proved all too easy to fill. Island factions deepened along familial fault-lines.

The surviving Sentinels marched home on foot. They shouldered their weapons, wearing clean parkas of gray. Sparrow led them to the bridge, then halted.

"Welcome to ELF Country," the twiggy sign proclaimed. Bearded Brian rode with them on a bicycle, his friend Loon balancing on the bar. Mukwa, bearing fresh scars, shuffled in the rear. The Naturals who'd stayed behind waited silently on the far side, ready to reunify. Returning fighters—men and women—arrived in wagons, unsteady on solid ground. They'd traded 500 hp motors for one-horse carts. The mariners looked ill with the change. Surviving Beaver captains Miller, Redding, Keller, and Bauman were led by the friend of Keith Two-Crow, Captain McCann. They had made the six-mile wagon ride, along with their families and crews.

The Greenes drove Annie Doyle. The widow's once-rosy face was wilted from weeping. Niece Maggie was there, holding tight to young Nick. Shattered by grief, they supported each other. Half of the island's three hundred were gathered; Deputy Williams wore his badge, and Father Peter shepherded his flock from Holy Cross to the crossing.

Both taverns, Shamrock and Comber, had closed, staff and stool-sitters coming to pay their respects. Alice, barkeep and owner of the 'Rock, dabbed a wet eye in remembrance. She'd been pulling pints for Doyle and Hanny since they were green-horns.

The Martins were there, being neighborly with the Nats. Amy Gillespie, township clerk, led a bicycle brigade of local government. An Ojibwe faction rode their ponies from Indian Point. They were there to support Samantha, their eldest and matriarch, who waited in welcome. The Indigenous supported Mukwa as well, if he'd have it; though the oft-troubled Muck had scorned them before.

Arriving at the little bridge, the islanders stood their ground on the north bank of the Jordan. For a moment, all was still but the river.

Naturals, on the south side, waited in ELF Country. Pastor George stood ready to bless the food-heavy tables. The elves—farmers, fishermen, and artisans—had prepared a feast, part memorial, part giving-of-thanks. Children in both crowds, eye-ing each other, were eager to unite. Social lines for the next gen-eration, if there was one, would be blurry.

Samantha, Grace, and Miin stood upon the bridge, all three women colorfully dressed. Grace held a smudge pot, wafting both sides. Samantha handled a jug of her elixir—strawberry wine. She'd infused it with medicine, and each of the crossers would be offered a sip. Miin tapped a hand drum, keeping time with the current. Made of island cedar and deer hide, Miinan—indigenous to the island—had stretched it herself.

The Jordan burbled its boggy song. October maples, bereft of chlorophyll, were all aflame. Birds and bees had grown quiet, summer susurrations shorter by the day. Samantha, silver hair brightly braided, raised her hands and rotated. Her voice carried, addressing both sides.

"You have won a victory at the bridge. The north is safe, so we are safe, at least for now. Your courage, your sacrifice, has bought us time. Time we must use to our advantage. We gather to mourn those who have died. Their bodies won't be returning, but we offer their spirits a home." She paused. Miin's drum did some speaking, as did Grace's clean sage.

"We gather to welcome home the warriors." Samantha nodded to the Sentinels, to boat captains and their battered crews. "Physically, they've returned, but mentally they might be wandering." She looked to her foster Mukwa, shoulders hunched in the rear, and also to Sparrow, whose bright eyes were blurry.

"To deal out death, and to witness death, is no small thing. Trauma bites like a bullet, cuts deeper than blades."

Those who fought at the bridge processed their visions—*body parts bobbing in a sea of flames, boats smashed and sinking, the entrails of horses, a flaming tower, the deadly drones.*

The scent of sage displaced their scent-memories of diesel and death. Miin's mini drum silenced the mammoth horn. As each soldier and sailor walked the span, they took a draught of strawberry sunlight. By the time they crossed over, all loads had lightened. Setting foot in ELF Country, they were welcomed with hugs and handshakes. Pastor George led the singing, joined by Father Pete and his Holy Crossers.

Once the food was blessed, plates were quickly filled and people mingled. There was venison, wild turkey, fresh fish, and roasted veggies. Farmers brought pies and growlers of foaming homebrew. Island kids ran barefoot with their ELF counterparts. Miin's acolytes, tree-tuned, showed off their budding green skills. Michael Martin and Josie Greene raced each other, hand over hand, up wild grape vines and into the canopy.

The island's Indigenous tethered their ponies. Lighting a small fire, they waved the troubled Mukwa—or was he Muck again?—to join them. The big man, muzzle still scabby, stood tall, sniffing his options. The elves, of course, would have him—there was always room for El Oso—but their scent was icy, an overflow of grief. There was an earthy smell to the Greenes, the Martins. These farmers would welcome his labor, but Mukwa, blooded by battle, preferred a sword to their plowshares. He definitely avoided Samantha and little sister, Miin. A pity party from his foster family would be unbearable.

A spicy aroma wafted from Ojibwe firekeepers. Mukwa missed his Lakota brothers—Big Ben, Shaggy Wolf—their sage, tobacco, and flowery cannabis. Shaggy had promised to visit soon, before the winter, winking a golden eye and howling as the Beaver boats steamed away. Decided—comfortable in his latest skin—Mukwa shambled towards the tethered ponies. White Bear growled *boozhoo,* joining the braided men and women from Indian Point.

Bearded Brian, blue eyes brimming, found Miin. They embraced, and he introduced his friend. "Blueberry, this is Loon. Maang, meet Miinan."

"*Aanii*," the teacher said, smiling her welcome.

"*Boozhoo,* Blueberry," the younger boy responded. He fixed her with his loon-eye. Miin felt an icy shock, then a flash of familiar. Loon nodded, feeling it too. "I know you," he said. "I've seen you before."

She opened herself, an eager tree leaning in. Miin searched the recent past, then suddenly she had it. *Nighttime. Midsummer. Uncle Keith still alive. Scouting the mainland in his beat-up canoe. Mukwa in the bow, Two-Crow astern. Petoskey, hanging town, noosed corpses dangling from street lamps. The spotlight walking across the waves, searching for them, almost finding, almost pinning.*

That was the night they'd been saved by a loon. Territorial and angry, the water bird drew the spotlight, allowing the scouts to escape. And now here he was, their savior, this little boy.

Miinan bowed. *"Miigwech. Chi-Miigwech."*

Maang bowed in return. "It was nothing. I'd been spying on those Chosen. Your canoe was so curious, your signatures so strong. An old crow, a bear cub, and you. Your aura was different then. It's grown a lot, but I recognize it now."

They smiled at each other, like to like. Brian, their go-between, was glad to see it. "Speaking of growing, Miin, how's the green-training? Your students? Your tree academy?"

The first-year teacher shrugged. Looking skyward, she laughed suddenly. Josie and Michael, impossibly high, had ascended a towering pine. The juveniles, arboreal, laughed from its crown. "I can't keep up with them," she said, smiling through a sigh. "I hope you two want teaching jobs."

Epilogue: The Caged Bird

SEVENTEEN DAYS SINCE HAWK HAD SEEN THE SUN, seventeen nights without moon or stars. Imprisoned in a padded cell, there were no tallies on her wall. Instead, she etched her flesh with a fingernail. Three clumps of scabby fives and two newer lines calendared her confinement. In the concrete bowels of Panzer Pharma, Nighthawk's moon-clock kept ticking. Even caged, the ELF warrior sensed the orb's fullness, its phase. The moon had been a mere crescent when she sprang Campbell from Chow's cabin, fighting the guardsmen in the dunes, firing the harbor with her flaming arrow. Since then, Luna had waxed to fullness and waned again.

Her own lunar cycle Schark appropriated with a pill. "I need you to stop menstruating," he explained, voice-filtered and faceless. "Panzerland needs your eggs. You don't mind, little bird, if I investigate your ovaries? Filch a few from your fallopian nest?"

Hormone injections followed. Ever-clinical, he'd named them all. Hawk struggled to remember—follicle stimulation? Gonadotropin? Ultrasounds increased as her harvest day approached.

Dr. Schark was depriving Hawk of her senses. He kept his bird blinkered and blind. Enhanced interrogation he called it, proceeding to monologue at length. The doctor loved to talk, though only through screens. Torture by tongue—it left no marks. He wanted information and tried every trick. She'd been drugged, kept awake, facing good cops and bad. There'd been carrots, there'd been sticks; she preferred the latter. *Do your worst.*

His minions called him Sharkey, and he seemed to run the whole show. The Big Boss was bossless as far as she could tell. His moods varied wildly, his punishments too. Two weeks ago had been bad; she'd etched those days deeper. Schark had been in pain. Something big had gone wrong. Some scheme of his was stymied. Muscled techs had burst in, bearing Boss Sharkey on a laptop-palanquin, the unhinged man screaming from his screen: *"Greenies! Terrorists! Severed the bridge!"*

Lab-coated goons used electricity, zapping her silly. His staff, high on testosterone, bruised her as well. She'd been starved and then stuffed, dehydrated and then drowned. Nighthawk got through it, just along for the ride. The physical punishments lessened as her retrieval day approached. They needed healthy eggs, uncracked and unscrambled.

Hawk etched her next tally—number eighteen—sensing it was morning. The month was October. Through concrete, she extended green-feelers and faced the waning crescent, or at least where she thought it would be. *Gaia, give me strength.* She'd talked, she'd confessed; told the truth and also lied. The injections had been many, the interrogators skilled. Schark was pleased with his birdie and her songs. Hawk's only consolation was that the Big Boss talked too. Socially distanced since collapse, the arch villain ached for an audience. Hawk feigned compliance, retaining what she could.

Etch completed, her sharp ears caught footsteps in the corridor. Then her cell door was opened by brawny staff bearing screens. Sharkey's voice, low and melodious, spoke from a tablet: "Good morning, Patient Hawk. And how are we feeling today?"

Despite the bridge setback, his mood was on the mend. Always scheming, Boss Schark had moved on. Future-focused, the man had a plan.

"Today is harvest day. Please relax and follow the directions of your care providers—my assistants, Mr. Wermer and Ms. Frau. Trust me, Ms. Hawk, this procedure is pro-life. It protects our freedoms, as I'm sure you will see."

Frau, a no-nonsense woman wearing scrubs and an N95, pushed play on a screen. Hawk listened to the terminology of in vitro fertilization, the too-happy testimonials from before. They diagrammed what would be done to her—the catheter, the needle. The corporate promo ended. "Any questions?" Hawk didn't bother.

The medical staff got to work. Schark's access to information was impressive. This video, for example, a digital relic—the reproductive habits of the rich. She consoled herself. The actors were dead now, clients too, extinct with all the rest. Good fucking riddance. Thanks to Gaia.

The gynecological team, gowned and gloved, were ready. Her straps were tightened, an IV was inserted—anesthesia? She fought the chemical twilight, forcing herself awake. They cinched her feet in stirrups, lithotomy position. Schark, on his screen, was down there too, under her hood; the man of cunning wanted it all. An ultrasound tech assisted the surgeon. There was a live video feed; Nighthawk viewed her invasion. She saw her ovaries, her clustered follicles, grapes on a vine. They vacuumed them all, every daughter, every son. They robbed her nest blind. And then it was over. The staff were packing up. She was cold. She was crying.

Schark consoled her from his screen: "There there, little birdie. You did great. You have no idea what you've done—for science, for Panzer, for me. Your DNA will be analyzed, your genomic resistance to disease, decoded. Your ova will be utilized, I promise, every last one. With your eggs I will breed the next generation, Covee-compatible, inheritors of the Earth.

"Plus, there's money to be made, and why not? Plenty of survivors out there, the top one percent, in their billion dollar bunkers. But what point is survival if you can't pass it on? Well-heeled matrons want grandkids; Fortune 500s, to father a son.

"The time for Virals is ending. They've served their purpose, the Chosen, the Cons. The spreading is nearly over. The planet has been de-peopled. My great flood of virions has washed it clean. It's time for the Garden again, a Neo Eden, armed guards at every gate. Black tie will be the new fig leaf. Every member an Adam, an Eve. My garden parties will be exclusive, invite-only, and strictly VIP."

This Ends Book Two of Sudden Quiet

Acknowledgments

These pages are haunted by dead poets: Mary Oliver, Kenny O'Dell, Keats and his Nightingale, Margaret Wise and her Moon—I acknowledge you. But my greater debt is to the living, especially my Indigenous mentors, for they have breathed life into this story. Courtney Miller, Kenny Pheasant, Waubeshig Rice, the Kwe Singers, Hadassah GreenSky—*miigwech*! Thank you for seeing me truly, and for helping me see the truth in others. *Chi-miigwech*!

ABOUT the AUTHOR

Joshua Veith is an educator, adventurer, and outdoor enthusiast. He graduated from the University of Michigan, later earning an MA in Literature from Eastern Michigan University. Today, Joshua lives with his wife and two sons in northern Michigan, fishes and hikes in the same spots that Hemingway enjoyed as a young man, and teaches a literature class on JRR Tolkien. As a public school teacher and writer, Josh strives to be an Indigenous ally, recognizing that traditional relationships with the environment offer the most sustainable pathways for humankind's interaction with the planet.